PENGUIN BOOKS

THE HOUSE WITCH

and the Charming of Austice

T0322210

ABOUT THE AUTHOR

Delemhach is the Canadian author of the popular series The House Witch and is already hard at work on the sequel series, The Burning Witch. When they aren't following the whims of their unfortunately intelligent cats, Kraken and Pina Colada, they are teaching music privately to their students. In their spare time outside of writing and work, they enjoy cooking, reading, hiking, spending time with family, and trying not to remember their socially awkward moments.

THE HOUSE WITCH

WITCH

and the Charming of Austice

DELEMHACH
Emilie Nikota

PENGUIN BOOKS

PENGUIN BOOKS

UK | USA | Canada | Ireland | Australia
India | New Zealand | South Africa

Penguin Books is part of the Penguin Random House group of companies
whose addresses can be found at global.penguinrandomhouse.com

First published by Podium Publishing ULC, 2022
First published in Penguin Books, 2024
002

Printed and bound in Great Britain by Clays Ltd, Elcograf S.p.A.

The authorized representative in the EEA is Penguin Random House Ireland,
Morrison Chambers, 32 Nassau Street, Dublin D02 YH68

A CIP catalogue record for this book is available from the British Library

ISBN: 978–1–405–96707–5

www.greenpenguin.co.uk

MIX
Paper | Supporting
responsible forestry
FSC® C018179

Penguin Random House is committed to a
sustainable future for our business, our readers
and our planet. This book is made from Forest
Stewardship Council® certified paper.

To the Royal Road readers who first made the story popular and have showered me with their encouraging comments and helpful insights. This longtime dream would not have been possible without you.

Especially my fan-turned-editor, Pika Trebond, who has been an incredible human and supporter. They are the first to see each week's latest chapter, and their excitement and love of the story has helped motivate me on some of the toughest of days. Pika, you have been instrumental in this endeavor for quite a while, and I cannot thank you enough.

CHAPTER 1
COFFEE KLATCH

Fin stirred on his pallet the morning after the prince's birthday ball, the embers low in the hearth. Despite his position on the floor and the fire having dwindled down, the witch found the room incredibly warm. It made him grateful that he wasn't fully dressed and …

Wait … what?

Fin's eyes blinked open slowly before the events of the previous night came flooding back to him, jolting him awake. Looking over to his right, Fin saw Annika Jenoure sleeping peacefully beside him in a similar state of undress.

All at once, Fin felt his insides melt.

He'd gone after her …

He'd played his hand and wound up with the most gorgeous woman on the continent in his arms throughout the night.

Leaning over, Fin brushed a kiss against Annika's temple and slid closer to her. Relishing the feel of her smooth skin against his, he relaxed against her.

The dark-haired beauty let out a soft grumble, and Fin's smile brightened. He loved that he had just discovered that she was not a morning person. Her feelings on the matter differed greatly.

"Morning," he greeted merrily.

Annika groaned irritably, then turned onto her other side, but she did so so suddenly that it caught Fin by surprise. Her new position had her forehead pressed against his bare chest, her soft breath tickling his skin.

"Do you want some coffee?" Fin whispered, already summoning more firewood to stoke the flames and boil water for the brew.

"Mmmmnffgh what?" Annika mumbled incoherently.

"Coffee. Do you want some?"

"What … is … coffee?"

Fin's eyebrows shot up. While he knew that the Daxarian serving staff wouldn't be aware of what the brew was—as its beans were a foreign export from Troivack—he had expected Annika to have tried, or at least heard of, it. He *had* thought it odd that none of the nobility had ordered the drink when he had initially purchased the first few bags …

"Wait here." Fin kissed Annika's temple and rose from the pallet.

The lady promptly fell back into a demi-sleep as she felt her muscles and thoughts at ease for the first time in what was—most likely—years.

Annika was drifting pleasantly between the realm of a heavy sleep and gradual wakefulness when a strange smell overcame her. It was smoky … mouth-watering … intriguing …

"Alright, my lady, give this a try."

Frowning in displeasure, Annika attempted to open her eyelids despite feeling as though they were weighted down with stones. Blearily, she searched around unsuccessfully for her tunic, until Fin handed it to her.

Standing slowly, she pulled the garment over her head with a small moan. Smiling, Fin placed a clay mug with a rounded bottom in front of her, filled with dark liquid. It looked like tea but blacker.

"Give it a try." Fin was sipping from his own cup while watching her with a cheeky glint in his eyes that suggested he was anticipating something amusing.

Annika gave him a dubious glare before lifting it to her lips and taking a tentative sip.

The bitterness bit her tongue, and she was about to spit it out but managed to swallow at the last minute. For some reason, Fin seemed so intent on …

"Oh." Annika's eyes widened, and the muscles in her face relaxed. It was like her body was responding to the sun after months of darkness. Goosebumps rose over her arms and legs in pleasure. The ebbing warmth began to fill her and clear away the last vestiges of sleep. "This tastes like crap but … Gods, I didn't know how much I needed this." She took another mouthful.

"I'm surprised you even have taste buds after drinking so much of your moonshine," Fin teased, while sipping his coffee. He took a seat at the table as Annika did the same. He leaned the side of his head into his right hand while the other hand cradled his own mug. The steam from his cup curled wistfully in the golden glow of dawn, making pretty patterns in the air before cooling.

"It's an acquired taste, but it still requires *taste*," she retorted indignantly. The glint of humor in her eyes had an unsettling effect on the cook.

Fin's coffee cup paused its journey to his mouth as his heart skipped a beat.

Everything was perfect.

He was sharing his favorite moments of the day with the woman he loved after spending the entire night with her. The world was quiet, the coffee warm, and the sun poured in from the window like honey. The light cast Annika's tousled hair and easy smile in an angelic frame, and Fin knew from the bottom of his heart he would remember that moment with her for the rest of his life.

Annika reached over and tapped his nose with her index finger. "I don't have much longer here, so maybe do more than just stare at me."

Giving his head a small shake, he straightened and took another mouthful of coffee. "Do what, exactly?" Fin asked, lifting an eyebrow skeptically as Annika stood and yawned.

"Well, a morning kiss isn't out of the question."

"Ah. I kissed you before you woke up so …" Fin's cheeks flamed red as he suddenly avoided her gaze.

Annika's fingers rested against her chin as she gazed at Fin mischievously. "Why are you being so bashful, hm?" She stroked her jaw thoughtfully as the redhead wrapped both hands around his mug and took a sip. "I mean … we already …" She trailed off, giving him a cheeky smile.

"I know!" The redness in Fin's cheeks crept up to his eyebrows. He risked a glance at Annika and realized that she was moving closer to him as cautiously and quietly as a cat. Jumping out of his seat, Fin rounded the table.

Annika turned a slow, sly smile on him and rested her hands on the well-loved wooden surface between them. "What seems to be the issue, *lover*?" She drew out the word *lover*, making Fin turn nearly purple as he both cringed and smiled.

Annika raced around the corner of the table, but Fin was quick. He shot over to the other side, maintaining his distance from her. The lady changed her direction nimbly, only to have him do the same in defense.

By the third attempt, Annika feigned another direction change and managed to grasp the sleeve of his tunic. They laughed until their sides ached throughout the entire chase.

"Alright, you crazy man, what is this about?" She wrapped her arms around his waist, holding him firmly against her hips.

Fin peered down into her happy face and gave in immediately. Closing his arms around her and reveling in the pleasant shock that flushed through him at touching his lady again, he smiled. "Alright. As wonderful as coffee is, there is a nasty little affliction that comes with it. I didn't want to ruin this morning with anything."

Annika's look of mild confusion was blended with concern.

Fin sighed, tilting his head back and looking to the ceiling. Though admittedly, his exasperation was all for show. That morning, he didn't have a care in the world. "Kiss me and see if you know what I am talking about." His head dipped closer to her, eyes occasionally dropping to her mouth.

Still perplexed, but of course wanting to be accommodating, Annika lifted her heels off the ground to bring her lips to his. The kiss was soft, pure, and the couple felt as though there was a fire between them lighting their insides. With their hearts beginning to beat a little faster at the gravity-defying pull they felt, Annika remained uncertain about what the redhead had been talking about. That is, until he let out his soft contented sigh.

"Your breath could wilt a meadow," she exclaimed before she could stop herself.

Fin roared with laughter and pulled her into a tight embrace. "Ah well, my lady, I hate to say it, but *your* breath could kill a unit of perfectly healthy knights."

Annika partially broke their embrace as she leaned her head back with raised eyebrows. The spark in her eyes indicated some impending verbal sparring, when there was a sudden pounding on the castle kitchen door.

"FIN! FIN! THE CAKE WAS AMAZING! FIN! C'MON! YOU'RE ALWAYS UP THIS EARLY!"

At the sound of the prince's shouts—which more than likely woke the entire castle—the couple sprang apart.

Annika darted to the garden door only to suddenly whirl around and rush back to Fin with a panicked expression. "My brother is having you followed, remember! I can't be seen leaving here!"

Fin's mind raced. Prince Eric would take one look at Annika dressed in men's trousers and tunic, with her mussed hair and swollen lips, and have all kinds of dangerous observations that could be repeated to *anyone*.

"Hide." Fin ushered her over to the stack of potato bags, but she wrenched her hand from his and shook her head.

"FIIIIIIIIIN! I HEAR YOU MOVING AROUND IN THERE! ARE YOU IN TROUBLE? SHOULD I GET THE CAPTAIN? OR MY DAD?!"

"No,.Eric! I'm fine, just give me a moment to tidy some junk away from the door!" Fin answered hastily, before turning back to Annika.

"No. Put me behind the door, then distract him so I can slip out. If I'm gone too long, people will notice! I need to get back before the maid, my brother—"

"FIIIIIN, HURRY UP!"

Not having time to finish her explanation, Annika rushed to the door with Fin on her heels. Once positioned, Annika gave him a firm nod, and the redhead threw open the door.

The prince stood in the center of the entrance, wearing only a plain tunic and trousers. Clearly, he had escaped his room before his governess could get his outfit sorted. The freshly aged eight-year-old beamed up at his friend. Then, without any warning, he threw his arms around Fin's waist and hugged him tight.

The previous tension in Fin faded away as he bent down and picked Eric up, returning the embrace. The fact that he managed to pull the child farther into the room, and Annika was able to slip out unnoticed, was an added bonus.

Placing the lad down again, the cook stepped back with his hands on his hips. "I must admit, it is obvious to me you are approaching manhood quickly."

The boy giggled in pleasure. "I know! Soon I'm going to be even taller than you!"

"Possibly! So tell me all about your birthday. I only got to see a little bit before I came back to serve the late-night meal."

With that, the duo resumed their normal morning activities. Fin prepared snacks for Eric, and the eight-year-old regaled him with the most interesting parts of the previous evening.

After nearly an hour, the prince's poor disheveled governess came to fetch her ward. The woman appeared to have gotten around to her own festivities the previous night, as Fin assessed her pale face and the faint odor of ale around her.

The cook had nearly completed the servants' breakfast, shortly after the prince's departure, when his aides joined him. Hannah looked antsy, the knights looked exhausted, and Peter looked … strangely exuberant.

"Good morning." Fin greeted each of them with a warm smile.

Both Sirs Lewis and Taylor looked a little green, while Sirs Andrews and Harris appeared oddly pale and shifty.

"Coffee?" Fin asked, looking to Sir Taylor—who had become quite vocal about his need for the beverage in the morning.

"Yes," the knights answered in unison.

"Enough chitchat! What happened?!" Hannah exploded, pounding the table with her palms. Sirs Taylor and Lewis winced.

Fin's eyes jumped to the petite blonde, who was already red in the cheeks.

"Er … what happened to you lot?" Fin raised an eyebrow in the direction of the knights as he blushed deeply.

Everyone shared worried glances.

"Out with it, Ashowan. Don't try to avoid the question." Sir Andrews had an edge to his tone that immediately made Fin respond with a half smile.

Failing to give his captive audience an answer, the cook instead rubbed the back of his neck and avoided their gazes. The group let out aggravated moans.

"Really, Fin?!" Sir Andrews complained, exasperated.

"All that stress for nothing?! I swear, Heather has been sick for two weeks because of the worry you give us! How could you have missed that opportunity to confess to Lady Jenoure!"

"It went well. I'd rather not say more … for … personal reasons," Fin managed to say, his hands coming up defensively.

"Judging by the pint-sized cloak tossed over the apple bags here, I'd say our cook did just fine," Peter announced with a bright smile. He held up the black cloak, which was very obviously meant for someone far shorter than the cook.

Fin closed his eyes and sighed. Perhaps he really was terrible at hiding his nonsense …

"So what happened to all of you last night?" The cook tried to change the direction of the conversation yet again, as he waved his hand and breakfast continued preparing itself.

Everyone shifted uncomfortably, and Fin felt himself go still.

"Is everyone okay? Did anyone get hurt?" His heart twisted in his chest.

"Oh, we're all fine … physically anyway," Sir Andrews muttered, while sharing a meaningful look with Sir Harris.

"Speak for yourself," Sir Taylor added as a cup full of coffee floated into his waiting hands.

"Some things can't ever be forgotten." Sir Harris looked uncharacteristically somber.

"I didn't know you were there!" Peter cried out.

Even Hannah became distracted with the state of the knights.

"Alright, let's start with you." Hannah pointed to Sir Andrews who sported dark smudges under his eyes and a haunting aura.

"Peter persuaded Sir Dawson to leave his post. Harris and I followed to make sure he wasn't in trouble. Little did we know *we* should've been the ones to be protected." Sir Andrews shivered.

"I don't understand." Hannah frowned and turned to Peter, who made a point of avoiding her gaze.

"They heard Peter being amorous with another man," Sir Taylor snapped. He drained his coffee in a single gulp and slid the cup back to Fin in his demand for more.

"You slept with a Troivackian?!" Hannah demanded in an incredulous tone, her hands rising to her hips.

"I didn't know it'd go anywhere when I flirted with him! Besides, Karter is a—"

"Oh, it's 'Karter' now?" Hannah's arms were crossed across her chest as she scowled up at Peter. The man looked as though he wanted to run straight for the garden door and flee for the woods.

"Perhaps we—" Fin began while trying to exude a calming tone.

"Not a word from you! I have some questions for Peter that he better answer truthfully!" Hannah trilled, her voice rising in hysteria.

Fin glanced at the knights who wore matching expressions of *maybe we don't try to get in the way of this.*

Fortunately for Peter, they were interrupted by someone who could take the situation in hand.

"Good morning, everyone! Fin! My love, you must tell me how—" Katelyn Ashowan strolled into the room, rosy-cheeked and beaming. When she caught sight of Hannah descending upon Peter, however, she halted. "What seems to be happening here?"

"This man I thought to be a good fellow slept with the enemy!" Hannah snapped, her eyes glittering in anger.

Katelyn looked to Peter who gave her a desperate, pleading look. Her gaze shifted to Fin, who gave a single shoulder shrug.

"Well, just because someone is from an enemy land doesn't make them an enemy. Not every citizen is their leader. Hannah dear, why don't we go for a walk. I'd like to return to the barracks and check on some of the knights, unless, Fin, you need her this morning?" Katelyn asked respectfully as she reached out and gently clasped Hannah's hand.

"No, no! Go right ahead." His overeager response earned Fin a deep scowl from the blond maid.

Kate patted the young woman's hand and guided her outside, leaving the men to wait with bated breaths to ensure Hannah wouldn't change her mind and fly back at them.

Once the duo was at the end of the garden path, the remaining group took a collective breath of relief.

"We should try to rein in Hannah a bit more," Sir Andrews declared, shaking his head.

"I'll say … at this rate, I'll be kissing her feet and begging her to marry me in no time." Sir Harris was gazing longingly at the open doorway where the women had disappeared.

Sir Taylor cuffed him up the back of his head. "Knock it off."

"So what happened to you two?" Fin redirected the conversation eagerly as he addressed Sirs Taylor and Lewis.

The two men responded by sharing a silent forbidding look.

Sir Lewis shook his head under Sir Taylor's gaze, his stress growing more and more apparent.

"We got drunk with your mom!" the man blurted out, while shrinking away from Sir Taylor.

"*YOU WHAT?*" Fin thundered, taking two menacing steps closer to the men—who immediately took three steps backward.

"It isn't anything bad, Ashowan! She found us guarding the place and asked us to come in and share an ale … Next thing we knew we were deep in our cups playing a few good—"

A knock on the castle door silenced the men.

"Mr. Ashowan? I'd like to have a word with you." The unforgettable voice of Captain Antonio rang out from behind the door.

Fin felt his face pale as he swallowed with great difficulty.

If the captain was coming to speak with him, that meant there was new important information pertaining to the war … or he had in fact been noticed at the ball. The cook didn't know which was worse.

In a matter of minutes, his morning tranquility evaporated into nothingness, and Fin began mentally steeling himself for the next wave of chaos.

CHAPTER 2
THE CAT'S MEOW

Fin stood staring at the captain with his arms folded across his chest as the aides filed out the garden door. Oddly, Sirs Lewis and Taylor had nearly run from the room the moment the captain entered.

Captain Antonio peered around the kitchen with his one good eye, his shoulders stiff and his cheeks tinged with pink. The man seemed to be avoiding looking at Fin, which only made the cook all the more anxious as he waited for the leader of the knights to speak.

"Ashowan, I am very sorry to have to deliver this news to you …" The captain cleared his throat and widened his stance.

The redhead's heart stopped.

They knew.

He'd gone to the ball and was about to be fired.

Gods, did they know about Annika and him already?

"You missed … Lord Piereva having the new bard dancing against him under a literal beam of light in front of every noble in the room."

Fin blinked. Then remembered he "had not heard" of the events yet.

"You're joking," he managed at long last. Fortunately, the captain was too distracted with trying to maintain his composure to notice.

"No. I swear to the Gods, I wish there was a way you could've seen it. Though it may not have been as funny to you as the rest of us. Have you met Lord Piereva?"

Fin raised an eyebrow as a slow smirk climbed his face.

"Many times."

The captain was nodding distractedly when he finally registered what the cook had just said.

"Why have you met Lord Piereva 'many times'?"

"The earl often has diarrhea and wants to discuss his food."

The captain was completely caught off guard by the response and snorted before he could stop himself. "That is interesting information. It would explain the man's disposition for sure."

Fin nodded, using every ounce of his inner strength to feign seriousness.

"I am sorry I missed such an event. He is an unpleasant man. Pardon my saying so," the cook added, while feigning a somber attitude.

The captain shook his head, his features immediately drawing taut.

"How someone like Lady Jenoure and the earl could be related, I'll never know."

"Troivack often treats the heads of their families like Gods. The women are expected to be silent, strong breeders from what I'm given to understand." Fin felt his jaw set as his mind threatened to envision Annika being raised in such an environment.

"The saying 'two heads are better than one' can be applied to an entire populace when it comes to genders. A pity they don't realize the benefit of this."

Fin nodded before he realized there was still an odd tension in the air. Something was off with the captain. The redhead turned a skeptical eye to the man, and the knight—being his usual perceptive self—seemed to acknowledge that he needed to dive into what was troubling him sooner rather than later.

"Er … Ashowan. I … As you may have heard, I lost my wife many years ago."

Fin felt his eyebrow lift.

"Last night I was on my way to my mother's cottage, when I encountered Sir Taylor, and he invited me to join himself and Sir Lewis in your cottage with Kate …"

Fin felt his fingers grip into a fist.

"Well, I … err … She is an incredibly charming woman and … I do not mean to cross the line or pry into—"

"Captain?"

"Yes?"

"For the love of the Gods, are you trying to tell me you want to court my mother?"

The captain of Daxaria's military said nothing for nearly a minute before he finally met Fin's gaze.

"I am. She is unlike any woman I have ever met."

"Captain, wouldn't someone with your position in the court be expected to marry a noble?" the cook asked in choked tones.

"Er ... well ... I've always been a lower noble, and I've earned a good deal of favor with the king through the years ..." The captain cleared his throat. "My position is appointed based on skill. It does not factor in ranking or heirs, so I have a bit of leniency pertaining to my domestic interests." The captain looked like a young awkward man attempting to ask a girl's father for permission to go for a stroll. The fact that he was well into his sixties was irrelevant.

"I see." Fin didn't want to ask the next obvious question, but he knew the conversation would drag on for longer than he'd prefer otherwise. "Captain ... are you trying to ask for my permission?"

Captain Antonio coughed and awkwardly covered his mouth as he tried to maintain his composure.

"I ... I ... of course your mother is a grown woman who can make her own decisions ... However, you and I have on occasion crossed paths in an informal setting, and it would feel strange if I should pursue a carriage ride with her should you object."

Fin lowered his forehead to his hand and began rubbing soothing circles into his temples.

"Captain, my mother isn't aware you know about my father. Which also dredges up the small matter of her still being married to Troivack's chief of military. Not to mention she hasn't heard anything from or about him in decades. Have you thought this through at all?" the cook asked with mounting tension.

"Your mother has not laid eyes on your father for more than twenty years. Should worse come to worse, she could formally appeal to the magistrate of Rollom for desertion. Leaving her open to—"

"—Alright. You've given this some thought." Fin let out a long sigh. "I honestly cannot speak for my mother. I can only say that should you disrespect her or attempt to harm her, I won't be fair in our next fight." In truth he was sounding drastically calmer than he felt.

The captain bowed slightly, his face slightly paler.

"I will treat your mother—"

"That's enough. No more. Nope. No. Good day, Captain." Fin shook his head firmly, hands on his hips and his eyes fixed on his worktable. He couldn't look at the man quite yet.

The captain opened and closed his mouth twice, before clearing his throat, then turning toward the garden door and striding out with an unnatural rigidity in his shoulders.

It took Fin nearly an hour after the captain's departure to settle into a peaceful rhythm of prepping vegetables and shaping pastry. Yet with all the welcome of a mage at a witch's wedding, the thought slammed into the cook's mind all the same.

"Godsdamnit. It isn't as though my mother will be interested anyway …" The redhead rubbed the back of his neck and focused on taking slow peaceful breaths.

He needed to think about the positives.

For one, the captain hadn't known about his attendance at the ball. Another blessing was that no one had noticed Annika leaving the kitchen as far as he was aware.

So what if his mother wanted to pursue a relationship with … with …

Godsdamnit. Fin knew he had no right to feel protective or annoyed for his mother … but the idea that she could be at the mercy of someone who wasn't only physically more powerful than her, but politically as well, perturbed him deeply.

Fin braced his hands against his worktable and hung his head.

I should just wait to see if she wants to meet with him. No use in getting worked up over eggs not even lain yet … Taking a fortifying breath, the cook brought back the image of Annika's smile from earlier that morning.

He felt a grin of his own stretch across his face as he allowed the warmth of the memory to reach all the way to his toes.

Picking up his knife, Fin returned to work just in time to notice his familiar's return.

Kraken strolled into the kitchen and peered up at his witch for a few moments peacefully before leaping up onto one of the chairs.

Lifting his gaze, Fin stared at the fast-growing kitten.

"Where have you been all night?" he asked airily, his mind drifting further from the captain, and instead deeper into pleasant thoughts.

"I hope my witch knows how much I've worked for his cause one day. It'd be nice if he … oh. Oh, he smells different today. Did he finally succeed in mating for kittens? I hope he remembers what happened to him this time. I swear, if I thought pooping on his bed would help, I'd—"

Fin reared back so quickly he nearly fell into the fire.

"DID YOU JUST TALK?!"

The feline stilled immediately.

"KRAKEN?!"

"… What is my witch on about? He couldn't possibly have heard me. We haven't ever been able to communicate before … I do hope that he isn't going craz—"

"SON OF A MAGE!" Fin's eyes were bulging out of his face. "YOU JUST TALKED ABOUT POOPING IN MY BED AND MAKING KITTENS AND, AND—"

Kraken's ears flitted back.

"What in the … meow? Meow?" The cat turned his face partially away. Kraken stated the "meow" as a human would, making it all the more disturbing.

The redhead rounded the table and snatched up the cat, staring at him closely.

"This has to be a familiar thing … how does that make sense though?! We've barely been around each other lately, how could we have deepened our bond? Speak! What has happened?"

Kraken began to wriggle furiously in the redhead's grasp.

"MEoooW!" The fluffy feline sounded even more unsure in the word as he repeated it.

"Speak, Godsdamnit! What in the hell is—"

The castle door opened as Kraken began sliding from the witch's grasp. Distracted, Fin looked to the doorway to see Annika standing there stunned.

Fin stared at Annika.

Annika stared at Fin.

Kraken stared at Annika.

A pleasant shock ran through the witch, making him release the cat back onto the chair he had been seized from. Seeing his chance, the feline leapt away in the name of freedom.

"Wait! No! Kraken, get back here! Speak to me again! Son of a mage!"

"Meowmeowmeowmeow—ouch, Godsdamnit! Meowmeowmeowmeow-meow!" The feline raced out of the room, slightly stumbling over a sharp stone, and was loping across the castle lawn in a matter of seconds.

Annika was watching the entire scenario unfold wordlessly, an unreadable expression masking her face.

"It isn't as crazy as it looks," Fin protested awkwardly. He already knew it was *exactly* as crazy as it looked.

The lady stared at him for a long time before slowly walking over to the cook.

"Fin, have you been drinking?"

Annika's morning …

Annika had barely had time to don her sleepwear before the dreaded maid her brother had placed in her presence as a spy rapped at her door.

Annika sat up, blinking wearily. She didn't even have to feign her exhaustion.

Zuma entered and gazed at the viscountess for a moment longer than was appropriate before curtsying. "My lady, what would you like to wear to meet Earl Piereva?"

Annika felt her previously joyous mood disappear abruptly.

"I cannot see my brother this morning. I already have two meetings arranged by lunch. He can wait until tomorrow. I will try to visit him before supper," Annika ground out flatly. She had never relished acting like a spoiled brat, but when it came to irritating Zuma, she found herself making all kinds of exceptions.

"The earl will be most displeased if—"

"Know your place, Zuma." Annika turned a dark glare to the maid, who stared back with glittering hatred.

That was all Annika needed.

She stood and strode over to the woman, who curtsied only once she was standing toe-to-toe with her mistress.

"Do you know who you serve, Zuma?"

The woman didn't answer immediately, and so Annika reached out and grasped the maid's chin.

While she wasn't inflicting harm, the woman still flinched.

"I work for you, my lady." Zuma's voice was too calm. Too controlled.

"I see. You serve me, yet you question my schedule and decisions. A servant I barely know, who is already disrespecting me, is pushing my brother's agenda." Annika's eyes flashed.

Zuma felt her confidence sink as she realized that Lady Annika Jenoure was not an air-headed noble to be easily manipulated. She had to warn Earl Piereva that his sister could not be underestimated ... that she was as vile and ... as conniving as a ...

"You've shown nothing but duplicity and insolence since becoming my maid. Go ask my brother if I will receive a gift credit for returning you." The scorn dripped from Lady Jenoure's words as her eyes darkened to blackness. A coldness that made Zuma shiver seeped through her skin.

"M-My lady, to refuse a gift such as my—"

"Again you challenge my judgment. *Again* you overestimate your importance." Annika's hand dropped from Zuma's face as Clara silently entered the room.

"Very well, maid. I will do as you wish and treat you as one of my own servants. You will be confined in a cell until the earl leaves for Troivack. No one but myself will be allowed to visit you. Anyone who tries to defy this order will be treated as a spy against His Majesty King Norman Reyes."

The Troivackian maid's face paled.

She can't be serious. She wouldn't risk angering her brother. Even if she is more intelligent than he believes ...

"Clara, please call for the guards."

In a matter of moments, three Daxarian guards had received their orders and escorted Zuma to the dungeons.

Annika knew such a punishment would breed antagonistic gossip. The King of Daxaria was known for disapproving of nobles who abused their power—especially when it came to harsh punishments of the serving staff. A staff member being sent to the dungeons was nearly unheard of in the castle, and even outside the inner court in the homes of nobles it was deeply frowned upon.

Once the woman had been carted off, Annika prepared for her day, while pretending to not notice Clara's expectant glances.

After she was washed and dressed, Annika turned toward the door, only to find Clara blocking her.

"Is there an issue?" the viscountess asked patiently, despite automatically recounting the number of knives she had hidden on her person.

"You did not come back to your chambers until this morning. Where were you?" Clara asked pointedly while examining Annika from head to toe.

"Not that it is any of your business, but I had an emergency at my estate in Austice. I have a special guest arriving this afternoon for the midday meal."

Clara stared skeptically at her mistress before Annika grew impatient.

"I just punished someone for their disrespectful behavior, don't make me do so again for consistency's sake," she snapped, before regaining control over herself. *Exhaustion blended with anticipation is not a winning combination, Annika.*

"Where are you heading to, mistress?" Clara's tone was mild, despite her intention being far from it.

"I need to confirm the menu for my date with Lord Nam this afternoon," Annika replied as she swept past Clara.

Once outside, Lady Jenoure proceeded down the corridor with her chin held high and her expression impenetrable. Her inner thoughts were a different matter entirely …

Godsdamnit, was it too soon to sleep together?! Should I ask him to forget all about last night and instead we slow things down? She nodded a greeting to Lord Gauva as she approached the staircase.

He could still have second thoughts. I jumped into this without a contingency plan, which is unlike me … this could go up in flames … Annika descended the stairs toward the banquet hall while passing several tired serving staff and nobles alike.

I jumped on any sign of hope from him, which was presumptuous. I was too desperate … Gods. What has become of me? I don't even know him! Annika's steps faltered as she realized that she was repeating one of the reasons Finlay hadn't wanted to pursue their time together.

Entering the banquet hall, she barely registered the signs of the festivities that must have only wrapped up an hour or two before her arrival. There were still sleeping knights on the floors, food left out, spilled ale everywhere …

I'll go see Fin. Annika turned toward the kitchens. *I am a noblewoman simply seeking breakfast without wanting to deal with sticky floors and slurred greetings,* she reasoned to herself as she turned down the east wing corridor.

It isn't like it would be so strange if I should go and ask for a cup of, oh what was that beverage called again? Coffee? Or would I seem too desperate? What if I am being too cumbersome after our night together by returning only a couple of hours after we've parted?! Annika's stomach began to twist in a way it never had before.

What if I become like some of the simpering women that wait day and night at the threshold for their lovers to return? Annika shuddered but didn't stop her progression to the kitchens.

As she approached the kitchen door, a sensation of doom settled over her, and she paused.

No. Fin has been kind, respectful, and trusting of me. He is unique, clever, strong ... Her heart was doubling its normal pace.

She needed to get a hold of herself again.

He is the man of my dreams, the man that I love ... everything is wonderful.

Reclaiming her confidence, Annika pushed open the kitchen door— to find the redhead shouting at his cat.

"—Speak, Godsdamnit! What the hell is—"

They all stared at each other—when the cat was eventually released and ran away "meowing," Annika continued staring at Fin. The only thought she found herself able to repeat in that moment was:

The man I love ... the man of my dreams ...

CHAPTER 3
UP IN ARMS

Annika stared at Fin across his worktable as the knives magically prepared the food for dinner.

"So ... you heard Kraken speak to you," she began hesitantly.

"I did. I'm not completely sure ... but that isn't the weirdest part of my day!" Fin knew his pride was on the line when he began speaking with a defensive tone. He had to try and salvage the situation before Lady Jenoure began regretting her decision to be with him.

"... What was the weirdest part of your day?"

"Captain Antonio wants to court my mother."

Annika's face grew strained as she processed the new information. She didn't want to insult Fin or his mother inadvertently, but she was uncertain whether or not laughing was at all appropriate ...

"Oh," was all that came out of the lady's mouth.

"I still don't know your plan for you and me. Does this interfere with us in any way?" Fin asked, unable to mask his hopefulness.

Staring at the open garden door where the fluffy black feline had just escaped, Annika felt her heartbeat double its normal pace. "Fin ... Do you really hear your cat speak to you? If so, I need to know sooner rather than later."

Annika was doing everything in her power to be even-tempered and reasonable. Even though within her mind, an obnoxious buzzing was beginning to increase in volume.

"I've never heard Kraken before today and I ... er ... it's a familiar thing ..."

Despite the obvious tonal doubt in his words, Annika latched on to Fin's explanation.

"I see. I suppose I understand that there are parts of your abilities that may seem ... odd."

She didn't understand, but she didn't want to start an argument on their first day of ... Gods knew what. Shoveling the occurrence away in her mind for another time, Annika remembered why she had wanted to come to see him in the first place. It was then she recalled how uncharacteristically nervous she was being back in the same room as Fin.

"I am expecting an important guest to arrive around the midday meal. If you could arrange a luncheon to be set for the rose maze, I would be greatly appreciative." Her voice seemed to be coming out of someone else's mouth. There was no way she could sound so proper and removed from a discussion with Fin, the man she had spent a passionate night with not even a day ago.

"Of course, my lady, I will see to it myself ..." Fin glanced over her shoulder, then at the castle door before lifting a cheeky grin. "When will I be seeing you again?" he queried in lowered tones.

Annika felt her cheeks flame in pleasure as she realized that he was just as eager to see her as she was him.

"Today is important for my plan, so it might be best if we do not see each other until things settle down. I will come as soon as possible." Annika couldn't meet his gaze for some strange reason.

"I understand. I don't suppose you might tell me about this plan at all?" Fin prodded gently. He didn't want to let on how insecure her reply had made him. He had genuinely hoped that with his confession and their coming together, there would be no further secrets between them, and he wouldn't have to stay away from her nearly as much as before.

She's still a noble and I'm still a cook ... that doesn't magically go away ... he reminded himself sternly. Even so, the enchantment of their night and morning together began to grow tinged with the gray of reality.

"I will. I just didn't want to say anything beforehand, but I—"

Ruby, the Head of Housekeeping, suddenly strolled in through the castle door, causing Annika to stop speaking abruptly and feign her haughty noble persona.

"Mr. Ashowan, the— Oh! Viscountess!" Ruby dipped into a low curtsy. "Pardon the interruption, I was merely tasked with sending for the Royal Cook." The older woman kept her eyes cast downward dutifully.

Annika shot an apologetic glance at Fin before regaining her look of cool superiority.

"Not at all, Ruby, I was merely giving the cook my instructions for my luncheon with Lord Nam this afternoon." Taking a graceful step toward the doorway, Annika gave a kind smile to the Head of Housekeeping before she disappeared from sight.

Turning back to Fin with a raised eyebrow, Ruby addressed him seriously. "You must have displeased the viscountess greatly for her to look so coldly at you."

Fin almost laughed.

"Er, nothing I can think of. I believe Lady Jenoure was merely intent on making sure her meal with the Zinferan goes well." Clearing his throat casually, Fin changed the topic. "You were asked to send for me?"

Unconvinced, Ruby continued gazing skeptically at the redhead. "Mr. Howard wishes to speak with you. He sends for you quite often, for a man who claims to want nothing to do with you." She said the last part more to herself than to Fin, and so she missed the mischievous smirk on his face.

"Very well, I will alert my aides and be up to see him shortly. Will it be the council room?" he queried, while beginning to untie his apron from his waist.

"No, this time he has requested you in the captain's quarters."

All levity in Fin's mood disappeared. Fortunately, Ruby failed to see this.

"I see." He stalked over to the garden door, his stomach churning as he tried not to think about his discussion with the military man only hours before. He knew he was being called to look over another battle plan but found himself dreading the encounter wholly.

On his way to the barracks, Fin addressed his aides working at the end of the garden path on the vegetables for lunch, asking them to return to the kitchen in his absence. It wouldn't do if the serving staff came to distribute the meals and witnessed Fin's magic at work without him there. At least with the aides present, it wouldn't seem as suspicious that the tasks were completed.

The group all agreed—albeit with several moans and groans over being subjected to the heat of the kitchen hearth and ovens—picking up their materials as Fin turned back to the castle.

Annika sipped her teacup rigidly with her eyes downcast. Lord Nam's pained expression had become the norm during their courting dates together, and this afternoon was no different. While the summer sun beamed down on the couple, Annika wore a drab high-necked gown. It was gray and thankfully a light chiffon dress. Despite her intention to appear as humble as possible, though, she had dared, out of a small sense of pride, to risk a pair of simple pearl earrings encircled in diamonds.

She caught the eye of a footman standing near the mouth of the maze and saw him give a nearly imperceptible nod to her.

It was time.

"I-I hope you don't mind, Lord Nam, I've invited a dear friend of mine to join us. She came to visit for the prince's birthday, but unfortunately was unwell the night of the ball." Annika knew it was incredibly poor manners to invite a third party to a courting date. She hoped that this "error" of social behavior was met with the disappointment she was aiming for. She even pretended to be nervous when she glanced at the Zinferan and nearly cackled aloud when she saw his look of annoyance.

"I barely saw you last evening at the ball, and now you throw another person into our time together? This insult to my character—"

"Presenting Lady Marigold Iones, daughter of Duchess Roberta Iones."

A young woman with long auburn hair that glowed like embers in the sunlight appeared at the entrance to the maze center, silencing the Zinferan. She wore an extravagant cream-colored gown with intricate gold embroidery around the gauzy hem and cuffs. Garishly large diamonds dripped from her ears and matched the necklace adorning her pale throat. Her hazel eyes were bright, and as she strolled farther into the garden, Lord Nam's jaw slowly opened.

The Zinferan noble rose from his seat as Lady Marigold neared, while Lady Jenoure smiled into the rim of her teacup.

"Good day, Lady Iones. I am Lord Nam." The Zinferan bowed, and she curtsied in response. Lady Marigold's eyes were already alight with pleasure as she noted the extravagance of Lord Nam's garb and his entourage behind him.

"Good day. I see you have the acceptable amount of servants with you," she observed bluntly. An observation that would normally earn her a look of disapproval or disgruntlement from the Daxarian nobility only garnered a look of pleasure from the Zinferan.

"Doesn't everyone?" he scoffed.

Lady Iones cast a disparaging look at Annika, who pretended to be very enthralled with the cloud formations overhead. "Tell me, those pants you're wearing, were they made by—"

"The famous Zinferan stylist Eun Gim? Of course. Why would I not fund one of the greatest talents of our land?" Lord Nam asked with a playful smile on his face as he watched the lady with growing interest.

"—Especially when he is said to be very exclusive with who he sells to." Lady Marigold raised an eyebrow, clearly impressed.

Annika cleared her throat. "Lady Marigold is visiting from Sorlia— She was one of the ladies considered for marriage to yourself. I hope you don't mind the awkward situation." Lady Jenoure blushed and hunched her shoulders over the table.

Both Lady Marigold and Lord Nam rolled their eyes, then realized that they had responded identically.

They exchanged a meaningful gaze before the young Lady Iones turned back to the viscountess. "How is it *you* were supposed to be the finest match for our guests?" she asked childishly.

"I-I … er … His Majesty is very kind and hoped I would lay my mourning for my late husband to rest. Another reason I believe was that he didn't want to risk placing any pressure on your father's legacy." Annika gave a dutiful nod of her head. After all, Lady Marigold did technically rank above her.

Marigold folded her arms gracefully while lifting an eyebrow in Lord Nam's direction.

"Tell me, Lady Jenoure, would you be opposed to my picking Lord Nam's brain regarding the textiles of his homeland? You seem quite … comfortable with your tea."

The volume of insults and violations of courtly behavior were staggering, and Annika could've kissed the bratty woman for all she cared.

"Not at all. It is splendid weather to enjoy a peaceful cup of tea. After all, solitude is best for reflecting on the proper humility for a widow like myself—"

Lady Marigold gently placed a hand on Lord Nam's arm and smiled up at him.

"Tell me, how did you manage to convince Eun Gim to make *only* a pair of pants? I can tell that your jacket, while of high quality, is not made by the same hand."

Once the two rounded the corner of the exit, followed by at least three members of Lord Nam's entourage, Annika leaned back with a broad smile. Pulling out her flask, she topped her cup up, and crossed her legs. Her posture was that of a woman of leisure—as opposed to the timid mouse she had feigned to be.

The remaining two members of Lord Nam's entourage shared skeptical glances as they noticed Annika's change in disposition, but she couldn't be bothered to care. Knowing dear old Lord Nam, he wouldn't listen to anything they had to report if it had to do with her. She had infuriated him at every turn with lectures of propriety, humility, and frugality. The fact that he could've sworn her off and returned to Zinfera had been no small risk. Luckily, it had all paid off.

In truth, Annika had thought it would take a great deal more manipulation to make Lady Marigold desirable to any respectable nobility. However, it was as though Lord Nam had been sent by the Goddess herself. The couple suited each other all too well.

"I must avoid any brats they breed at all costs," she muttered to herself with a small chuckle.

Closing her eyes, Annika enjoyed the warmth of the sun on her face as she pondered the coming days.

Her next biggest challenge would be handling her brother. Lord Phillip Piereva was going to try and force her to marry Lord Miller. She planned on playing up to his pride and the fact that she no longer had to get married as a means to refuse, but she knew that in itself was a risk.

Her other option was convincing Lord Miller to flee of his own accord. Encourage him to travel and study on his own before the Troivackian king could enlist him in the war. That move would be an even greater gamble, however, as he could easily turn around and tell King Matthias of her suggestion, betraying her to further protect himself. It certainly wouldn't be beyond most Troivackians to do such a thing …. While Annika no longer was under the King of Troivack's law and command thanks to her marriage with Hank, she would still be hunted for defying Matthias. Then, far away or not, it would only be a matter of time before the Troivackian king would have her killed.

Annika was about to head back into the castle to try and get a nap in, when she heard her brother's unmistakable growl behind her.

Slowly, she turned and saw the footmen standing by the maze exit with panicked expressions. They had clearly tried to prevent Lord Piereva from interrupting her but had failed miserably.

"Where's the pansy Zinferan you're supposed to be on a courting date with?" he snarled once she had risen and curtsied.

"He stepped away for a moment with some of his entourage," she answered, while keeping her eyes downcast. Her heart began to pound as she wondered what had brought him to her.

"You refused to meet with me."

"I had to meet with the suitors for our final courting times before giving His Majesty an answer this evening," Annika answered emotionlessly.

"Your answer will be Lord Miller of Troivack. Why not inform the Daxarian king of this now and be done with it?"

Annika didn't have to look up to know Phillip was glaring down at her.

"It could be seen as suspicious activity for me to make the decision early, and it would be an insult to—"

Lord Piereva snatched her arm and wrenched it upward, forcing Annika's eyes to lift to his as she yelped in pain.

"You defy me?" he demanded. "I heard you sent away my gift this morning to the dungeons. Did you think I wouldn't learn of your insult? That you should shame your own kinswoman and have her barred— It's as though you don't trust your own brother in his judgment of character."

One of the footmen who had been watching the scene unfold had fled—most likely to get help.

Gods. If Lord Nam comes back and sees this, he might feel some kind of pity for me and acquiesce to marrying me, Annika thought irritably. While her arm did hurt, she had experienced far worse pain before. She also knew that if he tried to break her arm, she would kill him, if need be, before he could reach that level of violent frenzy.

"Your 'gift' was putting on airs and being disrespectful. She is a maid and thought she had the right to question me, despite my Piereva bloodline. I didn't think you'd want such disrespect to pass, brother," Annika explained, forcing her voice to sound thin and weak.

She could tell her words made him hesitate. She had played to his pride countless times, but alas, it seemed he was in a particularly foul mood that day.

"That maid was a gift to help you remember who you truly serve. I see you have a problem with that." His grip on her arm turned bone-crushing, yet she kept her face controlled and turned down.

"Hm? Is that it? Why so quiet, sister? You've always been a brat, perhaps you've forgotten that I—"

"Lord Piereva, you will release Lady Jenoure this instant." The unmistakable voice of the king made the earl's head snap around. The man glared for a brief moment before dropping his sister's arm.

Norman strode forward, his hazel eyes flashing as he stared down the earl unflinchingly despite their size difference.

When he reached the bear-sized Troivackian, the king braced his legs apart, clasped his hands behind his back, and waited with a hardened expression. "You forget your manners. Kneel."

Lord Piereva was about to bark at his sister to do the same but saw that she had already lowered herself. It was then with sudden clarity that the earl knew who his sister was truly loyal to.

Bending his knee for the briefest of moments, the lord tried to rise again, but Norman held up his hand stopping him.

"I have received a number of reports concerning your behavior as of late, Earl Piereva. You've been harassing the staff, threatening some of them, and now you assault an esteemed member of Daxarian nobility."

Lord Piereva's lip began to curl.

"Your behavior is becoming increasingly hostile and disrespectful, and it will cease this instance. I have sent a letter to King Matthias with an account of each of your offenses, and it has been agreed upon that you will be imprisoned until a vessel arrives for you from Troivack. Lord Piereva, you are hereby suspended from the Kingdom of Daxaria until further notice."

Standing all too swiftly, the earl rose with a roar. "MY KING WOULD NEVER AGREE TO SUCH A—"

Mr. Howard had silently appeared over the king's right shoulder and proffered a rolled parchment with the Troivackian king's official seal.

Lord Piereva's eyes narrowed.

Captain Antonio appeared flanked by his highest-ranking elite knights and clasped irons over the earl's wrists.

"Foolish man. I'll have you beg my forgiveness on your knees after we've slaughtered every last one of your people in the war." The earl's growl came as he regarded the shackles around his wrist with a brief moment of hesitancy.

Norman continued staring at the earl without a flicker of emotion, but the guards didn't take him away; instead the king took a step closer, smiled, and said: "You have a bit of food in your teeth."

He then turned on his heel and walked away, as calmly as he had entered.

Shouting and swearing loudly enough to be heard throughout the castle, Lord Piereva was escorted off the castle grounds to the Lendenhoff Holding—the prison for nobles that was scarcely used.

Annika was left standing nearly alone in the garden, unsure of what to think or feel after what had just happened.

Slowly, she walked toward the remaining footman, a young man who was clearly very shaken by the events. "Once Lord Nam and Lady Marigold return, please inform them I am going to lie down for a time." The poor lad couldn't even speak, but he did manage to nod after meeting her concerned gaze.

When Annika exited the maze, she passed by Norman who was watching her brother be forcefully escorted away with an unsettlingly cavalier stance. The two shared a wordless nod before she continued on to the castle, leaving the king to his thoughts.

With a sigh, Norman closed his eyes and began to mentally prepare himself for what he would have to do before the ship for Piereva arrived.

I'm going to have to tell Finlay the second half of the message from Matthias ...

Mr. Howard returned to Norman's side after personally witnessing the earl leaving the castle grounds.

The two men then began their silent journey back to the castle.

How am I supposed to tell him ... ? Norman gave a somber nod to the guards at the doorway as he mounted the steps. *Troivack's chief of military will be the one coming to pick up Lord Piereva, and when he does, he will be staying for three days.*

Turning down the corridor, the king headed back toward the barracks where the very witch he was thinking of worked on battle plans. Norman's quip to Lord Piereva about the food in his teeth had been a response that he had imagined the cook likely to use when he felt like being particularly vexing ...

It felt oddly wonderful to use on an enemy.

With another inaudible sigh, Norman decided he didn't need to tell the witch just yet about his father's pending arrival. The redhead had seemed in good spirits for once when the official reply from King Matthias had come in, and for some reason, Norman didn't want to dampen the younger man's day.

With his thoughts turning to his own son and unborn daughter, Norman tried to fathom what kind of father would sow such deep pain and anger in their own kin. Not to mention how meeting the man who sired Finlay Ashowan could be anything, but definitely not inconsequential.

It will be interesting indeed to see what Aidan Helmer is like in the flesh.

CHAPTER 4
TROUBLESOME TIMES

Annika strolled into the castle after watching her brother's arrest, her skirts clutched in her hands, and her head light with emotions. All that mattered was that she returned to her chamber before anyone could see her true feelings. As she tried to process what this new development meant for her strategy concerning the war, as well as her relationship with Fin, her vision turned inward. Blindly turning toward the servant's stairwell, Annika was suddenly grabbed and hauled through a nearby open door.

Immediately, more than a decade of training overtook her, and she jammed her elbow sharply back into her abductor's ribs. After a hasty instep that had the person release her, she whirled around with a knife already in her hand drawn from her sleeve.

Only to see Fin standing in front of her wincing and hunching over his ribs.

Blinking in surprise, Annika immediately began apologizing. "I'm sorry! I didn't mean to—"

He stepped closer to her, and slowly, but firmly closed the door behind her. Taking two steps closer, the witch had Annika's back pressed firmly against the wooden surface, with one hand remaining pressed to the door. His other hand raised and gently stroked the side of her face.

"Are you alright?"

Annika stilled. She was confident that she had just cracked one of his ribs, and yet his focus was entirely on her. It was intense, and disconcerting, and … and …

She blushed.

"Of course I'm fine. I—"

"Your brother grabbed your arm pretty roughly, is it bruised?" Fin's eyes moved down to the arm in question, but Annika was distracted with the question of how in the world he knew about the event.

"Were you … spying on me?" she asked slowly.

"No. It was strange …" He looked thoughtful as he tried to explain what he experienced properly. "In the past, I could sense if someone was in extreme pain, or felt intense fear, but today with you … it was like I could see you and hear who was talking to you. I knew where you were just by a feeling, but I couldn't see anything else." Fin frowned slightly. "In truth, since we've been together, my abilities are doing strange things. I need to talk about them with my mother and—"

"Does your mother know about us?!" The color drained from Annika's face as she stared up at Fin, her heart racing.

"No! No, no … I mean everyone suspects we've … you know … because, honestly, getting to the ball took a lot of effort from my aides, my mother, and Jiho …" Fin trailed off and cleared his throat quickly. "No one knows about the details. What I meant was, I need to ask my mother about changes to my magic. I've been putting off talking to her about them for a while, as it usually leads to an interrogation but—"

Annika sighed and let her forehead fall onto Fin's chest.

"Your inability to keep secrets concerns me."

"The amount of secrets you insist on having concerns *me*." Fin chuckled.

Wrapping her arms around the redhead, Annika hugged him gently. She still wasn't convinced his ribs weren't smarting fiercely from her attack.

"At least this part has always felt strangely easy," she mumbled while allowing herself to feel soothed by his closeness.

"As long as our attraction isn't the only thing that comes naturally," Fin remarked while returning the embrace. "So what happened with your brother after he released you? I couldn't hear any more after his threats. Though I need to get back to the barracks soon, so I don't have much time," he added morosely.

"It's fine. I'll tell you la—"

Fin pulled free from her hold and stepped back. Fixing Annika with a somber stare, he shook his head. "No. There is no room for so many secrets in this relationship. You asked me to trust you, and that's what I'm doing, but you need to trust me, too."

Annika felt her anger spark. Folding her arms across her chest defiantly, she didn't speak immediately.

"I didn't say I wouldn't tell you, only that I would tell you later! You just said that you needed to leave."

Fin mirrored her and crossed his arms. "When will you then? There has been nothing but vague answers and promises for quite some time about telling me your plans. If I'm really going to gamble it all, you need to be more forthcoming with me."

Annika didn't even consider his words before replying.

"Fin, we *just* started whatever this is. It takes time to explain, and furthermore, I'm not going to be an open book within a few hours!"

"I'm not asking you to be an open book, I'm asking you to tell me important details that I should know!"

"If it is imperative that you know, then I will—"

"No, you won't! You like controlling everything and being the one pulling the strings, only I'm not on the opposing side of you anymore, Annika. I'm on *your* side, and we are supposed to be doing this together."

The sound of footsteps passing by the door had both of them fall quiet. Once the silence had returned, Fin let out an agitated breath.

"I should be getting back. Excuse me, my lady." Fin stepped over and opened the door, leaving Annika alone in the room with her steaming anger, and her disquieted thoughts.

When Fin reentered the barracks and returned to Captain Antonio's private office, he found the king had returned from whatever duty he had been called away for, and all the men were talking quietly.

Slowly Fin eased himself back by the map spread across the captain's desk, and the group raised their eyes to him. The king's gaze sharpened as he recognized that the cook's former jovial mood had dissipated, but he decided not to question the matter further in front of the others.

"One of our sources has reported that fifty thousand men are ready to sail in Troivack," Captain Antonio announced, pointing at the capital Troivackian city of Vessa.

The king nodded pensively. "Not to mention the most recent reports stating that there are soldiers already here on our shores. We don't know their numbers, or if they are in more than one of our cities."

"When exactly did we become aware of the threat of war from Troivack?" Fin asked, his mind gradually shifting back to the task at hand.

"Just after the Winter Solstice two years ago. Though last winter was when the threat became more concrete," Captain Antonio answered gravely.

"How many soldiers did His Majesty Matthias have at his disposal at that time?" Fin leveled everyone with his stare.

"Perhaps fifty-five thousand if our reports were accurate," Lord Fuks replied while his eyes began to slowly widen. The lord was beginning to piece together what Fin was building to.

"That means he could have begun smuggling those men onto our shores for two years, for the first wave of attacks. After that, they could've begun recruiting to bulk up their forces." The witch straightened and stared at the map with his arms folded frowning. There was something off about the whole thing … Something they were missing …

"He wouldn't have posted even five thousand men just here in Austice, we would have noticed it, especially with our food levels. The city is packed as is, and there aren't many places to hide. Not to mention Troivackians tend to stick out in our country." Lord Fuks began stroking his chin thoughtfully. "Even if the Troivackian king continued sending his men supplies, five thousand soldiers are hard to conceal."

As everyone stared at the map, a sudden bone-chilling thought crossed Fin's mind. Lord Fuks said the very words in the redhead's mind, having reached the conclusion moments sooner.

"He could've placed men in every city. If we summon our armies to Austice for when the ships come, we will leave the cities without enough protection if, perhaps, five thousand trained Troivackian soldiers are already hiding within their walls."

A weighted silence fell over the group.

"We need to investigate every building in every city. We can leave no stone unturned." The king's quiet voice broke the tension, and he turned a calm face to each man before him.

"We need to find these men—and dispose of them immediately."

Fin entered his cottage wearily that night, his mind full of anxiety pertaining to the war. He knew he had done everything he could to aid King

Norman and his men in explaining how his father could strategize, but he wasn't confident he'd done enough.

In truth, he doubted he really was the best person to give insight into Aidan Helmer's mind, but the only other person who could provide the council with better information was Katelyn Ashowan. It had never been considered as a possibility to ask for her help even for a moment, as Fin refused to taint his mother's peace with knowledge of her husband.

Turning toward his pallet that was already set out for him in front of the hearth by Kate, the redhead let out a long sigh.

He hadn't liked how he'd spoken with Annika earlier. While he did want her to communicate more openly, Fin knew he should have approached it more tactfully.

After all, she was a woman who had survived as long as she had because of her ability to play her cards close to her chest. She wasn't going to suddenly tell him everything the moment they began ... being together. It made perfect sense, and Fin knew he would need far more patience with her if they were to work.

He'd wanted to try and seek her out before retiring for the night, but Annika's warning earlier in the day, to give her space until her plans had time to settle, echoed in his ears.

Resigning himself to several sleepless nights, Fin collapsed onto his knees, then face-first onto his mat. Kraken was still avoiding him too ...

Letting out a long sigh, Fin couldn't help but reminisce about his peaceful morning where things weren't quite so stressful.

Despite his new worries and earlier reservations, sleep claimed the witch without hesitation, though his dreams were not of a pleasant nature.

It was past midnight when a strange pressure on Fin's chest woke him from a rather nasty dream about a fire slowly consuming his kitchen. As he tried to open his eyelids, the weight of relaxation beckoning him to once again fall unconscious suddenly lifted when he registered a tickling sensation on his neck.

Opening his eyes, Fin found himself staring up into the glowing green gaze of Kraken. The feline's pupils were the size of marbles.

"Good evening ... witch." Kraken began awkwardly. *"We have much to discuss now that you can ... hear me."*

Fin closed his eyes and squeezed them shut. He did not want to deal with the possibility that he was sinking into insanity. It was probably a

32

witch, familiar, bond thing, but in the middle of the night was not when he wanted to reason it all out.

"In the morning, Kraken … can't we do this … in the morning?"

"Witch, you have the most unpleasant of existences. You are awake and busy at first light, and do not find time to rest until deep into the night. Now is the best time." Stepping down off Fin's chest to sit beside him, the feline patiently waited, tail swishing to and fro, as the redhead sat up.

"I also recognized a look of disappointment in your new mate when we were last seen conversing. Tell me, does the interesting-smelling female not like cats? Or was it that she thought your mind furred?"

Rubbing his eyes, Fin leaned his back against the legs of one of his dining chairs that was firmly tucked into his table and faced his familiar.

"What is it that is so important to talk about right now?"

Kraken stared up at Fin without a sound, and the witch began to wonder yet again whether or not he had been hallucinating the entire exchange.

Gods … what if I am crazy … what if I never actually spent the night with Annika … is Annika even real? Fin's hand came up and pressed against his mouth. Perhaps this was what had happened to his father. Aidan Helmer had gone mad. Completely crazy. Perhaps Fin in his child-hood had appeared to him as the devil … or a very threatening bovine …

"Do you really have no questions?" Kraken chirped irritably. *"Your familiar can communicate with you beyond what is the norm. Do you not wish to get to know me? Are you so self-centered that—"*

"Good Gods. Are you in your young adult agonies?" Fin asked with a pained expression. It was common knowledge that young adults had no shortage of pains as they battled the task of growing into the world and their minds.

"I know nothing of which you speak! Now, I have been busy studying and earning my new position with—"

"Fin? What're you doing up in the middle of the night?" Kate opened the door to Fin's room with a yawn.

"Hairballs! For someone who hates fellow humans you are surrounded by them!" Kraken sauntered away, his fuzzy haunches brushing Fin's arm as he moved.

Rubbing the back of his neck, the redhead didn't answer his mother immediately as she stepped farther into the living space. Kneeling down in front of her son, Kate watched Fin closely, a concerned expression pull-ing her features taut.

"Were you talking to yourself just now?"

Fighting down the urge to snap, Fin let out a long breath. He was exhausted and anxious ... he didn't even know what exactly had happened to Lord Piereva after he had grabbed Annika.

"I've started hearing my familiar. As in, I hear him talk to me, and he understands what I say." He lifted his face to his mother to gauge her reaction. "Am I going crazy?"

Kate studied him for several moments before slowly seating herself on the ground with her back against the fireplace.

"No. I do admit, it is not common for witches to hear their familiars. However, it is more likely to happen amongst deficient witches. I have a theory, though it is just that. A theory."

Fin waited expectantly.

"I think deficient witches don't always separate themselves from their familiars as much as pure elemental witches do. I think the pure powered see the relationship more as master and beast, whereas deficient witches are more likely to see them as friends." Kate's eyes moved over Fin's shoulder and nodded at Kraken who was watching the exchange from the shadows. "Call Kraken over; we need to have a conversation. All of us. Fin, my love, will you translate for me please?"

The redhead turned his chin over his shoulder, and with a long breath he finally did as his mother ordered.

"Kraken, my mother has questions for you."

"*Glad to see at least one witch in your family has a good head on their shoulders.*" Stalking back over to the Ashowans, Kraken seated himself and glanced back and forth between them while only giving one slow blink up at his witch.

"*Alright, what is it your mother cat wants to know, you overgrown kitten?*"

CHAPTER 5
FAMILY FEUDS

"I see." Kate had a finger pressed to her mouth as she frowned thoughtfully. Between Kraken and her son, she had just been filled in on the development of Fin's new ability. As she listened to him describe the experience, her mind had begun whirring to life.

"Fin, I think your decision to pursue Lady Jenoure has brought you closer to the essence of your abilities." Standing, the healer began to pace in front of the fire while the redhead remained seated on the ground, wondering if there would be any chance of getting back to bed before dawn.

"How do you suppose?"

"Well …" Katelyn stopped and stared down at her son pensively. "A home is supposed to be filled with love and openness, isn't it? When you think of a 'home,' you don't think of it as a place where people who love each other cannot be together. I think with you embracing your feelings and pursuing your relationship—even if it seems unlikely to end well—"

"Thanks, Mum."

"—even if it seems unlikely to end well, it is what a home should have." Kate finished scowling down at Fin. "I think you can only now understand Kraken because you aren't fighting against rules that have no place in a home."

"Your mother is a wise woman. Could you please tell her to scratch under my chin at her earliest convenience?" Kraken looked to Fin pointedly then back up to Kate.

"I can't keep track of all the things my powers involve off the top of my head." The cook sighed, ignoring Kraken's glare when he failed to relay the message.

Katelyn's studious gaze softened. As she crouched down in front of Fin, she reached out and gently stroked his cheek. Drawing his eyes up to her own, he knew he couldn't hide his true feelings from her. She knew him too well.

"My love, I think you are taking on more than you should. It might be time to start admitting your limitations," she remarked quietly. "It will be better for them in the long run as well if your potential and abilities are maximized and not spread so thinly. What task is draining you the most? Is it all the preparation of the food or—"

"It's the hours. Being in the kitchen from before dawn to after dusk, and helping the king on top of it all—"

"Helping the king? Ah. That young knight—Harris, I believe? He mentioned that you've been doing so. What is it exactly you have been helping him with? His diet plan? Is he recovering from substance abuse and needs more fluids delivered regularly?" The intensity of her questioning paired with exhaustion made Fin's mind go blank.

"Could we do this in the morning by chance?"

Kate blinked, breaking free of her focused intent. During her years as a healer, she was used to waking and being alert for long painstaking hours. This meant that when a new dilemma to unravel presented itself, she wasted no time in delving in—a tendency that had not always boded well for Fin.

"When else can we talk about this?" she asked pointedly.

Fin glared at Kraken who was the culprit of starting the poorly timed discussion, but the familiar only stared back smugly.

"Look. I can't continue working with no sleep and pulling off sixteen-hour days," he snapped angrily.

"You need to request shorter hours! Have someone else take care of—"

"I'm not talking about this now. I'm going to sleep in the kitchen. Good night."

Standing abruptly, Fin stormed out of the cottage leaving both his mother and familiar alone. The witch headed back to the kitchens, wondering briefly why for once he was not being followed by a Troivackian knight, but he didn't have the energy to dwell on it.

Upon crossing the threshold, it took Fin only a breath to realize he wasn't alone in the room.

"Who's here?" he called out while taking a sideways step away from the door to place his back against the wall.

"What the— Good Gods, Finlay, do you never sleep?" The king's voice crested the silence. As the witch's eyes adjusted to the light of the room, he recognized the pointed beard tip in the shadows belonging to his ruler.

"Are you alone, Your Majesty?" the witch asked with a sigh, already guessing the answer.

"I am. I just came down for a bit of ale and a think." Norman turned back to the mug in his hands, his posture for once slightly slumped.

As Fin stepped farther into the room, the hearth and every candle gently rose back up. The kitchen was cast in a cozy glow, and without a word, the redhead wearily retrieved a mug of ale of his own before joining the king at the table.

"Why are you up still?" Norman asked, taking a sip and keeping his gaze fixed on the fire in front of him.

"My mother can be chatty at night. I came to get some sleep," Fin admitted before realizing the connotations of his statement.

"Ah, sorry to intrude. I will be back up to my chambers shortly." Norman took another gulp of ale.

Fin looked to the monarch and saw in the hazy light the shadows that plagued the man. The war hadn't even begun, but the stress was written in every deepened line around his eyes and forehead.

"Do not worry, Your Majesty. Sometimes we all end up carrying burdens that threaten to break us. Having some quiet and an ale can be good for perspective. Or tea if you prefer."

"There could be five thousand troops in Daxaria waiting to attack our citizens, the Zinferan military has not yet been secured, and my wife is going to have our daughter before reaching a full term, which means one or both of them may perish."

"… I'm sorry to say ale is the strongest alcohol I have."

"Don't worry. It does just fine for times such as these. Any more and I wouldn't be able to carry on." The king's thumb gently rubbed against the rough mug, his mouth pursed as though he wanted to say something.

"Mr. Ashowan, there is something I wanted to wait to tell you. However, the more I think on it, the more I believe you should know sooner rather than later." Norman turned to look at Fin, the half of his face illuminated in the firelight somber.

The witch felt his heart skip a beat. Whatever it was the king had to say, it was not good.

Norman made sure that Fin was fully focused on him as he braced himself for an unknown reaction.

"Your father is coming."

The flames in the room burned brighter, and the smell of electricity made the hair on Norman's arms stand at attention as Fin stared back with a blank expression.

"Why?"

"I had Lord Piereva arrested today, and the Troivackian king is sending his chief of military to retrieve the earl. He will be staying with us for a few days to bear witness to the betrothal between a Daxarian and Zinferan noble." The king kept the witch fixed under his attention.

Fin's grip around his mug tightened, and his heart raced wildly. "My father is coming here. When?" he repeated slowly in a daze.

"My guess would be that it will be a couple of weeks."

"I don't like this, sire. Something is … wrong about the entire situation. My father is up to something. So is the Troivackian king if he warranted the earl's arrest so easily …"

"I was thinking the same thing, to be honest. We can try to figure out what they may be planning tomorrow." The king finished the last of his ale, his gaze turning to the mug in his hands.

"Your Majesty, I might need more help for my duties. Either in the kitchens or … somewhere else if I am going to spend half my days with you. While my magic can continue to work while I'm not in the room because it is still in my home, it does drain me more if I'm not in the same space. Especially as I am not able to handle any of the tasks by hand, it means my magic is doing my entire job while I work with you." Fin felt his cheeks flame as he spoke.

Norman turned a tired smile to the witch. "Your aides aren't helping you as much as you'd like?"

"No, it isn't that … They don't really know how to cook for the most part. Not the way I can."

"No one can cook the way you can, Mr. Ashowan," the king complimented with a regal nod.

"I guess I just … I'm sorry. I don't know what I'm saying." Fin sighed and shook his head. He regretted even trying to broach the topic. What kind of person pestered the king, who carried the weight of his country, in the middle of the night?

"You need a break," Norman offered gently, his tone patient. "I understand. I feel similarly, though I suppose I have more nights to myself and sleep than you do."

The king pondered silently to himself for a few moments before speaking again.

"Very well. Mr. Ashowan, you are doing your country and crown a great service as of late. All while performing your regular duties, and yet you are not receiving any recognition or promotion at this time. How about I give you a week off to recuperate. In exchange"—the king held up his finger as Fin opened his mouth to protest—"I want you to investigate Austice. I want you to try and find where some of the soldiers may be hiding. Go to some of the local taverns and try to hear any rumors that may be going around. Try to learn if there have been any large groups of Troivackians milling about. We recently lost an informant in the city, and having a pair of eyes I can trust will be worthwhile."

Fin considered the offer with his mind working sluggishly. It would be nice to have a bit of a rest from his duties, even if he was technically still working …

"Thank you, Your Majesty. I will do my best to figure out where the Troivackian soldiers may be, and I'll try to rest and get my head on straight before my …" Fin cleared his throat. "Before Aidan Helmer arrives."

Norman nodded and gave Fin a small smile before clapping the witch on the shoulder. "Thank you. Now, I better get up before my wife wakes and decides she would like to be cross with me. Get everything ready tomorrow for your absence, and then start your time away the day after. To hide our true movements, we'll use the excuse that you are investigating some of the local vendors for better bulk deals for the castle."

Waving over his shoulder, the king left the witch alone with his thoughts, closing the door firmly behind himself.

Fin slowly rounded the table over to the fire and did his best to focus on the lovely idea that he would get some time to catch up on rest. Slowly, he stretched down on the ground, not wanting to think about the possibility of seeing his father again.

He didn't even want to consider what the man might try to do should they lay eyes on each other again …

Fin had nearly reached the soothing depths of sleep, when a final thought shattered his peace.

What will my mother do if she finds out her husband is coming?

~~~~~~~

As the cook pounded the dough on his table, the aides watched him nervously. They had never seen the cook's eyes so bloodshot, or his face so pale.

"Did you … get *any* sleep, Mr. Ashowan?" Heather squeaked. She had only just returned to working with them, having come down with a nasty lung infection the weeks prior.

"Not really. Hannah, you're on apples; Sir Taylor, you—"

The kitchen door burst open, and Fin nearly swore out loud. He was not in a good mood that morning, and his nerves were burnt to a crisp.

A lady Fin hadn't ever seen before entered, dressed in finery grander than anything he had ever seen. She wore a silvery dress that sparkled slightly in the daylight, with emerald and sapphire jewels glittering on her throat, ears, and hands. She sauntered in and studied the cook from head to toe as though calculating his exact value as a butcher would in front of the pig pens.

Behind her was none other than Lord Nam.

"Are you the cook?" the woman questioned imperiously.

"I am."

Fin returned her stare and didn't bow. Technically she had not introduced herself, so he *technically* was not being rude.

Giving him a far slower, hungrier lookover, the woman smiled up at him. Fin had to fight off the urge to cringe away from her. It was somehow abundantly apparent what she was thinking while looking at him.

"Well, you certainly are a sight for sore eyes—which is exactly what I've heard around the castle." The noblewoman glanced over at Lord Nam, who was studying Fin for himself with a haughty eyebrow raised.

"We have come to offer you a position in our future household. You will be paid double what the king is offering, and you will accompany us wherever we travel to serve as our own personal cook. While I've certainly had better cooking in Sorlia, your knowledge of Zinferan dishes has impressed my beloved." The woman then cast a brilliant smile over her shoulder to Lord Nam, who immediately smirked back as though they shared some kind of inside joke.

Fin's eye twitched.

"You're a long way from home there, sweetheart. Our cook doesn't need to put up with the likes of you."

Everyone turned in shock to stare at none other than Sir Harris, who was staring at the woman with open disgust.

It was then that the rest of the occupants of the room noticed that the woman dressed in the most expensive clothes and jewels the kingdom could offer and the slightly disheveled Sir Harris were, without a doubt, siblings. The identical auburn hair, hazel eyes, and even the shape of their jaw … it was irrefutable.

"Oh, you putrid little rat! What in the world are *you* doing here!" the woman shrieked as she descended upon the group, making everyone but Hannah and Sir Harris take several steps back.

"I work here. I'm surprised you're risking your precious shoes on a kitchen floor to offer a job to someone," Sir Harris sneered with flushed cheeks.

"Get out of my sight! You! Cook! Fire this man immediately! He is a blemish to this castle and any nobility that may have the misfortune of crossing paths with him!"

"Beloved, who is that man?" Lord Nam stepped in farther to the kitchen while trying to peer around his alleged fiancée to see whoever she was shouting at.

"No one!" Swinging around hastily, her eyes flashing dangerously, the lady blocked Sir Harris from view of Lord Nam.

"Pardon me, Miss … ?" Fin began, his voice a growl.

"*Miss?!* Do I look like a commoner to you?" she demanded before throwing her chin in the air. "I am Lady Marigold, daughter of Duke Iones!"

"Easy mistake to make if I don't hear an introduction." Fin shrugged, feigning innocence. Before either the lady or lord could chastise him for his lack of apology, he added on to his statement, "After all, you did not address a knight of Daxaria with a formal introduction."

All the color drained from Marigold's face.

"A … a knight? Do you mean to tell me that little urchin is a—"

"My lady, I do not recommend referring to a man entrusted with guarding the lives of our king and queen with such disdain." Fin bowed his head, his tone emotionless.

For a moment the harpy failed to make a sound.

Then, in a whirlwind of indignity, she grabbed Lord Nam's arm and headed for the castle door.

"A lowly knight is nothing to a future duchess," she cast out with a cruel laugh.

"Say that to me when our country burns with war," Sir Harris boomed with shaking fists at his sides.

Lady Marigold swung around, her face stretched into a cold smile.

"I doubt I'll have much of a chance to say anything to you ever again, even during a war because I can tell you'll be what you've always been. Expendable."

CHAPTER 6
TURNING TIDES

The silence that permeated the kitchen was stifling. For several moments, no one looked anywhere near Sir Harris, as he stood wordlessly seething in his sister's absence.

Peter and Heather had dutifully stepped farther away from the knights as the air crackled with the promise of violence.

"So … I take it you have some family drama?" Fin asked lightly.

"What a bitch!" Hannah exploded suddenly, her fists curled at her side. "What rank of nobility do I have to be to pummel that woman without being sentenced to death?" Hannah whirled around to face Sir Taylor who jumped at the sudden movement.

"Er … she's the daughter of a duchess? Well … right now only three other noble families rank on her level. Whomever she marries will more than likely inherit the title of duke unless …" Sir Taylor glanced at Sir Harris in obvious discomfort.

"Unless I claim the title for my own damn self."

No one had seen Sir Harris as anything other than sarcastic or teasing in any given scenario, so the man who stood before them now with rage burning in his eyes and a steely set to his jaw was all the more frightening. How could there be two extreme personalities in one being?

Fin turned to the knight cautiously. "Sir Harris, I don't mean to pry, but—"

"I'm a bastard." Sir Harris's fierce gaze moved to the cook. "My mother was the wife of a blacksmith who was commissioned by the former Duke Iones for a decorative sword. It literally killed the man to make it. He had been in poor health for some time, but the pay was too generous to pass up when he knew he was dying. Within a fortnight the duke came to our house and offered my mother half the agreed price or nothing. Unless she ..." Ire choked the words from him. No one made him finish the sentence as understanding settled over them all.

"Is he dead?" Hannah demanded, her eyes glinting wickedly.

"Yes."

"Good. My to-do list is shorter," she said, seething, as she turned her glare back to the closed kitchen door.

Sir Taylor scratched the back of his neck awkwardly. "Careful there, Hannah. If you're heard talkin' like that, you could be exiled or flogged ..."

Fin looked at Sir Taylor carefully. After studying him for a moment, the cook's gaze moved to Sirs Andrews and Lewis.

"It occurs to me now, I don't know nearly enough about all of you. Sir Andrews, I know your mother was a seamstress, but that's the extent of it."

The trio of men glanced at one another with unreadable expressions. However, the wordless communication that the three often shared took longer to be settled this time. Sir Harris was oblivious to the exchange as he stormed over to the ale barrel, snatched a mug from the shelf, and poured himself a drink to the brim. Peter and Heather shrunk toward the garden door hopefully.

Hannah gazed at the auburn-haired knight worriedly, her anger taking a back seat to her concern before she then moved her attention to the trio.

"Out with it!" she snapped.

Sir Taylor turned, a small frown on his face at her tone. For the first time in a long time Hannah hesitated, before dropping her gaze, chastened. "I'm sorry. I'm too riled up after that woman."

The knight nodded appreciatively before turning to Fin.

"I am the highest ranking of us kitchen knights. My father is a lower-ranking baron in Xava, and I'm his eldest. I will be inheriting the title baron once he passes, as well as seeing that my six younger brothers are taken care of."

Sir Lewis surprised everyone by speaking next.

"I am the youngest son of my family. My father was a respectable knight, and we own several acres with tenants just south of Xava. I have three older sisters, and given that they are nearly two decades older than myself, my eldest sister's husband inherited the majority of the land. My mother found out she was with child shortly after my father's death—a second marriage you see."

Fin nodded; envisioning Sir Lewis as the youngest amongst a brood of domineering women seemed fitting.

Sir Andrews shifted uncomfortably but received an encouraging nod from Sir Lewis that had him stepping forward.

"I am the illegitimate son of Earl Laurent. My mother was his mistress even before he entered into his marriage with Lady Isobel Laurent. Though I came more than a decade after the marriage ..." Sir Andrews shifted awkwardly. "After I was born, my mother was cast out. It would seem Lady Laurent was only willing to tolerate her existence so long as there were no bastards."

Fin's jaw dropped.

Lady Isobel Laurent had been his dance instructor in the times leading up to the ball. She had been a prim, regimented woman, a cousin to the king ... though that was through the marriage to her husband, Sir Andrews's father.

"I never knew the nobility liked to make their lives so much more difficult," Hannah remarked, awed.

"You think my father or Andrews's gave a rat's ass about the price their commoner lovers had to pay?" Sir Harris barked, slamming his tankard down on the ledge. "Did you know I met my father twice before the old bastard died?" Sir Harris poured himself another ale.

"The first time? I was four. He came when my mother had sent a letter pleading him for enough coin for firewood so that we wouldn't freeze to death. The villagers had scorned her as a used woman, and so they all turned their back on us. They didn't care that they'd known her all her life, or that she had no choice in becoming a mistress." Sir Harris downed the tankard. "He came. Gave her three coppers and told her that was all she'd be getting if the child his wife bore next was a boy."

The room was deathly quiet.

"It would seem the Gods have a twisted sense of justice because all he got was Marigold. Then he never could get that cold bitch of a wife pregnant again." Sir Harris's back remained turned to them as he finished the second tankard. "He didn't return until I was fifteen. He gave me an

44

old sword and said if I wanted to inherit the dukedom, I'd have to take it for myself. Told him I wanted no part of it. I didn't want anything he had touched." Disgust dripped in Sir Harris's voice as he poured a third ale for himself.

"Then, the glorious day of his death. I received an official summons from the magistrate of Sorlia. Imagine my surprise when the duchess and my sister saw me and learned of my existence. To this day, unless Marigold marries, I can lay claim to the title. Of course there have been several attempts to have me … dealt with. So I disappeared. I joined the Royal Knights six years ago when Captain Antonio stumbled upon me working as a mercenary."

No one moved to stop the man from finishing the third ale. Everyone stood frozen to the spot.

"What would happen if you … if you tried to claim the dukedom?" Sir Andrews risked asking.

"Oh, my dear father had several stipulations. I had to have served in the military for at least five years and completed a year serving a noble household to learn reading, writing, and have the basic understanding of how to run a dukedom. An impossible task should the Duke or Duchess Iones not want it to happen."

"I see … how would one learn anything about such a role if not from your deceased father?" Peter piped up for the first time that morning while sharing a worried glance with Heather.

Hannah had still yet to forgive him.

"There are three other dukedoms in the kingdom, remember? One for each city. I just so happened to have served under Duke Rubeus Cowan in Rollom a year after Captain Antonio found me." A ruthless chuckle escaped Sir Harris's lips.

"Clever old git that the captain is, he knew more than he would ever let on. Knew exactly who I was and what the will's stipulation was. Of course I've had my suspicions that he acted on the orders of the king … Otherwise I have no doubt Duchess Iones would've put a halt to my join-ing the household of Duke Cowan."

The mounting tension in the air was broken by Sir Taylor when he blurted out loudly, "Gods, man! You mean to tell us you could be the next Duke Iones?!"

Sir Harris turned around with a cold smile that was eerily similar to the one his sister had given him earlier that morning.

"I never said I wanted it. Never planned on going after it. I wanted to go after my own fortune, but I must say …" He trailed off with a choked laugh while shaking his head. "That brat of a sister is making me rethink a few things. I don't think I can let someone like *her* wield power. Not with a war on the horizon. You know what, Mr. Ashowan? I should follow your example. You are my boss, and I should take it to heart, I think."

Fin looked at his other aides perplexed. "Me? I'm a witch not a noble."

Slamming the mug down on the ledge, Sir Harris turned to stare at the cook with a mad glint in his eye. "No. You found your own reason and strength to go after your fate. You didn't let others push it upon you, or let it be taken away. So I think now, I'm going to do the same."

Then, without a second look back Sir Harris strolled out the garden door without another word, startling poor Heather and making her squeak as she leapt clear of his path.

"He was swayed so easily." Fin blinked as he watched the back of the knight retreat down the garden path.

"Not everyone is as dense as you," Sir Andrews muttered under his breath. When the redhead shot him a narrow-eyed stare, the man had the good sense to look away.

"Some people survive by protecting themselves, others by adapting. I think Sir Harris is the latter," Sir Lewis observed with a frown, once again demonstrating his recently enlightened point of view. Ever since his time under Fin, the man had turned from slack-jawed lackey to … something of an enigma.

"Or he always had wanted it and just needed an excuse to feel like it was alright," the witch added thoughtfully after shooting the knight a brief look of surprise.

"I'm worried what his sister will do," Sir Lewis continued, staring at the doorway.

"You think she'll try to stop him?" Peter asked, stepping forward to rejoin the group.

"Harris just mentioned that they'd tried to have him dealt with … then there is the fact that his mother died in a fire shortly after his father's death—"

"I beg your pardon?" Fin's attention snapped to the knight in alarm.

"Aye. He joined the mercenaries when he was sixteen? Seventeen?" Sir Taylor looked at Sir Andrews, who nodded to confirm the information.

An icy dread crept into Fin's stomach.

"Hannah, go find Sir Harris," he instructed with an edge in his tone.

The blonde looked at him, perplexed.

"You're the only one of us who can calm him down. Bring him back here. We need to figure out how we can help him become the next Duke Iones and keep him alive in the process."

Pulling the drawstring tightly on his sack, Fin straightened. His mother stood behind him in the doorway of his bedroom wringing her hands anxiously. It was the first morning of his week off his duties, and Kate was not taking his departure well.

"I don't like that you're staying in the city. Why not save your coin and come back at night to sleep here?"

"Because it's a long walk back and I think it'd be nice to stay somewhere near the sea," he lied easily. The truth was he knew it'd be suspicious behavior for him to poke around Austice then keep returning to the castle.

"You grew up around the sea, you've gotten your fill," Kate snapped irritably.

Fin turned with a smile to face her. She had been the same way when he had been preparing to come work for the king.

"It's only for a week. I'll be back before you know it. Besides, you're barely here, anyway. You're either with the queen or seeing to everyone else's ailments." Fin planted a dutiful kiss on his mother's cheek. "You used to go to Rollom for weeks at a time without me."

"Yes, but I knew you'd be safe at home!" she exclaimed, following her son as he approached the door. "Your familiar hasn't been back since you left the other night, and you haven't told me about Lady Jenoure and I-I— Finlay!" She called out as he placed his hand on the door.

With a sigh, the redhead turned around and embraced his mother.

"It's only for a week. Kraken is fine, I can feel him somewhere in the city. I might even find him while I'm there. Lady Jenoure and I are … fine. Just relax! Maybe invite Hannah and Heather over to have some tea, the Gods know that Heather needs to be less afraid of the rest of the kitchen staff and Hannah needs to be a little less violent …"

Kate made a face that was a mix of hesitancy and concern. "You aren't painting them as the most ideal of company, you know. Perhaps I'll invite the rest of your aides over with them … I would love to hear more about all these alleged adventures you seem to have gotten into since arriving. That Captain Antonio is quite an interesting man as well, wouldn't you say?"

Fin's smile dropped and he turned back hastily to the door before Kate could see.

"Have a lovely week, Mother."

If he were being completely honest with himself, Fin was more than a little apprehensive about leaving the castle grounds. He just didn't want his mother to see and make him feel like an even bigger coward than he already was.

The truth of it was that Fin barely left the area that qualified as his home, and it had been that way since his childhood. Staying where he could protect himself and those he cared about made the most sense to him, so he hadn't ever taken any unnecessary risks by wandering around in the great unknown. Even the journey to the castle had been fraught with anxiety. Were it not for his ability to defend himself reasonably well, Fin would never have bothered taking a job on the opposite end of the continent. Festivals and other gatherings off grounds were short visits for him, and the redhead preferred it that way.

Now however ... something inside him was different. Risking his life to be with Annika had made him feel restless somehow. As though he'd cut away whatever was holding him back from growing.

The moment his foot cleared the perimeter of the king's lawn, Fin felt his magic leave his body. It was always a strange sensation that he tried not to think about. If he had to liken the feeling to anything, it'd be akin to being untethered and cast adrift into a sea of unknown ... Like a ship that had cast off without sails or oars.

In a matter of moments, Fin was strolling amongst the crowds of Austice. The freedom to follow the currents of people and not feel every object's, person's, or plant's presence was somehow quite peaceful.

He didn't feel what everyone was craving, didn't sense the general mood, didn't feel inanimate objects hum with the desire to be of use ...

Another sense had been closed off, and as a result, Fin felt his other five shoot skyward.

It was exhilarating, passing by bakeries and groups of gossiping women without any tickling sense to force out of his awareness. He watched people's faces as they went about their daily lives, consumed in their own thoughts, not noticing his attention on them. The smell of the sea and food cooking, the sounds of chattering and laughter—it was a wall of white noise that was somehow pleasing.

After walking for nearly an hour, the witch decided to grab a bite to eat at a pub that he was nearing on the right side of the road. As he headed toward the establishment, Fin failed to notice three cats that had stilled to observe him from the shadows of an alleyway as he passed by. The pub had a varnished wooden sign with black lettering that jutted out proudly from the building's whitewashed walls. It swung cheerily above the door announcing its name to the world: THE ALL OR NULL.

As Fin took the step down off the street and reached for the pub's door handle, a voice sounded behind him over the noise of the street.

"Turning tail and running already? Good to see those socks are keeping your feet so damn warm."

Fin swung around, his eyes wide. Before him stood Annika dressed in peasant garb, her long hair tied and hidden under a kerchief, and her beautiful face smudged with dirt. She looked like several other women he had passed that morning on the road … only there was no hiding her fierce gaze.

Taking the step back up to stand directly in front of her, Fin stared down at Annika in the daylight as though in a trance. As he drew closer, the viscountess faltered and her cheeks heightened in color at his proximity, though she continued openly glaring at him.

"Well? What do you have to say for yourself?"

He stared down into Annika's burning dark eyes that made his heart skip a beat, then surprised her by smiling and reaching down to take her hand.

"Come inside with me, I'd like to buy you a meal."

CHAPTER 7
A ROAD LESS TAKEN

Annika sat across from Fin in the cheery pub and studied him closely as he sat sipping his ale contentedly. Their food had come swiftly and sat enticingly in front of them. Chicken sandwiches stacked thicker than the average man could fit in his mouth, along with a bowl filled with apples, grapes, and berries.

She hadn't spoken since Fin had guided her by the hand into the pub, and she had waited calmly while he spoke to the serving wench and placed their order.

At long last Fin turned to stare at her, a small smile on his face.

"You thought I was running away from you?"

Annika's dulled anger flared up once again.

"I haven't heard from you since the day before yesterday, and then I learn from my maid that you are leaving the castle grounds with a bag."

"So you dressed as a peasant and followed me?" Fin asked slowly, his smile replaced with a look of curiosity.

"Nonsense. I was already dressed this way. Since the arrest of my brother, I've decided to stay at my estate in Austice. I sent out a decoy carriage then disguised myself in case any of his men decided to seek revenge," she snapped.

"Then you finding me in the crowded street was a happy coincidence?" His dubious tone was not lost on Annika, who folded her arms and crossed her legs in response. It was a wonder no one realized she was nobility—no peasant woman would dare to look so bold.

"You walked down the main street of Austice and took only one right. You then continued your way down toward the sea; I happen to have to take a similar path to get to my estate." She shifted then, realizing that a couple men at a nearby table were glancing at her curiously.

"If you aren't running away, then what are you doing?" Annika demanded while lowering her voice and leaning her elbows on the table.

"His Majesty asked me to take care of some business for him. I will be returning to my duties in a week." Fin's expression became shuttered, and it was clear to Annika their last encounter had resurfaced in his mind.

"You don't have to tell me," she retorted while picking up her sandwich and taking a very unladylike bite out of it.

"Very well," he countered smoothly while picking up his own sandwich and biting into it himself.

The two ate without sparing another word and when they finished, Fin paid the bill. He held the door open for her and, once they faced each other in the bright street, looked properly discouraged by their pending farewell.

"Guess I will see you back at the castle sometime ..." Fin's right toe had just turned to leave when Annika edged closer to him.

"Why don't you just stay with me at the estate?" she blurted out suddenly, her eyes darting around at the people who strode by them.

"I ... er ... uh, is that ... appropriate?" Fin blushed while lowering his voice even further.

"Not at all, but I have minimal staff who are overpaid not to wag their tongues or comment. There have been several instances where they have been tested, and they have all proven themselves. Come. Don't pay for a tavern with bedbugs, just ... at least come so that we might talk a bit more." Without realizing she had done it, Annika was clasping Fin's hand in both of her own.

Looking down at her two small hands grasping his own calloused scarred one, Fin blinked several times as though in disbelief before lifting his eyes once again to her.

"As long as it won't cause problems for you," he agreed, his cheeks beginning to deepen in color.

Annika smiled radiantly as Fin laced his fingers through her own. Stepping forward shyly, he directed their steps farther down the road toward the water.

"Do you even know where you're going?" she asked after the giddiness of him holding her hand in public had worn off.

"Not a clue," he announced, suddenly stopping in his tracks, making Annika laugh.

"Alright then, come with me."

As the couple walked, they noticed that no one spared them a second glance, as they appeared like any other unremarkable young peasant couple. It baffled Fin because, to him, the graceful way Annika moved seemed like a dead giveaway that she was on another level entirely.

"Another right here." Annika steered him to an even narrower side street, working them farther south into the city. Fin frowned when he saw at the end of the road there was nothing but the rocky cliff wall that the city was built into.

"Do you live in a cave?" he speculated dryly.

"Aren't you the court jester, hm? Just follow my lead." Annika gave him a wry smile before tugging him along.

They passed by quaint gardens with flowers and vegetables all lovingly tended to by the residents of the city. The homes with their rust-colored tile roofs grew smaller and smaller, until they became quaint cottages rather than tall, narrow houses. Hidden just before the street ended by the cliff was another quieter road that continued down the hill.

At first Fin wasn't sure what it was that was so strange about the road, until he realized that not a single home faced the street. There was neither a window nor a hole that could provide a view, and its cobbled street was worn and broken in several spots. The air of still desolation chilled Fin in a way he didn't fully understand, and he was about to say as much to Annika as they drew even closer to the sea, when she tugged him toward a dirt turnoff that he would have once again missed were it not for her guidance.

It was a wide drive that sloped down into a stony beach that was completely hidden by the strange setting of the homes and cliff. As they turned down the road, Annika glanced around them carefully, then picked up her skirts and began the journey down. Fin noted that while the road did slant down until they were at the water level, a stone archway marked the rise of another hill on the other end of the beach.

"Where is your estate?" Fin asked as the road leveled out beneath his feet and he stared out over the rocky beach at the horizon. Merchant ships dotting the waters appeared peaceful to him from such a distance.

"Just around the bend of the hill." Annika panted slightly before shooting him an excited smile.

Fin joined her in climbing what she claimed was the final hill, admiring the rising view and privacy as he went, and then he rounded the corner and stopped dead in his tracks.

A courtyard large enough to fit several carriages and a grand regal manor stood before him; it was carved into the cliff with stone balconies jutting out of several open doors and rooms. Gauzy curtains fluttered in the fresh sea breeze, while roses of various colors climbed the walls by the base. A fountain stood in the center of the courtyard with various mythical sea creatures wrapped around a large rock where at its top sat a mermaid. The water that flooded out came from somewhere within the rock the mermaid sat upon, and Fin would've taken longer to admire and examine the piece of art, but he noticed two lines of servants coming down the front steps.

Fin released Annika's hand then and instead grasped the sack over his shoulder more firmly.

It had been easy to forget Annika was a viscountess when they both lived under the roof of the king back at the castle. The extraordinary home and wealth of servants in front of him, however, brought back the reality all too vividly.

"Come, Fin. Remember, not a single soul amongst them will breathe a word." She gave him a reassuring nod before turning back to her home.

As Annika approached her servants, she stripped off the covering for her hair and straightened her posture.

Clara appeared from within the open front doors that rose in peaks and had stained-glass windows glittering like jewels in the sun.

"Why am I arriving before the carriage?" Annika demanded without saying anything about Fin who was approaching the lines of servants cautiously. The serving staff curtsied dutifully to Annika as she passed, creating an impressive wave as she moved, but as the redhead drifted by, they stared through him as though he weren't there.

"Troivackians attacked as you anticipated," Clara answered briefly before glancing over Annika's shoulder and raising a thin eyebrow. She then turned back to her mistress with a masked expression.

"He is to be my guest. Please prepare his room," Annika declared forcefully as she spared only a brief look over her shoulder at him.

"Yes, Viscountess." Clara waved her hand at two serving women who marched back into the keep immediately. "Will his room be next to yours, my lady?"

Fin was quite certain there was amusement glittering in the maid's eyes.

"Yes," Annika snapped, her cheeks turning crimson. "I'm going to freshen up and change. Have the solar prepared, I want to hear what happened to my carriage."

"Of course, my lady; would you like a change of clothes prepared for Mr. ... ?" Clara looked at Fin pointedly; the good-humored sparkle in her eyes was not lost on him, and it made him give the telling reaction of blushing.

"His name is Mr. Wit. Now one more word from you and I will deduct your pay," Annika added churlishly.

Clara made the wise decision to curtsy submissively before rising and gesturing toward the redhead to follow her. Annika had already swept through the doors and disappeared within the keep, leaving the witch, the maid, and majority of her serving staff in the wake of her whirlwind arrival.

If he didn't know better, Fin would've thought that Annika was being shy because of him, but surely the composed, confident woman he knew wouldn't feel such things ... right?

Standing with his shoulder propped against the open balcony doorway, Fin gazed out over the sea pensively. His arms and ankles were crossed as he tried not to think about the room behind him that felt too lavish to be touched. There was a cream-and-gold-threaded carpet on the floor, and chairs and a couch that matched with their wooden feet and handles gleaming from a fresh polishing. The bed was a four-poster bed with crisp white linens, gauzy curtains draped around it, and a fireplace with a magnificent stone mantel was the cherry on top of Fin's intimidation. At least with the seaside view he didn't feel guilty in enjoying ...

A soft knock at the door had him turn around, and he found himself staring at Annika, her hair brushed until shining, falling around her shoulders and back with only a small section tied back; she was wearing a white flowing gown without sleeves. A gold bracelet encircled her wrist and gold dangled from her ears. The dress was made of a chiffon, and unlike anything a noblewoman of Daxaria would dare to wear.

"You ... You look ..."

"Ah. When I'm here I ... I dress as the Troivackian noblewomen do during the summer. We tend to not worry about thick clothing or small amounts of leg." Annika kicked out her right foot to reveal a slit in the dress that climbed up until a spot little above and over from her knee.

Fin swallowed with great difficulty.

"You look quite different yourself." Annika nodded at the fine cream-colored tunic Fin wore with the gold thread embroidered down its front. "As annoying as Clara can be, she proves herself useful more often than not."

He nodded. Focusing on anything other than the slit in the dress was proving to be incredibly arduous for him. Then again, they were completely alone, in a room with nothing to interrupt them ...

"Shall we go hear what happened to my carriage?" Annika asked quietly as though sensing the shift in mood.

Fin worked on clearing his throat, but only managed to bob his head again before gesturing toward the door.

Smiling nervously, the viscountess exited before him, leaving the redhead to say a silent prayer to the Goddess that no harm would come from his risky decision to live and breathe within the same walls as Annika Jenoure.

Sitting in the solar, Fin waited patiently as the serving staff brought in a pitcher of water and a tray of fruit before Clara began to speak. It was made even more uncomfortable when they bowed before leaving, and Fin felt himself want to cringe and leave with them.

"Your decoy carriage left as planned, with Zuma disguised as you in a cloak, and me following in the carriage behind. We were perhaps about halfway down the main road when the Troivackians attacked. They killed Zuma, and attempted to interrogate the footmen regarding your whereabouts, but fortunately Captain Antonio arrived as per the arrangement and arrested them. We will hear if there is any luck in the interrogation over the next few days, though it's doubtful."

Annika didn't move or say a word as she stared at the fruit in front of her and periodically tapped the finger that rested against her thigh.

"Were any of them men my brother arrived with?"

"No, they weren't. So without a confession or reliable evidence, it will be difficult to add this to his crimes."

"Where are they keeping them?"

"In the magistrate's cells. We won't risk having them anywhere near the castle or Lord Piereva."

Annika didn't say anything as she continued mulling over the situation tentatively.

"Pardon me, mistress, but are we sure Mr. ... *Wit* here, should be hearing these details?" Clara asked while sliding her gaze over to Fin for only a moment.

"Everyone will have heard about this; it makes no difference if he knows as well," Annika dismissed the concern easily. She was still lost in her own thoughts, though, as she turned the situation over and over in her mind.

"The knights should interrogate anyone who saw the men moving through the streets before the attack and try to figure out from witnesses where they originated." She leaned back into the sofa with her arms folded.

No one said anything for a long while, and during that time all Fin could think was how he should have been searching Austice already. The men who attacked Annika's carriage were likely from the very group he was supposed to be locating ...

"I think I may head back into town for a bit and peruse around. I've not really seen the city since moving here," Fin spoke out as the thought of anyone attacking Annika unawares flashed through his mind, bringing about violent urges.

Both women looked at him before sharing a quick glance.

"Very well, I'll walk you back to your room." Annika stood at the same time as Clara, unnerving Fin even more somehow. The two were clearly very in sync with each other.

The trio walked back through the winding narrow halls without uttering a word to one another. The sound of the crashing waves far beneath them and the call of gulls were the only sounds thrumming through the keep.

At long last, Clara curtsied and excused herself when they reached what looked to be her own chamber.

Feeling increasingly sheepish, Fin walked beside Annika and wracked his brain for something to say. Fortunately, she saved him the trouble.

"Should we talk about our argument? Strangely we haven't discussed that at all ..." Annika pretended to be casually looking out the windows as they walked, but Fin could see the tension in her forehead.

"We haven't. To be perfectly honest I was just happy getting to see you so suddenly that I hadn't thought of it since we met this afternoon."

Annika's cheeks deepened in color as they neared their respective rooms.

"I can't always tell you everything." She turned to face him. Staring squarely up into his bright blue eyes that seemed even more brilliant from being by the sea, she did her best not to become flustered.

"I can't always go on blind faith," Fin countered with equal sincerity.

The two shared a long-suffering silence.

"Where does that leave us then?" Annika asked tightly, her heart skipping several beats.

Unsure he had the ideal answer to such a question, Fin opened his mouth to reply, only to have the sound of incoming footsteps make him usher her into the nearest chamber door with him close behind.

"Where that leaves us is with each other. Faults and all. I agreed to try this, Annika. I know I have a ways to go to be worthwhile to you as anything more than a … a …" He couldn't find the words. Instead, he cleared his throat and looked away. "Regardless, perhaps we could try to meet each other halfway?"

Annika fidgeted slightly before she let out a breath she hadn't realized she'd been holding.

"We're in it together, Fin. Good or bad, that's what we said when this started." Annika agreed with him, a swell of warm hope filling her. She looked up at Fin, her gaze so uncharacteristically vulnerable that all other thoughts left his head.

Reaching out, Fin drew her into himself, and once she was in his arms again, there really was no way they could argue against finding a middle ground. Especially when part of the middle ground involved crisp white linens and a room all to themselves.

CHAPTER 8
FIN'S KITCHEN NIGHTMARE

Fin awoke the next morning feeling better rested than he had since beginning his position as Royal Cook. He had wondered if he would have trouble sleeping on a bed stuffed with goose feathers instead of the floor, but the witch found that it was an unnecessary worry in the end.

After he finished dressing and had planted a kiss against Annika's temple, he had quietly retreated from the room, acknowledging that she would not be awake for several hours. The sun had not yet risen, and Fin knew he could get a lot done in the day before his lady awoke.

Perhaps I can find some useful information in Austice and get back in time to have lunch with her.

The thought put a spring in Fin's step as he walked purposefully back down the winding corridor toward the stairs he had first climbed upon arriving. The morning was pleasantly cool, but there was a taste in the air that gave hints of the heat that was awaiting the citizens of Austice once the sun rose.

It wasn't until he was halfway down the grand staircase that Fin crossed paths with another person. An elderly maid carrying an armful of fluffy white towels was mounting the steps with her tired eyes cast downward as she walked.

"Good morning," Fin greeted.

The poor woman let out a yelp and nearly fell down the stairs in shock.

"Oh my— Good morning, Mr. Wit! Forgive me, I didn't hear you!" She took several calming breaths while placing a pale wrinkled hand over her chest. "I am terribly sorry. I didn't anticipate you or Lady Jenoure to be awake for many more hours, it will be a bit of time before breakfast is prepared in the dining hall—"

"Oh, please don't fuss. Sorry for startling you, I actually just need to know where the kitchens are. I am more than happy to prepare ... er ... grab my own breakfast." Fin felt his awkwardness resurface. He didn't need them to know just how far beneath their beloved mistress he was.

"Of course not, Mr. Wit! You are a guest here! I will escort you to the dining hall this instant— Oh. The towels." Turning around on the step to peer down at a young maid who was crossing by the foot of the stairs, the elder called out. "Delores, please show Mr. Wit to the dining hall, and tell the cook to get his meal ready immediately."

Fin cringed internally. While the soft mattress may have agreed with him, the excessive servitude most certainly did not. However, he could tell that the older maid would be far harder to goad into having his way, and he preferred his chances with the younger woman.

After descending the rest of the steps and standing in front of the maid named Delores, Fin observed that she was perhaps only a few years younger than himself and was incredibly pale for the time of year.

"Come with me, Mr. Wit." She curtsied politely, her dark eyes downcast, and Fin had to stop himself from bowing in response.

The morning was getting out of hand.

"Delores, was it?" Fin asked as she straightened.

"Yes, sir."

"Right. Please call me Fin, and—I promise that I sincerely mean this—don't take me to the dining hall. The kitchen is where I actually requested to go." He gave her an apologetic smile that, instead of endearing her to his request, had the reverse effect of making her take a step back with a frown.

"Sir, I am more than capable of relaying any messages to our cook about what you would like to eat."

Fin wanted to rub his eyes in frustration, but he could tell that wouldn't convey the right tone.

"Delores, I wasn't making the request because I doubt your capability. I just am more comfortable having my food in the kitchen when I am the only one eating." He held up his hands in defeat, his weariness over the situation climbing rapidly.

Was there something truly grotesque in the kitchen that made it such a strange request?

The young maid peered at him as though he were a few eggs short of a dozen, but tentatively she bowed her head in acceptance.

As they began to move across the grand entrance of the estate in the same direction she had been heading, Fin decided to try and break the awkward silence that had stretched on between them.

"Have you been working for Lady Jenoure a long time?" he asked conversationally.

Delores slowly turned and stared at him. Her expression indicated that her opinion of him was rapidly plummeting.

What in the world is wrong with these people? Fin began to grow increasingly worried for the staff in Annika's estate ... was she a complete monster to her own servants when she wasn't at the castle? Were they terrified of anyone "friendly" with their mistress? What in the world could it be?

After a couple minutes of prolonged silence, the maid reached the end of a short hallway that was just off the dining room. Placing her hand on the kitchen door, Delores shot him one last questioning look, and it was all Fin could do to remain calm and not break the door down in exasperation.

Opening the door for him, the maid hastily leapt away from its entrance and scurried off before whoever, or *what*ever, was inside could see her.

"Who is it?!" a voice boomed out menacingly.

Fin jolted at the bellow and immediately felt himself internally reach for his magic, only to find it wasn't there. This paired with the maid's behavior set him even more ill at ease ...

Stepping forward cautiously, the redhead revealed himself in the doorway. The man staring back at Fin matched the voice that had first exploded from within the room.

A large burly man with a thick black beard and massive muscular arms stood behind a cooking table. A Troivackian. His dark eyes glared at the intruder for a moment before easing back into a pained look of respectfulness.

"You must be Lady Jenoure's guest."

Fin was relatively certain he could detect a note of disdain in the man's voice.

"That I am, and you are … ?"

"Raymond."

"A pleasure to meet you, Raymond."

He grunted.

Fin entered the kitchen and cast an appraising eye about the room while trying not to be obvious about doing so. It was well stocked, if a little cluttered and messy on a few of the shelves that stood around the room. He was pleased, though, to see that despite there being the occasional spilled potato, or dusting of flour, the place wasn't dirty.

It was perhaps half the size of his kitchen in the castle, but the one particular feature that had Fin stop in his casual perusal of the room was the open stained-glass door that looked out over the sea and let in a refreshing morning breeze.

Taking a deep breath of salty air, Fin turned with a smile on his face, unaware that he had been examining the kitchen with his hands behind his back as though he were a teacher reviewing his student's work. However, this was not lost on Raymond, a man a few years older than the redhead, who was clearly losing patience with the intruder in his kitchen.

"What a lucky man you are." Fin grinned.

Raymond's hostile expression shifted to open bewilderment.

"You get this fantastic breeze to cool you down so that this room isn't stifling. Not to mention the view is spectacular." As he spoke, the redhead kept his gaze fixed on the horizon where the soft touches of a pink dawn began cresting over the sea in promise of another brilliant sunrise.

"What can I do for you, Mr. Wit?" The terse reply succeeded in making Fin turn around, his eyes cutting to the Troivackian with interest.

"I was hoping to eat my breakfast here and watch you work." The witch walked over to the kitchen table and folded his arms over his chest.

"You'll be more comfortable in the dining hall, sir." Raymond's physical response to his visitor joining him at the table was a curling of his lip.

"I like to watch people cook; I won't be a bother." The redhead looked around the room and spotted a stool that was the perfect height for the table, no doubt the same one the cook himself used for his meals.

Bringing it over to the table, Fin made himself comfortable and stared up at the man who looked ready to punt him over the balcony edge.

"What is it you'll be having?" Raymond ground out, his teeth gnashing.

"Hm, I think I wouldn't mind scrambled eggs and a bit of bread. If there is any herb butter or bread that would be welcome. If not, some jam will do." Fin smiled and waited. His face lit up as though he were about to receive a gift.

Instead what he got was a curt response.

"You must be used to that hoity-toity new cook at the castle." Raymond turned around with a grumble, which had him missing the stricken expression his guest made.

"What's this about the new cook? I hear he's ... he's decent." Fin cleared his throat awkwardly.

"More than decent apparently—or so everyone keeps telling me since they've tried his food." He muttered more to himself than to the redhead. "He's making people fussy. Puts it in their heads that they should have whatever they want."

Fin was at a loss for words then. He didn't know how to take the ... insult? Compliment?

Instead, he contented himself with watching Raymond crack a few eggs into a bowl. It always interested him how other cooks prepared their food, and sometimes he became inspired with new recipes or methods. Settling down, he dismissed his earlier unease over the comments Raymond gave and waited earnestly to watch his breakfast be made.

Sadly, however, what Fin witnessed next quashed any former levity.

He watched the cook give a few halfhearted turns of the eggs in his bowl with a fork and sloshed the barely mixed liquid into the pan over the fire. Raymond then turned his back on the rapidly burning eggs in the pan that was far too hot and snatched up a loaf of white bread. Fin watched him cut the bread much in the same manner as a butcher would cleave a chicken's head.

By the time his food was sitting in front of him, the redhead barely felt hungry at all. He stared at the plate for several moments without moving, his expression that of a broken soldier.

"What's wrong with it?" the cook snapped after several moments.

Fin slowly raised his face to the man, his right eye twitching.

"Raymond, do you hate me?"

The massive man scowled down at the redhead.

"I don't know you well enough to hate you, but you aren't a favorite of mine," he managed to break out. "Why're you asking me that?"

Fin stood slowly, still staring at his plate as his hand went to his mouth. He said nothing, even as the reach of dawn grew behind him.

After several moments of watching his sorrowful expression, Raymond had had enough.

"What in the Gods' name is the matter?!"

Fin jumped and began shaking his head.

I can't go causing a ruckus in Annika's home. It wouldn't be right ... Fin's hands were on his hips, as he still continued staring at the food. He was struggling to find the right words.

"Raymond ... I ... I can understand if you dislike me, and perhaps prepared breakfast in such a way to communicate that, but—"

"In what way?" the cook barked.

"Like ... like it was a job. A job you cared nothing about. Food is ... food is life. It can start the day right; it can make a day better. It can heal or harm. It brings people together and is there when people are alone. Food is to be respected. It is a gift, and the best kind of gift. The kind where the Gods and mankind work together to create something whole. Something for the better." Fin turned toward the rising sun over the water and walked to the balcony doors. His gait was that of a man on his way to the gallows.

"There is no home without food. A place of rest and recovery should be sacred, and the offering of food should be treated and prepared with great appreciation and care."

Fin turned around and found that Raymond was looking at him as though the witch had two heads that spoke in foreign languages. He also noted that the estate cook wasn't the only member of the audience anymore. The elderly maid from earlier, and Delores, stood in the doorway with matching blank expressions.

"I'll show you." Fin stepped forward briskly. Rounding the table and nudging the catatonic Raymond out of the way, he picked up the basket of eggs and the egg bowl that had been discarded.

The staff wanted to stop him, but they were torn with their desire to ask how a crazy man wound up coming home with their brilliant mistress.

That is until Fin cracked four eggs faster than they could blink and had them beaten to golden smoothness in a moment with a whisk he had plucked from a pitcher filled with seldom used cooking utensils.

He carefully poured the mixture into the pan, then lifted the pan in and out of the flames, turning the solidifying eggs over gently. Without even looking, he reached over into a clay pot that held salt, and seasoned the mixture sparingly, before adding another dusting of pepper. The briefest thought of how Fin knew where the ingredients were without asking did cross Raymond's mind but was quickly dismissed as mouth-watering aromas began floating around the room.

"Aren't those just eggs he's cooking?" Delores whispered, confused, to the elderly maid at her side.

The senior didn't have time to answer before Fin had the eggs divided onto three plates. At one point he held out his hand, as though expecting something to fly into it ... but that was ridiculous. Giving his head a shake, the redhead walked over to a bag of apples—once again showing that he somehow knew where everything was as though it were *his* kitchen.

He sliced the apples up with such skill that no one thought about stopping him anymore. Everyone watched entranced as their guest worked, unable to move or speak. Somehow, even though he didn't do anything supernatural, it was as though when he cooked, it was ... magic.

Annika slowly sat up in her bed while giving a long breathy yawn. She hadn't slept so deeply in a year. Smiling to herself, she glanced over to the side of the bed where Fin had lain the night before only to find him gone.

Frowning, Annika wondered how he had been able to leave the room without waking her.

She had just swung her legs over the edge of her bed, intending to find and ask him all about his stealthiness, when her chamber door burst open and in rushed Clara.

"Up! Get up! You need to see this!"

"What in the— Clara! You forget your place, you—"

"Mr. Ashowan is in the kitchen with Raymond."

Annika's eyes widened. "Oh, Gods."

Slipping a robe over her nightdress without another hesitation, she bolted from the room with Clara on her heels.

The viscountess darted past maids and footmen who all bowed and curtsied but who Annika barely acknowledged in her rush to save Fin.

Raymond was a former squadron leader for the Troivackian army. If Fin annoyed him, there was no small chance that he'd be thrown off the nearest balcony without a second thought, even if there happened to be closed glass blocking it ...

Throwing the kitchen door open, Annika found herself staring at the backs of several members of her serving staff. Momentarily slowed by the perplexing obstacle, she finally managed to push through their shoulders and found her jaw dropping open on its own accord when she beheld the sight before her.

Fin stood behind Raymond, his arms wrapped around the ex-Troivackian military leader, as he gently guided his meaty hands into slicing a peach.

"—Thinner slices, yes, you don't want to give out quarters, it's unnecessary when using them to garnish a plate, and— Oh, good morning!" Fin greeted Annika with a knee-wobbling smile.

After a few beats of silence, Annika's brain began to work again, albeit somewhat brokenly. All she could think over and over:

Man of my dreams … Man that I love …

Turning around to head back to the dining hall, she wondered if Fin had brought any coffee with him on his "vacation."

CHAPTER 9
A DARING DEBUT

Annika sat at the dining hall table with her face pressed into her hands, trying to make sense of what she had just witnessed.

Sir Raymond Barso, ex-squadron leader of the Troivackian military, known for fighting entire battles with nothing but a club and still coming out victorious …

Had Finlay Ashowan's arms wrapped around him, showing him how to slice … a peach.

Clara slowly stepped closer to her mistress, her face composed and cool. She looked her normal self. Only someone with an eye for subtleties would be able to see the occasional flutter of her throat, indicating that she was trying desperately not to burst out laughing.

Yet Annika didn't even have to look to know that was exactly what was happening.

"Clara, please ask Mr. Ash— Wit. Mr. Wit, if he has any coffee with him."

The maid didn't dare speak, only let out a strangled high-pitched noise before sweeping back to the kitchen.

Annika gradually began to readjust her mental focus to her day plans. She had to search the city for where the Troivackian attackers had come from, and she had to try and find where they were hiding. Then she had to find out how the interrogations were going …

The sound of clay plateware hitting the wood of the table made her finally raise her eyes to see Fin standing to her right, setting down the miracle brew she had requested while giving her a small smile.

"How'd you sleep?" he asked quietly as the staff who had been spectators to Raymond's cooking lesson filed by at the end of the dining hall to return to their duties.

The dining hall was actually a good deal smaller than those in most estates owned by the upper nobility. However, the four large, peaked windows that ran along the end of the room gave a spectacular view of the sea and made the room feel airy regardless of its size.

"I slept great," Annika replied softly as Fin placed a plate of eggs with perfectly sliced peaches in front of her, and a piece of toast slathered in butter and jam.

Upon hearing a contented sigh leaving Annika's lips at the sight of the scrumptious-looking meal, Fin set down his own plate with a pleased smile and drew up a seat beside her. Admittedly the meal looked infinitely more appetizing than what poor Raymond would grub up each day; then again, the former soldier didn't really have any formal training as a cook.

"Will you be heading into town today?" Annika asked while picking up her utensils and laying a napkin on her lap.

"I will. I have things to investigate, though it sounded yesterday as though you will be doing a search of your own," Fin answered before shoveling the food into his mouth without a hint of aristocratic manners. It caught Annika off guard, having been more familiar with his more cultured education and insight. Then again, it wouldn't make sense for him to be educated on table manners or noble graces …

In time, I'll teach him, she thought to herself while shaking her head with a smile.

Fin paused his inhalation of food to glance up at her and enjoy the morning glow in her cheeks. She looked happy, and that was all that mattered. He could put up with awkward maids and unqualified cooks if it meant he got to see Annika looking somehow … whole.

The two passed the rest of the meal sharing pleasantries and idle thoughts, both relishing their first unharried morning together.

Fin sat wearily in the pub and stretched his legs out lazily. His hand wrapped around a tankard, he surveyed the room while feigning more drunkenness than he felt. He had asked a few inconspicuous questions around at local inns and with shopkeepers about any suspicious activity or people who could have been coming or going. Yet none of them could say they'd noticed a surplus of Troivackians in the city. Or at least that's the story they all seemed to stick with. After resolving to search abandoned buildings and seedy taverns on his own, Fin's quest had led him to his current location.

The Wet Whistle was well equipped as a dodgy locale for underhanded business. With its sticky floors, musty smell, and shady clientele, it didn't take much imagination to assume that dangerous people could be lurking in one of its darkened corners.

Making sure he was in the center of the entire room, under the brightly lit chandelier, Fin aligned himself to be an open target to be pickpocketed or …

"Oyy, pretty boy there!" Fin was in the process of lifting his cup to his lips when he heard the call he had been waiting nearly an hour for. He smiled into the rim and took a sip.

"You! Didn' you hear 'im the firs' time?"

Slowly lowering his ale, Fin did his best to school his expression before gazing up at the group of three men that had approached him. The one standing in the middle had a large gut hanging over a worn leather belt, and both a double chin and face that were unshaven. The last one who had spoken was a young man, perhaps twenty at most, with a blond mustache and bloodshot eyes.

The third of them was the quietest and most reserved. He was also the tallest. He glared down at Fin; his black shoulder-length hair easily managed to stay swept back off his forehead thanks to its lack of hygiene.

"N-noo! Hi! How're you!" Fin feigned his innocent expression best he could. Slurring his speech while he was at it to make himself seem an even easier target.

"Ye got coin?" The youngest of the men spit as he cackled in a deranged manner.

"Not much! Jus' visitin' my aunt! Wanna have a drink!" Fin greeted nonsensically, a large, dazed smile on his face.

"Well, les' see the coin then, hey?" the older, larger-bellied man pressed as he rested his rough palms on the table's surface.

"Pfft, I left it with my aunt! Jus' gettin' a pint before headin' back." Fin stared blearily up at them. "Good thin' too! Had a group of Troivackians try to rob me earlier, can ye believe it?!" he exclaimed innocently while draining the last of the ale.

The trio of men fell silent then and exchanged glances before stepping back and whispering to one another. Fortunately for the redhead they'd just tried to rob, the youngest member was too inebriated to control the volume of his voice. However, given that it was a three-way conversation, the man's input was quite fragmented.

"… Again … They keep … What do we …"

After several moments, the men turned their attention back to Fin who grinned up at them.

"Lad, mind takin' us to where you saw these men?"

Son of a mage … that isn't any good. Maybe if I drunkenly stumble around, they'll take me to where they last heard about them. Or …

A new idea popped into Fin's mind then as he stood with a stretch, making the men eye him even more suspiciously when they realized how tall he was.

"I'm actually quite tired from my travelin', so I think I'll head back to me aunt's." Fin began heading toward the doorway, when the man with the greasy black hair stopped him with a hand to his chest.

"Empty your pockets."

Grateful that he hadn't been lying about not having any more coin on him, Fin obeyed.

With a snort, the heftier of the three men stepped forward. "You know what we do to people who don't pay the admission fee?" His breath reeked of rotting teeth.

"Apologize for not letting them know there *was* an admission fee?" Fin's mouth worked before he could stop it. The man's breath was so potent that he had forgotten to slur his words as he leaned his face away from him.

… It then dawned on him that he had just goaded his mugger.

The man with greasy black hair grabbed Fin by the front of his tunic, yanking him down toward him. "What's that you said?" His eyes glittered.

"Well, s-sir, how can I know 'bout a fee if I wasn' told sooner?"

"Red, I don' like 'im. Somethin's wrong here. You with the knights or somethin'?" The black-haired fellow jerked his chin at his friend he'd called "Red."

"Yer right. What do ye think yer playin' at there?" Red stepped forward and pulled out a dagger that glinted in the hazy light of the room. The low whispers that had been humming around the tavern since Fin arrived suddenly fell silent.

"Not with the knights. Just visiting town." After hastily assessing the situation, Fin knew that the only way he could get out of the situation and not draw attention to himself was to take a few punches. He wasn't looking forward to it, and he tried to edge closer to the door just in case.

"Why you pretendin' to be drunk?" The black-haired man's lip curled.

"Was hoping to enjoy a drink in peace. A drunkard isn't the greatest of conversationalists."

The trio frowned in unison.

"Why you usin' big words? You sound like one of them noble people."

"I was educated."

"Think you're better than us, do ye?!" The youngest one burst forward raising his fist high in the air.

Fin knew he should've taken the blow, but the lad's movements were so clumsy the cook's pride wouldn't allow it. He easily leaned back out of the wide swing, and the young man fell with his fist, crashing into an empty table.

Fin stood with the black-haired gentleman and the one named Red. They watched the youth attempt and fail to get back up for a few moments in silence.

A small, disappointed sigh escaped Red's lips as the boy grabbed on to a chair, then somehow slipped and bounced his forehead off the table, knocking himself unconscious.

"Your son?" Fin asked sympathetically.

"If I say no, don't tell his mam," Red replied before realizing who had asked the question.

He turned to face Fin who was shaking his head and running a hand through his hair, his cavalier attitude disarming them.

"I have a younger sister a lot like him. She likes to take a swing at people." Fin sighed.

"You let a woman throw knuckles?!" Red rounded on him, alarmed.

"You try tellin' her no." Shuddering to himself and leaning into the story, Fin casually crossed his arms. "A man pulled a knife on her once and she nearly clubbed him to death with a pan. Didn't leave anythin' for me to take care of." He hung his head in feigned shame. He had adopted their style of speech as he spoke, hoping it wouldn't make them any more wary of him. He did this while mixing as much truth to his tale as possible … He'd heard that it helped make lies more believable.

While his speech pattern had jumped around, he knew mirroring the men as much as possible would help distract them from the fact.

"She doin' the dirty work for ye? Can ye even fight when yer no bigger than a fishin' rod?" Red chortled. The man with black hair continued watching Fin carefully.

"Used to get in a lot more brawls before she grew up. Now I spend more time tryin' to stop 'em than start 'em." Fin shook his head wearily.

Red and the black-haired man shared a look, then turned at the same time, each delivering a blow to Fin's middle.

"Can't have that now, lad." Red patted him on the back before clocking a fist into Fin's temple.

Still gasping for air, Fin could feel his subconscious reach for his magic, only to find nothing was there. A moment of panic flooded his mind as other people around the pub seemed to take up fights as though it were a game …

That's it. It's a game. They just like to fight. Fin managed to soothe his momentary floundering with the realization before straightening with a smile, picking up a chair, and chucking it at the two men who stepped aside easily. Red's son, however, had finally gotten his sea legs back and was promptly clobbered back to the floor by the missile.

The two men looked at each other, then to Fin who smiled and raised his fists despite a pounding pain in his head. The pair ran at him with battle cries, and then the fight truly began.

Annika sat at the dining table awaiting Fin's return while poring over the reports she had received on the progress made during the interrogations with the Troivackians who had made the attack on her carriage. Most of the prisoners were characteristically stoic, but one of the men had said something about "his group isn't ever privy to confidential information."

As the viscountess began to ponder this slip of the tongue and what it implied, Clara swept into the room with a frown.

"What is it?" Annika asked without looking up from her parchments.

"There was a strange occurrence at one of the seedier pubs in Austice … My lady, have you heard of the Wet Whistle?"

Annika straightened at that. Of the pubs in Austice, it was ranked as one of the highest crime-ridden establishments. Fights and shady deals were discovered all the time. At any minute of any day, something nefarious was happening within its walls. Its patrons knew to keep their mouths shut so that no charges were ever laid, and the owner was as mysterious as any spy. No one knew his name, or what he looked like … but people knew that anyone who brought the knights to the pub couldn't expect to live long.

"What's happened?" Annika wondered if it had something to do with the Troivackians she was looking for.

"Well … a fight broke out."

"Yes?"

Clara's large eyes glanced down to the floor, and Annika could've sworn she saw the woman's throat tremble.

"After everyone settled down, apparently there was some kind of … group singing the entire pub took part in that drew the attention of the knights who mistook it for a full-blown battle. The knights apparently joined in, and now …"

Annika waited, at a loss over what in the world was happening.

"There's a street festival, mistress. The Wet Whistle is even giving out some of its food to the beggars on the streets."

There was a beat of silence, during which Annika stood slowly.

"What … in the world … could have—"

Clara couldn't hold back any longer; she burst out laughing, her normally effervescent pale complexion growing pink with delight.

"… I swear to the Gods, do you mean to tell me that *Fin* ended a fight and they all wound up … friends?!"

"Ended the fight?! My lady, your beloved cook started it and *won* the damn thing, then offered to cook for everyone— And yes! They all seem rather fond of him!" Clara was beyond caring about her language as peals of laughter wracked her body. Annika pressed her fingertips into the top of the table and stared blindly for a moment at its polished surface.

Clara had just calmed down, when it was Annika who burst out into hysterics of her own. Next thing the women knew, they were clutching their sides with tears running down their faces, unable to stop howling over the absurdity that always seemed to follow Finlay Ashowan.

CHAPTER 10
WOMEN TROUBLES

Fin wiped his brow with the back of his hand as he handed out the last plate of food to a particularly inebriated gentleman who reeked of fish. Picking up his ale and giving Sal, the cook for the Wet Whistle, a brief pat on his back, the redhead exited the small kitchen to join in on the festivities.

As he shouldered his way through the packed pub and made his way onto the street, Fin smiled as he passed by a group of knights and some of the seedier patrons he recognized from the brawl. The group was cheering over some kind of gambling game with dice, and not one of them appeared hostile as they all laughed and shouted in good fun.

The witch was still trying to wrap his head around how the impromptu festival happened, when he strode by two men talking quietly under one of the shadowed eaves of a run-down house.

"—Going to have them come at different times. Can't be suspicious."

Fin slowed his pace and pretended to become interested in a shop window that was only a few yards away from the duo. He wasn't able to make out their faces, but something about them pricked his instincts.

"They're getting pretty rowdy these days; this'll be good for them." The man who spoke had a smooth voice, and his words were enunciated clearly, indicating he was nobility …

"Your group has been here the longest, right? Pity about the carriage, that—" They suddenly stopped talking, and Fin could feel unseen eyes fall on him. He frowned and tilted his head at the shop display of hunting knives, trying to look captivated by their prices.

When the men still didn't resume their conversation, he made a show of stepping back and staring up at the faded sign.

Unfortunately, neither of them seemed inclined to risk talking further with Fin being within earshot, and so he turned and continued down the street that was thrumming with people. Food carts had come running at the whiff of a business opportunity, and some of the townspeople had even come and strung up lanterns between the buildings.

In half a day, the street had been transformed from a dingy cesspool of criminals and shady business owners to a place of glittering joy and fun. Women and children frolicked amongst the crowd, laughing freely and chatting with their friends, while the men discovered interesting discussions and games waiting for them.

There was a merry mood all around, making Fin smile to himself as he leaned against the corner of a building and surveyed the scene before him. In reality, he was waiting for the two men he had been eavesdropping on to move from their position so that he might glimpse their faces more clearly under one of the lanterns.

He saw them talk to one more person, who was obscured from Fin's view due to the crowd, but only for a moment, so perhaps it was nothing.

Taking another drink from his cup, Fin glanced momentarily up at the night sky and was heartened to see the waning moon shining brightly above him.

As his eyes slowly fell back down to the street, Fin's heart skipped a beat when he saw a lock of silky black hair pop out in the crowd.

That couldn't be Annika ... I mean, it's late. I had said I'd most likely be back for dinner, but she wouldn't take such a risk and— Fin's inner monologue was cut short when he saw Annika's beautiful face turn in the crowd, her dark eyes peering over every face.

Of course she would. She must've become worried and wanted to make sure I wasn't murdered in an alley. Pinching the bridge of his nose, the redhead cursed himself for being so thoughtless. He didn't want to draw attention to her in case it put her in harm's way, but how could he—

"Well, hello, tall and dreamy." The sultry tones of a woman drew Fin's eyeline to the right, where he found himself staring at a beautiful woman with dirty blond hair that hung loosely around her in large curls, bright red lips, and light brown eyes. Her bodice was pulled tightly enough that it looked as though it could burst open if she so much as sneezed—though given the amount of cleavage she was displaying that must have been the point.

"Er … Hi. Excuse me." Fin turned to look back at the two men who remained in the shadows, and then to Annika, but she had already disappeared in the throng of people. He began to step out of the shadows to take a proper look for her when the woman rounded on him and stepped in front of his path. She was practically shoving her breasts against his chest—she was tall for a woman—and between those assets alone Fin was effectively hemmed in.

"Not much real fun out there. A few townie bumpkins. You seem like you're looking for something special." She smiled up at him beautifully. Her eyes were somehow … hungry and desperate …

"I am, but you're not her. Have a good evening." Fin attempted to sidestep her, but she was oddly determined as she grabbed his tunic and leaned up hastily to kiss him. Fin dodged the attack, but only partially succeeded as her red lips careened into the side of his cheek.

Immediately, he stepped back and tried to wipe the oily cosmetic off his face, but the prostitute only took another step toward him, backing him up farther and farther.

"I don't know if this kind of approach has worked in the past for you, but you need to stop." Fin's gaze turned icy, as he refused to budge another step, and stared down at the woman who finally hesitated. "Herding me back and accosting me isn't doing yourself any favors. Not to mention, I'm broke. Now have a good evening, I'm going to go find—"

"Oh, come on, let's just chat! I'm sure we could work out a—" The woman had reached out to grab Fin's arm as he finally successfully moved away from her, when a small hand suddenly caught the woman's forearm and halted her in her tracks.

Glaring up at the prostitute, Annika had appeared from the shadows. She was once again wearing peasant clothes, though the ones she wore were incredibly unflattering. She wore a plain gray skirt that fell just above her ankles, a black tunic, and a white handkerchief that hid most of her hair. The only sign of her ebony tresses was the dark tendril that had been freed from the bun at the back of her head.

"You're going to leave my husband alone, or I'm going to make you eat your entire jar of lip paint."

Fin was too stunned from being referred to as "husband" to register how sincere Annika was in her threat.

The prostitute showed only a moment of consideration before she laughed. Her condescending notes made Annika shift her grip on the arm, and the burst of pain made the woman suddenly choke.

"Be gone," Annika hissed, thrusting the woman back several steps.

After a moment of staring just over Fin's shoulder, the prostitute turned her gaze back to him. "Enjoy the short leash." She barked like a dog, giggled, and whirled away back into the crowd.

Turning and staring up at him with pink in her cheeks, Annika began speaking angrily. "I swear, just because I helped get rid of her, she has the nerve to— Why are you staring at me like that?"

"You … you called me your husband." Fin blinked as his gaze moved down, and he watched as Annika's eyes widened.

"No, I— Well, I did, but only because I didn't think she would leave you alone unless I said so." Her voice trailed off to a mutter as she suddenly turned her attention to the crowd awkwardly.

"I liked hearing it."

Annika blushed, unable to look at him, or say anything in response.

Fin smiled as he returned his attention back to the shadows where he had been hoping to see the men, only to find that they had left.

"Damn." He frowned as he stared at the spot where they had been.

"What is it?"

"The men … They were there, I was waiting to see their faces, but—"

"Oh, the prostitute distracted you for them." Annika shrugged as she leapt to the conclusion swiftly.

Fin turned to her, startled. "How do you figure that?"

"A high-ranking prostitute who becomes that aggressive toward a commoner isn't likely, especially given that she was beautiful. I don't doubt she has serviced far more powerful men, or even nobility—" Realizing that she was accidentally insulting Fin, she turned to face him quickly with apology already forming in her mouth.

"How do you know she is a high-ranking prostitute?" The redhead hadn't even registered the slight and was more intrigued with the reasoning, much to Annika's relief.

"She was dressed in more expensive material and had moderate-quality makeup. Also her teeth are perfect." As she spoke Annika reached up and began trying to wipe off more of the red lipstick from Fin's face.

"So she might know who the men are?" Fin began scanning the crowd looking for the blond hair, while missing the look of irritation that momentarily creased Annika's face.

"Yes. Or her madam might."

Fin looked down at her, ready to issue an apology and a farewell before chasing after the woman, when he registered the look of annoyance.

"You keep me waiting for dinner, have been drinking all day, won a brawl fight, and somehow started a street festival. Now you want to go chase a prostitute." Annika folded her arms over her chest.

"I ... I am sorry that I didn't send word about not being able to make it back for dinner. This has to do with what the king asked of me, though, I'm sorry. You've made it clear you want us to keep certain facets separate from our relationship, though, remember? I doubt you're going to tell me all about your day, right?" he reminded her while placing his hands on his hips.

"I don't wind up getting kissed by strangers and starting pub fights that could get me stabbed!"

"No, you just *get* stabbed and then bury bodies in the woods," Fin countered evenly.

Annika's eyes widened, and her nostrils flared.

"Good thing I bloody well don't tell you more— You do realize you just blurted that out in the middle of a *Godsdamn festival*?!"

Several heads around the couple turned at Annika's raised tone, and people gradually began adjusting their paths to give the pair a wide berth.

Fin had just opened his mouth to reply when Red stumbled over to him with his son, who turned out to be named Sasha, and the man with black hair, a family friend of Red's named Tom.

"Lad! What a turnout! I haven't had this much fun since Tom an' I met twins that— Oh. Who do we have here?" Red turned with a lecherous smile to face Annika. Both Fin and Tom cuffed him over the back of his head.

"Lorraine will kill you before dawn at this rate," Tom growled.

"How's it going?" Sasha drunkenly leaned toward Annika who was not taking kindly to the interruption.

"It was going just fine until a moment ago," she snapped while shooting Fin a scathing look.

"Well, how 'bout I make it aaaaaall better!" Sasha sluggishly rested his hand on Annika's shoulder.

Before Fin could intervene, she had the hand peeled off and bent back painfully, bringing the young man to his knees.

"Don't touch me."

Fin stepped forward hastily before Red or Tom could get angry and gently pulled Sasha free from her hold.

"You'll be fine, Sasha, but you aren't having the best of days. Maybe take a seat." Fin patted the whimpering young man's shoulder sympathetically.

"Oyy! Is this that sister you were tellin' us about?!" Red demanded indignantly while pointing a sausage-like finger at Annika.

Rounding on Fin faster than a hawk hearing a mouse in a field, Annika exploded.

"YOUR *SISTER?! GODSDAMNIT!*" Annika turned away and began storming back toward the crowd.

"Hey! That isn't what he meant! I-I-I didn't say you were my sister!" Fin called after her, but he couldn't even attempt to keep up with her as she wove in and out of the flow of people with near inhuman speed thanks to her smaller stature. Before he'd even taken three steps, she was on the other side of the street.

Letting out an aggravated sigh, Fin turned to the trio of men who all watched, shifting their stances uncomfortably.

"What … is wrong with the women in your life, lad?!" Red finally managed, making Fin begin rubbing his forehead.

"Probably me. I tend to make people go a little crazy." The tone of defeat went unheard amongst the men.

"Red, there was a particularly pushy prostitute I noticed earlier. Red lips, tall …" Fin found himself at a loss of how else to politely describe the woman.

"Aye, you met Sultry Sandy! Bit out of your price range, lad." Red shook his head sympathetically while Tom merely nodded silently in agreement.

"I'm not interested in … that … but who is her madam?" Fin asked, his focus turning back to the important task of finding the king valuable information.

The trio of men all shared confused expressions before answering.

"That'd be Madam Mathilda," Tom replied, watching the redhead carefully. "Why do you want to know? She's a mysterious woman … not many people have seen her."

"Kind of like the owner of the Wet Whistle?" Fin asked slowly.

"Yeah—only we don't even know the name of the tavern owner," Red remarked while eyeing the tankard clasped in a passing knight's hand. Sensing that his new friends were about to disappear back to enjoy the festivities, Fin rushed his questions.

"What is my best chance of talking with Madam Mathilda?"

"You could try goin' to the house where all the girls live. It's just 'round the corner." Tom brandished his empty tankard down the slope of the street.

"Good luck, lad, no one has seen the madam 'side from her closest friends."

Barely registering the warning, Fin set off toward the end of the street, determined to get the answers he needed, and then he was going to have a long talk with Annika.

They couldn't keep fighting over their work …

With a sigh, the redhead braced himself for the coming hours, somehow sensing that his exciting day was not over just yet.

CHAPTER 11
THE HEIGHT OF THE NIGHT

Fin rounded the corner of the street where the festival had inadvertently started and found himself staring at a sea of colorful skirts and heavily powdered women. Several drunk gentlemen were draped around the ladies, not to mention a good number of knights.

Ducking his head in case any of the military men were from the castle, Fin managed to step in over the threshold into the establishment without notice.

When he was certain that he was tucked away from errant gazes, the redhead raised his chin and blinked several times to adjust to the brightly lit room. The moment his sight returned to him, he sneezed. The new assault on his senses came from the overwhelming scent of perfume and incense that was so thick he nearly gagged.

Once he had recovered enough to risk swallowing, Fin scanned his surroundings. The room was far larger than he would've guessed given the size of the front of the house, with an oak bar taking up a third of the space against the left wall. Wrapped around the entire perimeter above them were banisters leading to the rooms the clients could retire to with their chosen companions. There were bright pinks and reds in the curtains and carpets everywhere, while the furniture was polished to a shine.

It somehow seemed like the room was aching with the bright colors and rosy-cheeked patrons ...

Stepping farther into the building, Fin surveyed four burly men who watched the room from each corner. Clearly they were there for the protection of the women, but the redhead also worried that they could prove problematic if he needed to do a bit of sneaking around ...

"Hi there, gorgeous, you looking to get a*head* in life?"

Unable to stop the bemused smile on his face from the poor pun, Fin looked down to stare at a young woman, who barely looked over fifteen years of age, scantily clad in a sheer chemise, and a black silk robe tied around her waist that made her look like a mourner. His amusement disappeared immediately, and instead he stared at the young girl with wild curly blond hair and big blue eyes with a frown that made her take a step back.

"Ah, sorry if I upset you, sir! The girls did tell me not everyone would like my humor—"

"How old are you?" Fin demanded.

The girl straightened and jutted her chin out indignantly. "Sixteen! Why does that—"

"Gods. What's your name?" He covered his eyes and tried to not dwell on this new dilemma.

"Chastity."

Fin stared at her for a beat before speaking again. "Your real name?"

"Chloe. Ah! Dangit! I'm not supposed to—" The girl clamped a hand over her mouth when suddenly a tall slender brunette with a beauty mark painted on her left cheek appeared between the two.

"Would perhaps a more worldly companion suit your tastes, fine sir?" She batted her eyelashes, while simultaneously herding Chloe behind her. Fin immediately respected the new woman for clearly protecting her young coworker. She wore significantly less makeup than her coworkers, and from the look of it, wasn't the slightest bit inebriated.

"Sorry, I did not mean to cause a stir." Fin sighed. He knew young prostitutes were not uncommon, but it was more likely that poor young women would seek a husband for a few years before the whorehouses. For a girl like Chloe to be there meant she had been truly desperate, or someone had sent her to work there ...

"Quite alright." The new woman breathed with a smile. "We are still training Chastity, but I'm more than willing to repay your patience." She lifted her hand and was moving it toward Fin's chest when he moved back with a shake of his head.

"No, thank you. I'm here with a business query for Madam Mathilda; where might I find her?"

The woman stiffened, and as if on cue, the nearest guard approached them.

"Everything alright here?" His bald head gleamed in the bright light of the room.

"This man says he has … a proposition for Madam Mathilda." The brunette shrank away from the redhead as though she had just learned he had leprosy.

"Er, yes." Fin noticed that the man in front of him was making eye contact with at least two other guards in the room.

"I'm new to town, and uh …" Fin looked around and was pleased to see that there wasn't an abundance of attention aside from the guards directed his way. "Have I done something?"

The brunette cleared her throat awkwardly behind the guard as she backed away until she had merged once again with the crowd.

"I can count the people who've met Madam Mathilda on one hand. She don't take kindly to strangers stickin' their noses in her business," the guard responded with a growl.

"I'm just looking to find out why she would intervene in *my* business," Fin countered vaguely.

The guard's wiry gray eyebrows shot up. "Madam Mathilda interfered in your business?"

"She did."

The guard frowned and eyed Fin up and down cautiously.

"Go have a drink. I'll be right back," he ordered gruffly before giving the redhead a shove in the direction of the bar.

Without having any more coin, Fin acquiesced to taking a seat on one of the tall stools, but he waved off the bartender when the man sidled up for his order.

In hindsight, Fin knew he should've been more skeptical when he was suddenly given a free drink, but he was too busy scanning the crowd looking for any Troivackians to give it much thought. Besides, he'd been pacing himself well throughout the day, a single drink wasn't going to interfere with his ability to think …

His first mouthful of the strangely bitter yet sweet concoction, however, snapped his attention to the barkeep, who was already moving away from Fin's side of the bar.

Giving his head a shake, the lights in the room began to shine to the point of haziness, and Fin found his fingers and hands exploding with strange sensations of tingles and lightness. The guard was returning to his side through the crowd, and the moment he was within earshot, Fin began to ask, "What did you …" but the room was beginning to rock slightly, and so he found himself forgetting his train of thought.

"Come with me. The madam's assistant wants a word with you," the guard uttered quietly while pulling Fin to his feet.

For some reason, the redhead found himself smiling exuberantly. He felt great! Everything was cheery, people were having a good time, he was going to talk to Mathilda then go back to Annika's estate and talk with her. He'd be all set in no time at all!

Fighting the urge to hum, Fin allowed himself to be guided up the wooden staircase to the second story with zero resistance. Peering out over the excitement below, he found his grin becoming even broader until his entire face felt sore. Everything seemed to magically glow and heighten the euphoria he was basking in.

The guard had just realized that the redhead was not right behind him and turned back, annoyed, to grab him by the elbow. Being quite content with his place in the world, Fin had no qualms with being pulled along. His newfound carefree attitude, however, meant he was slow to react when he careened into a hooded figure that was exiting one of the rooms.

"Ahh, sorry about that!" Fin beamed as the fellow he'd bumped into righted himself.

Once the figure had regained his balance, Fin found himself staring down into the very surprised gaze of Mage Lee.

"Hi there, Lee! How're you doing tonight!" the witch cheered, patting Lee's shoulder as though they were old friends.

The mage was stunned into speechlessness.

The guard began pulling Fin along again before the elder could recover from his shock.

"Bye, Lee!" the redhead waved happily as he resumed being dragged along the balcony.

Mage Lee stared after him perplexed, unable to move as he tried to make sense of what had just happened. It was in that state that his wife found him as she too exited the room.

"Alright, we better get back, I just got inspiration for my book and— What is it, dear? You look like you've seen a ghost." Candace Lee righted her robes as three prostitutes filed out of the room behind her with dreamy smiles on their faces and only partially dressed.

"You go ahead of me; I think I saw ... I don't know what I saw ..." Giving his head a shake, Lee began reluctantly walking in the direction he had seen Fin being carted off, even though he was unsure of whether or not he wanted to be involved in the cook's affairs.

Gods, please don't tell me that bloody witch is in trouble. Please just let it be that he is here for a good time ...

Sitting alone in an office that was tucked inconspicuously in the farthest corner from the stairwell, Fin looked around while still unable to stop smiling to himself.

Unlike the downstairs, the room had a masculine quality to it. With an expensive green carpet beneath his feet, and a large oak desk in front of him with a fireplace behind it, the room was cozy. What was even more surprising was how quiet it was given the amount of noise both outside on the street the window looked over, and in the bar area beneath his feet.

Fin's focus shifted to the painting of a horse hung over the fireplace with a gilded frame, and for some reason, even that seemed like a reason to be happy. As he began considering standing up and perusing the room further, the door opened, and in walked a lissome woman wearing a stylish forest green dress; she had chestnut brown hair, almond-shaped brown eyes, and a thick red book under her left arm. She appeared to be barely older than Fin yet carried herself with all the confidence of a captain.

"You're the gentleman who insisted that Madam Mathilda interfered with your business?" she began briskly without sparing him a glance.

"I am." Fin smiled at her, but he received a blank look in return.

"I see. How is it that Madam Mathilda came across your path?" Seating herself behind the desk, the woman opened the book, and plucked up a white quill already dipped in ink with a business-like efficiency.

"One of the girls here was sent to accost me earlier to distract me."

The look of annoyance that flashed across the woman's face was borderline frightening.

"Sir, our girls are meant to drum up business by—"

"I find it hard to believe Sultry Sandy needed to drum up business so aggressively." Fin smiled innocently, but his words had the desired effect of making the woman in front of him stiffen.

"You're certain that it was Sandy who was propositioning you?" she asked hesitantly.

Fin turned his cheek where he had no doubt remnants of the woman's lipstick still existed, despite both his and Annika's best efforts.

A dark expression fell over the assistant's face as she stood and marched over to Fin. Grabbing his chin roughly and jerking it over so that his cheek was better exposed to the light, she wiped her thumb against the mark. Rubbing her two fingers together, she examined the texture in silence for a moment before turning back to her desk and seating herself.

"What business were you conducting that Sandy allegedly distracted you from?" The woman folded her hands over the crisp pages of the book and waited for the reply.

"Well, that's what I'd like to talk to Madam Mathilda about. I also don't believe I got your name." Fin's sunny disposition showed no signs of dimming, despite the bluntness of his words.

"I am Elizabeth Nonata. Assistant and manager when Madam Mathilda is elsewhere. You will discuss your business with me and tell me exactly what happened." Her authoritative tone made it clear to Fin that she was not a woman who had an abundance of patience.

"I won't," Fin replied breezily and stood up. "I will come back another day to try and catch her. Good evening."

Elizabeth snapped her fingers and immediately the guard who had escorted Fin to the room opened the door and filled the frame, his arms crossed.

"You will stay here until you tell me exactly what it is that is going on. This now concerns official house business," she explained coolly.

"I'm aware. Which is why I will discuss it with Madam Mathilda. You legally cannot hold me here."

At the mention of the law, the woman's eyes glinted dangerously. "You think the magistrate of this city will take your word over—"

The guard cleared his throat before tentatively stepping farther into the room while closing the door behind himself. Apparently he was more intimidated by the assistant than he was any male patrons.

"Miss Nonata, he seemed to be quite chummy with … *Lee*, who was with us this evening …"

At that, Elizabeth stood and rounded her desk, staring at Fin with a glint of curiosity. "Is that so?"

Giving a small effortless shrug, Fin tried to choose his words carefully. "Well, for obvious reasons, I don't like talking about knowing a mage of all things, but—"

A sudden knock on the door cut Fin off immediately.

Elizabeth's gaze jumped to the guard, and after a moment of shared eye contact, she gave him an affirmative nod.

Turning to open the door, the man used his body to block Fin and Miss Nonata from view.

"Private busi— Why … uh … Royal Mage Lee! What brings you here to—"

"—Oh, good Gods. Ashowan! You in there!" The unmistakable voice of Mage Lee made its way into the office without any issue.

"Hi, Lee!" Fin called back jovially.

"Son of a … Miss Nonata, you didn't give the gentleman in there … that special brew the sailors brought you, did you?"

Elizabeth's eyes widened as she turned to stare at Fin with new-found concern.

"I did, why?"

"Oh Gods … can I please come in?"

In another moment Lee stood in the room staring at Fin with open distress and vexation.

"Ashowan, how're you feeling right now?"

"Great! Everything is quite wonderful right about now! I feel tingly and— Hey! Hey, we should try whatever that drink is with the others back at the—"

"You are *not* allowed to go back to the castle in this state. Not ever."

"Castle?! Mage Lee, is this man nobility?!" Elizabeth's alarm was making her voice rise in volume. Lee shushed her hastily then let out a long, aggravated sigh. Before responding, he shot Fin an annoyed eye roll as the man continued smiling like the village idiot.

"He's not nobility but he is … a problem. Especially if his judgment is altered," the mage grumbled bitterly.

"I don't care much for your tone, Lee; that tenth fountain was entirely your own doing, you know," Fin jumped in indignantly.

"Why is he here in my office asking to meet Madam Mathilda?" Miss Nonata demanded after shooting the redhead an incredulous look.

"Gods, I don't know; he's …" Lee's shoulders slumped forward in defeat. "Could I please speak with him privately? I'm sorry for the trouble."

Elizabeth's lips pursed, and for a moment, it seemed she wouldn't condone the meeting at all. After giving a closer appraisal of Fin's dopey grin, however, she conceded with a curt nod.

After a few awkward stares and shuffling, Mage Lee and Fin were finally alone.

"Alright, you dunce, what are you doing here?" Mage Lee implored wearily.

"His Majesty sent me here," Fin replied good-naturedly. "Why're *you* here, Lee?"

Clearing his throat awkwardly, the mage shifted his weight. "Private business, Ashowan. What do you mean the king sent you here? You expect me to believe His Majesty sent you to a high-end prostitute house?"

"He didn't send me *here* here. Just getting done what he asked took me here. Does Mrs. Lee know you're *here* here?" Fin waggled his eyebrows, making the elder turn crimson before closing his eyes in exasperation.

"She was here with me but— That does not concern you! Do you even know *who* it is you are set on annoying here tonight?"

"Well, no, because everyone is being real cagey on letting me meet her!" Fin sighed as his gaze suddenly moved to the window, his eyes losing focus as he continued staring dazedly outside.

"What is it?" Lee snapped after a moment.

"That window's glass is very well cleaned, don't you think?"

Lee looked to the ceiling and begged the Gods for the virtue of patience.

"I don't think that, no. Fin, you are currently irritating one of the biggest black market business owners of the city. One word from Elizabeth Nonata can have you disappear at any time, and not even your family will dare to say your name once Madam Mathilda's men are through with you."

There was a moment of silence as Fin slowly turned his face back to Mage Lee.

"Lee, don't be so worried! After all, I annoy the king on a regular basis, and I've not been decapitated or imprisoned once!"

"Miss Nonata is different; she isn't— Wait. You're aware you annoy His Majesty? Do you do it on purpose?!" The mage's incredulousness had his tone rising swiftly.

Fin didn't bother to answer, and instead he began to hum to himself as he stood and strolled over to the window and looked down into the street where the festivities were still carrying on. Mage Lee continued trying to think of a way to handle the delicate situation, but after several moments had to silently confess that the greatest challenge of the whole scenario centered around one important fact …

How much of the witch's thought process was induced by the drug he had taken, and how much was just Finlay Ashowan being his usual pain-in-the-ass self?

CHAPTER 12
FAILING SIDEWAYS

Fin watched with a dazed smile on his face as Mage Lee paced back and forth in front of him. The old man was stroking his beard frantically and had his staff clenched in his hand. His eyes searched the floor blindly for answers to questions the redhead didn't feel overly concerned with.

"Lee?"

"What?" the mage barked abruptly.

"I'm feeling a bit hungry, I think I'm just going to step out to the festival and—"

"The festival … yes … wait a minute. You wouldn't happen to have anything to do with the festival that randomly broke out, would you?" Lee rounded on Fin with a mad glint in his eyes.

"Well, that is quite the accusation to make! I mean how could I, a lone person, start an entire—"

"Godsdamnit, it *was* you." The mage closed his eyes and took a deep breath. "I need to advise the king to never send you out of the castle for errands ever again."

"Nothing bad has happened! Don't worry that pretty little mage mind of yours! Go with the flow and ride the wave of life!" With a daft smile still on his face, Fin clasped Lee's shoulders and then tried to move around him toward the door.

He wasn't having any of it, however, and proceeded to rap the witch on the head with his staff.

"Snap out of it. I need to figure out a reasonable explanation for you asking after Madam Mathilda so that you aren't a person of interest to her ..." Lee resumed his thoughtful pacing.

"What if I want her to be interested in me?" Fin countered before a look of horror crossed his face, his smile finally eradicated. "Oh no. That sounded wrong. Please know I didn't mean that way! I can't have her thinking that I'd ever be interested in anyone else. I—"

"Who can't you have you thinking you're interested in anyone else?" The mage turned around hastily and gave Fin his undivided attention.

Fin slapped a hand over his mouth and shook his head like a child who had eaten something they shouldn't have.

"Ashowan, do you by chance have a woman you are courting?" A slow smile started to light the mage's face.

The redhead continued shaking his head.

"Affianced then?"

Fin paused his frantic head shaking, then frowned, finally removing his hand from his mouth. "I don't think we're any of those things ... at least not yet, though I suppose that was implied. I mean, I hope it was ..." It was the witch's turn to begin pacing with a frown, leaving the mage to watch in awe.

"So, Mr. Ashowan, you're having difficulties with the fairer gender, hm?" Lee scoffed. "Well, I knew it was a matter of time. You need a woman to goad some sense into that head of yours, though I must say, I already pity the lass who decides to put up with you."

Fin stopped his pacing and let out a wistful sigh. "She's amazing. I think I'll go see her."

The redhead had just strode past the mage when he found himself being halted by Lee's grip on the back of his tunic.

"Hold it there, you idiot. We still need to find a way out of this mess."

"Oh, for Gods' sake." Fin sighed exasperatedly before slapping Lee's hand off his shirt and lunging for the door. Throwing it open before the mage could stop him, he called out: "Ms. Nonata! Please come baaaaa— Ow!"

Lee had successfully clubbed Fin in the ribs with his staff and thrown him back into the room, but it was too late. The damage was done.

Elizabeth Nonata strode back in and regarded both men coolly with Fin hunched over his middle, and Lee looking even more agitated than before. Rounding her desk, and seating herself again, she made no move to retrieve the quill she had laid down before.

"So, gentlemen, what is it you wish to tell me?"

Fin opened his mouth and Mage Lee once again attempted to cover his mouth, only the redhead was ready for that, and so the two ended up in a childish scuffle that had Elizabeth Nonata pursing her lips and raising her eyebrows.

At long last Fin shoved Lee back into his seat so forcefully two of the legs began lifting off the ground. Turning back to the assistant while slightly out of breath, he finally managed to speak.

"I'm looking for whoever paid off or told Sultry Sandy to distract me. She interfered in my business, and I figured the only person who could've had that say over her would be your madam. I didn't mean to irk the owner of the house." Fin gave a small bob of his head; the drug had evidently worn off enough that he no longer needed to smile incessantly.

Elizabeth Nonata seemed to consider the argument carefully before replying.

"Sandy is under the protection of this house, and that means I cannot allow you to question her. I can, however, promise she will not interfere in your business again."

"I need to know who she was covering for." Fin jumped in before Mage Lee could stop him.

"Sandy was most likely aiding a client, and if it is a client, we will protect his or her privacy." The assistant stood, her dismissal of the two imminent.

"She interfered with another client, and I believe it is my right to know." Fin held his ground then.

A sardonic expression overcame the woman's face as she eyed Fin from head to toe. "Pardon my saying so, but you do not have the means to be a client here, that much I can tell."

Not caring a whit that he had been condescended to, Fin crossed his arms and stilled his features.

"Not myself. Mage Lee. We are looking for the men together; however, he was taking a ... dinner break with his wife." Fin cleared his throat while ignoring Lee's strange guttural noise that was a mix of an outraged denial and a pleading whimper. Fin guessed that the elder was bordering on apoplectic.

Letting out an agitated sigh, Ms. Nonata pointed to the door. Her answer was clear.

Slowly, the two men left her office without another word. Lee looked pained, and Fin crestfallen.

As they walked, Fin noticed the guard who had escorted him up hung back by several feet, but he followed them all the same. As they strolled for a wordless moment along the upper floor staring down into the pit of excitement below, the redhead suddenly slowed his pace.

"I really do need to find out who Sandy was covering for. It's a hunch but—"

"Wait a moment. Do you mean to tell me you just risked the wrath of one of the most dangerous crime rulers in Austice based on a *hunch*?!" Lee's distress rose substantially.

"A good hunch! C'mon, you know my hunches are good." Fin looked around at the blithesome glowing lights of the room in a daze.

"What I *know*, Mr. Ashowan, is that the Goddess must've laid down horseshoes in the soles of your feet for all your damn luck."

The witch sighed while ignoring Mage Lee's strange compliment. Not only had Fin failed, but he had angered Annika in the process.

Not to mention that, according to Mage Lee, he would most likely be followed for a few days and potentially roughed up at some point just to be sure he learned not to bother Madam Mathilda's house.

Yet somehow, despite his failures and pending trouble, Fin still had an oddly good feeling about the night. Then again, the drug was still singing in his blood … at least the initial wave that had made him unable to control his face had worn off.

The men descended the stairs down to the first floor, only to find that it had grown even more crowded as people enjoying the festivities had filed in to close off their nights in the arms of a woman or two.

As Lee and Fin attempted to shoulder their way through the crowd, they found themselves being herded closer and closer to the wall farthest from the bar where several men had their mouths attached to the women's necks, or their hands wandering over places that would've earned them a hearty slap in polished company.

They had made it about halfway through the room, when Chloe broke free from the crowd, pulling with her an inebriated middle-aged man with flushed cheeks. He was well dressed—most likely a merchant—and had his mustache waxed straight.

Fin stopped, his euphoria unable to properly process the emotion that tore through him.

Mage Lee's gentle hand on his shoulder appeared immediately. "I know it doesn't seem right, but we cannot cause more trouble than we already have."

Just then, the merchant Chloe had been tugging along stumbled as he cleared the last ring of patrons, sloshing the contents of his cup, a ruby red wine, all over Chloe's dress.

Releasing his hand and giving a small gasp, she stared down at the stain that began at her breasts and ran all the way down her front to her hemline.

"Ahh, don't worry, dress won't be on ye long!" The man proceeded to half shove the young girl against the wall in front of the two onlookers, completely oblivious to their presence.

Fin moved before Lee could stop him; he seized the man by his shoulder and thrust him back. The guard who had been tailing them was held up in the crowd, though he tried valiantly to move faster.

Still holding his shoulder, Fin flashed a predatory smile down at the customer who was at least half a foot shorter than him, and slight of build.

"What is the meaning of—"

"Ever seen a ritual killing?" Fin's words paired with the maniacal glint in his eyes made the gentleman visibly gulp.

For a long drawn-out breath, no one knew what was going to happen, until Fin suddenly adopted the most flamboyant voice Lee had ever heard, and suddenly popped his hip out.

"Because, handsome, that's what this dress looks like it's been through! The fabric needs to be washed immediately! Chastity, darling, please stay as you are, we don't want that wine staining anything else. Now, how about you be a dear and go grab a clean towel, vinegar, and laundry soap from the barkeep. If he doesn't have those things, perhaps some white wine. This hunk of gorgeous here will go help you!" Fin gestured toward the guard who arrived and appeared equally as stricken as the mage who watched with his mouth agape.

"W-Who are you?" the merchant asked, as he tried to reconcile the murderous man who had first grabbed him, and the effeminate pansy who was kneeling in front of the young prostitute tutting over her garb.

"I'm the Head of Housekeeping here! Madam Mathilda's house doesn't get its sterling reputation for nothing! All the girls must be shining and perfect for our esteemed guests." Fin gave a flourished wave over his shoulder as the customer stared back and forth between Fin and the guard who looked equally confused.

"Chop chop! No time to waste— We *cannot* be having Madam Mathilda waste money unnecessarily on such things!" His words worked in motivating the drunken man into action as he turned back to the crowd. The guard was clearly uncertain about whether or not to leave Fin alone with Chloe, or to protect and help the patron who was looking at him expectantly when faced with the wall of bodies.

He eventually chose to help the paying customer after the man's second unsuccessful attempt to head to the bar, leaving Fin, Mage Lee, and Chloe alone.

Shifting the black robe that had absorbed a good amount of the wine, Chloe stared down at Fin with pursed lips.

"Why'd you have to do that?" she asked with tears beginning to rise in her eyes.

"This is chiffon. It's expensive, and you would've been in more trouble for ruining this than that man's night," Fin informed her with his usual voice.

"R-Really?"

Fin looked up at her. He doubted the truth to his words, but the truth would've burdened everyone.

"Yes."

Standing up, Fin peered over the heads of the crowd and was satisfied to see that the guard and patron had just reached the bar.

"Are you out of your mind?" Mage Lee demanded in hushed tones in his right ear.

"It's a bad stain!" Fin defended heartfully.

"Is that why you looked ready to snap his neck?" Lee demanded.

"I was not—"

"He will take that woman to bed, Fin. You can't stop it."

The silence that ensued made the mage turn to study Fin's profile and found that he looked so openly broken, it caught Lee off guard. Looking to the young woman who was trying to pull her skirts taut to avoid the stain spreading, Fin felt a helplessness settle in that he didn't like one bit.

"Is … is that woman the one you were talking about earlier—" Lee began, referring to Fin's love life from earlier.

"No. No, she isn't. She just is too young to be here. Most girls her age are looking for husbands … Unless they truly have no choice."

"Much like Hannah. I understand why you—"

"Who?!" Fin's head snapped toward the mage so quickly he could've given himself whiplash.

"Your kitchen aide. After you started joining in on the war council discussions, I investigated your aides. The blond one, Hannah? Her father was a nasty drunk. Tried to sell her off when she was fifteen … he died before the deal could go through. She had to raise her brother, though, so she found work at the castle— But you must already know all this. Why are you staring at me like that?"

Fin's eye twitched. "Remind me to bake that woman a pie."

"I don't think pie will—"

"Well, it's something!" Fin's drug-addled brain was too stressed to handle such heavy topics.

The guard and patron who was hoping to share a bed with Chloe reappeared then, much to Fin's disgust and relief.

"Here." The guard thrust the towel at Fin, along with the vinegar.

"Perfect, thank you, darling. Remind me, what's your name?" Fin resumed his flamboyant persona when he addressed the brothel's muscle.

"Erm … Name is Gord."

"Gord, you scrumptious devil, please see if you might find another garment for Chloe here!"

"Chloe?" The merchant turned and stared confused at the young woman who suddenly looked fearful.

"Ah! My mistake! My mother's name; you know, *Chastity* here just makes me think of her! Tell me, what's your mother like?" Fin asked the patron as he dropped to his knees again and began dabbing at the fabric.

The gentleman blinked several times, the color in his face draining. After a few moments he finally managed to say, "M-My mother never really paid me much attention growing up … it was more about my brother …"

"Oh, dear. That can't have been nice; was your father any better?"

"N-No." The patron suddenly looked as though the weight of the world was pressing heavily against his shoulders.

Fin looked at him compassionately.

"You've struggled a lot then?"

"I have. I've made a name for myself, and I ship the finest goods from … from …" he trailed off, sorrow marring his face. Gord the guard proved to be a feeling sort as he reached out and patted the merchant's shoulder sympathetically.

Mage Lee watched astounded as, once again, the witch affected his surroundings in the most baffling way imaginable.

"Oh, Lee, why don't you make yourself useful and get a chair for the guest," Fin called out in a mothering tone.

Mage Lee looked at Gord and the merchant who appeared to be lost in the vulnerable moment, making them consequently useless before turning his gaze up to the ceiling. He realized it was time to seriously consider if the witch in front of him was correct in his belief that mages were, in fact, cursed.

CHAPTER 13
WINNING BY DEFAULT

Elizabeth Nonata had just finished logging her account of the situation pertaining to the tall redhead she had learned was called Finlay Ashowan, and the Royal Mage. That being said, she was beginning to question if Lee really was a mage or just liked to wave his fancy stick around and claim he was.

If Lee was who he said he was, however, she didn't like that castle business was finding its way to her doorstep, and she hoped that after the nuisance that was Mr. Ashowan had his legs broken, he'd be less inclined to drag further attention to the establishment.

Standing and stretching, she strode over to the window and noted that the festival was winding down.

Good. I can finally go to sleep. This was not supposed to be a busy night … Ah well. Mathilda will be happy that we had a sudden profit wave.

Momentarily closing her eyes, Elizabeth took a fortifying breath and then turned and exited her office.

Her mind was already drifting to the goblet of wine she was going to savor before gratefully climbing underneath her crisp linen sheets. Her thoughts were so far from her present, in fact, that she didn't notice anything amiss at first.

No, it wasn't until she had nearly reached the first corner of the balcony that she realized the normal chaos that deafened her was at a tolerable hum.

Peering down onto the bar floor, she noticed that several patrons and her workers were all facing something that was under the balcony walkway. Whatever it was, Elizabeth couldn't quite see from her position.

Worry fluttered in her chest as she quickened her step while lifting her skirts ever so slightly in her hand to make sure she wouldn't trip.

Lithely she descended the steps, only to find that she was then too short to see what was happening, and too far away to hear who was talking through the many shoulders and ruffled skirts. It sounded like a woman weeping and a man asking questions …

Frowning ever so slightly, Elizabeth's eyes raked through the crowd searching for one of the guards she paid handsomely to keep business running smoothly. When she eventually did manage to find not only one but all of them, she was deeply irked to realize that all of them were watching whatever attraction was occurring with exclusive interest.

Muscling her way to the nearest guard named Sing, a brick wall of a man, she faced him with cold fire leaping from her eyes.

"What is the meaning of this?" she hissed.

"Your new Head of Housekeepin' is solvin' our patron's marital disputes." The guard known as Sing replied with a whisper as he lifted a finger to point to the scene, his eyes still transfixed.

"My new what?"

"Head of Housekeepin'. That guy the mage keeps callin' 'Ashowan'?" the guard replied, his eyes not once leaving the scene.

Elizabeth resisted the urge to kick the man in the shins. "Sing?"

"Yes?"

"Break his legs in front of everyone."

"The mage?!" Sing was so mortified by the suggestion that he finally turned to look at his employer.

"No, Ashowan's!" she snapped.

The guard's mouth closed, and his expression drew down into one of sadness.

"But they're just gettin' to the part where we find out whether or not Mrs. Keedle is having an affair with his brother!"

"Now!"

The reluctance Sing was unable to hide did not help Elizabeth's mood in the least as she watched the man gradually muscle his way through the crowd.

Once he had disappeared, she waited for the screams to start, for the crowd to gasp and shift awkwardly away, but that didn't happen. The longer she waited, the more concerned she was, and it didn't get any better when she saw Sing slowly making his way back to her, his face pale.

"What happened?" she demanded as soon as he had returned to her side.

"T-The Royal Mage says he would like to speak with you in your office. He's comin' through now."

Elizabeth's lips pursed. The entire situation was spiraling out of control, and if there was one thing that was guaranteed to put the assistant in a black mood, it was problems with meddling patrons.

Mage Lee slowly made his way to the stairs; the moment he laid eyes on the infuriated woman, he cast his gaze downward. Unable to properly face Elizabeth's wrath, he wordlessly gestured to the staircase as the crowd suddenly broke out laughing over something Fin had said.

Upon entering the office, Elizabeth could feel the rage she had kept under control downstairs begin to peak. Slamming the door firmly after the mage had cleared the threshold, she descended upon the elder like a murderous banshee.

"What the bloody hell do you think you two are doing?! We've had an arrangement since the beginning, Lee: you do not interfere in this house's business, and word never gets out about your visits. Even though we both know there would be no better advertisement for the house." Hands on hips, she loomed over the man who was doing his best not to cower.

"I know, and for that I am grateful. I promise, however, that if you try to break that man's legs, it will only mean bad things for your establishment. Ms. Nonata, I would not intervene lightly. If you break Fin's legs in front of a room full of wealthy merchants and knights, the king himself might become involved."

That quelled her rage enough to make her pause.

"Lee, who the hell *is* Mr. Ashowan?!"

"A pain in the ass—"

"No! No ambiguous replies, I want an honest to Gods answer. Who. Is. He?"

"He's … He's a cook!" The mage floundered while trying to properly explain without letting on just how important Fin was.

The redhead was the embodiment of a headache and was helping advise the war council for the kingdom, his mother was going to be delivering the next prince or princess and helping to keep the queen's life out of danger as well.

And worst, yet most important of all …

He was a Godsdamn house witch who also happened to be a hero that helped save hundreds of people from Hilda the water witch who had attacked not so long ago …

"A cook." Elizabeth stared back at Lee flatly. Despite her placid expression, Lee wasn't fooled. He knew an even greater storm was brewing inside the woman. "You risk my wrath by trying to convince me that the king of the continent would become involved should I discipline a *cook*."

"Ms. Nonata, please, there are some things I cannot say!" Lee was beginning to back up as the woman drew nearer.

"Mage Lee, you are henceforth banned from ever returning to the house after this evening. You and that meddlesome redhead aren't to even sniff in this direction. I am breaking Ashowan's legs *tonight*, and you, Lee, are going to be grateful that I don't do much worse to yourself." Her eyes were wide and had a mad gleam in them that had the mage swallowing with great difficulty.

The office door opened then, and in stepped none other than Finlay Ashowan, his legs perfectly intact. He brought with him a wine bottle and a single glass, but he knocked gently on the open door while surveying the drama with a sunny smile.

"Ah, sorry to interrupt. Ms. Nonata, I believe this is your favorite beverage? Your bartender seemed to think so."

Mage Lee stepped forward and quickly took the bottle and glass from Fin, in a halfhearted effort to avoid them becoming weapons Elizabeth Nonata could use.

"What happened downstairs?" Lee jumped in, unable to hide his curiosity.

"Oh, Mr. Keedle needs to go home and have a long talk with his wife, but I think they'll be alright. I don't believe she actually slept with his brother, but he needs to apologize for taking to bed anyone he can pay to."

The assistant slammed her palms on the desk, silencing the two men before she stalked over to Fin, the shadow of death following on her heels, eager for whatever carnage she was prepared to create.

"You. Don't expect to be needing your boots for quite some time." She growled up at his infuriating face. She knew the drugs were making him more careless, but this was ridiculous.

"While I am all for preserving my footwear, I'd like to ask you, Ms. Nonata, is it your business that I have intervened with?"

The silence that rang in the room was deafening. Lee doubted he'd be able to save the git no matter what he did.

"Just as you are angered and ready to do me considerable bodily harm. This all began due to my inquiring to speak with the one responsible for doing the same thing to me. Do you see now how you mishandled the situation since the beginning?"

Elizabeth punched him in the groin.

Fin doubled over and collapsed on the floor at her feet, while Mage Lee winced for the younger man. The mage set the bottle of wine and glass down on the desk behind him as an excuse not to look at Fin's pained expression on the floor.

"Now that you've had time to reflect on your words, Mr. Ashowan, would you like to reconsider what you've just said?"

When he was unable to do anything but wheeze, Elizabeth turned her back on Fin, and strode swiftly back to her desk. Now she just had to wait for the guards to do the last bit of dirty work and the whole situation would be—

"Ms. Nonata!"

Both Sing and Gord burst into the room, both of them nearly tripping over Fin who was still curled up on the floor.

"Godsdamnit, what now?" She exploded furiously.

"T-There are knights serving under Viscountess Jenoure's house h-here to retrieve Mr. Ashowan. They were quite adamant that he not be harmed."

This time, it wasn't only Elizabeth Nonata who was stunned. Lee, completely perplexed, looked at Fin on the ground. When the assistant and mage shifted and locked eyes, the elder shrugged.

"Even I don't know about this one."

Stomping back over to Fin who was slowly picking himself up, she grabbed him by the front of his tunic and gave him a firm shake.

"WHO THE HELL ARE YOU?!"

Mage Lee was rubbing his face and trying to convince himself that he was actually asleep back at the castle, and none of the absurdity had actually happened.

It was then that two lines of knights marched through the open doorway. Both Gord and Sing were easily shoved aside, and Elizabeth stared dumbstruck at the group before turning back to Lee looking more than a little helpless and unhinged.

"First, he knows you. Then you say the king would become involved if his legs are broken, now knights serving the Jenoure household are in my study. Did the king have a bastard I'm unaware of?!"

Mage Lee shook his head, his hand covering his mouth as he genuinely had nothing left to say.

Releasing Fin's tunic and flinging herself behind her desk, Elizabeth collapsed into her chair and watched Fin slowly bring himself back to a standing position. Her face was twisted with a deranged expression ...

Wordlessly, the redhead walked over to the desk, his shoulders ever so slightly hunched around his aching middle, and set to uncorking the wine bottle. He filled the glass nearly to the brim and then set the bottle down.

"Have a good evening, Ms. Nonata, it's been a pleasure."

Smiling, Fin turned and followed the knights out of the room with the mage following hastily behind him, clipping his heels as he went.

Instead of descending the stairs back down to the main room, the guard named Gord guided them to a back stairwell away from prying eyes; it led to the alley beside the establishment, where only a few drunkards lay on the ground unaware of the world around them.

Exiting into the alley, the knights opened the door to a sleek black carriage that sat waiting for them. As Fin stepped into the cushy interior, Lee was about to follow him, when the witch turned sharply and stopped him.

"Er, Lee ... this is taking me to Lady Jenoure's estate, not the castle."

The mage stared blankly up at him.

"I just saved your hide in there and you are telling me you are not going to give me a ride back home? Also, why in the name of the Gods is Lady Jenoure sending *you* a rescue team?"

Fin had been concocting the lie ever since learning who exactly was sending in the cavalry on his behalf, and so he gave his prepared answer.

"I came to town for His Majesty and was looking for a place to sleep. Lady Jenoure's maid Clara offered me a room to stay in at Viscountess Jenoure's estate. In return I'm helping their cook improve on a few dishes."

The mage frowned. That much made sense, but still ...

He glanced back at the row of knights.

"Why did the viscountess concern herself with rescuing you? Furthermore, how is it she *knew* you needed rescuing?"

"I'm not entirely certain myself. I'll let you know if I get the chance to talk to her. Thanks for your help, Lee!"

Without waiting for the mage to say or ask anything more, Fin ducked inside the carriage and closed the door hastily.

Annika sat with her arms crossed and a glare on her face. Her expression was visible thanks to a candle that was held in a glass bowl in a small compartment behind Fin that had a glass door.

"Hi, love," Fin greeted weakly.

She said nothing.

"It really wasn't all that bad. I—"

Annika said nothing, but somehow Fin still cut himself off.

"Look, I know I—"

Once again feeling the words die in his throat, Fin wondered if Annika was secretly a witch capable of stealing his voice.

"The situation was in hand, it just—"

The carriage jostled them around as it moved, but Annika continued staring stonily at him.

"I'm sorry." Fin's shoulders slumped forward in defeat.

An odd noise that almost sounded like a laugh drew Fin's attention to the small window behind Annika where she could shout to the driver if need be.

"Fin, you do realize the mess you've created tonight?" Annika demanded quietly.

"I don't think it's that bad!"

"You just painted a massive target on your back with Madam Mathilda's business. I'm guessing you didn't find out any information on the two men you were watching, and you— Why in Gods' name are you smiling?!"

"I was drugged." Fin continued grinning. While the effects had lessened since he had initially taken it, he still found his face naturally collapsing into a grin when faced with his beloved.

"Do you even know what they gave you?!"

"Not a clue!" Fin began to hum as he watched Annika's beautiful face in the faint glow of the candle.

The viscountess began rubbing her eyes furiously, the black hood of her cloak falling back to reveal her shining dark tresses.

"How did you know I was in trouble?" Fin tilted his head as he asked, easily becoming mesmerized by her.

Peeking up at him for a moment, Annika sighed and leaned back into her seat.

"That's a story for tomorrow morning when I'm not ready to kill you." Her eyes strayed to the carriage door wearily.

"If it makes you feel any better, you're probably the third woman tonight to feel that way!"

With a long moan Annika straightened in her seat and stared defeatedly at Fin.

"There's someone other than Elizabeth Nonata?"

"Yes— I'm also curious how you know about her, but I guess we'll come back to that. Yes, I hired a new kitchen aide! Her name is Chloe, though she isn't too happy with her career change. I kind of insinuated she was a lad with a spot or two to the man who was trying to sleep with her back at the house."

"You ... Good Gods. Why?!"

"She is only sixteen," Fin remarked, shaking his head.

"There are prostitutes younger than that Fin! Why in the world would you ... Godsdamnit. You've really made a mess of everything."

"Hardly, she gets a new job, and it's one less young prostitute having to do something they don't want to do. I know if we had a daughter with no options, I'd want someone to step in."

That made Annika pause. Fin gazed at her warmly, and next thing she knew she found herself blushing.

With another sigh, she conceded for the night. The bleeding heart of a man sitting across from her was still smiling, and it was a problem as his smile was a weapon against her anger. As was the bone-collapsing fatigue she felt. Dawn was only an hour or two away, and all she wanted was to crawl into bed with Fin beside her.

"Annika?"

"What is it, Fin?"

"Thank you for saving me."

"You're welcome."

"I got punched in the groin so I might not be able to—"

"No more talking for tonight." Annika closed her eyes and leaned her head against the wall of the carriage.

Good Gods ... man of my dreams ... man that I love ...

Fin slowly moved over next to her and pulled her head onto his shoulder. Kissing her hair, he shut his eyes with a smile that may not have had anything to do with the drugs in his body.

CHAPTER 14
MINDING THE MADNESS

Fin awoke with a faint pulsing headache, and an unpleasantly nauseous stomach that immediately had him wary of any food or coffee. Slowly he opened his eyes, his mind sluggish and a little hazy.

Reaching out to his side, he tried to grasp Annika's hand to give it a small squeeze, only to find her side of the bed was in fact empty.

Sitting up swiftly, and nearly vomiting as a result, Fin found himself staring at Annika who stood at the foot of the bed, her one hand holding a goblet, her other arm wrapped around her middle with her hand gently resting in the crook of her elbow.

"Good morning, Finlay."

At the use of his full first name, his stomach grew even more uneasy.

"Morning … erm … have I slept long?"

"Oh, it is just about midday; how're you feeling?" Her tone was light, and her expression unreadable. At the rate his stress was rising, Fin would not have been surprised if he vomited imminently.

"Not the greatest …" He eyed her hesitantly as he adjusted his position in the bed.

"It's interesting, you see, I'm not perfectly clear on what drug you were given last evening. Tell me, do you remember anything?" She casually stepped over to his bedside and handed him the goblet that was filled with water.

Taking a grateful sip from the silver cup, Fin's mind began to stretch itself.

He remembered walking into the house belonging to Madam Mathilda, and talking to the young girl named Chastity—or Chloe rather …

Then there were odd flashes and scenes, but some of them felt more dreamlike …

"Erm … was I speaking to a crowd at one point?" He frowned while trying to figure out the jumble of images.

"Oh, at one point you were quite the entertainment of the house. You gave public counseling to some of the patrons of Madam Mathilda's, trying to help them better their marriages and all."

Fin knew he shouldn't have, but he chuckled a little.

"That sounds … amusing."

"Oh, I'm glad it does. Did you enjoy making Royal Mage Lee panic?"

"That part wasn't a dream?!" Fin's alarm smothered all joviality.

"Oh no. You owe that man a great debt. From what I'm given to understand, he saved you from getting your legs broken by sticking by your side and trying to calm down Elizabeth Nonata for more than an hour."

Fin immediately began scanning the room for something to be sick in. Sensing this inevitability, Annika bent down and handed him the empty chamber pot from under the bed.

Once he was finished relieving his stomach, he reached for the goblet of water that Annika had placed down on the bedside and took another deep drink to wash away the acidity left in his mouth.

"The part where I saw knights come to rescue me, was that …"

"Men under the command of the Jenoure house."

Fin paled again, but thankfully stopped himself from being sick again.

"I am unbelievably sorry for making you have to send … oh Gods. Who saw them?" He looked into her calm brown eyes, his panic etched in every line of his face.

"No one saw you leave with them thanks to an inconspicuous back stairwell."

Rubbing his face wearily, more and more fragments of his memory began to come back, though Fin almost wished they hadn't.

"How angry with me are you?"

"I feel very little pity for your current state," she answered shortly. "How could you be so dense as to accept a free drink from a business that had been hostile to you?!" Her volume began to rise and Fin visibly winced.

"I haven't had any problem before with—"

"Why in the world did you not investigate what kind of woman Madam Mathilda is *before* insisting on seeing her?" Annika demanded next, the fire in her dark eyes burning hotter.

"No one who told me about her mentioned that she was—"

"One of the major underworld leaders?"

"… Exactly."

Annika dropped her forehead to her hand and began rubbing it in soothing motions.

"Fin, I know you are not a foolish man. You understand people relatively well, but you are naïve to the world. I blame your magic. You haven't needed to rely on wisdom to survive in a long time. If ever," she muttered to herself defeated.

"I … admit there is much I don't know, but I did learn things that will help me."

"At a greater cost than the information is worth!" Annika snapped desperately. "Fin, please, please tell me what exactly the king asked you to do."

At that his spine went rigid.

"Will you share with me *your* plan pertaining to our relationship? The war?" he asked cautiously.

"The plan for us I concede that you should know, but there are political matters I cannot discuss; it'd be treasonous."

"Aren't I in the same situation then?" Fin countered defensively.

"Fin, you're being reckless and I'm genuinely worried!" Annika exploded, her expression becoming openly vulnerable. The witch was taken aback by this new show of emotion.

"I knew I'd most likely start a brawl in the pub I went to. I wanted to find information from the people once they deemed me acceptable. Or better yet, to try and needle out information from the owner. Then next thing I knew I'd created a festival, but it was that or the brawl would've spilled out into the street," he explained quietly, while reaching out and gently grasping Annika's hand.

She shook free of his hold.

Turning around she pressed the heel of her palms into her eyes.

"Godsdamnit, Fin … what're you doing to me?" Her voice was quiet, but steady, and the redhead felt his heartbeat triple its speed. "Before you, I'd write you off and or have you shipped off for causing so many complications to my plans. I wouldn't give a second thought to my methods or have … *feelings*!" The last word of her rant dripped with despair and disgust.

"Why is it bad that you're feeling things?" Fin's quiet voice made Annika turn back around, the stress on her face bordering on pain.

"I've survived this long because I can be distant. Assessing and making logical decisions is important, because a second guess? A hesitation? I will not be effective in my job. I will not survive. Hank made me … made me promise that if I ever fell in love to … to never … GODSDAMNIT!" Annika Jenoure was in tears, and Fin was holding her the second he saw them.

Unbeknownst to the embracing couple, outside the chamber door was a crowd of servants. However, only one of them had her ear pressed to the keyhole of the door. Clara leaned away and whispered to the group that had gathered.

"Oh, she loves him alright."

The cluster of servants broke out in silent smiles and excited jumps. Clara shared in their joy, but a small frown was creasing her normally flawless complexion.

"What is it?" Raymond asked while matching the maid's hushed tones.

"These two need a lot of help," she admitted, the trace of worry in her voice making the excitement die back down. "Get back to your duties; I think she'll take a little while to settle down from the sounds of it."

"Gods, did she even cry for Hank's death?" one of the newer maids whispered to Raymond as the group began to step away from the chamber door and scatter back to their positions.

"I think once, but I can't say for sure. The old man never wanted her to," he replied gruffly as they moved farther away from their mistress's bedroom door.

"I haven't really met this Mr. Wit fellow … what do you think of him?" the newer maid asked with a conspiratorial note in her voice.

"What I think"—Clara's cool voice cut into the conversation, making both servants jump and turn quickly while both curtsying and bowing—"is that we are in for quite a bit of fun. Honestly, you should have seen our lady yesterday in the brothel …"

Annika's evening after her confrontation with a certain redhead during the festival …

Storming away from Fin and the men who believed her to be his sister, Annika made her way back into the shadowed alley where Clara lurked waiting.

The maid only had to watch the hurried pace of her mistress to know that something was wrong. Not wanting to jump to conclusions, however, she waited. After Clara handed the noble her cloak, Annika huffed and set off farther down the alley where she would eventually exit on the next street over.

"So ... I take it Mr. Ashowan is fine?" Clara asked when she had caught up with Annika's breakneck pace.

"Oh, the giant numbskull is doing great! Throwing a festival event for the hell of it and chasing prostitutes!" Annika uttered scathingly.

Clara halted and blinked in surprise at the viscountess. "You mean to tell me that he has already strayed?"

"What do you mean 'already'?" Annika turned on her maid, a crazed glint in her startlingly calm face.

"I meant that it seems you two are having troubles quite early on ..." Clara arched a thin eyebrow. "My lady, might I be so bold as to ... inquire what exactly happened?"

"There's no time. I have to make sure he doesn't get himself beaten to death." Annika grumbled with the subtlest note of hysteria.

Knowing the Royal Cook's propensity to land himself in trouble, Clara didn't need to question her mistress's urgency.

The women made their way to the waiting carriage that had parked farther up the street that ran parallel to the festival; once inside, the two changed their clothes swiftly. Annika covered her hair with a cap and dressed as an errand boy to a midlevel merchant, while Clara changed into a low-cut pink dress and let her long blond hair fall from its usual tight bun.

"Which whorehouses are in this area?" Annikka asked distractedly while pulling on her shoes.

"Hm ... there are three that I know of. There is Madam Tulaney, Mister Danier, and of course ..."

"Godsdamnit. Madam Mathilda." Annika threw the carriage door open with significant force, allowing the cool night wind to enter their stuffy confines.

"You think that's the one he went to?"

"Tell me, Clara, where would someone go to get in the most trouble imaginable of those three options?"

The maid didn't reply, but instead hiked up her skirts and followed her mistress who had already taken off at a sprint.

~~~~~~

Upon entering the crowded house belonging to the one and only Madam Mathilda, Annika scanned the room hastily for the signature fiery red hair she had come to know intimately. After several moments, she realized she couldn't find Fin, which was odd given his unnatural height …

Thinking quickly and moving through the crowd, Annika figured one of three things could make him hard to see. Either he was on his back with one of the paid women, in the office with the assistant or even the madam herself, or sitting down. The last option was preferable.

Pushing herself closer to the bar, Annika did her best to keep her face turned toward the ground so that none of the nearby patrons might recognize her. She had finally managed to wedge herself beside the oaken surface, when she spotted Fin sitting on the opposite end.

Letting out a small sigh of relief, she watched the way his sharp blue eyes surveyed the room. He was doing the smart thing and watching the guards of which there were …

Supposed to be four.

One for each corner of the room.

Annika risked lifting her face up enough to try getting a better view of her surroundings to locate the missing guard.

It took a moment, but she finally found the paid muscle on the second-floor balcony, locking eyes with the bartender and giving a nod, then holding up a single finger. Fin's back was to that part of the balcony, and so he missed the exchange.

Annika's heart skipped a beat as she then watched the bartender reach beneath the counter, pull out a strange vile, and pour its contents into what looked like a glass of milk …

Annika's mind immediately shifted through the poisons she knew of.

She needed to warn Fin or find a way to administer an antidote as quickly as possible. Then again, he wasn't completely unaware of how dark the world could be. Surely he wouldn't …

The viscountess watched in dismay as Fin failed to spare the bartender a second glance as he was handed the beverage. He drank what was given without even looking at it, and Annika felt her heart stop. She immediately began pushing her way through the crowd around the bar when she noticed the missing fourth guard appear back in front of Fin. He had moved exceptionally fast given that moments prior he had been on the upper balcony. Perhaps there was a back stairwell …

Where the crowd had moved to quickly get out of the bald guard's way, they would not for Annika dressed as a page boy, and so she found herself being pressed farther and farther away as Fin was pulled along with a strangely peaceful smile on his face ...

Confused, Annika doubled her efforts, but the guard and witch were already on the second floor.

Fin suddenly stopped and stared out over the sea of people as though marveling at a beautiful sunrise. For a brief hopeful moment, Annika thought he might be able to see her and she could signal him. Instead, the guard retrieved him and began pulling him along the balcony once more.

Annika finally broke free of the crowd and had one foot on the stairs when she saw something she couldn't believe.

Mage Lee?! She stopped in her tracks.

Her heart racing, Annika saw Fin speak briefly to Lee who had just exited one of the rooms, then once again the cook was tugged away. The elder stared after the redhead, openly dumbfounded, without moving to follow the man, and Annika nearly screamed in frustration, when Mage Lee's wife exited the room.

Unable to properly process what she was seeing, Annika stood frozen. Three women left the room after Candace Lee and headed to the stairs— exactly where the viscountess stood.

Turning to the railing and pretending to be searching the crowd, she could hear the giggles and feel the brush of lace brush behind her as the prostitutes joined the throng of patrons below. Once the women had successfully passed, Annika mounted another step, only to see Mrs. Lee heading straight toward her while Mage Lee ... followed in the direction Fin had been taken.

Annika let out an audible sigh and turned to the railing so that Mrs. Lee would pass without recognizing her. Once she was certain that no one else was behind her, she collapsed onto the step, her shoulders slumped.

Gods ... what in the world did he get himself into?

Steeling herself, the viscountess stood back up and headed straight to the bar. She trusted Mage Lee would take care of Fin; even if the two of them usually battled like cats and dogs, there seemed to be an understanding there.

Now, she just needed to find out exactly what the witch had been dosed with, and to find out who he was being hauled off to meet.

The moment her foot touched back onto the first floor, Clara was at Annika's side.

"You distract the bartender, I'll get behind the bar and steal a bit of the powder they put in his drink," Annika ordered her maid quietly as they began to move in unison.

The two had been in similar situations during the years they had been together, and so they worked together with the utmost efficiency and understanding. Neither of them needed explicit communication to know what needed to be done. The only wild card in their usually flawless operation being the one and only Finlay Ashowan, the one they were trying to save.

CHAPTER 15
AN UNEXPECTED GUEST

*A*nnika's *night continued ...*

Giving the vial a shake, Annika frowned at the powdery substance and gave an experimental sniff.

"This is ... odd. It smells like a drug that I know ... but I think it's cut with something else."

Clara nodded while pretending to lounge against a pillar. The cook still hadn't emerged from the room with the woman Annika had learned was called Elizabeth Nonata. The viscountess had gathered the name from one of the other girls while pretending to inquire where her "master" might be able to submit a donation to the house. She of course had been pretending to be the page boy for a merchant, and fortunately most of the occupants of the room were too inebriated to be suspicious.

Thus far her disguise was going over quite well, though she had a few choice words that she kept to herself when some of the other patrons began suggesting that "the small errand boy" should join them in their evening activities.

"What is the drug you know of?" Clara asked, bringing Annika's attention back to the task at hand.

"It's called kava. More or less makes the taker experience height-ened sensitivity to light and euphoria mixed with relaxation. Could make someone be pretty trusting. If it were cut with perhaps something that would make the mind a little foggy, it'd be quite the deadly combination."

Clara nodded, when her blue eyes suddenly became fixed on the balcony above.

"Fin and Mage Lee are coming out now. They look fine."

Annika let out a sigh of relief. Finally, she could get him home, put him to bed, and come the morning, give him her scathing reprimand.

As she watched Fin draw closer to the stairs, her mind began to turn to a question that she hadn't had much time to dwell on.

What exactly is the king having him do? Earlier he was looking at those two men … I wonder if this has anything to do with witches. Or perhaps the Troivackians … but no. I'm investigating the origins of the Troivackians involved in the carriage attack, His Majesty wouldn't send someone as inexperienced as Fin into the city to look for the same people …

The tall redhead touched down onto the main floor and began to cross around the perimeter of the room, when he suddenly stopped. He was talking to someone …

The crowd started growing quieter and quieter, setting Annika's already frazzled nerves even further on edge.

"Well, why is it your wife's fault for not showing affection the way you'd like her to? She loves you, doesn't she?" Fin asked innocently, his voice carrying throughout the room, which was fortunate for the curious patrons wanting to hear about the captivating drama unfolding before them.

Why does he sound like he is mimicking a woman's voice? Annika wondered with growing dread.

"But … but why doesn't she rush out to greet me when I come home?! I'm gone at sea for months sometimes!"

"Would you rather her angry with you for always being gone? Does she not get you a bath and have a warm supper prepared immediately?"

"… I know. But … but …"

"Have you tried telling her this?"

"Well, I don't want to seem … everyone will laugh … I'm a man!"

"Alright, listen here, silly goose, there's nothing wrong with telling someone how you like being treated! Especially your wife! You there, yes, you sexy biscuit, do you tell your wife when you feel something is lacking?"

Annika turned to Clara, her face stony.

"Summon my knights. I'll stay here until they arrive." Annika's words were choked.

Fortunately, Clara didn't hesitate in springing to action. She darted around the crowd that was rapidly growing more and more enthralled with the dramatic scene playing out for them, and she slipped out the door without anyone noticing.

All Annika could do was wait. Wait and hope to the Gods she didn't have to do something even more drastic to save his drugged-up arse. As she bided her time, she couldn't help but repeat to herself over and over what had quickly become her mantra since growing closer with Fin.

Man of my dreams ... man that I love ... don't get yourself killed so quickly.

Present day ...

Fin strolled along the sunny street with nausea wrangling his stomach thanks to the remnants of the drugs he'd been fed.

He and Annika had yet to have their full discussion about work, as a messenger from the king had come for her shortly after she had calmed down. Fin had quickly made himself scarce, and after a hasty promise to avoid trouble for at least a day, the two had parted for their separate schedules.

Sighing heavily, the redhead decided to avoid Madam Mathilda's side of town, and instead try farther north in the city. He'd investigate closer to the castle to see if there were any abandoned buildings that could offer a good viewpoint to a group of enemies.

The walk uphill was normally something Fin found relatively easy after growing up on Quildon with its steep rolling slopes, but under the hot summer sun, and still feeling ill from the previous night, it felt as though he were treading water with weights shackled around his ankles.

He had just reached the end of a shadowed alley that exited onto a road that ran parallel to the main road of Austice, when he slumped against the wall of the nearest building. Taking a moment to bask in the feeling of the cool stone he could feel through his tunic, he closed his eyes and braced himself for the unforgiving heat he would once again step into on the next sunny street.

Fin opened his eyes again wearily and turned his head to his right; at least his trek back down the hill would put the sun to his back. He had just straightened himself out when he noticed a woman staring at him. Her long straight hair was pure snowy white, and yet she couldn't have been older than his mother. Her blue eyes were such a pale shade that they almost appeared colorless, which somehow made her eerie despite standing in a bright street with people surrounding her.

Yes, she looked like a snowdrop in the middle of summer, but her striking looks weren't what bothered Fin …

It was the way she was looking at him with open dread, fear, and perhaps a hint of sickness.

He had never been looked at in such a way, and Fin felt himself hesitate before momentarily looking around to see if she was perhaps staring at someone else. Everyone that passed by him, however, were moving targets, and she was quite fixed in her focus. He shoved his hands into his pockets and pushed away from the wall, fully aware that there was no mistaking who her attention was on.

Swallowing with some difficulty, Fin stepped back into the heat, and gave the woman a wide berth. He didn't know why her expression disturbed him so much, but it was twisting his stomach into knots.

Unconsciously, the redhead hunched his shoulders and strode by her with mounting apprehension.

"Gods … are you … Katelyn's boy? Finlay?" Her voice was breathy and weak.

Turning swiftly, the witch stared apprehensively, and he was once again alarmed when the woman cringed away from him.

"Please … please don't look at me like that. You look too much like him."

It was as though Fin had been dunked in an icy bath when he realized that this woman was talking about none other than Aidan Helmer. His father.

"I'm nothing like that man. Whatever he did to you, I am sincerely sorry." Fin's hands were clenched in his pockets as he felt the growing urge to vomit.

"Oh, I … I am so sorry. I … that was a terrible thing to say. Please, I-I am a friend of your mother's. My name is Sky. Perhaps you've heard of me?" The woman took two tentative steps forward as though still uncertain of whether or not he would attack her.

Fin blinked several times, his mind blank.

"We were close friends years before you were born; in fact … I'm an … an air w-wit—"

The speed with which the redhead stepped forward to stop the woman from saying anything more in the bustling street caused her to squeak, her eyes growing wide.

"Might we have a talk somewhere more private?" Fin breathed hastily, his tone apologetic.

The strange woman named Sky stared up at him, appearing every bit as terrified as a field mouse.

That is, until she gazed into his eyes.

Visibly relaxing, but still a little dazed, she nodded.

"My house is just down the road, why don't you step in for a cup of water?"

Fin bobbed his head slowly and indicated she should lead the way.

As they walked, he still couldn't shake the hesitation he felt at the sudden encounter. Then again, he had not faced a witch while being powerless in many years.

Sky's house was one that simultaneously blended into the street, and yet stuck out with its odd circular doorway painted a rich green with a bold brass knocker in its center. The inside was equally contradictory with one half of the main sunny room being sparse with a lone potted tree in the corner and hand-sewn pillows resting in front of the fireplace, while the other half was cluttered with jars of herbs and tinctures that Fin was all too familiar with seeing.

"I thought you were an air witch," he observed when he noted the fresh cut flowers and drying herbs.

"I am," she replied shortly as she crossed over to one of the pillows on the floor and seated herself.

Slowly, Fin moved to join her while waiting to see if she would explain the two very different styles of the room that indicated an earth witch also lived there.

"I take it you are one of those people who prefer not to be open about having witches as acquaintances?" Sky asked, her eyes gazing outside the house instead of at her guest.

Fin grew more wary as the woman revealed how very little of him she seemed to know.

"You said you were friends with my mother?" He changed the topic, hoping to glean more about her.

"Ah yes ... yes. Before she chose to marry your ... your father."

The clenching in Fin's stomach made him hesitate in his next question.

"You seem scared of me. I hope you can understand that I am not like Aidan." The somber note in Fin's voice finally made Sky turn her attention to him, though the silence in the room somehow made this even more unsettling.

"You look like him in nearly every way, but … your eyes. I believe those are like your grandfather's."

Fin's eyebrows shot upward. He had heard little of his mother's life before her marriage to his father. Mostly because she was always preoccupied with patients, or schooling …

"What were my grandparents like?"

"Strict. Serious. A little cold … your grandmother was an air witch, your grandfather a water witch. Your two aunts took after them. I believe I—"

"I have aunts?!"

His outburst made Sky blink rapidly and straighten her posture. "Your mother never told you? Well, I suppose she was never really on good terms with them … still. It is surprising."

Fin tried to process the information he had just received but found it difficult to comprehend. Just as he opened his mouth to ask another question, the front door burst open.

"Alright, Sky, don't for a second think I'm going to forgive you if the reason you forgot to meet us at the market was to stare at a flock of seagulls again. I don't care if you think you might be blood related somehow, I've told you that—" The woman who had appeared was clad in a brown skirt and a deep green tunic with a mustard yellow handkerchief tucked in a black leather belt around her waist. Her dark hair puffed away from her scalp in an impressive Afro, and her ebony skin looked warm to the touch.

She carried with her two satchels overflowing with vegetables that looked to be quite heavy as she plunked them down on the worn kitchen table. Turning with a swirl of her skirts, her burst of movement stilled immediately when she laid eyes on Fin.

"Oh. Hello."

As the woman turned to stare quizzically at Sky, the obvious question shouldn't have needed to be asked. Yet the air witch's response was to smile dreamily at the woman, who took matters into her own hands, clearly familiar with the scenario.

"I'm Adamma, and you are?"

"Fin. Nice to meet you."

Adamma was about to say more, when in burst two more people carrying sacks of flour, both sweating profusely.

"Aunt Adamma, remind me again why you can't carry one of these?!" The first to speak was a young man who looked similar to the woman named Adamma, only his hair was cropped short to his head, and his skin appeared to be a few shades lighter.

"Because I'm your elder and you are living in my house for free," she reminded him while placing her hands on her hips.

"Then why do we have to buy flour in the middle of the day when it is the absolute bloody hottest time?" It was a young woman who had spoken. Fin was guessing the young man to be her brother given the particular shade of skin tone they shared, but where she differed was her wild wavy black hair, and a sullen expression. A young woman not yet in her twenties … a fearsome age indeed.

"Because when I tried to wake you both earlier this morning, you each had creative threats for me." The woman named Adamma reached out and gave a stern yet gentle pinch to the girl's cheek. An action that was not well received.

It was then the two youngsters noticed Fin, making them both freeze. Despite the skeptical looks given between him and Sky, the air witch still seemed set on watching Adamma wistfully, completely oblivious to the awkward tension.

"Children, this here is Fin. Say hello, and let's try and get Sky to tell us why he is in our house," Adamma remarked briskly, taking the situation in hand.

Finally snapping out of her reverie, the air witch stood and strode over to Adamma's side.

"This here is Finlay Ashowan. Kate's son," Sky explained with a sweep of her arm.

"Wait, Finlay Ashowan, the Royal Cook?" Adamma's surprised but excited smile was so dazzling that even Fin found himself caught off guard. He was surprised that even the younger siblings reacted to the news as well.

"Really?!"

"The house witch?!"

Fin blinked in confusion. The children seemed to know more about him than his mother's friend. He stood awkwardly and wiped his sweaty palms on his pants in anticipation.

Noticing his confusion, Adamma stepped forward and shook his hand.

"Don't mind us, we've just heard a thing or two from my brother, their father. I believe you've worked a bit with him. His name is Kasim. Kasim Jelani."

CHAPTER 16
FACING FORWARD

Fin had been moved to the table and was waiting for someone to speak once again. Kasim's children were staring at him with a mixture of awe and curiosity, while Adamma had a more unreadable expression.

"This day has taken a few turns I didn't anticipate … Sky, you seem to have had some issue with my father given your reaction to me." Fin began trying to wrap his mind around the situation.

The air witch shifted in her seat and her eyes dropped thoughtfully to the rough table surface in front of her.

Adamma reached out unconsciously and gently rubbed her back, shooting her an encouraging smile while doing so.

For once, Sky didn't gaze up longingly at the woman and, instead, took a deep breath.

"I did. Shortly before your parents were to marry, I told your mother not to go through with it. I told her to abandon the betrothal. Your father hadn't done anything truly wrong, but he was always talking about pure witches and there was a … a hunger in him. Something about it all felt wrong."

Fin winced. While he didn't hold an abundance of memories of his father, he did know that if something or someone got in the way of achieving something he desired, he'd burn through whatever it was. No matter the cost.

"Did he hurt you ... badly?" the redhead asked with a heaviness in his chest that ached.

"Not ... that time. Kate told him her concerns, which were ... exacerbated by my own, and he soothed those worries away. To be honest with you, I don't know how much of his determination to wed her was his desire for her healing power, and how much was his love for her."

"You think he loved my mother?" The note of disbelief in Fin's voice succeeded in making all eyes rivet to him.

"Well, I ... I cannot ... speak for another's feelings. I do not know." Sky glanced desperately at Adamma.

The woman reached out and gently clasped Sky's hand in her own, before turning her gaze to Fin.

"I didn't mean to cause any distress," Fin remarked hesitantly, unsure of whether or not he should apologize when he had only been responding with a matter-of-fact attitude.

"It's alright. Ever since the final meeting with your father, Sky worries about angering others. It isn't normal for air witches to be so conscious of others' moods; they aren't as grounded as the other elemental witches."

Swallowing with great difficulty, Fin tried to look again at the air witch but found that it was growing more difficult by the second.

"If you don't want to tell me what happened, I completely understand." He tried to soften his voice as much as possible.

"It's alright ... perhaps the Goddess wanted to use you to help me. To face my fears and try to put them behind me. Especially after the other day when I met with—"

Adamma squeezed Sky's hand.

"Stay on task, love; what do you want to tell Finlay?"

Sky's shoulders slumped ever so slightly forward, but the redhead could see that she was gathering strength to go on.

"It ... It was after you were born. Your father came to me to ask if I would join the cause ... his 'purist' movement. He wanted all deficient witches to be placed as lifelong servants to pure witches, and for the pure elemental ones to be in charge of all kingdoms. He believed government and the covens should be the same thing, and that they should rule each continent." Taking a fortifying breath, she managed to finish her sad tale.

"I said no, and that I didn't like how he kept insisting your mother should be supportive without questioning his ideals, and he ..."

"—Attacked Sky brutally and threatened to do much worse." Adamma jumped in when it became clear that the air witch wasn't going to be able to speak in detail about what happened.

"I fled as far north as I could and haven't been south of Sorlia or Xava in nearly thirty years."

Fin nodded and attempted to clear his throat while also ignoring Kasim's children as they shifted uncomfortably and averted their eyes. They seemed to know the story, but his presence upon its retelling was another matter entirely.

"I am sorry for the pain he caused you." Fin felt the familiar crushing burden of his father's sins, and for a moment, his childhood seemed not so long ago.

"It is not for you to apologize for," Adamma said firmly.

"She's right. Thank you for listening to me, Fin. I'm sorry if this was difficult to hear." Sky's milky blue eyes remained dropped down.

With a small nod, the redhead straightened and looked to the door. It was probably a good time to leave ...

"Is it true that you're more powerful than a pure elemental?" Kasim's son suddenly blurted out, earning a stern glower from his aunt and an elbow to the ribs from his sister.

"Er ... I don't believe so." Fin felt his cheeks and tips of his ears turning red.

"What? Dad said he was expecting a proper spar with you when you first met! He said you called down lightning!"

"Lightning doesn't sound like the property of a house witch," Adamma commented slowly, her gaze turning suspicious.

"A house witch can protect their home and those living within it. I suppose the form it takes with me is lightning," Fin explained, leaning back in his chair and not quite meeting anyone's stare.

"You speak as though you are not the only house witch," Adamma prodded gently.

"There was only one other recorded in our coven, but it was hundreds of years ago. As you know there are very few reports that were kept safe for so long." Fin shrugged.

Adamma frowned and looked to Sky.

"Our coven keeps paper records on their island," the air witch explained, for once speaking on time in the conversation.

It was Fin's turn to become curious.

"Adamma, both you and Kasim have said you come from another kingdom, but neither of you have ever mentioned which one."

Adamma had a small smile when she turned to stare at the redhead again.

"Ah, that is because our people tend to try and remain isolated from other kingdoms. However, I suppose since we all seem to be baring some secrets, I will tell you our homeland's name. My brother and I hail from the kingdom of Lobahl."

There was a strange reverberation in the air after the name was said, as though the name itself bore power.

"Our land lies to the west of Daxaria, far from its shores, and is east of Troivack, somewhat closer, but still very far."

Fin felt his head fill to the brim with questions; however, before he could utter a single word, Adamma cut him off.

"Knowledge of our land is coveted, and to share an abundance of information could lead to exile from our home shores ... even if we have no intention of returning ever again."

"I respect your country and its laws," Fin began slowly, and he noted the glint of warning in Adamma's eyes. "Might I know the reasoning behind such strict secrecy? That will be my only question," he assured hastily, his tone sincere.

The Lobahlan leaned back in her chair and folded her arms across her chest, her face masking her thoughts.

After a few moments of silence, she let out a small breath.

"Other kingdoms cannot envy what they do not know. We do not want to take any risks of unwanted attention."

Fin bobbed his head subserviently.

"I understand."

Standing slowly, the redhead nodded his head once again to Sky, then to Adamma.

"I best be on my way then, but it was lovely to meet you all."

It was then both of Kasim's children exploded from their seats at the same time and began speaking hurriedly at once.

"Wait!"

"We have questions!"

Fin stared bewildered at the two of them as the boy stepped forward.

"I don't think my sister or myself got to introduce ourselves ... my name is Urick Jelani, and this is my younger sister, Nina Jelani. She's an earth witch, and I'm a ... I'm a ... water witch."

Fin noted the awkward shift of the boy's eyes as though embarrassed.

"I'm a weak water witch," Urick finished lamely after a moment of an inner battle.

The young man then lifted a goblet that rested on the table, and Fin watched as it filled to the brim with cool clear water. "This is all I can do."

Without saying a word, the redhead stepped forward, took the goblet, and emptied it into his mouth. After swallowing the drink, he met Urick's gaze with a wry smile.

"To me that was the best power I've seen all day."

"You didn't even offer him a cup of water on a day like today?!" Adamma scolded Sky who was too busy looking out the window once again to hear her.

"What I'm wondering is … is *how* did you become more powerful? I know my dad talks about how mutated witches are 'the chosen,' but for the most part they are … weak." Urick looked embarrassed to even say the word, but Fin showed no sign of offense and instead waited.

"I know because only my dad is a witch, and not my mum, that there's a chance I'm just always going to be significantly weaker but … Nina is a respectable earth witch. I have to be able to be better than I am!"

By the end of his explanation the boy had worked himself up into an anxious state, and Fin felt deeply empathetic with him over his frustrations.

"Well, being honest with you, Urick, sometimes that is just how it is, and that's okay. In my circumstance, I spent as much time in my 'element' as possible, and taking work in the castle expanded what I was able to do."

Urick looked crestfallen, and Fin found himself scrambling to find a way to soften the blow.

"Keep in mind, your powers rely on your personality and how you accept yourself. You might try becoming more confident or finding friends or places that make you feel like you belong. You might also try thinking about what the element means or represents to you and get a little … creative with what a cup of water can do. For example, I'm pretty sure if that were frozen and you hurled it in someone's direction you could do a great deal of damage—"

Adamma was giving him a death glare that would've impressed his mother. Fin cleared his throat awkwardly, but he was pleased to see that Urick was already looking somewhat cheered up by the notion.

"If that's everything, I—"

"Wait!" Nina cried out again, as she threw herself around the table and hurried up to him to stand beside her brother. "Could you please spar with my aunt!"

Fin blinked. Upon seeing his blank expression, this only goaded the young girl on, making it apparent that the siblings really weren't all that different.

"You see, Sky refuses to spar, and so I've only ever gotten to see Aunt Adamma face off with my dad, and, and it'd be really amazing if I got to see another witch use their powers … for educational purposes!"

His eyes moved to Adamma who was obviously suppressing a smile. Something told the redhead that the children had been desperate for a little magical excitement for some time.

Even Fin had to admit he'd be interested in giving it a try. His tutor had never bothered teaching him to spar given his abilities, but with the way things were going more recently …

"I wouldn't mind it, though I have very little experience with such things. The other issue, of course, is that I have no power when I am not on the grounds of my home," he explained apologetically.

Everyone's face fell in the room, and Adamma frowned slightly.

"You have … no powers whatsoever right now?"

Fin shook his head.

The kids looked as though they had just been told there'd be no cakes for dessert and the aura of disappointment was devastating.

"Our sparring grounds are deep in the king's woods. Sky blocks the sound, and I set traps in the earth to alert us of anyone approaching so it is quite private," Adamma began to offer, casting Fin a hopeful glance.

After a moment's hesitation, the cook reasoned that the worst-case scenario was that he had no powers to spar with, and best-case scenario that he could magically let loose a little.

"Alright. I have to finish doing a bit of work here in town, but I should have a bit of time afterward. I need to be finished by dinnertime, however … otherwise, my … er … *companion* will have my head."

Adamma gave an excited but understanding expression.

Perhaps she was just as eager as Kasim's offspring to see a sparring match.

Fin followed Adamma into the woods from a more southern access point that was hidden from any casual onlookers from the castle.

Not a bad place to potentially come up for a rear attack ... Fin couldn't help but have his mind turn to the recent battle strategies he had been consulting on with the council.

The farther the group traveled into the woods, the thicker the trunks of trees grew until it would take all of them holding hands around one just to encircle it. The deeper they went, the deeper the sense of old magic sprung from its thick foliaged ground. Fortunately, the sun had lowered enough that the day's heat had eased, and the trees provided enough shade that it was even cooler still.

"This should count as your home, yes?" Adamma called over her shoulder. "It is 'technically' on the castle grounds. Kasim assured us His Majesty wouldn't mind. Not that he really asked ... but His Majesty seems the understanding type I'm told."

Fin smiled, but let his eyes lose focus as he searched for his magic. He'd be lying if he said he hadn't been missing it fiercely. At first it had felt like a release when he'd been roaming the streets of Austice, but as he found himself experiencing difficulties when it came to locating the Troivackian soldiers, the more he had missed it.

As he reached his senses out, his heart began to sink a little when he felt not even a twinge of his power returning.

"What happened there?" Urick had stopped several feet in front of Adamma and was pointing toward a long path of brush that had been cleared as though a cannonball had been blasted leagues into the forest.

Adamma leaned forward frowning.

"Perhaps there was another battle here, but ... this is peculiar..." She laid her hands on one of the nearest trees.

"They're saying it was a man who came flying through here." She remarked while glancing at the extensive tunnel of damage that ran farther than the eye could see.

All at once Fin's memory snapped to Jiho being launched deep into the woods when they'd had a spat weeks ago, and for some reason, he burst out laughing.

The group turned and stared at him bewildered.

Yet as he laughed, it suddenly began seeping into his skin.

His magic.

It was like warm golden light gently pouring itself through every pore of his skin, filling him up and warming him with its love.

It felt good to be home.

Once he had calmed down and straightened, Fin stared back at them with a magical glimmer in his eyes.

"I'm the one responsible for this. I had a bit of an ... argument with a friend one night." When the group shared uneasy glances, Fin let himself grow a little more serious. "He was perfectly fine, and believe me, he gave me a couple good jabs to pay me back."

While the women looked exasperated, Urick grinned.

"Well, is this a good enough space to spar?" Fin changed the subject and gazed at Adamma who suddenly was looking oddly sly ...

"I suppose so. I also suppose I might not have to go as easy on you as I thought I would, judging by the damage I'm seeing." She gestured toward the long tunnel of broken branches made by Jiho.

The redhead placed his hands on his hips and replied, "Oh, don't worry, I can't have the kids be completely bored with me. Maybe you two should stand on the other side of the barrier, though." Fin nodded to the siblings who oddly became even more pleased by the order.

Both Urick and Nina were beginning to become more than a little excited about the show they were about to witness, and both Fin and Adamma shared a look of understanding as the children's enthusiasm heightened their competitive moods.

If Fin were being honest? Even he was a little curious to see if perhaps he may even win ... after all, he'd never tested his power like this ever before.

CHAPTER 17
WINDED

Leaves rustled gently under Sky's feet as she walked a full circle around Fin and Adamma. The sounds of the forest gradually became quieter and quieter, until there was nothing but an eerie silence in the invisible bubble. Fin stood with an idle expression, while Adamma had a wild glint in her eye.

Kasim's children stood outside the perimeter, and once her proofing was completed, Sky joined them. The air witch had managed to block all sounds louder than a speaking voice so that everyone could hear what was said, but that whatever commotion was caused wouldn't draw unwanted attention.

"How far do you want this to go?" Adamma asked as she began strolling around the perimeter, her eyes trained on the redhead.

"Either I'll be unconscious or I'll say when I want it to stop. My mother is a healer, remember, and not far away. What about you, Adamma? When should I call it off?"

She laughed.

"I mean no offense, house witch, but"—Adamma held out her hand and summoned a long broken tree branch from behind Fin that worked perfectly as a staff, forcing him to dodge in order to avoid getting clubbed over the head—"my element is better suited for sparring."

It was the redhead's turn to laugh.

"Perhaps. Or perhaps I'm going to sit your ass in time-out, then get you the best cookies of your life."

Adamma's jaw dropped, but the excitement in her gaze turned hungry. "One way to find out."

"Indeed, though it is only fair I have a weapon myself." He nodded at the staff in her hand and held out his hand.

It took a few moments, but suddenly Fin's frying pan flew into one hand, and his broom into the other. Fortunately, he had placed them in his cottage prior to his vacation, so no one should've noticed the unnatural activity.

After an affirmative nod between the two witches facing off with each other, Sky called out: "Begin!"

Roots around Fin suddenly sprang up, knocking him down to his knees; the ground surged beneath his feet as though made of liquid and created hill after hill.

She was powerful alright.

Gritting his teeth with a smile, Fin magically launched his frying pan right at Adamma's head.

The waves beneath his feet stopped momentarily as she had to duck the missile, though it clipped her in the shoulder when it pulled a U-turn to fly back to Fin's hand.

"Not bad, house witch," Adamma called out as she gave him an appreciative nod and rotated her shoulder experimentally.

"We can send a missive for my mother afterward," Fin reminded her, more seriously.

Adamma nodded in agreement.

The ground suddenly opened beneath Fin's feet and swallowed him whole.

Enclosed in darkness and dirt, Fin couldn't breathe, and yet he didn't panic. This ground was his home; he requested the earth to open a tunnel for him. Not much liking him disturbing the worms and bugs' work, the earth agreed instantly. The moment it happened, Fin's pan shot out in a blur. Running after it, he could hear the yelp of surprise from Adamma.

He exploded from the tunnel to see that the exit had come behind the woman who was using her staff to fend off the dogged blows the frying pan was trying to deal.

Kasim's children were cheering wildly on the sidelines, and even Sky looked more interested in the match.

Before Adamma could do something else to Fin, he sent his broom to join the pan. As soon as that happened, however, Adamma released her staff and commanded it to handle both of his weapons. Freed from trying to battle the pan and broom, the earth witch snapped her fingers, and tree branches snaked down and coiled themselves tightly around the redhead.

The pan was managing to crack and splinter the staff as it struck repeatedly against the same spot.

"Your defensive moves aren't bad, but you have a relatively weak offense," Adamma called as she strode around the battling weapons, only to have the broom suddenly snap out and trip her.

"I'm not really trying all that hard." Fin huffed out the words as more and more branches began to reach for him. Some were beginning to wrap around his throat.

A green aura was beginning to emit from Adamma, her eyes glowing and swirling.

"I won't stop until you're unconscious or until you—"

The earth witch stopped suddenly and turned around sharply to stare in the direction of the castle.

"A group is approaching. Perhaps six of them?"

Fin stilled despite the branches still holding him.

Then he heard it.

Or rather, them.

"FIN! FIN, WHERE ARE YOU?!"

The unmistakable voice of Hannah broke through the trees not far off in the distance, and Fin felt his mouth break into a smile.

"It's fine, Adamma! They're friends of mine. They know about me." He called down to the witches present.

"HANNAH! THIS WAY!" Fin called out, already excited to see his friends.

In a few moments, the four kitchen knights followed by Hannah and Peter skidded into sight.

The knights all wielded either a gardening tool or paring knives as they fixed cold stares onto Adamma.

"She's a friend! We're just having a sparring match for the kids," Fin called out when he realized how it looked.

The group collectively sighed and relaxed.

"Gods, we thought you'd gotten into trouble only two days into your vacation!" Sir Andrews called while relaxing his hold on the rake in his hand.

"Well, get on with it! Things have been pretty boring without you getting into trouble," Sir Taylor shouted as he slowly meandered over to where Sky and Kasim's children stood.

Nina was staring up at the bear of a man with a mixture of awe and shock.

"A-Are you a knight?" she squeaked.

"I am indeed. Sir Taylor at your service. That there is Sir Andrews, Sir Lewis, Sir Harris, and then we have Hannah and Peter."

"You're friends with knights?!" Urick asked excitedly as he stared up at Fin who was still grinning while suspended several feet above the air.

"They're not so bad once you get to know them," the redhead hollered back, earning a few mischievous smiles from the knights. "How did you all know where I was?" he asked suddenly with a frown.

"Hannah snitched your pan the second you left, so when it suddenly flew out of the room we knew something was up. You're lucky none of the aides who're helping in your stead noticed!" Sir Harris explained as Hannah shot the knight a look of pure betrayal.

Despite her blatant disregard for his privacy, Fin laughed.

"Come on, get fighting. I've been curious about this for ages!" Hannah demanded, her cheeks growing red.

"Yeah! You teach the hell out of these kids and clobber her!" Sir Harris cheered, delighted.

Adamma turned to stare back up at the redhead, her expression far more sober than it had been moments before. "You have good friends, house witch."

"The best," Fin agreed, his smile faltering as he admitted the truth.

"Oyy! Enough of this mushy shit! I'm craving some violence!" Sir Harris whined.

Adamma's demonic smile returned and her energy flared. "Don't worry, sir. You will have it."

The branches suddenly tightened their grip around Fin, choking him mercilessly. He managed to command his pan to evade the magical staff and attack Adamma once again, this time knocking her out from the back of the knees. Fin was released immediately, though he stumbled momentarily from the fall.

The pan was back in his hand as the broom and staff continued battling.

Adamma was also back on her feet, only she was glaring.

"You toy with me. I don't even see your magic essence. I am not going all out on you, but you can release more power than that."

"Yeah, Fin! It's for the children!" Sir Harris called out while grabbing Nina's shoulders from behind and giving her a shake that made her giggle.

It wasn't her that made Fin pause, however. It was Urick and his hopeful gaze, with its clear need to see ... something unexpected. Something to show that even a "weak" witch could become powerful.

A true home gives people hope.

Fin stepped back and closed his eyes.

"Adamma, don't hold anything back."

"This might kill you, house witch," Adamma explained though there was an unmistakable note of curiosity in her tone.

"It won't."

"Well ... if you're certain your will has already been drafted ..."

Fin's eyes remained closed, but he could feel the earth rumbling beneath his feet, could feel Adamma's power, and while it wasn't quite as strong as Kasim's ... She was charging up for something big.

I will remain safe in my home. Not a scratch.

Fin chanted silently, and when his eyes opened, the roots of the trees were all rushing toward him, the ground was opening, everything was dragging him down, ready to snap his bones and bury him alive.

Then, there was an explosion.

Blue lightning cracked around the entire area, and errant twigs and leaves began to hover off the ground from the electrical charge in the air. The blast had been Fin's shield encircling him and holding him in place while incinerating anything that sought to bind him. The ancient symbols that crackled in a perfect sphere prevented him from being moved anywhere without his consent—including into the gaping hole that had opened up to consume him. Hovering above the hole, his eyes were filled with nothing but blue lightning; Adamma's skirts were beginning to hover as electricity touched down around her. Fin strolled forward as though his feet were on land; any branch that tried to pierce the shield was immediately singed to a crisp, and Adamma began backing away.

Fin lifted his hand, prepared to blast her clear out of the forest (albeit safely), when a bloodcurdling scream rang out.

Both Adamma and Fin turned and saw Sky shrieking and crying with her hands over her ears as she shook. The knights around her had jumped away, while Nina and Urick tried to touch her, but her shaking only grew more violent as a result.

All magic from Adamma ceased as she rushed over to Sky and wrapped her arms around her. As if this broke the final thread, Sky collapsed into a crouch on the ground, but the Lobahlan didn't let go for a single moment.

"It's fine, love, I promise I'm not hurt. See? We're just sparring. It's okay," she whispered against Sky's hair, rocking her back and forth. Fin had dissipated all lightning, and with his feet safely back on the ground, stepped forward worriedly. He crouched down to be within eyeline of the air witch.

"I'd never hurt Adamma, I promise," he whispered as misplaced guilt began to bloom in his chest.

Sky's eyes rose at his voice, only when she saw him, it was suddenly very apparent it wasn't Fin she was seeing.

She was seeing a ghost from her past. Or rather … a demon.

A burst of air flung Fin backward and would've sent him flying back into a tree were Adamma not quick in having a branch snag down and grab him.

Only Sky wasn't through facing the past. A fierce wind began whirling around Fin, one that was too strong for anyone to get near.

Then he felt it. The air being forced out of his lungs.

Gods, she will kill me. The second the thought entered his head, Fin's shield returned. Dropping to his knees in the safety of his lightning, he gasped for breath.

He then realized that his sphere was beginning to be lifted off the ground. He rose higher and higher, Adamma's shouts to try to calm down Sky barely audible over the roaring wind. It wasn't until he was a few feet from the tops of the trees that Fin realized the true jeopardy he was in.

If she raised him high enough, he wasn't at home anymore. He was in the sky, his shield would fail, and if she held him there, she could easily suffocate him.

"Godsdamnit!" Fin realized that Adamma probably wasn't considering this when she was trying to calm the woman down.

Sky needs to stop. She needs to …

The redhead had an idea, and even though he wasn't sure whether or not it would work, he had to try. He just needed to try something slightly different than when he'd faced Hilda … Back then he never would've believed he'd have the strength to do it, but … there was a chance … maybe.

Fighting against the wind was nearly impossible, but with a last-minute dive, Fin was able to grasp one of the last branches to be passed before he hit the open skies. Using all the strength he had, he hauled himself down, the tree becoming engulfed in his shield, and thus stopping the winds from touching it. Clambering down as quickly as he could, Fin eventually came to the final problem of the long ways to the ground where there weren't any branches. Desperately, he scanned around and spotted his broom plastered to a nearby tree trunk by the gale force winds. Summoning with all his might, he managed to draw it into his shield and held it level.

Reaching out, Fin grabbed hold of its shaft and hung beneath it as he gently lowered it down to the ground while keeping his shield intact.

He was starting to run low on energy. He could feel his burning magic inching closer to his life energy. He couldn't stop, though. If he did, he'd be killed.

Sky was still trying to blow him far away, and so, with heavy steps, Fin stepped closer to her. He forced his shield wider and wider to cover the ground around him to keep him anchored. When he stood face-to-face with Sky and Adamma, his eyes were still burning with his lightning. As she stared up at him, the fearful shine in Adamma's eyes was not lost on Fin.

"Stop it! You're making it worse by scaring her!" she screamed over the howling wind.

Fin noticed that she and everyone else had their legs holding them to the ground by roots. However, Sky also wasn't focusing her efforts on them so much as a particular redhead.

"If she gets me above those trees, she can kill me! I have a plan, trust me!"

Adamma didn't look at all convinced, but Fin could feel himself getting too close to the end of his reserves to wait. He reached out and grabbed Sky from Adamma, hauling her into his shield.

Both women screamed bloody murder at him, but the moment Sky was in his shield, her powers ceased like a candle snuffed out. It wasn't easy to smother her magic, and a few of the symbols in the sphere shifted and glowed gold, but it worked.

Fin wrapped his arms around her so that she wouldn't see the lightning in his eyes begin to turn gold and white.

"I'm not my father, Sky. I will not hurt you. You just need a time-out."

Alone in his shield without her powers, Sky collapsed on the ground sobbing and shaking.

Crouching down and scooping her into his arms again, he rocked the woman slowly.

"You're safe in my home, I promise," he whispered, his throat aching.

~~~~~~~

"This isn't good!" Adamma shouted over her shoulder to the knights and children. Outside the shield everything had fallen into a calm, but the earth witch was watching Fin's eyes through the shield and saw that he stared blindly ahead of himself as he held Sky and soothed her.

"Why not? Our cook has the situation in hand. He's lettin' her cool down. What was that whole windstorm about anyway?" Sir Taylor asked while brushing dirt off his clothes.

"No, look at his eyes. He's hit the end of his magic; if he keeps up like this, it'll kill him."

All four knights snapped to attention

"What do we need to do?" Sir Harris stepped forward immediately.

"I-I-I don't know! He's suppressing her powers somehow, but if he releases her and she tries to kill him again, I don't know if I can stop her. I'm almost tapped out, and worst of all, she might hurt all of us if we try to stop her."

"So we're just going to let him die?!" Hannah shrieked, her hands balled into fists.

"Aunt Adamma, I ... I can knock her out," Nina spoke up softly then, her eyes wide and terrified.

"I-I-I don't know. I—" The woman was clearly torn between caring about the safety of her niece and Fin.

"THERE'S NO TIME!" Hannah cried out, pointing as the shield surrounding Fin began to turn white.

Rounding on Nina who was growing paler by the second, the largest of the knights took charge.

"If that witch tries to blow him away again, you club her hard, got it?" Sir Taylor addressed the girl with a growl, but with a swallow she nodded.

"FIN! YOU CAN STOP! WE CAN HANDLE HER!" Sir Taylor roared through the lightning.

At first they weren't sure if he'd heard, but then, bit by bit, the shield dissolved.

Fin immediately collapsed onto the ground unconscious, and there was nothing but quiet and the soft sobs of Sky filling the deathly still forest.

Everyone was beginning to relax, when Hannah screamed.

"SHE'S SMOTHERING HIM!"

Everyone's spine stiffened as they stared wide-eyed at the unconscious redhead.

Sure enough, Fin's pale face was beginning to turn purple, and yet he didn't stir.

Sky continued hiccuping over him, uttering the words: "Never again, never again will you hurt me. No. No. Never again ..." Her eyes were closed as tears ran down her cheeks.

Nina stepped forward and summoned the club Adamma had been using, only she was suddenly propelled backward by another thrum of air. She would've been thrown into a tree trunk if Sir Taylor hadn't caught her in time.

The winds were starting to gather again, though markedly weaker than before, when suddenly an iceball the size of a man's fist careened into the back of Sky's head, knocking her unconscious.

Everyone waited to make sure the woman was truly asleep and watched with bated breaths to see Fin's chest resume its usual rise and fall.

After several terrifying moments, a slightly raspy gasp escaped the redhead's mouth. He didn't wake, but the most imminent danger had been dealt with.

It was then that all eyes turned to Urick who stood wide-eyed and shaking with his fists clenched.

"M-Mr. Ashowan w-was right, t-that *is* useful."

CHAPTER 18
COLLIDING COURSES

Norman stared down at Annika's bowed head with gritted teeth. Even Ainsley knew better than to say anything.

"We haven't had much time to talk, have we, Lady Jenoure." The king observed his distant tone not affecting the woman who curtsied before him in the slightest.

Standing slowly, Annika faced Norman with a mask of innocence as she clasped her hands demurely in front of herself.

"We have not, sire. Not since the meeting with the suitors following your son's birthday party, and the arrest of my brother."

Something shifted behind Norman's eyes, but neither of the women present could identify it.

"Would you care to explain to me how Lord Nam and Lady Marigold Iones have become … smitten?" The note of pain in his voice made Ainsley bite down on her lower lip.

"I may have been … less than ideal to the man. However, I wouldn't say that I was entirely unagreeable," Annika replied mildly.

Norman's eyes were beginning to bulge from his head in a most concerning manner.

"You do realize that Lady Marigold, as a result, will have to return to Zinfera to continue garnering favor from the Zinferan emperor?"

The viscountess responded with a pleasant smile.

"You *also* realize if that woman manages to insult *anyone*, they could choose not to support Daxaria in the war?" Norman asked, his voice rising.

"Which is why they will have to send a message of their marriage, and you insist that they stay here for a year so that the new duke and duchess might settle matters here before paying Zinfera a visit," Annika responded calmly, her face the picture of serenity.

Norman closed his eyes and took several deep, calming breaths.

"Lady Jenoure, you are privy to a great deal of … political flexibility because we share an understanding. However, your underhanded way of handling the matter of your marriage without conferring with me cannot be ignored."

"Your Majesty, you said yourself the Zinferan emperor declared that either myself or Marigold would be acceptable. I have done nothing to—"

"Don't play that card with me, Lady Jenoure. You're on very thin ice as it is."

It was then that Annika's face finally hardened into seriousness.

"Sire, I genuinely did not believe that I was doing anything truly damaging. Daxaria has its army through this marriage, and if we keep both Lady Marigold and her intended here until the war is over, then—"

It was Ainsley who interrupted Annika this time.

"Norman, we need to tell her. Word is about to come out regarding … you know. She should be prepared." The stress in her voice made both the viscountess and king turn and stare at the queen, whose rounded belly rose and fell with each soft breath.

With a sigh, Norman let his chin fall to his chest. Closing his eyes for a brief moment, he then raised his head and stared sharply into Annika's keen gaze.

"Marigold's dowry and political appeal to Zinfera is that she is a daughter in a dukedom that has no apparent male heir. Her husband is set to inherit the title. You had the same appeal, which is what made you both viable candidates; however …"

A strong sense of foreboding filled Annika.

The king stole one glance at his wife who looked as discontented as he did.

"Marigold is set to lose the dukedom title and all the estates, land, and money save for her dowry in less than a year."

Annika's face turned ghostly white.

"How can that be? The deceased Duke Iones was frugal to a fault! He made many smart financial decisions that should set—"

"Because he has a son. An illegitimate one that I've been … secretly aiding for many years in hopes that he would lay his claim on the title and lands. I believe he will be a better leader and addition to the nobility than whatever ponce Lady Marigold chooses to marry." Norman bit out the last sentence in a rare moment of pettiness.

Annika looked as though she were about to faint. Which was so unlike her that even Norman's anger faded to concern.

"Lady Jenoure, I realize this might come as a shock to you, but—"

"Why now? Why is the son coming forward *now*?" Even more uncharacteristic of her, the viscountess spoke informally and without her former composure.

Decidedly ignoring the show of rudeness, Norman answered.

"When I spoke with Sir Harris, he indicated that Lady Marigold may have recently spoken to him and been … well … herself. He declared then that he couldn't sit by and let her get her way any longer. Then he got the support of his friends—you know how Mr. Ashowan tends to—"

"Fin did this?"

The room fell unnaturally quiet.

The king stepped forward with a raised eyebrow.

"I was unaware you were on a first name basis with the cook."

"He helped me the day I got stabbed, and he didn't ask questions," Annika evaded smoothly, but whether it was convincing enough was hard to tell.

"How odd that you acted formally toward him the day we convened in his cottage."

"It was an official meeting, Your Majesty."

Before the king could question her further, there was an odd commotion heard just outside the bedchamber. By the time Norman strode over hastily and opened the door, Annika already had her hand on the small decorative dagger that hung from her belt.

Upon opening the door, however, the king found himself staring at Katelyn Ashowan who was facing a young blond maid Norman recognized as one of Finlay Ashowan's aides.

"What is the meaning of this?" the monarch boomed.

Both women immediately dipped into curtsies.

"S-Sorry, Your Majesty," Hannah puffed; she clearly had run a long way. "I-I was just trying to … to tell—" The blond aide's eyes then landed on Annika behind the king and her eyes rounded.

"To tell Mrs. Ashowan something?" the king prompted again, this time his voice gentler.

"It's Fin! I mean, Mr. Ashowan!" Hannah announced, her volume noticeably increasing for some reason, her eyes occasionally darting to Annika in the room behind him. "There was an accident, and I was coming to get his mum to help!"

Katelyn Ashowan turned to the king immediately, her posture rigid but her voice was in full command. "Your Majesty, I apologize, but I must tend to my son. Please send word if the queen's condition changes."

Then, without waiting for a reply, the healer swept off while tugging Hannah along hurriedly.

Norman watched them retreat in the direction of the servants' stairwell with a deep frown. He hoped the witch hadn't landed himself in anything too serious … Mage Lee had mentioned there had been some trouble in town with Finlay, but the elder had been relatively vague on the details.

When the monarch turned back to his bedchamber, he was startled to see that Lady Jenoure no longer stood waiting. In fact, she was nowhere to be seen.

Turning a questioning eye to his wife, he became even more alarmed to see a look of stunned concern on her face.

"What is it, dearest? Do I need to call for Mrs. Ashowan? Where in the world did Lady Jenoure go? It—"

"I'm fine … she took the secret passageway while you were talking to the women outside." Ainsley's voice was quiet, but her eyes were trained on the passageway door on the other end of their chamber that only three people knew about, her thoughts unknown.

"It isn't like her to run from me," Norman began slowly, hoping to prod some more information from his wife.

Ainsley didn't say anything, though, only continued staring at the door, lost in thought.

She didn't want to say anything to her husband just yet. Not until she had a chance to talk to Annika alone …

She had to find out for sure if what she'd just seen actually had happened.

Ainsley's best friend, political stooge, and trained killer working for the crown of Daxaria had panicked and fled at the news that the cook, Finlay Ashowan, had been harmed in an accident.

Given everything that had just been uncovered moments before, the pieces to the puzzle began to form a partial picture in the queen's head, and all too quickly, Annika's best friend had a pretty damn good idea what was going on.

This is a far bigger problem than we realized ... Resting her hands on her unborn, Ainsley began rubbing slow anxious circles. *Gods ... this is so sudden* ...

Kate stared into her son's pale sleeping face for several moments before pulling up the chair that had been brought in from the cottage's main room into the bedroom.

The truth of it all was that one could do very little to heal a witch once they had begun using their life energy instead of their magic. Rest was often required, and usually their abilities would be weaker for an indeterminate amount of time, but how long Fin would sleep was unknown.

With a sigh, Kate stood and exited the cottage to face the worried kitchen aides and Adamma's niece and nephew. The earth witch had taken Sky back home to get some rest and make sure she wouldn't become violent again. Aside from a minor concussion, the wind witch's greatest injury was not a physical one ...

"There's nothing to do but wait. Fin didn't suffer any other real injuries aside from a few scratches and bruises, but what ails him is not something that is easily healed. It's a matter of the soul more than the body. I'm also worried about how this affects Sky ... sometimes when witches use their energy force the results can be semipermanent. If the caster dies, then it becomes a curse of sorts." Katelyn Ashowan was beginning to speak more to herself than the group that was rapidly growing more alarmed by her words.

A strange crack echoed in the cottage, making Katelyn turn to peer in, when Hannah interrupted her.

"You mean, Fin could have permanently taken her powers if he'd kept going?" the petite blonde asked suddenly with a frown.

"At the cost of his life, yes. It is a most unholy thing to do as it is essentially stripping away a piece of another witch's soul."

The group settled into an uneasy silence, when a faint call originating from the castle drew their attention.

"We need to be getting back to work, we've already been gone far too long ... Ruby will have to report to Fin about us being absent ... er ..." Sir

Andrews trailed off and awkwardly began to back away from the cook's cottage. "Pardon me, ma'am."

The knight then darted away from the cottage, leaving a puzzled Katelyn to stare after him.

"What in the world was that about?"

"Oh, Andrews is a little dodgy around you given that you're Fin's mother and also courting with our captain. You're tied closely with both his superiors, you see," Sir Harris volunteered breezily with a bright smile on his face.

Katelyn turned scarlet at the mention of her recent outings with Captain Antonio.

"Ah … I see … yes, well … best be off, you lot. Can't have a short-staffed kitchen!"

The aides all smiled and waved farewell to Katelyn Ashowan as they traipsed back to their posts, each wondering if their beloved cook would be better sooner rather than later.

Entering back into the cottage, the healer headed back to her son's room and froze in her tracks.

Fin was awake. Sitting up, and wearing an oddly dreamy smile on his face, he stared toward the open window.

"Wh-What?!" Katelyn rushed forward and placed her cool hand on her son's forehead drawing his attention to her. "Finlay! How in the world are you recovered this quickly?!" She continued to fuss over him, but he remained oddly quiet. A pleasant breeze wafted through the window that made her pause.

She had closed those when she'd performed a magical examination … She'd even locked them.

How had they come open?

"Sorry to frighten you, Mum. I think I just need a good night's sleep. I'll be alright by morning. Make sure you go check on the queen. You mentioned before I left you think she will go into labor in a few weeks." Fin yawned sleepily, and closed his eyes again, his expression peaceful.

Shaking her head over the oddity of the day, the elder Ashowan turned to the cottage to begin preparing a cup of tea. She needed time to think before her evening stroll with the captain …

Annika paced her chamber floor while chewing on her thumbnail. She hadn't returned to her home in Austice. Despite the danger of her brother having her murdered, she couldn't just leave Fin when he'd been bedridden …

She knew the king wasn't through talking to her, and she needed time to form a new plan. Things were tenuous at best, and she needed some way to firm up the relations with Zinfera without being forced into a marriage …

A small knock at Annika's door had her stop and storm over. Who in the world needed to talk to her when next to no one knew she was there?

Upon opening the door, the viscountess found herself staring into Ainsley's slightly rounder face. The queen's flat expression didn't lighten as she pressed herself into the chamber before Annika could stop her. She wore nothing but a velvet robe that she'd left open and a chemise—yet the monarch seemed completely unperturbed by her state of undress.

"You're supposed to be in bed!" the viscountess blurted, her mind finally stepping out of its flurry of plans and worries.

"A small trip to your chamber is good for me. I'll just sit while we have a little chat, hm?" The queen waddled over to the four-poster bed and cast a wry glance over her shoulder.

Annika rushed forward and gave her friend a hand as she lowered herself atop the ruby coverlet.

"Now. How long have you been sleeping with the cook?"

The viscountess didn't even bother to lie. After the beat of momentary surprise and widened eyes, she let out an unladylike groan.

"I knew you'd catch on after today …"

Ainsley let out a disapproving sigh. "I know he's attractive, but Annika … you're risking your entire country's safety for him. Do you realize that? You can't marry him."

"I can handle this, Ainsley, I promise. I can make sure Zinfera forms a firm alliance with Daxaria for the war that doesn't rely on my marriage."

"Is it something you can muster in less than two weeks? Because if they sign the treaty and then discover that Nam is going to be denied one of the privileges he was expected to receive from the marriage, they could see it as underhanded dealings. They could grow very hostile toward us, and then we have an entire other nation we have to be wary of."

"I just didn't know about the bastard son … I would've been in the clear …" Annika muttered as she began rubbing her temples that were beginning to throb.

"You're not being as careful as you usually are. You usually know everything before we tell you," Ainsley observed gently. "Under different circumstances, I would be thrilled that you have fallen in love to the degree that you're pulling away from your line of work. However … Annika, I will not gamble the safety of the entire country for you to marry a cook. I want you to find happiness, and if it were with a marquis at the very least I'm sure we could manage something, but we won't risk it for an already … tricky pairing."

"You mean you won't risk it for the cook who saved hundreds of people, yourself, the king, and your children included?" The viscountess's voice had a hard edge that Ainsley had never heard from her friend.

"Yes, that cook. Annika, I know you resent me saying these things, but I have to be a queen first. There are millions of people in this country, and I need to protect them. If I have to choose between the happiness of two people or the safety of every man, woman, and child under my reign, you know what I have to do."

Annika knew her friend was right. Knew it was the right choice.

Still … she wasn't so easily defeated.

"Will three days be too much time to give me? I still think I can save this," Annika asked, her mind straining against the confines of her skull.

Ainsley studied the viscountess's determined face; her desperation, and hopefulness, were palpable.

"Fine. Three days. If you don't find some miracle solution by then, you have to marry Lord Ryu. I am truly sorry."

Annika nodded somberly.

Slowly standing back up, the queen gripped one of the posters of the bed to right herself while waving off her friend's hand. She was almost at the door when she turned around, her hands cradling her lower back.

"Even if you somehow pull it off, you know we still can't sanction your marriage," Ainsley remarked slowly.

At this, Annika smiled.

"Oh, you will. He'll be ennobled, and regardless of how poor he is, I'll marry him. It might take a few years, but we'll get there. I know it."

CHAPTER 19
KRAKEN'S SMOKE SHOW

Fin awoke the next morning feeling refreshed and ready to resume his search for the missing Troivackians, but he also wanted to try and see Annika before he began.

After passing out in the woods while trying to suppress Sky, he had awoken to the comforting warmth of Annika's hand in his, her lips pressed against his forehead.

The odd thing was that when he had opened his eyes, she truly had seemed to have a faint golden glow around her ... but then again it had been some time since he had gone unconscious from overusing his abilities.

The more likely explanation was that it could have been a dream.

Either way, he needed to let her know what had happened. If she hadn't received word from anyone about his whereabouts, and he had once again stood her up for dinner ...

She would be seething mad and picking out the best wood to use for his coffin.

Well ... the sooner I face that storm, the better.

Rising with a stretch, Fin stepped out into the main room of his cottage to see that his mother had already left for the day.

A note on the kitchen table informed him that she had to attend to the queen, but that she wanted to speak to him soon.

With a sigh, Fin admitted to himself that he would have to be a little more forthright with his mother in the near future if he didn't want to feel like an ass for putting her through so much worry.

Fin approached Annika's estate clutching a bouquet of sunflowers he had picked from a small patch that had grown near the edge of the king's forest. He knew they weren't extravagant, but hoped she was the type to like flowers. She had liked the rose he had brought her after all ... then again roses were significantly nicer than—

The clatter of hooves and the crunch of gravel coming up the laneway behind Fin made him turn around. He was surprised to see Annika's carriage drawing up alongside him; where had she gone so early in the day?

The carriage halted beside him, and the door opened. The Troivackian beauty sat on the bench wearing a gauzy light blue dress underneath her cloak and stared at him with a small frown.

It took Fin a moment to stop gawking at her loveliness, but when she gestured to the opposite bench with her hand, he cleared his throat and handed her the flowers he carried.

She blinked in surprise as he climbed into the carriage and seated himself.

"Everything alright?" Fin asked tentatively as she failed to signal the driver to continue.

Giving her head a small shake, Annika reached out and shut the door then called for the footman to continue on.

"Are you recovered enough to be out and about?" she asked, her gaze roving over him, making the redhead feel incredibly self-conscious over the sweat and grime he had accumulated from walking in the humid morning.

"So it wasn't a dream that you were in my room," he muttered, unable to stop himself from blushing.

"No. I happened to be at the castle when I heard you were in an accident. I checked in on you and you woke up briefly while I was there, though you were pretty out of it."

Fin nodded seriously as the carriage pulled up to the front doors. The witch hastily jumped out, then made sure to offer his hand to Annika as she stepped down.

The two walked up the steps while the serving staff all bowed dutifully to them, and one stepped forward to take her mistress's cloak.

Once back in the cool building, Annika gestured for Fin to follow her back up the stairs. They passed by several serving members who didn't dare look him in the eyes, and the redhead somehow knew that there had been a bit of … excitement, thanks to him.

Annika didn't say a word until the door closed behind the redhead in her bedchamber. Setting down the bouquet of sunflowers in a nearby vase, she turned to face him with her arms folded across her chest.

"Why the hell are you always in trouble?! First you're in a brawl, then you're drugged, then you're going to have your legs broken, and *then* you nearly die from fighting some random witches' match?!" Annika exploded.

Fin winced, knowing that she was entirely within her right to be angry. She must have eavesdropped outside his window and learned about why he had once again not returned to the estate the previous day.

"Furthermore! You've now made things ridiculously complicated by encouraging Duke Iones's illegitimate son to inherit the title and lands," she concluded, her former gusto dropping off into defeated tones. Wearily, the viscountess reached down the front of her dress and procured her flask.

"What does Sir Harris have to do with anything?" Fin questioned slowly, making Annika pause in taking a drink.

Slowly lowering the flask and screwing the top back on, she fixed him with a somber stare, and Fin then noticed the dark bags under eyes. She hadn't slept well it seemed.

"Fin, you know how I was set to be married to one of the three suitors?"

"Yes?"

"Well, there was one other noblewoman that the Zinferan emperor would've accepted becoming betrothed to one of his lords. A lady whose hand in marriage meant a Daxarian title for her husband. However, if, say, a secret son were to appear and take that title …"

Realization washed over the redhead's face. The color then proceeded to drain from every inch of his skin.

"What does this mean now?"

"It means I have three days to figure out a new Godsdamn plan to get out of a forced marriage."

"What are the options?" Fin demanded, stepping forward as cold dread gripped his heart.

"The crux of the issue is to find a way to appeal to the Zinferan emperor to sign the treaty even if Lady Marigold doesn't have a dukedom to offer. She is still a noble, and her dowry is … impressive, but it isn't as good a deal."

The redhead fell quiet.

"I can try to ask Jiho if he has any ideas on what the emperor may want or what he could be convinced to take instead. The tricky thing is we are trying to persuade someone we don't really know."

"Oh, I have a pretty good idea the kind of person the emperor is. A proud man. One who is prone to changing his disposition, and a little bit hedonistic. Unlike our dear Lord Nam, however, he is intelligent."

"You've met him?" Fin asked, surprised. It was well known that the Emperor of Zinfera didn't like to leave his kingdom.

"No. I've met his nobility and his subjects, though. I know how to read a man from his reputation. Still go and talk to Jiho, however, but instead ask if there is anything questionable about Lord Nam's title, wealth … anything. If we can find out the emperor was trying to offer an under-handed deal himself, we have grounds to fight back. He won't like us, but after some expensive gifts and a few years to recover, the emperor should be fine with Daxaria …"

"I'm not sure how fond I am of blackmailing an emperor," Fin informed her uneasily.

"It's not blackmail, love. It's politics." Annika walked up to Fin then, her hands on her hips. "You know, I do believe it has been quite long enough since you kissed me."

Fin laughed before wrapping his arms around her waist and pulling her closer to himself.

"To think I was worried you would be angry with me about missing dinner again."

"Oh, I'm furious, but I am flexible in how I handle that particular feeling." Her voice had dropped to a hush as she stood on her toes and brushed her lips gently against his.

It took another hour or two before the couple left the chamber, but when they did, Annika didn't recall ever being angry to begin with.

"So it'll be soon then?" Slapping his cards down on the overturned crate, the Troivackian soldier stared up at his superior. The man stood over the small group of men that were in the middle of their third round of games that day.

The group of five hundred soldiers milled about the abandoned building listlessly. All windows and doors were boarded firmly shut, and the only source of light was from the various candles around the room. The only glimpse of the outside was a small broken slat in a round window at the back wall of the building.

"Yes. After the chief of military leaves Austice, he will send a missive to our king's ship, and once that reaches him, we will begin the siege. Ideally the city of Xava will fall before he arrives. It'd be significantly easier if we aren't having to worry about counterattacks from the south."

The men all grinned amongst each other. Everything was going to plan.

"OYY!" One of the men hollered as a large fluffy black kitten landed in his lap.

"Ahh, that beast. Go easy on him, Jas, he's keepin' the rats at bay for us." Reaching down, the superior of the Troivackian unit plucked up the kitten and began rubbing his belly, only to have the feline playfully bite at his hand.

"He keeps stealin' our food." Another of the men grumbled while taking a deep drink from his bottle of Troivackian moonshine.

Oddly, the kitten's head swiveled over to stare at the one who had spoken and glared, making the soldier shift uncomfortably.

"Cats are smarter than most people give them credit for." The superior chuckled as he placed the animal down.

"Whatever you say, sir. I tell you, I cannot wait to get out of this Godsforsaken land. I—"

"FIRE! FIRE! EVERYONE GRAB YOUR BLANKETS!" one of the soldiers shouted from the back of the building, gesturing wildly toward the small room they were using to store their food. Everyone could see the faint glow and the haze of smoke beginning to creep out.

As the men bolted from the table, Kraken gave the abandoned moonshine bottle a quick sniff. Once he confirmed his suspicion, he knocked it over, its contents spilling all over the wooden surface and card game spread out.

Leaping onto the table that was in fact a wooden cart wheel propped up on buckets, he wandered over to the edge. Three lit candles that had dripping wax rolling down their sides sat innocently.

With a sharp jab of his paw, he managed to knock the tallest of the three down, and hastily scampered away as the table exploded into flames.

Clambering up the nearest wooden pillar, Kraken pulled himself up onto the balcony that wrapped around the entire structure. He sauntered past the men's pallets where the other kittens under his command had successfully emptied a number of waterskins that had in fact been filled with moonshine.

"*Come, we must clamber out the window now. We will drop the final candle from atop!*" Kraken called out over the rising panic of the soldiers below.

The soldier named Jas coughed as the curling black flames climbed higher and higher around him, the severity of the situation beginning to settle in, when he glanced up and had to blink through the smoke to be sure he was seeing things correctly.

Approximately fifteen kittens were all leaping up and squeezing through the small round window that had a single broken slat near the peak of the roof.

He then saw the unmistakable tuft of black fur on the balcony above of the very cat that had been loitering around them for more than a week ... only ... the cat had a candle in his mouth.

"What the fu—"

Kraken dropped the candle, and the entire balcony burst into flames as if by magic. The feline jumped up and scrambled through the slatted opening, ignoring the cries of the men from inside.

Upon landing on the ground, Kraken could feel the heat from the fire that raged within the building, even though the flames had not yet consumed the outer walls.

"*Kraken, sir!*" One of the kittens burst out, making the fluffy feline whip his head around quickly, only to find himself staring at a puff of smoke.

"*What is it?*" he asked while double-checking that he saw each of the brave young kittens that had volunteered for the job.

"*Your ... Your fur is...*"

Kraken looked and noted that he was smoking slightly. Dropping onto his back in the dirt, he squirmed around until he was quite certain he was completely put out. A handy tip James Paws had taught him.

"*Come, kittens, before the fire reaches the street.*"

Fin was walking up the street toward Sky and Adamma's house to check and see how the air witch was managing after the previous day, when he saw the black cloud curling up in the north end of the city.

"Oh Gods, that is a huge fire," he marveled worriedly. "I wonder what happened ..."

It was then he felt the faint brush against his trouser leg.

Looking down, Fin broke out into a bright smile at the sight of Kraken gazing intently up at him.

"There you are! I've wondered where you've been." The witch chuckled as he reached down and plucked up his familiar.

"I've been fine. Would you happen to have any water?" Kraken relaxed comfortably in Fin's arm as the redhead then resumed walking.

"I don't, but I'm on my way to see some people that will."

"Oh good … so. Have you succeeded in making any kittens yet?"

"Kraken!"

"What?! What is it?! I can explain the ash in my fur! I swear I—" The black cat grew a little more rigid in his witch's arms.

"What about the ash in your fur?" Fin demanded, immediately worried.

"Oh … nothing I … walked too closely to a candle."

Kraken intended to tell Fin everything eventually, but right then … all the feline wanted to do was to find a nice bowl of water to drink, and perhaps some cool stone to lie down on and take a nap.

He hated to say it, but his witch was a little sensitive about people being harmed. Kraken doubted his witch would be happy to hear that his familiar had more or less smoked out an entire unit of the Troivackian army. There probably were some that were injured, but … at least he'd hunted down some of the rats that were going to try and attack his family.

CHAPTER 20
AFTERMATH TAXATION

Seated at the table with Kraken snoozing peacefully in his lap, Fin studied Adamma's weary face. The woman looked as though she hadn't slept a wink, and Sky was nowhere in sight.

"I can't apologize enough, Mr. Ashowan." Adamma's hands were wrapped around her tea mug, its aromatic steam tinted with lavender and mint. "Sky has made great improvements since that time with your father, but I fear seeing you and … and your powers unraveled all of that work."

Fin's stomach clenched painfully. Sensing this, Kraken burrowed himself into his witch's middle, making the redhead begin to thoughtlessly pet the beast.

"I don't blame Sky for what happened, Adamma. There was no way to know beforehand that she would try to kill me. Even she had said once she saw my eyes that I didn't seem like my father," Fin reassured gently.

The corners of Adamma's mouth tried to turn upright but failed to make the full journey into a smile. Huddling her shoulders over the table, the vibrant woman from the day before was gone and in her place was an exhausted, heartbroken spouse.

"How did you and Sky meet?" Fin asked instead. He could see how hard Adamma had worked to heal the mind of her loved one.

"Oh, quite by the hair of the Goddess." She chuckled a little, the first hint of a real smile touching her face. When the earth witch noticed Fin's confused expression, she explained.

"In my kingdom it's an old saying. We believe that meaningful encounters of fate happen because the Goddess tied a strand of her hair between two individuals. It is a fate that cannot be broken as it is touched with her divinity."

Fin smiled; he hadn't heard the saying before but couldn't help but enjoy the notion.

"I had just arrived, and I was all ready to hunt down my oaf of a brother, whom I had assumed had been abducted and was toiling away under the cruel Daxarian king."

Both Adamma and the redhead chuckled at that horrifically incorrect assumption.

"I had quite literally just stepped off the dock, when I heard what sounded like a child shrieking … I, of course, marched down the hill to the beach to go rescue them, only to find a woman with snowy white hair making parchment boats swirl around each other in the water for some local children. They were all having a marvelous time …" Adamma's eyes shone as her mind delved deeper into the past.

"Then their mothers and fathers came. Snatching their children and lecturing them on being careful around the mad witch. They mentioned she was living on the beach that ran under one of the docks and well … my curiosity was piqued."

Fin nodded along to the story. It sounded as though they had overcome a great many things in their time together. "Where is Sky right now?"

Adamma blinked slowly, drawing herself back from the past.

"In our bedchamber. Resting. She isn't speaking to me yet … your mother was here first thing in the morning, but all Sky could do was cry." Closing her eyes, the earth witch scratched her left eyebrow wearily.

Feeling at a complete loss as to what to do, Fin glanced down at the mass of soft kitten fluff in his lap. Cracking open one bright green eye, Kraken thrust his head into the redhead's hand. Somehow, the action created a sense of peace in Fin's chest. He couldn't fix everything for his mother's old friend, or take away Adamma's burden for that matter, but there was something he always *could* do …

Standing and cradling Kraken against his chest, the redhead rounded the table and gently placed the feline in Adamma's lap. She opened her eyes in surprise, but Fin was already moving with purpose.

"Does anyone in the house have foods they won't eat?" he asked while approaching the table under the window that was covered with dried herbs and tinctures.

"Oh, uh … Nina hates fish, and Urick hates some of the leafier foods," Adamma answered hesitantly.

Fin nodded to himself as he began rummaging around some of the sacks that were stacked at the end of the table.

Confused, Adamma watched him for a few moments as he began assembling various foodstuffs he found around the main room.

"What is it you think you are doing, Mr. Ashowan?"

"I'm going to cook for all of you. Now, would you mind telling me where I could find some cheese and fruit?"

Sky lay motionless on the bed, her eyes staring blindly out the window as wondrous smells gradually began filling the house. A trembling in her stomach let the air witch know that she was hungry, but crushing disappointment and guilt weighed her down onto her sheets. She didn't deserve food when she hurt people … Kate's son, Adamma, she'd even nearly harmed Nina …

The latch to the chamber door clacked as it lifted, and despite not turning to see who had entered, Sky knew it was her niece and nephew by their footfalls.

The siblings crossed the room and rounded on her, blocking the view of the window as they slowly lowered themselves down to crouch before her.

"Aunt Sky, Mr. Ashowan made us all food, but Aunt Adamma isn't letting us have any until you eat," Nina began gently.

The air witch remained silent.

"He's the best cook in the kingdom is what all the nobles have been saying," Urick jumped in, unable to hide his growing admiration for the redhead.

Sky's eyes began to water.

"Aunt Sky, don't cry!" Nina looked to her brother desperately. "Just … try his food. He made soup even though it's summer … he let it cool down and apparently cold soup is something some people eat …" the youth prattled on nervously.

Urick picked up one of the sliced strawberries on the board he was holding and pressed it to his aunt's mouth.

"Aunt Sky, if you don't eat this, you're going to make it weird," he pleaded, his awkwardness palpable.

The woman's eyes did flicker then. She looked to her nephew, her gaze softening at once, and opened her mouth. She never could say no to him … not since the day she saw him swaddled in his mother's arms.

A perplexed expression suddenly crossed her face as she chewed.

Blinking, Sky slowly sat up then reached for a wedge of soft cheese on the board. After she gobbled nearly half of the fruit and cheese that Urick had brought, she turned curiously to the bowl in Nina's hands that had a sprinkling of what looked to be a mix of parsley and chives atop a creamy steaming soup.

"M-Mr. Ashowan calls this soup the 'Everything Is Right with the World Soup.' I don't get it, either, but it smells amazing. It's mostly potatoes and milk from what I saw but—"

Sky suddenly dove for the bowl making Nina jump, but the siblings watched in amazement as the first spoonful of soup made the faintest blush of pink appear in their aunt's cheeks.

During her entire meal Sky hadn't said a word, but a glint in her eyes made both Urick and Nina share hopeful smiles.

"Aunt Adamma is downstairs with Mr. Ashowan," Nina started quietly, but stopped swiftly when a look of uncertainty returned in Sky's eyes.

Urick was quick to speak then. "His familiar is here, too! A really fluffy black kitten; he's named Kraken. Though Mr. Ashowan says we can't leave any bread out or the cat will steal it …"

A touch of mirth appeared on the air witch's face, and not wanting to waste an opportunity, Urick offered his hand to her. With a smile, Sky accepted the gesture, and stood. She nodded gratefully at Nina who was in the process of letting out a very tense breath.

The trio made their way out of the chamber, down the narrow corridor with its creaking old floorboards, then down the winding stairs to the small alcove that was set off the large main floor.

Sitting at the table that was fully set with more food for everyone were Finlay Ashowan and Adamma. A fluffy black kitten sat at attention on the herb table, the tuft of white fur on his chest akin to a small badge.

"Shall we have some lunch together? It looks like you've eaten, but we'd love it if you'd join us," Adamma asked warmly.

Sky couldn't bring herself to look Fin in the eyes, but she nodded.

Once seated, everyone dug in and immediately began exclaiming over the food. The redhead regaled them all with tales of his mother's best healing stories, and the children told him funny anecdotes from their time growing up.

It was a wonderful afternoon, and when everyone had finished, Fin began to clear the table.

"No, no, you are our guest and you have already done enough," Adamma chided as she stood and wrenched the dirty dishes from his grasp.

Opening his mouth to argue, both of them were stopped when Sky's quiet voice interrupted.

"How did you make even the berries taste better?"

Fin turned to the woman and regarded her kindly.

"I know which ones are ripest, but in my personal opinion ... it's because of the intent I put in preparing them. I wanted you to have food that comforted you and gave you a bit of gumption." He looked apologetic at the last part of his explanation, but the air witch didn't look insulted in the least.

"Well ... it worked. I must admit ... I don't think you are as powerless off the castle grounds as you believe," she explained softly.

Fin laughed then, but Sky's stricken expression made everyone tense immediately. The redhead shifted self-consciously under her stare.

The breath of silence lasted only a moment before Sky spoke.

"You have Kate's smile." The air witch's face lightened, and everyone in the room shared looks of happiness and relief.

Placing his hands on his hips, Fin turned to Kraken.

"Well, I think we need to get going. If I stand my companion up for a third night, she really might kill me ... or, worse yet, refuse to rescue me."

Everyone laughed, and the redhead took the opportunity to head to the door. Bending down, he picked up Kraken from the table as he passed. The feline seemed quite content to be carried.

"I hope you stop by for a visit again, Fin," Sky called out.

Adamma smiled to herself, reassurance smoothing out the wrinkles in her forehead and beside her mouth.

"Also, if you could, please ask your mother if her friend in Troivack received the message safely."

Fin froze.

Turning slowly, he stared wide-eyed at the air witch.

"What friend in Troivack?"

"Oh, perhaps a little more than a week ago?" Sky looked to Adamma who nodded in confirmation, though the two women looked perplexed at Fin's reaction. "That was when your mother tracked me down. She asked if I might use my air magic to send a missive to a friend of hers in the Troivackian castle. I sent a note to a cousin of mine who is a part of the Aguas Coven there, and they were supposed to get a reply back to her quickly."

"Did my mother say who she was writing to?" Fin asked faintly.

Sky shook her and shrugged wordlessly.

Blood thrummed in Fin's ears; he was vaguely aware of himself thanking them and saying farewell, but he walked back to Annika's estate in a daze.

Was his mother in contact with his father? Was she pleading with Aidan not to come? Or perhaps she was officially asking for a divorce …

The questions continued to grow more fevered, until Fin found himself in the courtyard leading up to Annika's estate. While he was giving his head a shake, the same elderly maid who had dropped the arm full of towels on his first morning there rushed out.

"Mr. Wit, there is a … a man here asking for you. He … He called you a different name. Ash something or other. Though he described you perfectly …" The woman was wringing her hands and appeared to be quite distraught.

Fin felt his heart drop into his stomach. "Everything will be alright, Gemma. Where is Anni— Lady Jenoure?"

"My lady is in town, and I don't know when she will be home. I've asked Clara to go retrieve her."

Nodding, Fin handed Kraken to Gemma, making the woman pause in momentary confusion.

Striding up the rest of the way to the great doors, Fin could hear two male voices bellowing at each other even before he could touch the handle to the entrance.

One of them sounded quite familiar …

"UNHAND ME AT ONCE! I AM HIS MAJESTY'S TRUSTED MAGE AND—"

The witch stepped into the entryway in time to see Raymond pinning Mage Lee's arms up behind his head. The giant Troivackian obviously found his opponent as inconsequential as a bag of flour. Lee's staff lay on the floor out of reach.

"YOU!" the mage thundered, spittle flying from his mouth upon laying eyes on Fin. "SUMMON LADY JENOURE THIS INSTANT! WHAT THE BLOODY HELL IS—"

"Raymond, he is the Royal Mage to the king. Maybe don't break him like you do chicken necks," Fin called out mildly.

Lady Jenoure's cook cast the redhead a disappointed glance, but he released Lee and took a few steps back.

"I'll talk with him in the solar. I'll come check your biscuits afterward, alright?" Fin stepped forward and picked up the staff.

"Alright, holler if he gets troublesome again." Raymond growled under his breath as he lumbered off back to the kitchen.

Mage Lee turned and stared at Fin with the clear wish of causing him bodily harm.

"Shall we have a chat?" Fin gestured toward the staircase.

The mage straightened his robes with an indignant sniff, and the two men set off to have a conversation that the staff would no doubt be attempting to eavesdrop on.

Once they reached the solar and the doors had been closed, Fin strolled over to the open balcony doors, crossed his arms, and leaned his shoulder against the doorway.

"So how've you been, Lee?"

"You," the mage hissed.

"Me?" Fin asked innocently.

"Enough of your smartass remarks. What the hell are you doing here? You said that Clara gave you a room to stay in while you helped their cook, but why the hell is the staff treating you as though you're the master of—"

A look of realization dawned on the mage's face, and the witch felt all blood drain from his cheeks.

"Mr. Ashowan ... are you ... perhaps ..."

Fin's heart was about to explode as he waited for the next series of dreaded words.

"Betrothed to Clara, the viscountess's personal maid?!"

CHAPTER 21
AN ENGAGING ENCOUNTER

Fin had his mouth covered with his hand and his eyes fixed on the floor as the situation continued to grow out of hand. It was then that the viscountess herself burst into the room with Clara on her heels.

"Mage Lee! I am surprised to see you," Annika greeted the mage breathlessly, her normally impeccable appearance entirely disheveled. She wore a cream-colored gown that had very obviously been thrown on in great haste. Fin assumed she had been in men's britches before being summoned. Her long braid had several flyaways, and her cheeks were flushed.

"Viscountess, I am incredibly sorry for not properly announcing my intention to come. I had a very curious matter to investigate. Namely the arrival of your personal guard the other evening when Mr. Ashowan here was in trouble. However, I believe I understand fully now." His blue eyes twinkled merrily, and Annika's gaze flitted to Fin briefly before her cool mask of control fixed itself over her features.

"Oh?" She clasped her hands in front of her skirts.

"Yes, and please know that His Majesty will not be happy, though there are a few who will be more pleased …"

Fin stared at Mage Lee blankly. The witch was unable to speak or properly think past the massive misunderstanding.

Annika appeared to be holding her breath.

"The viscountess has only been close with a handful of people since arriving here in Daxaria, and one of those people was Clara." Mage Lee addressed Fin before he turned back to Annika. "Your maid handles every meeting, and household matter for you … so when Fin found himself in trouble, of course, Lady Jenoure, you would offer your personal armed guards to help. Oh, that means if married, you might have to quit the castle and come here," Mage Lee turned again to Fin on the last point, his face beaming in pleasure over the very valid reasons for his new "discovery."

The man was completely oblivious to Annika's stunned confusion.

"Mage Lee, I am afraid I am not entirely certain what you are talking about," she began hesitantly.

"His Majesty would be upset, of course, as I said before, but I can't say I'll be too tearful to see you go, Mr. Ashowan. Mr. Howard will most likely host a party … When is the wedding to happen? Will you allow Clara to continue working? I imagine Lady Jenoure may have something to say about that—"

Annika's eyebrows shot up as she finally realized what the elder was saying.

"Mage Lee, are you suggesting that Mr. Ashowan and my maid Clara are betrothed?"

The maid in question suddenly choked, then snorted, though she managed to cover her mouth when her mistress shot her a scathing glare over her shoulder. Clara wisely pretended to have been coughing.

"I understand this is a private household matter, Viscountess, and you have my sincere apologies for intruding. However, you know how attached the prince has become to Mr. Ashowan, and I must advise you to reconsider insisting he work for your household immediately after the marriage."

Annika looked ready to pummel the man. At least it appeared that way to both Fin and Clara who had come to recognize the slightest shift in her eyes.

"Mage Lee, I don't believe my dear maid will be getting married any time soon." Annika smiled prettily, making both Fin and Clara shudder.

The old man failed to notice and waved off her comment before grabbing her hands.

"Now, now, my dear. Your maid isn't as young as she was when you first arrived. She deserves her chance at love, though I must confess she will have a difficult road ahead of herself being wed to our Royal Cook."

Clara's blue eyes were fixed on the ceiling, her face growing pink as Fin covered his face, unable to watch the disaster continue to worsen.

"Mr. Ashowan, no need to be so bashful! Our viscountess has been incredibly gracious and accepting of you staying in her home while you court Clara. Why don't you two sweethearts stand together while we all discuss your coming nuptials."

Fin had managed to take a single hesitant step before Annika jumped back in.

"I would love to, Mage Lee; however, I do feel a migraine coming on, and I—"

"Oh, Mr. Ashowan can fix you the most wonderful tea. It has helped our king many times when experiencing such ailments. You know, with this week being Mr. Ashowan's time off, perhaps these two could take their vows in a couple of days and— Well now! I just had a thought! Isn't your mother at the castle, Mr. Ashowan? Why not have the ceremony while she is here! If you wait longer, Kate may be quite stressed if she is also tending to our queen and the new babe when the time comes."

Fin slowly began walking to the door to prepare the tea, his legs feeling as though they were wooden stilts. As he passed behind Annika, her hand shot out faster than anyone could see, and gripped his arm firmly, holding him in place.

"I'm not sure we should be planning Mr. Ashowan's wedding without him present." Without meaning to, Lady Jenoure's grasp tightened on Fin's arm almost painfully.

Mage Lee blinked at the viscountess's sudden move but shook his head dismissively once she released Fin.

"I understand, of course; however, this affects you as well, my lady. After all, will Mr. Ashowan permit Clara to continue working after they marry as I asked earlier? Oftentimes it isn't long after a wedding with two perfectly healthy people that there are children of their own. There is the likelihood that—"

"Mage Lee," Fin croaked. At the rate the mage was digging Fin's grave for him, he would soon hit the Alcide Sea. "Perhaps imposing upon Lady Jenoure, interrupting her day, and insisting she listen to a commoner's marriage plans when she feels unwell is a bit much, hm?"

Clara was partially hidden behind Fin and was visibly struggling to stop herself from laughing.

The mage looked crestfallen.

"For once I can see the sense in what you're saying." The elder sighed. "I did actually come here to deliver a message to you, Lady Jenoure. I suppose I will do so and take my leave."

Fin and Clara gratefully bowed and curtsied before backing out of the room and closing the doors to the solar behind them.

The two made it to the end of the hall before Clara lost all her composure and doubled over howling.

"Glad you found that funny," Fin remarked dryly.

"I've never seen her so close to harming someone out of pure irritation!" Clara continued laughing until tears tracked down her face. "Gods, you and I? How in the world did he think that up?" she wheezed.

"He was with me when Annika sent her guards to rescue us, remember?"

The maid settled down enough to straighten and wipe her face dry, though she was still grinning widely. It was the first time Fin had ever seen the woman show any emotion. Annika was a skilled actress, but the maid was often an icy wall of impenetrability.

"I see. So he believes that because Lady Jenoure is such a good friend of mine that she'd send her men to save you. I suppose it does make some level of sense."

Fin shook his head and began rubbing his face.

"There, there." Clara patted his shoulder. "Most of the time my mistress chooses a quick death for her victims."

"What do you think the message is about?" The redhead changed the topic glumly as they continued on their journey farther away from the solar.

"She receives messages pretty regularly from the king. It's odd that Mage Lee would be the one delivering the missive, but perhaps he volunteered in order to help you plan our wedding."

Fin looked to the heavens as Clara succumbed to another spell of hysterics.

"I beg your pardon?" Annika stared incredulously at the mage who had grown significantly more somber as he delivered his news.

"Yes, hundreds of Troivackian soldiers were discovered in one of the winter market buildings the commoners use. The fire drew our military, and they found that the door had been barred by some barrels that had been knocked over on the outside. Most of the men are fine, though a few suffered burns and some bad coughs ... a few even appear to have mental stress. Some of them are babbling about cats setting the place on fire ..."

Annika shook her head dismissively. "Mage Lee, this is all very …
shocking. However, why is it you are informing me of this?"

The viscountess knew the king wouldn't be so careless as to expose her
to the mage. There had to be something more to it.

"Well … my dear, I am sorry to say this, but there was incriminating
evidence regarding your brother discovered at the scene. Written orders
with his seal. He has violated numerous Daxarian laws by smuggling
the soldiers onto our shores, and there is a distinct possibility that the
Troivackians have been using this method in all major cities. We are
keeping the unit we've discovered isolated from everyone and everything.
We've sent emergency messages to all the cities to immediately search
their winter marketplaces so that we have the element of surprise and
ideally catch a significant portion of them."

Annika waited; she knew there was more … the discovery was a huge
one. It was massively helpful to their war preparation, but she could tell
that the old man was still beating around the bush.

"Well, naturally your brother's death will be demanded as a result. It is
up to King Matthias whether or not it is our executioner who will do the
deed, or his own. Then again it could also be the official beginning of the
violent aspect of war … It depends on whether or not the Troivackian king
tries to play the fool and responds by saying Lord Ptereva was acting on his
own accord in a treasonous manner to his own kingdom."

"Lee"—Annika reached out and gently touched the mage's whorled
hands—"my brother was a tyrant his entire life. I feel no remorse."

Nodding in understanding, the elder raised one of his own hands and
covered hers.

"My dear, I wish that were the extent of the news." With a sigh, he
pushed on. "The Daxarian court feels uneasy with you being so close to
His Majesty and the queen in light of this new development and … well
… we think it best if you stay away from court during the war. Due to the
attack on your carriage, you aren't entirely suspicious, but some fools still
feel the need to whisper. You're welcome to stay here in Austice, of course,
and His Majesty himself doesn't suspect your involvement at all, but it
would be a respectful show of how seriously your brother's misdeeds rests
in your heart."

Annika bit her lip, glistening tears rising in her eyes. "I understand. I
… I only want what is best for our king and queen. You know how much
I love them."

Mage Lee felt his heart constrict. Lady Jenoure had truly matured into a wonderful woman since becoming a Daxarian.

"I am sorry, my lady. We will all speak of your goodness to those who dare try to say otherwise."

Lowering her eyes demurely, Annika made a show of smoothing her skirts. Raising her chin regally, she met Mage Lee's stare.

"Thank you. You are a good man." Her voice warbled, but her brave resolve made Lee silently curse her misfortune.

The elder squeezed her soft hands, and after a quiet moment, he pulled himself up using his staff.

As he hobbled to the door, Annika stood as well, her stoic expression unchanging.

"You know … Lady Jenoure … perhaps a joyous event of a wedding might help take your mind off—" the mage began before Annika cut him off sharply.

"Mage Lee, with this grave news I need to be alone with my thoughts. I pray you'll understand." She added on the last part even though she wanted to shove the old codger down the front steps of her estate and have him gone.

For once, the elder wisely shut his mouth, bowed, and took his leave.

Annika sat back down in the quiet of the solar for a moment. She raised her hand to her mouth and let loose all she had held back during the entire conversation.

Then, she stood up to go find Fin.

"… going to be in so much trouble!" Raymond roared with laughter after Clara had regaled him with Mage Lee's assumptions.

Fin stood with his arms crossed and his chin to his chest. He didn't like waiting to get into a fight.

"Mr. Wit, are you sure there is supposed to be this much butter?" The burly Troivackian suddenly became distracted by the biscuit batter he was in the process of folding.

"Have I instructed you wrong before?" Fin answered without moving a muscle.

Raymond shrugged wordlessly while Clara continued chuckling to herself.

"Mr. Wit?"

The unmistakable cool voice of Annika broke the quiet of the room, making everyone turn and stare immediately at the viscountess who stood in the door, her face unreadable.

"Please follow me," she requested softly before turning and leaving the room.

The witch glanced at Raymond who drew a line across his throat, while Clara feigned hanging herself.

"Thanks. Traitors," Fin grumbled as the two of them burst out laughing again.

Once the couple was alone again in Annika's bedchamber, she turned and stared at him, her breaths began coming out oddly … as though … excited … or angry …

"Fin … I'm not going to have to get married." Her face suddenly broke into a smile so bright that her eyes watered.

"W-What?"

"My brother is on trial for breaking Daxarian laws, and I am expected to stay away from court for the duration of the war given my family tie with him. I will no longer be considered an acceptable marriage option to the Zinferans!"

Fin's jaw dropped. "Are you alright?!"

"Yes! Fin, I can't be in the castle, but we don't have to worry anymore, don't you see?!"

"Do you truly mean to tell me you feel nothing over your brother being sentenced to death?" the redhead asked warily while wrapping his arms around her.

"What you've seen of my brother was nothing in comparison to what he was like while we grew up. That man would happily kill me if I was no use to him. Does that answer your question?"

Letting out a relieved sigh, Fin allowed his forehead to drop to hers. "Then thank the Goddess. I was worried we'd be losing sleep over this for quite some time."

"Oh, we will be losing sleep, just not for that reason …"

Fin laughed, but then made sure to do his part to help her prediction, and so the two shared a passionate kiss as they felt the latest burden on their relationship dissipate.

Late at night wrapped in a certain redhead's arms, Annika awoke, but she wasn't sure what had stirred her. Blinking sleepily, she gazed over at the fireplace that glowed faintly in the darkness. Suddenly, she felt something … furry … graze her leg.

Annika let out a yelp that had Fin jerking awake in a heartbeat; the couple sat up, disoriented and in a state of complete undress. Annika already had a dagger in hand.

Then, their eyes rested on the fluffy black kitten that sat at the foot of the bed in the moonlight, kneading his paws on the sheets.

"Oh Gods … it's just Kraken." Fin collapsed back onto his pillow as the cat then began to prowl closer to his witch.

Annika took several calming breaths and released the knife she had grabbed from under her pillow, then briefly rubbed her eyes before reaching out and scratching the troublesome beast behind his ears.

"I don't want him in the bed all the time," Annika explained as she allowed herself to flop back onto her pillows.

Fin was already sound asleep and answered with an incoherent grunt, while Kraken's glowing eyes regarded her curiously.

With a yawn, the viscountess continued petting the kitten as sleep began to gradually settle back in.

Until she realized she smelled something smoky …

What was that?

Opening her eyes, she glanced around the room. Fin had put the candles out before they'd gone to bed, so nothing was on fire.

Annika lay down slowly while frowning.

Kraken gently bumped his head against hers, his silky fur making her smile, until she realized it was *him* that smelled like smoke.

Some of them are babbling about cats setting the place on fire …

Annika stared at the purring feline, suddenly wide awake as she realized that the Troivackian soldiers might not have been mad with shock after all.

"… Oh my Gods," she whispered disbelievingly.

The only response she got was a secondary head boop and a dollop of drool on the sheet beside her as Kraken settled in for the night, unaware that his secret had been discovered a little sooner than he'd planned.

CHAPTER 22
A BAD FEELING

Annika paced the chamber floor while gnawing on her thumbnail. Dawn had blessed the skies, and Kraken had slipped out at some point after she had fallen into a fitful sleep.

Fin was sleeping for an uncharacteristically long time, but he had mentioned that being a result of his overuse of power during his witches' match.

So the Lady Jenoure was left to her thoughts in the quiet of the morning, which of course equated to an increase in the likelihood that the poor cook would face an emotional explosion the moment he opened his eyes.

By the miraculous grace of the Goddess, however, a soft rap at the door pulled Annika away from her spiraling thoughts pertaining to the pyromania of a certain feline …

Tightening the sash to her robe around her waist, the viscountess steeled herself for the door, her mind a strange combination of foggy and alert.

Upon opening the door a crack, she found Clara standing, waiting in her usual black somber dress. Her face had become more expressive in recent weeks, yet still somehow composed. However, the moment Annika laid eyes on her maid, she could see the worry in the woman's face.

"The king and queen have summoned you. They've asked that you arrive in secret," Clara declared, her voice a disconcerting mix of quiet and weak. As though her message bore a death sentence.

Annika nodded firmly, her spine straightening.

Without another word, she closed the door and dressed. A pair of brown pants, black tunic, and black cloak disguised her feminine physique.

Fin didn't stir during her preparation, and with an odd impulse she didn't fully understand, Annika kissed his temple. He wouldn't know she had done such a thing and yet … somehow it mattered.

Exiting the keep through the back staircases in the name of safety, and riding astride a horse, the viscountess made her way toward the hidden hatch in the king's woods that led to a passageway. The tunnel ran under the castle, then up beside the chimneys to exit into the major bedchambers—the fourth door up the ladder of course being the king and queen's chamber.

As Annika entered the room while pushing past the tapestry that blocked the panel of wood, she kept her hood drawn out of precaution.

"Thank you for joining us so quickly," the king's quiet voice greeted her as she stepped farther into the room.

Dropping onto her knee, Annika bowed before slowly standing and lowering her hood in front of the king.

"My maid was unable to tell me what it was that made you seek my presence," Annika explained while casting a quick appraisal of the monarchs before her.

The queen sat fully dressed on the bed, her hand resting with a pained expression on the swell of her belly that … had it dropped lower? Annika was momentarily fixed on this shift before she regarded the king whose expression was unreadable.

"Lady Jenoure, I trust you received my message from Royal Mage Lee?"

Annika nodded while rising slowly to her feet.

"I am sorry that the events have transpired this way; however, you understand in matters pertaining to the war, I cannot afford to cause any further rifts amongst the nobility. There is going to be enough upheaval when Sir Harris sits in on the next council meeting and his intentions to inherit the dukedom are announced."

Annika made sure to remain expressionless as she bobbed her head.

"You will be required to stay away from the castle and most nobility for a year to allow this business with your brother to blow over."

She nodded again. She was waiting … there had to be more. Otherwise, why was Clara so stressed? What had the summons from the king entailed exactly … ?

"Do you have anything to say on behalf of your brother regarding his recent crimes?"

Annika finally raised her gaze to the monarch who was watching her closely, she realized, because he wanted to know if she was at all worried about her family.

"My brother and I have never been close, and while I do not wish to be the hand to end his life, I recognize he is too dangerous to leave alive. I will not plead against this ruling," she replied carefully and watched as a flicker of relief passed through the man's face.

"Regarding your marriage, it is presumed that you will no longer be the preferred marital option; however, this matter will be broached following Lord Nam's discovery that he will not receive the title of duke. He and Lord Ryu may wish to confer on the matter further. Lord Miller has respectfully withdrawn his candidacy in light of recent events and has already boarded a ship to return home to Troivack."

"Forgot about him …" Annika muttered before she could stop herself.

The king blinked in surprise at the outburst, and what appeared to be a hint of a smile passed over his face.

"He was not an exceptionally ambitious man." The monarch's good-humored expression faltered once more as he shifted his stance ever so slightly. "I am sorry, Lady Jenoure, that you will not be able to aid the queen when she gives birth."

Annika froze and regarded Ainsley's pale expression again.

"Have the pains already started?" she asked while feeling her throat constrict.

"A touch; however, Mrs. Ashowan is trying to suppress the birth with her abilities. The babe has dropped, so it won't be long now …" The queen's face was strained with worry, and Annika's heart ached. The king stared at his wife with open anxiety and love.

"Perhaps ask the council in an emergency meeting today if they will draw issue with my presence during the birth? Surely they will see that it is a womanly matter—and of course politics are not discussed during such a time." The pleading note in the viscountess's voice softened Norman's face considerably.

"I will put the question to them; however, I will admit it doesn't look likely … the fact that we now have thousands of Troivackian soldiers being held as prisoners across the kingdom is wearing on many of us."

Annika's lips pursed.

"If I may make a suggestion, sire?"

Norman gestured for her to continue.

"Ask every merchant in Sorlia to surrender their vessels and set the Troivackian soldiers afloat across the Obelia Sea. Make sure their proximity to the oncoming enemy vessels is as far and difficult to get to as possible."

The king stroked his beard thoughtfully.

"Transporting them will be difficult, especially with many of them already attempting to stage a coup and escape. However, it may also serve to confuse their efforts. The only other issue I might see is the merchants complaining about loss of funds."

Annika quieted for a moment before speaking again. "Offer them a substantial tax reduction for the next two years as thanks. It would financially even out their ledgers, and for some they would even be in a better position as they won't face the risk of losing any cargo or ships."

Norman sighed while shaking his head. "A good idea. However, wars are expensive. We will need to find ways to—"

The queen suddenly grunted and hunched over her middle, making both Annika and Norman rush to her side immediately.

"Doing alright, my dear one?" Norman gently clasped her hand, while his eyes searched her face.

"It does not feel right ... perhaps summon Mrs. Ashowan." Letting out a long shaking breath, Ainsley closed her eyes. Sweat was beginning to bead on her forehead, and Annika felt her pulse triple in speed.

"I'll ... I'll leave immediately then to evade notice." Annika felt her own stomach grow uneasy with distress as she realized that there was a chance that this would be the last time she'd see her friend.

"I will go send for her. Viscountess Jenoure, say your farewells. I am sorry to say that all I am willing to risk for you is a few moments." The king's gentle voice brought Annika's gaze to his, and when she stared into his hazel eyes, she could see the understanding there.

Once again, she was reminded why she remained loyal to a fault to the King of Daxaria.

"Thank you." Annika's voice came out a whisper while the queen gave her husband a strained yet loving glance, nodding ever so slightly.

Norman hurried from the room, and immediately Annika grasped Ainsley's hands in her own.

"You are not allowed to leave me, do you understand?" the viscountess demanded, tears immediately rising to her dark eyes.

"Oh, st-stop with the theatrics. That cook is making you overly emotional." Ainsley tried to laugh but winced instead.

Hastily raising her hand, Annika brushed the queen's brow as lovingly as she would her own sister.

"It was either my emotions or my figure that would become soft when it came to him."

This time the queen did manage to give a breathy laugh.

"Was it your suggestion that my brother's conviction made me unacceptable for a political marriage?" Annika asked, while staring intently at her friend's face. She had been wondering which of the nobles would have suggested her absence from court, but had a hunch …

"Well …" Ainsley took a deep shuddering breath as an unforeseen pain seized her body. "If it isn't a guarantee that I'll be around to keep you tame—"

"Don't you dare say such things," Annika's voice croaked.

She couldn't lose Ainsley … not like this.

"My friend, I'm in the best hands—your cook's mother's, in fact—but … if the Goddess wants me, I don't think any magic in this world will save me."

"To hell with that! You tell that blockheaded deity wench that she is going to leave you well enough alone, or I'm going to come to the forest of the afterlife and burn it down." Tears had begun spilling down Annika's cheeks as her grip on the queen's hands tightened.

Ainsley's smile turned sad as she reached out and gently brushed her thumb against the wet streaks on her best friend's face.

"Listen to me, I don't have long to explain before you must go. I need you to protect Norman and Eric should the worst happen. No matter what, do not let him rely on advisors to run the kingdom. I don't trust any of those senile idiots to do half the job he will."

Annika said nothing as her vision grew blurrier and blurrier.

"Finally, I want you to get that redheaded witch ennobled and make him one smashing success amongst the courtiers. If there's anyone who can make a peasant into a wealthy noble through conniving plots, it's you."

A small sob wracked Annika's body as she embraced Ainsley tightly, not wanting to let go.

"Promise me you'll do these things," the queen whispered, her own eyes beginning to mist as she fought off shuddering through another wave of pain.

"I promise. *You* promise *me* this isn't goodbye," Annika insisted frantically as she pulled away again. "You've been the best friend I've ever had. My first friend …"

Ainsley gave her hand another squeeze. "You have been my closest friend and confidante, and I love you like family. Now, please ... go."

Annika opened her mouth to insist yet again that Ainsley wasn't allowed to die, but the sound of footfalls nearing the door had her wrenching herself away and diving for the passageway.

With one final look over her shoulder at Ainsley's smiling face, Annika closed the panel, and fled the castle.

As if on cue, the castle door flew open and Ruby, the Head of Housekeeping, entered along with lines of maids carrying towels and a change of clothes. "Mrs. Ashowan has been summoned, Your Majesty. The babe is coming?"

Ainsley opened her mouth to reply but found her voice stolen by yet another surge of agony. After it had passed, she looked up and could see the worried glances the staff were sharing.

"It would seem that way."

Slowly returning to lie down in the bed, Ainsley couldn't help but note a deep sense that something was different.

For one, the child was going to be born even earlier than Mrs. Ashowan seemed to believe, but there was something else that she couldn't put her finger on. Something that made her wish that she had spent another hour with Eric the previous night when she had read bedtime stories to his eager ears. One more moment where she could tell him how much she loved him as she held him in her arms. One more moment kissing her husband's smiling lips.

Then, another jolt of pain seared through her being that stole any thoughts she could spare.

Annika burst into her bedchamber to find that Fin had already risen and left for the day, and somehow this made the ache in her chest all the worse.

Clara stepped quietly behind her mistress, removing the cloak from her shoulders. "The messenger mentioned that the queen had urged him to hurry with his missive ... is everything alright at the castle?"

Annika wanted to scream.

She wanted to do *something* instead of waiting idly for word to come. She had never been powerless before. Never been in a situation she couldn't think or battle her way out of. Yet there was absolutely nothing she could do. She couldn't even be in the room ...

All because her friend had wanted to try and help Annika and Fin be together somehow before she …

Turning toward the fireplace mantel, the viscountess grabbed a candlestick and hurled it blindly. She then proceeded to throw, break, and stomp on various items in the room without a word, deaf to Clara's concerned calls behind her. The ringing in her ears grew worse and worse, and she realized at some point that she was screaming wordlessly.

The thought turned over and over in her mind relentlessly.

My friend is dying … and I can't do a thing to stop it.

Strong hands suddenly gripped Annika's shoulders, forcing her to be still.

The smell of baked bread and coffee worked its way through her haze of grief, and then the quiet yet soothing voice of Fin as he pulled her into his chest broke into her senses.

The rest of her walls crumbled then, and Annika succumbed to sobs as her knees gave out. She would've fallen in a heap on the ground were Fin not holding her.

Carefully, he picked Annika up, carried her over to the bed, and laid her down gently.

"What's happened?" he asked worriedly as she continued to cry.

Her reply didn't make complete sense, but after a few moments of careful questioning, the message that did make itself clear was: "Your mother better be the best healer in the Godsdamn kingdom."

CHAPTER 23
FACING THE ODDS

Fin trudged up to the castle with his hands pressed in his pockets, his steps slow and heavy.

Annika eventually had told him enough about the queen's condition for him to realize the gravity of the situation. She had also revealed that to cover their backsides, he still needed to talk to Jiho to firmly eliminate any controversy over Lady Iones's marriage being acceptable to the Zinferan emperor.

Fin had left Annika's estate with the intention of both trying to talk with his friend, as well as to keep an ear out for news regarding the queen.

Kraken trotted alongside the redhead for part of the journey before veering off on his own. Fin was too lost in his own thoughts to think much on his familiar's vibrantly independent life.

As he stepped onto the castle grounds, he felt his magic surge through him, and then ...

It started.

Fin stumbled and clutched his head as multiple terrified feelings and images flashed through his mind.

The queen was in so much pain ... her fear and agony rang the loudest in his head, and all at once he understood why Annika's panic was so poignant.

Breaking out into a run, Fin charged toward his kitchen, his mind racing with the dread and despair of the castle occupants …

They were all so heartbroken …

His feet pounded down the grass as a new person's intense fear broke into the flurry—and it made the witch need to stop and clutch his chest to catch his breath.

Eric.

Eric was terrified, shouting, and crying.

Giving his head a shake, Fin tried to quiet the clamor in his head; he needed to help.

The cook began to move once more, his heart hammering in his chest, as he dashed down the east wall to his kitchen.

He needed to hear what was happening from his aides.

Rounding the garden edge, Fin bolted up the pathway and burst into the kitchen that was in complete chaos. Ruby stood by the hearth waiting for water to boil, and a team of maids and knights stood at the ready to help haul the buckets upstairs.

His arrival was almost completely missed, even by Hannah, Peter, and the kitchen knights who stood off to the side talking as they worked on preparing what looked like seaweed.

The sight of the long smelly plant only added to Fin's anxiety.

Katelyn ordered seaweed soup to be made for mothers who had given birth.

This meant she thought the babe was going to arrive soon.

"Mr. Ashowan!" Ruby's startled voice snapped Fin out of his panic. "What are you doing here? You aren't due to return until—"

"My mother is with the queen?" he demanded while moving swiftly toward the castle door.

"Yes, she is, but— Where do you think you're going?!" Ruby was hot on his heels as he exited the kitchen and moved through the halls that were deathly silent.

"Eric must be upset. I'm going to check on him and then see if I can help my mother. I've been her aide since I was a child and can help."

"Mr. Ashowan, there is an army of maids at her disposal, you aren't needed—"

"Ruby!" Fin swung around, his pale sweaty face startling the already distressed Head of Housekeeping into silence. "Any advantage we can give to the queen, we will. You know that as well as I do."

There was something about the strange light in the cook's eyes, his insistent tone, and his overall intensity that obliterated any objection the woman could think of on the spot.

Instead, the witch turned back around and continued his hasty stride to the servants' stairwell. Ruby continued to follow him, occasionally calling out for him to wait, huffing as she went.

Fin heard Eric before they'd even made it to the fourth floor. The shouts and weeping along with a great deal of scuffling rang out in the otherwise quiet castle. Upon reaching the king and queen's corridor, the cook saw two knights attempting to subdue the prince, while his governess stood off to the side, her hand clamped down over her mouth. Tears soaked the woman's face as Eric called for his mother over and over.

Fin didn't want to startle the knights by running to the child, but he walked quickly enough to create a breeze in his wake.

When the men finally noticed him, he was already in front of them. The knights shared confused expressions before Fin dropped down and wrapped the flailing eight-year-old in his arms. Lifting the boy free of the guards with surprising strength, he backed away from the queen's door and began carrying the child toward the servants' stairwell.

"No! No! I want to see my mom! MOM! MOM!" Eric was shouting and crying, his small face nearly purple.

"Eric, you need to let your mom work!" Fin managed with a grunt as one of the prince's kicks landed dangerously close to his groin.

"She's not working, she's dying!" Eric hiccuped as he broke down in sobs. Fin clutched the boy even more firmly to himself. The child's face was buried in his shoulder when the chamber door opened, and the king stepped out, his face ghostly pale. His eyes landed on Fin and his confusion made him blink several times. Then his gaze dropped down to his son in the witch's arms, and he quickly looked back up.

They shared a nod of understanding before Norman slowly retreated back to the room, his expression grim.

Fin retreated around the corner of the corridor, but he didn't take Eric downstairs as he originally planned. Ruby, the governess, and the knights stood motionless in their confusion. They knew the prince had a close friendship with the cook, but for the king to trust him to console the boy spoke volumes.

"Your mom is working, Eric, I promise. She's working to bring your brother or sister into the world," Fin explained when the child's sobs had settled down enough for him to be heard.

"D-Dad told me a sec-secret." Eric gasped out the words as another surge of weeping overtook him. "Y-You can-can't tell him I to-told you."

After reaching the opposite end of the castle's second floor in record time, Fin slowly sat down. His back leaned against the back south wall while he still held the prince against his shoulder.

"I won't tell him, what's the secret?" he asked quietly.

"I-I'm going to ha-have a sister." Eric wiped his runny nose on the back of his sleeve.

Fin managed a small smile. "So are you going to protect her from dragons?"

Eric sniffled and nodded.

"What about Kraken? Are you going to protect her from Kraken?" He brushed some of Eric's golden curls away from his forehead.

"Kra-Kraken is go-going to protect her, too."

"Hm, you should probably tell him how you two plan on guarding the princess. Would you like me to call him?" Fin asked as residual sobs jerked through the child's body.

"Y-You can call him?"

"I can. I just close my eyes like this." The witch shut his eyes and immediately reached out for the magical connection to Kraken. The cat felt far away, but that was one thing about a familiar … if their witch called them, they could always hear it …

And they would always come.

Opening his eyes, Fin saw Eric's tears continuing to spill down his cheeks, but he was less hysterical at least.

"Kraken is on his way, though he might take a little bit of time to arrive. Would you be able to wait for him here?" the redhead asked gently.

"Wh-where are you going?"

"I'm going to go help your mum."

At the mention of his mother, the prince suddenly began crying a little louder. His governess had finally composed herself enough to appear from around the corner, and once the sound of his tears beginning again reached her, she hurried forward.

"You need to wait for Kraken here. When he arrives, tell him everything that's going on, and he'll help, okay?" The boy nodded, but then threw his arms around the cook's neck in a vise grip.

After hugging him back for a long moment, Fin stared at the governess and gestured for her to come and take the lad.

Once Eric was safely stowed in the woman's arms, the witch stood and strode back to the king and queen's chamber. The two knights standing guard wore strained expressions as shrieks and grunts could be heard from within the room.

"Please tell Mrs. Ashowan I'm here to help." Fin's expression remained stony as the men glanced at each other, unsure of what to do. "Now!" he ordered, his voice carrying an unnatural boom.

The knights didn't have a chance to obey before the door opened and Ruby's reddened face appeared.

"Your mother says to come in." The woman's voice was tight with barely restrained emotion, and after setting foot in the chamber, Fin saw why.

The room was in complete disarray as maids fumbled around the queen uncertain of what to do. Physician Durand stood by the fireplace questioning everything Katelyn was doing, and the king stood to the side of his wife, holding her hand as she doubled over her middle. His face was as still as a statue.

The moment Katelyn saw her son, relief flooded her eyes.

"I need everyone except the king and Finlay OUT of the room!" she called out over the chaos.

The beat of silence that followed her order was immediately offset by loud protests and arguments from everyone but the royal couple.

Fin met the king's gaze then and saw the distraught agony he was narrowly keeping under control. The man was barely aware of what was happening around him as his wife's grunts seemed to grow even more feral.

Katelyn looked up from her position between the queen's legs, and when she realized the king hadn't heard her, she reached a bloodied hand out and gently touched his sleeve.

"Please, sire."

The orders and disagreements continued to boom for another moment or two, before Norman finally turned his attention to Katelyn. It took him another breath to process the request.

"Everyone will obey Mrs. Ashowan this instant."

The monarch's voice was uncharacteristically quiet, and yet there was a hollowness that struck everyone deeply.

The maids filed out of the room first, followed by Ruby who announced loudly that she would remain outside the door should they need more towels, which Katelyn confirmed was a good idea. The last to leave was Physician Durand who looked uncertainly at the woman usurping his professional duty, but one look at the king's face had him reluctantly heading out the door.

Once it was just the four of them in the room, Katelyn summoned Fin over.

"There are more complications than I would like to deal with. The baby is breech, she's early, and the queen has lost a lot of blood. To top it off, the contractions are becoming weaker and her ankles are swelling."

Fin felt sick.

The odds were bad.

His mother's stern expression reminded him that it wasn't over yet, and they had work to do.

Fin snapped his fingers, and towels began to stack themselves beside Katelyn, candles burned brighter, and his mother's instruments that had been jostled by one of the room's former occupants suddenly began sterilizing themselves in the steaming water.

"Your Majesty, I may need to perform surgery on the queen if we are to save the babe," Katelyn explained as she rested her hand atop the woman's belly. The golden glow appeared over the queen, and when it disappeared, Fin could see the stress in his mother's eyes.

"What about ..." Norman cleared his throat and licked his dry lips. "What about Ainsley?"

The queen suddenly reached out and grabbed Norman's sleeve; her sweaty face had taken on a gray tinge, and her body had begun shaking from the stressful labor.

"Save her. No matter what, you choose our daughter, you hear me?" Her eyes were wide and wild with pain and delirium, and the king's soul appeared to die as he stared back at his wife.

He suddenly dropped to his knees and kissed the back of her hand that he still held. His tears began to fall.

"No." Norman bowed his head over their hands. "No. You are not leaving us. Ainsley, we need you! We can't, I'm sorry!" The king shook as he refused to look at his wife who was losing more and more energy with each passing moment.

Katelyn pursed her lips, a move that signified she had more bad news, and Fin immediately took up the task of drying the instruments.

"Sire, I will need to operate regardless. The babe is stuck. If I leave them, they both will surely die."

"Don't give me those choices, you're a damn healer; you give them *both* an equal chance, you understand me?" Norman's voice suddenly surged in strength as he glared up at Katelyn, who had a brief sharp intake of breath before giving a small nod.

With one brief glance at Fin, she held out her hand, and wordlessly, he handed her the small blade and then gave the potent sleeping draft to the king to administer to his wife. There was no time to waste.

Norman stood by the open window, unable to continue watching the gruesome work happening behind him.

Everything was silent. Too silent.

Ainsley had taken the potent sleeping draft and had fallen into an unconsciousness that was too similar to the rest of the dead.

Occasionally the door would open and close as the bloodied towels were carried out and fresh ones were delivered, but other than that, there was nothing. No sound of life.

Staring out over his kingdom, Norman felt his hope slipping away with the day as nighttime settled over Austice.

He knew that things weren't going well behind him, and before he could stop himself, he wondered if by the next dawn, his entire world would have come to an end …

The king wondered if he would ever again see Ainsley's smile, or feel her strong presence beside him, or share an afternoon nap with her and Eric in their bed. Wondered if he could keep being a king without his queen …

And then, a weak cry broke out.

The cry of his daughter.

CHAPTER 24
FIRST

Fin peered into the sleeping princess's face, the rest of the world moment-arily forgotten as he beheld miraculous life that had just been born. Despite helping his mother with countless births, he rarely ever had to hold the infants. The newborn's mother or family members would imme-diately cradle them, cooing and crying over their new loved one. Not that he had ever cared or minded …

But this time was different.

The king stood with his back to them while Kate finished stitching up the queen who lay motionless on the bed, her daughter's first cries being soothed away by Fin.

Fin knew that the king would've been able to hear the babe's first weak shriek, as the room remained deathly silent, yet he still didn't move.

"Your Majesty, would you like to hold the princess?" he asked softly as his mother continued her work.

"Is Ainsley … is she … here?" Norman's voice sounded far away, his hands still clasped behind his back, his gaze fixed on the dark night out-side his window.

"She sleeps," Kate replied slowly. The king turned around hesitantly, sensing there was more to be said. "There was a lot of blood lost, and her heart is weak. I am using a great deal of power to keep her here. I can continue to do so for a few days at most; after that, if she does not wake and recover on her own ..." The witch's hands hovered over the queen's body, a faint golden glow encasing her. The monarch moved stiffly back to the bedside, his eyes fixed on his wife.

With shaking hands, Norman reached out, and clasped Ainsley's limp hand in both of his before half collapsing to his knees.

The princess in Fin's arms let out a small whimper and opened her eyes. She looked around blearily, and the redhead felt his heart skip a beat.

She was so small ...

"Sire, your daughter will need to eat soon, would you like to hold her before—" Kate asked softly while nodding toward the babe in her son's arms.

"Leave."

The growl from the king that interrupted the healer was directed at Fin. Norman's hazel eyes had somehow changed. They seemed sharper ... and smaller.

It was terrifying, and the redhead found himself unconsciously holding the infant even closer to his body than before in a protective gesture. The king didn't spare the child a single glance before he turned back to his wife and rested his forehead on his hands that still hung on to her.

Fin looked to his mother who regarded the ruler with deep sorrow and understanding. Her eyes slid to her son and, using her chin, she gestured at the door.

After a moment's hesitation, he took the hint, and with the princess swaddled in his arms, he walked out of the chamber.

Upon stepping into the corridor, Ruby and the guards jumped in surprise. They said nothing at first as Fin turned and closed the door behind him quietly.

"Does the queen need fresh towels? Those still look clean—" Ruby whispered before moving to grab the bundle in the redhead's arms, only to have him jerk back carefully.

This startled the poor princess into giving another weak cry, making the guards and Head of Housekeeping leap back in shock.

"Ruby, please summon the nursemaid for the princess. She needs to eat," the cook requested softly as he proceeded to gently rock the infant back into a more contented mood.

"The ... The princess ... ? Princess. My Gods, there is a princess!" Ruby and the guards burst out into bright smiles. The Head of Housekeeping even began to tear up as they all shared in the moment of joy, until Ruby realized Fin wasn't smiling.

The smile melted from her face.

"Her Majesty isn't well enough to feed the babe?"

Fin shook his head.

Horror and grief filled her eyes.

"Oh, no … Oh, no, no … She's …"

The knights immediately became somber, as they fixed the redhead with determined expressions. Before they could ask for details, Fin was already talking.

"She is alive, but … we don't know for how long. Whether or not she recovers is … uncertain."

Ruby's tears spilled over, though for a different reason than happiness.

"Oh Gods," she whispered brokenly before succumbing to sobs that the nearest guard sought to soothe by embracing her, his own eyes growing red.

"Ruby?" Fin's hoarse voice called out quietly. "The princess needs to eat. I do not know where the nursemaid or nursery is."

Pulling free from the guard's arms quickly, Ruby dashed at the tears on her face before nodding.

"I-I will go summon her. The princess's nursery is … the first door on the right after the turn. In the west end of the castle. She was going to be placed in Lady Jenoure's old chamber but Her Majesty wanted to sleep with the child until … until—" Ruby broke off and took a steadying breath.

Fin nodded and proceeded to head in the direction of the nursery. The child in his arms grew fussier as he did so, either because she was hungry or because the corridor wasn't as warm as the chamber she had just left, he wasn't completely certain.

Once he reached the chamber, Fin didn't think twice about magically lighting the hearth and every candle. His mother had told him once how important it was for the babes that had been born too early to remain warm. She had also said that normally there were some breathing difficulties for them.

Silently, Fin thanked the Goddess that it was summer and not winter for the princess. It'd be easier to keep her warm and wouldn't be as tough on her small lungs to adapt. Seating himself in a chair before the fire, he stared back down at the child. Her eyes were open, though unfocused, and she was watching him. In fact … he was the first person she'd ever seen.

"I'm sorry that you aren't getting the welcome you deserve," Fin whispered as emotions threatened to strangle him. "You're doing great so far."

The baby let out a small snort, making Fin smile before he could stop himself.

"You know, I never would've imagined in my entire life that I'd be the first person to ever hold or talk to a princess." He chuckled quietly. "Life's a little funny sometimes … and sometimes it is unfair. I'm sorry that it's already been a tough start for you. Your father is a great man, he just … he just is tired. Your mother …" Fin's smile faded, and his eyes grew misty as the princess peacefully listened to him. "Your mother is a brave woman who loves you more than you can imagine. I hope …"

The door behind him opened, and Fin turned expecting to see Ruby arriving with the nursemaid.

Except it wasn't, it was Eric.

The prince stared at Fin puzzled, as Kraken suddenly appeared behind him. The redhead guessed it was the child's bedtime from his sleep shirt, but Eric looked completely awake, his eyes still puffy from crying earlier.

"What are you doing in here?" the prince asked, stepping into the room.

"Eric, would you like to meet your sister?" Fin hastily blinked back the tears; it wasn't his place to tell the child about his mother's condition.

The boy stopped in his tracks, his eyes round in wonder as he registered the swaddle in Fin's arms.

"Come on over here," the cook called out quietly as the little girl in his arms moved at the sound of her brother's voice.

Eric's face was stricken as he tentatively moved closer, until he finally rounded the chair and gazed down at the infant.

His baby sister.

She stared up at him and let out a small sigh that made Fin's heart feel as though it were being squeezed.

"She … She looks weird. Why is she so tiny?" Eric stared down at the baby, his perplexed expression making Fin smile.

"She was born early, so she didn't have time to grow more. She was just too excited to meet you."

Eric lifted his finger and gently stroked her cheek.

Turning toward the touch, the princess immediately began to suck on her brother's finger, making him giggle.

"Why is she doing that?"

"She's hungry. Her nursemaid is coming to feed her soon," Fin explained as the princess suddenly frowned and squirmed in annoyance.

"Ah, she's unhappy that you aren't tasty."

Eric burst out in another fit of giggles, before taking his finger out of her mouth and gently patting her small head.

"What's her name?"

Fin froze. Neither the king nor queen had mentioned having a name picked out.

"I don't know yet. How about for now we just call her Princess?"

Eric looked somewhat disappointed, but he nodded. "When will Mom and Dad tell us?"

Fin's spine stiffened. "I'm not sure … your mum was very tired after having her, so she may sleep for a while."

Eric, too enamored with his new sibling, had completely forgotten his distress for his mother from earlier. Instead, he continued gazing with loving fascination down at his sister.

The chamber door opened again, and the nursemaid, followed by Ruby, entered. Both of them were pale and had obviously been crying, but fortunately Eric didn't notice as Kraken was sniffing the baby interestedly, making the boy laugh.

"Time for us to let the nursemaid feed the princess, alright?" Fin slowly stood and turned to the woman who carefully took the newborn from him.

"Can I go ask Dad what her name is going to be?" Eric turned to Ruby, who showcased her complete inability to lie as she burst out into fresh tears when gazing upon the young prince's eager face.

The poor woman fled from the room, and Fin was hasty in picking the young prince up and carrying him out into the corridor. Too distracted with the oddity of what had just happened, the boy didn't think to question why his friend was holding him.

"Not tonight, sorry. Maybe later. Both your parents are exhausted." As Fin stepped into the darkened hallway and shut the door behind them, he realized he had no idea where the prince slept.

"My chamber's that door." Eric pointed to the chamber beside his sister's, which explained how he knew where Fin was. "Why was Ruby crying?"

"She's … happy. Happy that the princess is here."

"So Mom is okay?"

Fin inadvertently gripped the child tighter as he opened his chamber door and noted the governess who was fast asleep in front of the fire.

"Your mom is sleeping," he repeated desperately.

Eric began to squirm then, and Fin hastily set the young child down on the floor.

"Something's wrong!" The boy rounded on him, his fists clenched at his side. "Tell me! You're my friend and … and friends tell each other everything."

At first, Fin's shoulders slackened, as he was unable to think of a proper way to handle the situation. Then after a moment, he slowly lowered himself down to kneel in front of Eric.

"Your mother had a really tough time giving birth to your sister, Eric, and your dad is … worried. My mother is doing everything she can to help her. You can ask your father about everything tomorrow."

The boy was breathing hard through his nose as he obviously tried to stay in control of his emotions.

"So my mom isn't dead?" he demanded.

"No," Fin answered evenly, making sure to hold the boy's stare.

The prince sniffled and wiped his nose using the back of his sleeve.

"Are you lying to me?"

The cook shook his head slowly.

"Then why is everyone so serious?"

"Eric, I won't lie to you, but your father wants to be the one to tell you about what is going on. I'm not supposed to."

The boy's lip quivered, and Fin could see his young mind working furiously to try and find a way to argue his answer.

"I'm sorry, Eric. The best thing you can do is keep your sister company. She is really scared and hasn't met anyone else yet. Do you think you can be strong and be there for her? She doesn't have anyone else."

The prince nodded firmly, his eyes still brimming with tears, but instead of displaying fear, his expression grew determined.

"You're going to be the best big brother." Fin reached out and ruffled the boy's hair, then stood.

Casting a judgmental eye at the governess who continued snoring away, Fin turned to the door.

He was about to take a step when small arms suddenly wound around his hips.

"I'm scared." The boy sobbed quietly into his side, and Fin's heart broke into a million pieces because of it.

"I am, too, but we have a lot of people to help us. So we have to do the best we can." The redhead turned and hugged the young royal back before he bent down and once again picked him up. This time he set the child down on his bed and tucked him in.

With a small chirp Kraken leapt up onto the green satin blanket and immediately sauntered over to Eric. The feline proceeded to nuzzle the child until he was rewarded with a fierce hug that probably hurt, but he made no move to stop the embrace.

"Kraken will stay with you all night, alright? I will see you in the morning."

"But Ruby said you … you're not back to work until next week," Eric said while leaning back into his pillows.

"Friends don't leave when they're needed." Fin managed a small smile, and then left Kraken and the prince for the night. Unsure of what the future held, and scared that Eric would soon have to say goodbye to his mother, the witch doubted he would be able to sleep at all.

CHAPTER 25
PHYSICIAN'S ORDERS

As Fin approached the king and queen's bedchamber after bidding good night to their son, Prince Eric, he could hear angry whispers in the dimly lit corridor, and he immediately felt dread burn his stomach.

What was happening now?

Once he was a few feet away, he recognized Physician Durand and the guards who stood in front of the door.

"What's the problem?" Fin asked, not bothering to lower his voice.

"Ah! Mr. Ashowan, precisely who I was looking for. Where might I find the princess? I need to give her a thorough examination before seeing the queen." Physician Durand shot a stern glare at the guards before giving Fin his full attention.

"The princess is in her nursery being fed." Fin gestured over his shoulder in the direction he had just come from.

Physician Durand gave a terse nod before setting off without another word. The guards looked stressed, and Fin could tell that something else was an issue.

"Mr. Ashowan, your mother has asked you to reenter the room, but no one else is permitted to," the one guard explained, sounding relieved.

Frowning over the strange instruction, the redhead stepped between the guards and opened the door.

The room had grown even darker in his absence as the fire remained unstoked. One of the only light sources was the faint glow of magic over the queen's body, which was how Fin could see his mother still kneeling beside the monarch with her hands outstretched.

With a flick of his eyes the fire roared back to life and one glance from Kate told Fin how weary she was.

"I will need to rest soon, but I can't go far from Her Majesty. Whatever Physician Durand does, he cannot perform any surgery or administer any medicine or ointment without my consent. I am trying to keep the queen's condition balanced, and any changes could endanger her further if I'm not tracking them closely," Kate explained as sweat beaded along her forehead.

Fin stole a glance at the king who continued holding his wife's hand, his eyes deadened.

"Can't His Majesty ban the physician from the room?" Fin turned to the king.

"I can; however, your mother and you will be under a great deal of scrutiny from the advisors and nobility." Norman's voice was hollow, but as he shifted his stare to the redhead, his meaning became clear.

"The court needs to become aware that my mother is a witch in order to accept what she's doing to the queen." Fin felt a cold sweat break out along his back.

"Yes. I won't be able to tear myself away to explain myself properly, so Finlay, it will be your responsibility," Kate explained while gazing down at her patient.

Fin felt every inch of him grow tense, but after one brief look at the queen's gray complexion and the king's despair, he knew he'd do whatever he had to if it helped.

"I … I will go speak with Physician Durand and explain to him first. After that, will you permit him in the room?"

"Only if he is calm and accepting of it. I don't have the stamina to fight with him," Kate said after receiving an affirming nod from the king.

"Very well. I'll go see him now." With a short bow, Fin excused himself from the room and mindlessly turned back toward the nursery.

He forced any fearful thoughts from his mind to the best of his ability, but his heart still pounded, and his stomach boiled. Fin was so consumed in his efforts not to think about what was happening that he didn't remember to knock on the nursery door, and instead he simply entered.

From the doorway, Fin found himself interrupting Physician Durand examining the princess in her cradle. The newborn flailed her tiny limbs and let out several weak shrieks as the nursemaid finished righting her clothes.

The princess must have already eaten … A small cough from the princess snapped Fin's attention back to the present.

"Move her back to the hearth. She needs the heat." The witch found himself already halfway across the room as the physician whipped his head around and stared skeptically at him.

"The hearth is too warm for her in her fragile state."

"She's too small to stay warm on her own," Fin countered quickly, plucking the child up in his arms before he could be stopped. As Physician Durand began to argue, the cook moved back to the hearth, and when the babe's cries ceased immediately, the physician fell silent.

The princess let out a long yawn, her eyes slowly closing as she found herself back in the comfortable spot by fire.

"I take it that was another nugget of wisdom from your mother?" The dryness in the physician's voice wasn't lost on Fin, and while he wasn't in the mood for such barbs, he needed to remember the man knew nothing about the queen's condition.

Which brought back to mind the very stressful scenario he was in.

"Physician Durand, there is something you need to know. Might we talk in private?"

The man raised a bushy eyebrow at him, but he nodded to the nursemaid who took her leave. Once alone, the pair then seated themselves in front of the fire. Fin still held the princess safely in his arms, though it seemed he had forgotten all about her.

Physician Durand smiled.

"You've a way with children. You'll make a fine father one day, Mr. Ashowan … though I must confess, you are a man of many peculiarities."

Taking a deep breath, Fin readied himself.

"Physician Durand … my mother is … she's a …"

The elder waited patiently for the redhead to finish his sentence, a gleam of curiosity in his eyes.

"My mother is a witch."

The physician's eyebrows shot upward. He then wordlessly readjusted his position on his seat and folded his hands in front of his belly. His eyes were alight with interest as he continued staring at Fin in silent encouragement.

"Specifically, she is a healer. The king and queen knew this and summoned her with that knowledge," he hurried on to say. "The queen and the princess would have more than likely died were she not here, but Her Majesty is …" Fin cleared his throat and looked away.

There was a moment of quiet that suddenly made the room feel darker.

"Mr. Ashowan, is the queen dead?" Physician Durand leaned forward, his face taut with worry.

"No. Though she might pass soon. My mother is sustaining her using her magic, but it isn't easy. She can't leave the queen's side, and while there is a chance she will recover, it isn't guaranteed. The issue is …"

"The king's advisors and other courtiers may have an issue with Mrs. Ashowan treating Her Majesty. Or worse yet, they may suspect something ridiculous such as her bewitching our king's mind. I don't know much about witches, but I do know that that is beyond their magical scope."

Fin nodded and studied the man a little closer. He was reacting calmly and rationally …

"I can see that my response is not what you were expecting?" Physician Durand smiled while lifting his elbows to rest on the chair's armrest.

"Er … not really, no …"

"I may not be the wisest man in the kingdom, Mr. Ashowan, but I am no fool. I've been treating the courtiers and knights of this castle for more than ten years. I know every sickness, pregnancy, broken bone, and death. Your mother appeared and started seeing some of the staff members, and eventually the knights. Oddly enough they would be miraculously healed. Broken ribs were mended like new, fevers and colds relieved after a gentle touch. I began to suspect something was a little strange …"

Fin noticed the kind glimmer in Durand's eyes and felt himself relax. The princess continued to snort in her sleep peacefully, and he instinctively began rhythmically patting her back.

"I can help speak on your mother's behalf to the courtiers and advisors; however, I do believe you will be the best person to answer any questions in place of your mother pertaining to her being a witch."

Swallowing with great difficulty, Fin nodded.

"Now, I am going to go see to the queen and determine from your mother how else I might be of some help."

"My mother might already be asleep, which is why she sent me to speak with you … she doesn't want you doing anything to the queen without confirming with her. Not because she thinks you aren't skilled or—" Fin added quickly, feeling the tops of his ears going red. "She … She is doing something that is hard to maintain."

For a moment the physician looked stunned, then seemed to reach some kind of conclusion in his mind and let out a long sigh.

"Very well. I will go to speak with the king then at the very least. Would you like me to move the princess's cradle for you?"

Fin blinked down in surprise at the sleeping baby. He had completely forgotten he was holding her.

"Physician Durand … do you know if the king or queen had a name chosen in advance for the princess?"

The man's amused expression grew somber.

"Our rulers stopped choosing names for their children after their third babe died."

Fin nodded after a moment of absorbing yet another piece of tragic news and turned his gaze to the flames.

"You need to rest, Mr. Ashowan. I can see the toll this day has taken on you."

Fin didn't answer as he continued to fight off the overwhelming sadness that waited to crash down on him on the princess's behalf.

She was a child who hadn't been held by her mother or named by her father …

"The princess will be just fine, Mr. Ashowan. Regardless of the queen's fate, this babe is spending her first night in this world warm and cared for. That is in no small part due to you. However, tomorrow there will be new matters to address, and so it is time for sleep."

Fin looked down quietly, unable to lift his gaze from the princess.

Physician Durand moved the cradle in front of the hearth, and Fin carefully laid the baby down. The elder clapped the witch on his shoulder and gently ushered him out of the room.

The nursemaid who had stood outside waiting, quietly reentered the nursery and closed the door behind herself.

Fin felt the coldness of the corridor in more ways than one, and he was only vaguely aware of Physician Durand bidding him a good night.

In a haze, the witch walked through the darkened castle and made his way to his cottage.

Not bothering to light the fireplace when he arrived, he instead entered his bedroom and was about to fall atop his mattress when, out of the corner of his eye at the last moment, he noticed a dark figure shift.

"Annika?" Fin recognized her spiced scent immediately. Magically, a candle floated in from the main room already lit.

The viscountess stood in her cloak and britches, her face stained with tears as she stared at him anxiously.

"Wh-What's happened? Clara says she heard that you went in while the queen was in labor and helped?" Annika was pale and shaking ever so slightly, the pain and stress sharp on her face, as she waited to find out her best friend's fate.

Without saying a word, Fin slowly reached out and embraced her. His body felt heavy and drained.

"F-Fin? Please, please tell me, did she … Is she … ?"

"She's alive, but …" He had to clear his throat. "She might not make it. The princess, while small, is … alive, and seems well."

Annika stilled in his arms, and then the trembling worsened as sobs wracked her body.

"Oh Gods. Oh Gods, Ainsley …"

The couple continued embracing, allowing their grief to rest between them, each hoping that the next day would bring better times.

Fin stood in front of the council room doors, his heart racing wildly as he heard the commotion of voices from within. He had never been in the room when it was filled with nobility. Only when it was the king, or the men who knew of his abilities …

"I will speak first, Mr. Ashowan. Would you prefer to say anything after the fact or simply answer their questions?" Physician Durand regarded Finlay carefully; it was obvious the redhead had not slept a wink. Dark bags were carved under his normally bright eyes, and there was a lifelessness to his face that spoke of his inner turmoil.

"I'll just answer their questions then go check on my mother."

With a nod, Physician Durand turned to the guards who stood waiting and signaled that they were ready.

The room was filled with immaculately dressed nobility all fighting amongst themselves. Some were standing and passionately arguing, others sat at the long table sharing heated discussions. The sun poured in from the windows behind them, casting a warm glow that felt out of place given the mood of the day.

Captain Antonio and Mage Lee were the only two men who weren't adding to the din of the room's occupants, but Fin found seeing their faces somehow helped his nerves.

Once the lords noticed Fin's and Physician Durand's presence, they began to quiet. Each of them stared perplexed at the new arrivals to their meeting.

"Durand! Who is this commoner with you? What is this about?" one of the lords demanded. He looked to be in his early fifties with a ruddy complexion and a bright green coat buttoned up to his throat despite the summer heat.

"Lord Laurent, please seat yourself, all will be clear in a moment." Physician Durand's quiet authority succeeded in settling down the men, though it was obvious that it wouldn't take much for them to once again become combative.

Fin clasped his hands behind his back and widened his stance.

It was going to be a disaster.

He could tell that much already.

"You all must have heard about Her Majesty the queen going into labor yesterday morning," Physician Durand began while stepping forward.

"Yes, and no one is saying a Godsdamn thing about what's happened!" another lord snipped from the opposite end of the table.

"I am aware, Baron Gauva. There has been a great deal to handle in light of yesterday's events. You see, the queen has given birth early to the Princess of Daxaria."

There was a stunned silence before the entire table broke out in polite but puzzled applause.

"However, Her Majesty faced several complications and is in a precarious state. It is unclear whether or not she will recover, and our king is understandably beside himself with worry and grief."

Every man in the room respectfully bowed their heads while some appeared openly shocked.

"The physician from Rollom is helping me tend to Her Majesty as she requires constant supervision in her weakened state, but the princess is quite delicate herself. Both of them must be treated with a great deal of care, and I am unable to do so on my own."

No one said anything for a moment.

"Why are we letting a charlatan healer care for Her Majesty? We have several certified and talented physicians here in Austice! We know nothing of this Mrs. Ashowan woman." It was Lord Laurent once again.

Physician Durand held up his hand, immediately silencing him. Despite his lack of title, the man could control the room with great ease.

"Mrs. Katelyn Ashowan is not a charlatan. She was trained as a professional physician in the city of Rollom and has all the credentials required to treat Her Majesty. She does not go by Physician Ashowan only because she prefers to be more informal with her patients. As for the reason she is preferred by our king and queen ..." Physician Durand cast a single glance at Fin who kept his eyes glued to the back wall.

The time had come, and Fin braced himself for the chaos he knew was about to unfold.

"Katelyn Ashowan is a witch. A healer witch to be precise. As she is currently with our queen, her son is here to answer any questions or concerns you may have. My lords, this is Mr. Finlay Ashowan, the Royal Cook here in the castle."

CHAPTER 26
FOLDING UNDER PRESSURE

Fin stared back at the men who regarded him with a wide range of emotions. Some were quizzical, some barely able to hide their disgust or concern, others were merely surprised. Physician Durand's announcement wasn't met with an outcry or with the immediate demand for Katelyn's execution at the stake, however. So Fin straightened his back and stepped forward, already trying to prepare what he would say in his mind.

"Good day, my lords." He bowed slightly and did his best to keep his face a mask of indifference.

"Physician Durand, surely you jest," Baron Gauva barked while ignoring Fin's greeting. "This is a humorous prank His Majesty is playing on us all, surely."

"Now, now, Baron. Surely you all are aware witches have existed for quite some time, and that condemning their kind is *illegal*." The slight emphasis Physician Durand placed on the final word had the baron clamping his mouth shut, but his cheeks betrayed his anger.

"If there are no questions, I should be heading back to my duties where—" Fin began stiffly. He was hoping that the men could fight it out amongst themselves and that he might slip away unscathed.

"Hold it right there! I cannot let this matter rest! Mr. Ash— Whatever it was, your mother is a properly certified physician?" Earl Laurent scoffed doubtfully.

"My mother apprenticed under Physician Gandly when I was ten years old. She studied under him for the required five years. After which, she proceeded to work as a partner with him for another year before taking requests throughout the city and the islands south of Rollom," Fin explained without any inflection of emotion in his tone. "She went on to treat the magisters of the city as well as some of the lower-ranking nobility."

The men around the table shifted uncomfortably while casting uncertain glances around themselves.

"Is there someone in the city of Rollom who could vouch for her background?" It was Earl Danen who put the question to him. The man's voice was commanding, but non-accusatory.

"I will be happy to provide a list of her former patients, though you already have one of them here."

Everyone sat up straighter with small frowns creasing their faces.

"Our foreign visitor, Lord Ryu, was a patient of my mother's for two years before he was well enough to return home to Zinfera."

The lords immediately began whispering amongst themselves, while Fin still remained resolute in his avoidance of any form of eye contact.

"How is it none of you are asking about the bloody fact that Physician Durand just informed us all that she is a witch?!" A man Fin had never seen before exploded out of his seat. He was in his mid- to late forties and wore a brown velour vest with a rich, deep red tunic.

"Yes, while we know of witches, it is that we do not know much about them. Your mother is a healer, but I thought witches could only work with the elements," a lord who spoke with a guttural voice pointed out.

"Witches in more recent years are experiencing mutated abilities to better help people," Fin explained quickly knowing that this was going to make things even more difficult.

"What sort of mutated abilities?" Baron Gauva questioned through narrowed eyes.

"The Goddess created witches to act as agents on her behalf to remain connected with nature in its truest forms. However, humanity has grown more complicated, and so our abilities have as well. My mother's abilities are linked with healing, which is an Earth element at its core—think of the new growth and recovery in the springtime. Pertaining to the queen, my mother is trying to help Her Majesty heal so that her physical being isn't overwhelmed."

"That didn't answer my question!" The baron slapped his palm down on the table. "I asked *what sort of mutated abilities*?"

Fin's teeth immediately set themselves on edge. He had tried to avoid facing that particular question for a reason.

"There are all kinds. It is tough to say exactly what the abilities are when it is a newer development. There was one witch who could fashion the most durable weapons you've ever seen. In fact, he was a resident of Austice until he died—some of you have probably heard about the work of Theodore Phendor."

The whispers that exploded at that announcement were louder than before.

"You mean to tell us the famed blacksmith and craftsman of Daxaria was a witch?!" This time it was Captain Antonio who called out stunned.

"Yes. Another mutated witch had the ability to talk to and understand all animals."

"So what's to stop this 'healer witch' taking over the queen's mind?" The outburst came from Earl Laurent who looked to his fellow nobility.

The room fell deathly quiet.

"Witches do not possess the magic to dominate anyone's mind or will in any way." Fin's firmness in tone made at least half of the council visibly relax, while the other half remained unconvinced.

"Mr. Ashowan is correct," Mage Lee suddenly interjected and stood. He leaned his gnarled hands on the table's surface and stared levelly at each man before him. "While I do not count myself as informed about witches as Mr. Ashowan, I can say that it has been well documented and proven that witches can *never* invade someone's own mind. It is not the will of our Gods."

Fin's gratitude for the man was so overwhelming he thought he might launch himself across the table and hug him.

"Mage Lee, were you aware of Katelyn Ashowan being a witch?" Earl Laurent asked directly after a beat of silence in the room.

"I was. However, as it did not interfere with Mrs. Ashowan's work or affect the royal family greatly, I saw no reason for the private details to be revealed. With the development in the queen's condition, however, things have changed."

"You yourself have just stated that you aren't as well versed on the capabilities of witches. What if this is the beginning of a hostile takeover from the Coven of Wittica? What if they are working with Troivack to bring about our demise?" Baron Gauva exclaimed, making Fin's right eye twitch.

"I don't know details pertaining to witches; however, I do know that it is not possible for them to—"

"What if you're bewitched right now!" Baron Gauva brandished a finger at the mage that earned him a sharp look.

"Baron, that is exactly the panicked line of thinking that led to the inhumane hunting and executing of witches in our history. You cannot create a reality that is separate from this one and persecute beings that have not done any harm." Everyone who didn't know the mage thought he sounded calm and in control. To Fin, Captain Antonio, Lord Fuks, and Mr. Howard, however, they all knew that the elder was cursing out the nobility fiercely in his mind.

"Not done any harm?! What about Hilda! That witch who flooded our city and endangered everyone!" Lord Gauva stood angrily.

"Then what about King Matthias? Does he represent all of mankind?" Fin suddenly burst out, unable to stop himself.

Every head snapped around to stare at him, but the redhead was too enraged to care.

"You judge all witches based off *one* misdeed? There are kings who have led armies that slaughtered thousands. In fact, it was only fifty years ago that witches stopped being burned at the stakes!"

Lord Gauva's expression turned murderous. "You dare talk back to me? You are nothing but a cook."

"For this meeting I was assigned by His Majesty to be a representative of witches, and as such will speak my piece." Fin's eyes flashed, as his fingernails dug into his palms.

The baron straightened and clasped his hands behind his back, meeting the redhead's ire head-on.

"Rafael, there are two knowledgeable people in this room explaining about witches and their craft, yet you seem determined to shout over them. Is it possible you draw issue with Katelyn Ashowan's economic status more so than her 'witch' status?" Lord Fuks interjected, his eyebrow arched mirthfully.

"Not at all—though it is peculiar how they are mere peasants and yet hold such power. Is that not ludicrous?"

"Believe it or not, witches are not well received by some, so they try to keep a low profile," Fin interjected coolly.

The baron, clearly dissatisfied with the way the conversation was turning, directed his attention once again to the cook. "What about you, hm? Are *you* a witch? Who are you to say that you are the best one for answering our questions?"

"How can he be a witch? He's a man!" Earl Laurent blustered with a wry chuckle.

"He just said our famous weapons maker Theodore Phendor was a witch. This means *he* could be one too!" Baron Gauva broke out desperately.

An uneasiness settled over the room, and no one dared say a word as Fin locked eyes with the baron who looked ready to sentence him to a nice pile of dry kindling with a waiting torch.

A strange calm settled in the redhead's chest as he stared at the noble before him. Fin couldn't explain why, but it was suddenly very clear to him that he didn't want to lie or hide anymore. Not when there had been so many accepting people thus far. Not when he had made friends and fallen in love with people who cared very little about the fact that he was a witch.

Straightening his shoulders, and suddenly appearing incredibly imposing, Fin answered Baron Gauva's question.

"Yes, I am a witch. A house witch, actually."

Everyone froze. Uncertain of how to respond.

Even Baron Gauva who had first fired the accusation looked stunned. Evidently his question had been intended to discredit Fin rather than oust him.

"Can you perhaps tell us what a house witch does?" Captain Antonio requested softly, his blue eye warm with encouragement.

"Well, I think many of you have enjoyed my cooking at least once by now."

A small flutter of chuckles ran through the men, and this reaction alone emboldened Fin. They weren't persecuting him; they weren't shouting at him ...

"My abilities center around creating a harmonious, comfortable home. A safe place with good food, and where its occupants feel cared for."

"Those are *feelings*, do you mean to tell me you can control emotions?" Baron Gauva sneered.

Captain Antonio didn't rise from his feet, but when the baron locked eyes with him, he cowered all the same. It was obvious on the military leader's face that he was a hairsbreadth away from punching the lord.

"No. I do not control people's emotions," Fin replied tersely.

"How about a demonstration!" Lord Fuks clapped his hands together and smiled jubilantly.

"Mr. Ashowan is not a court jester. You cannot demand that he perform for our entertainment." Captain Antonio snapped irritably at the chief of military who didn't appear the slightest bit chastened.

Fin sighed. He didn't like being a show pony any more than the next fellow, but even he understood how it might help the nobles fear him less.

Turning his attention to Mr. Howard, who was scribbling away on a piece of parchment for the king to review later, Fin held out his hand.

"Might I please have your vest?"

The assistant looked up abruptly. He clearly hadn't intended on being an active participant in the whole ordeal and was hoping to get away with his report unscathed.

Slowly, the man removed the article of clothing and handed it to Fin who held it up for all the men to see.

Fin then released it, only instead of falling to the ground, it hung suspended in the air.

There were a couple gasps and exclamations around the table, and then the vest proceeded to fold itself perfectly. It then floated down gently to the table and lay before the nobles awaiting judgment.

"You're right, Lord Gauva. Mr. Ashowan will have our linens pressed to a deathly stiffness. Whatever shall I do without a crease in my trousers?" One of the lords chuckled, and soon a few more had joined in.

"So you … can fold laundry with your ability?" Mage Lee asked pointedly. It was obvious he was trying not to laugh. He knew Fin was showing the least-intimidating side of his magic.

"I can." Fin then turned his attention to the glass pitcher of water that sat dripping with condensation on the table's surface and magically raised it. It floated around to each man's goblet, refilling each one before drifting harmlessly back to the middle of the table, and setting itself down.

"However will we overcome such evil?" Lord Fuks clutched his chest, and this time the entire room burst out laughing. Everyone except for Baron Gauva, who was turning purple in the forehead and was staring at the cook with deadly resolve.

The noblemen filed out of the council room all fanning themselves from the summer heat and talking excitedly. The meeting had proven effective in bringing the fear of witches down, while also distracting everyone for the briefest of moments from their worry for their queen.

Fin was one of the last people out of the room, his hands shoved in his pockets, and his shoulders slightly hunched—he was exhausted.

He had not once ever thought he would be publicly announcing what he was. He hoped that his doing so didn't hinder any more of Annika's plans for their relationship. Though she still hadn't told him about any of her plans in detail …

There always seemed to be some new crisis or work matter, or they were too busy—

"Fin? Why were you in that meeting?"

The redhead snapped out of his thoughts and looked up to see Sir Harris, who stood leaning against one of the stone pillars near the council room.

"Oh … I had to answer a few questions," he replied vaguely. He wasn't really in the mood to fully explain everything. "What're you doing here?"

"When I heard about the emergency meeting, I wondered if it was about the dukedom, and I got antsy. Sorry …" The knight looked sheepish as he gave a guilty smile.

Fin frowned in confusion until he remembered that Sir Harris was supposed to be working in the kitchen.

He waved his hand dismissively. "Don't worry about it. Things are a little chaotic today anyway."

"I'm surprised to see you back so soon, to be honest. I thought you'd be gone until the end of the week," Sir Harris observed while stepping alongside Fin as he moved.

"I don't trust you all with my kitchen unsupervised," Fin remarked idly.

"Hey, it wasn't that bad except for … er. Well …"

The cook stopped and turned slowly to face the knight.

"Except for what, Harris?"

"Isn't it nice weather for a run? I think I'm going to—" The soon-to-be duke tore off down the hallway, leaving Fin to chase him.

"HARRIS! WHAT DID YOU DO TO MY KITCHEN?!"

CHAPTER 27
CROSSING YESTERDAY'S STARS

A long time ago …

Fiddling with the sleeves of her dress, Ainsley stared out shyly over the sea of noblemen and their sons. The banquet hall was cast in a bright glow from the springtime sunshine, and everyone appeared to be in grand spirits as the men discussed the upcoming royal hunt, and subsequent feasts that were going to be had for the next few months as the king tried to decide upon a husband·for his daughter.

So far, Ainsley had curtsied and exchanged greetings with over a hundred and thirty-three nobles. All of them wore painfully polite smiles or could barely look her in the eyes. Not that she could blame them. She was easily ten times as awkward and shy as any of them. Being uncharacteristically tall for her age didn't help matters, and while she knew she was passable in her looks, her feet were bigger than those of some of the boys who were her peers.

"Ainsley, won't you answer Viscount Jenoure's question?" the king's low rumble of a voice almost made her cringe as she was snapped back to the present.

"I'm so sorry, my lord, what did you ask of me?" She turned shyly to the viscount who smiled warmly down at her, making her immediately feel a little more at ease.

"I asked if you've read any good books lately. Last we spoke you were quite taken with the tales of the Pirate Noone."

Immediately Ainsley's face lit up. "Oh yes! She is by far my favorite heroine thus far. The way she battled her enemies a day after giving birth with her babe in one arm and a sword in the other is one of the most exciting chapters I've ever read! Though recently I started a new book about a Zinferan empress who was secretly a witch and—"

"You must forgive my daughter, Hank. She should be spending more of her energies reading foreign policies and refining her stitchwork. It is kind of you to indulge her," the king interrupted while reaching for a bunch of purple grapes out of a golden fruit bowl.

Ainsley's face turned crimson as she refocused her attention on the glittering jewels in her forest green shoes.

"Nonsense! I still enjoy fantastical tales that inspire the mind. Why do you think I study the lore of the stars so avidly?" The viscount winked at Ainsley who was still too embarrassed to lift her gaze.

"Of course, it is good for a woman to read all sorts of stories, sire! It means she isn't a complete bore outside of council rooms and political dinners," Viscountess Mael Jenoure insisted while leaning down to block the princess from the king's view.

The monarch didn't bother responding as he was once again approached by a nobleman who steered a boy no more than ten years old by the shoulders.

"Ah, King Matthias Devark. Thank you for making the journey; this is your son I presume? Matthias the Sixth?"

The Troivackian monarch nodded and released the child.

Stepping forward and lifting his dark eyes, the boy bowed perfectly. He straightened himself, then turned to the princess and executed the same bow.

"I am here as the future king of Troivack, to offer for the hand of Princess Ainsley Cowan."

The room fell quiet, as Ainsley stared mortified at the boy. She wanted to laugh, or to pound her head against the sturdy table in front of her, but she knew neither reaction would be well received.

For once, her father intervened on her behalf.

"I will consider your offer seriously, young man; in the meantime, please enjoy the festivities."

The prince stepped backward into his father's waiting hands. If he was self-conscious about his bold announcement, he didn't show it. No, his cool dark eyes didn't convey a whisper of his true thoughts …

Ainsley fidgeted as the nobility in the room gradually became engrossed with their previous conversations, leaving her to shrink back into her chair undisturbed.

After another hour, the king was invested in a conversation with an earl from Xava, and so the princess took it upon herself to quietly excuse herself and silently drift through the banquet hall toward the doors. She stuck to the walls of the room and kept her eyes downcast, avoiding any unwanted attention or greetings entirely. Despite her height, she was quite adept at disappearing.

Once free of the crowd, Ainsley continued sidling down the corridors, until she reached the east wing exit. Finally free of the castle walls, she began to pick up the pace of her steps, until at long last her skirts were hitched in both hands, and she was flat out running toward the king's forest.

Ainsley didn't stop until she had broken through the first ring of trees, and once she had skidded to an undignified halt, she let out a long loud sigh while placing her hands on her hips.

"Is he serious?! He wants me to consider marrying a ten-year-old?! I'm sixteen! This is insane! Even if we wait until I'm eighteen, he'll only be twelve. Oh Gods, it isn't like the others were much better anyway …" Ainsley chattered to herself energetically while walking deeper into the woods. It was the only space she could freely say what she wanted to.

As she walked through the fresh greenery and marveled at the wildflowers that dotted the lush underbrush, the princess spread out her arms and enjoyed the feeling of the warm sunshine on her skin.

With her eyes closed, she took in the sounds of the forest, allowing them to soothe her. The chittering squirrels, the singing birds, and the faint echo of a woodpecker somewhere deeper in the woods drifted into her awareness. She tripped a couple of times over an errant root or two, but she didn't let that dampen her spirits. She had to enjoy every moment of the tranquility before stealing back to her chamber to get ready for the banquet.

Taking another deep breath in, the sharp snap of twigs behind her nearly made Ainsley jump out of her skin.

Whirling around with a shriek on the tip of her tongue, she found the new captain of the Daxarian knights standing behind her with his hands respectfully clasped behind himself. Bowing deeply before her, he waited for her to regain her composure before speaking.

"My apologies for startling you, Princess. It is not safe for you to be out in the woods by yourself."

The pained look the young woman gave him immediately made the man take an unconscious step back.

"With so many suitors in attendance, it—" Antonio began to explain quietly.

"I ... I ... get..." Ainsley tried to explain. Tried to tell him to go away. Tried to tell him that if she didn't get some time away from the castle, she was going to scream until everyone's ears bled.

But she couldn't.

She didn't want to bother anyone.

Didn't want the king to have another reason to disapprove of her.

It was bad enough that her mother died giving birth to her ...

"If I follow from back there, will that be alright?" the captain asked worriedly, pointing farther back in the brush.

Ainsley's blank stare turned to him, and that was when he saw something he didn't expect to in the Princess of Daxaria's eyes.

He saw sorrowful defeat.

"Never mind. I will go back to prepare for the feast." She turned and, assuming a dignified posture, began walking back in the direction of the castle. She still tripped just as often, but she at least tried to cover it up a little more gracefully ...

Captain Antonio didn't fully understand the guilt he felt, but he could tell that he had accidentally trodden on something that was important to the young royal.

To think I was just trying to be more mindful of the lass. Everyone seems to forget about her all the time ...

Cracking her neck wearily, Ainsley sat on her bed waiting for her maids to leave her for the night. Recently she'd been forced to wait until everyone was asleep, then steal away to the library to try and smuggle more books into her chamber.

When her tutors had reported her obsession with reading to the king, at first he had thought nothing of it, until he found her with her nose in a book at every social gathering. She would abandon any duty or task the second someone took their eyes off her and immediately procure a novella she had hidden in the room or on her person.

After that, the king had banned her reading non-educational books outside of an hour a day in the morning, and only one book per week. Even if she finished it sooner.

The truth of it was that the books were all she had to distract from the painful loneliness she felt. The other noble girls only gossiped about what others were doing or fawned over potential husbands …

After the moon had inched a little higher in the sky, Ainsley deemed it safe enough to escape. Slipping out of her chamber while wrapped in an ugly brown robe that she refused to throw away, she scurried down to the third floor, and stole into the third door on the left along the north wall.

There was a slight chill in the air that the princess felt in her bare feet but ignored as she snatched up a candlestick and hastily lit the taper in the darkness.

Wrapping her hand around the silver base, she readied herself to find the next story to fall in love with, when she lifted her gaze—and froze. There, with two books clutched to his chest, was a boy. A boy who was exactly Ainsley's height, with the same color of hair, but whereas her wide eyes were a dull brown, his were a captivating hazel.

"What are you doing here?!" Ainsley whispered while placing a hand on her chest. Her heart racing from the scare.

"I'm just … I'm just borrowing a couple of books to help me sleep. I promise I'll put them back in the morning, or … sorry that was rude of me! I'll put them back now. I never asked if this was appropriate or if—"

"No, no it's … it's fine." Ainsley let out a slow breath, once again feeling a calm settle over herself. "As long as you don't tell anyone I was in here," she insisted as her left hand clutched the lapels on her robe tightly closed.

"Aren't you the princess, though?" he asked, tilting his head curiously. "Can't you read or wander the castle however you want? It's your home after all. Though perhaps you aren't permitted in your guest's bedchambers. I could see that being an issue. Not that I'm saying you go sneaking into anyone's chamber, I'm sure you are perfectly respectable and … and … sorry. I tend to talk too much sometimes." The boy blushed, and for some reason, Ainsley found herself smiling.

"I don't mind … if anything I like that I know what you're really thinking."

It was the boy's turn to look bashful as he averted his gaze and fought off a smile of his own.

"You're … You're too kind."

"What's your name?" Ainsley asked quietly while moving closer to him.

"I'm Norman. Norman Reyes. A pretty boring name really … Norman. Change one letter and my name is 'Normal.' I'm the son of Baron Eric Reyes, we live a few leagues outside of Sorlia," he explained awkwardly, his eyes alternating between looking at her and the table in front of them.

"Oh, so you're here to marry me too?"

As soon as the words were out of Ainsley's mouth, she felt her face grow pale in mortification. She just sounded like the most presumptuous hussy in the world, and surely he would look at her like she was insane and—

"Well, I don't remember you being already married … but, yes, my father brought me here for … that reason." Norman blushed even more deeply.

"I don't remember meeting you," Ainsley admitted apologetically.

"Oh, you haven't yet. My father greeted your father earlier today while I hid."

Ainsley blinked in surprise.

"You … You said you liked it when I was honest, and I was honestly scared to meet you. I sound ridiculous, and I heard a ten-year-old even proposed to you properly already, but I didn't know if you'd think little of me because we aren't the highest-ranking nobility. Nor are we the richest family, but I like our home. It's not as large as a castle but we have a nice apple orchard and—"

Ainsley was smiling so broadly she felt as if her cheeks would burst.

"What about this one?" Norman lifted a tart from the small kerchief he had stuffed full of snacks for them.

"Is that raspberry? Of course I want it!" Ainsley snatched up the baked good and relished in its sweetness as Norman picked up the blueberry tart and bit in. A dribble of filling stained his chin, making Ainsley laugh out loud.

"It isn't that funny, you know!" he exclaimed with a smile despite wiping the mess up quickly. "I see you drop stuff all the time during the banquets!" he added when she continued laughing.

Somehow this observation only made her laugh harder.

"I know!" she gasped. "But no one sees it when I do it!"

"Well, I did," Norman teased before finishing off his tart. A snort suddenly escaped Ainsley's nose that was followed by an astonished expression as though she couldn't believe she could make such a sound, which had her rolling on the ground laughing again.

This time Norman wasn't immune to the humor, and he, too, burst out laughing as Ainsley managed to explain between snorts and gasps that the tart was coming out of her nose.

When they had settled down into a contented silence, the couple stared up at the blue sky together and watched the clouds drift peacefully by. Their bellies full of baked goods, and their faces glowing in happiness, they enjoyed the undisturbed quiet of the day. Ever since the night in the library, they had stolen every chance to meet and talk, or sometimes just to read together.

"You know that Captain Antonio man follows us every time we meet," Norman announced quietly.

"I know. He hasn't told my father anything, though, so don't worry," Ainsley replied, not wanting to break the good mood of the day.

"My father will put in an official request for your hand, but I'm worried," he began slowly.

Ainsley felt the unwanted fingers of reality reaching for her heart as she realized what he was about to say.

"You want me to talk with my father and tell him I want to marry you?" she asked, her expression growing taut.

"If he thinks we care about each other, it might help ... I mean your father wants you to be happy, right?"

Ainsley sat up, her former levity a distant memory as the notion of talking to her father began clawing its way into her mind.

"He wants what is best for the kingdom. I don't know what he was like when my mother was alive, but since I've been born, he doesn't look at me if he can help it. You know how this works, Norman. Princesses are pawns. Not that it's my father's fault ... He has to think about everyone in Daxaria. Not just about me."

"He's still your father. You should try talking to him. King or not, he should look at you and hear what you have to say."

Ainsley clutched her skirts tightly. Norman meant well, but he didn't understand. He hadn't grown up feeling as though love was to be earned, and only if there weren't more important matters at hand. She could feel her throat closing, and the fear settling over her like a cloud.

"Ainsley?"

Reluctantly, she turned to face Norman's calm yet determined hazel eyes.

"I want you to be with me more than anything, and if you want me there when speaking to your father, I will be. I'm never going to let you be alone again. I promise. I will do absolutely everything in my power to make sure we stay together."

Despite the kindness of his words, Ainsley felt tears spill over the edge of her eyes. She ached for the warm solace of Norman's love, and yet she struggled to see past the cold obstacle of her father, the king. Her father would never approve of her marrying someone who offered so little.

The young lord suddenly reached out and interlaced her fingers in his own, giving them a gentle squeeze of reassurance.

"I will make myself worthy to be your husband, and worthy enough to be the next ruler. Then I'll show you that a king can be a good father *and* husband, because I don't agree with you a whit that a man can't do all of it. It's going to be hard, but we can do it. I know we can."

Ainsley couldn't say anything more, couldn't *do* anything more as a surge of powerful emotions overtook her. So she simply allowed the boy she'd fallen in love with to embrace her as she cried, while wishing with all her might that everything he said was going to be true.

CHAPTER 28
REASSIGNED DUTIES

Fin stared around him, his hands on his hips, and his lips pursed. His aides stood behind him, glancing at one another and mouthing messages as they waited for his reaction.

He had walked through the kitchen the night the queen had gone into labor … However, he hadn't taken the time to really see what had been done in his absence.

With his abilities able to sense what had been moved, what had been added, and what had … disappeared. Shifting his feet slightly against the stone, he winced as he heard the soles of his boots stick to its stained surface.

Turning around slowly, his aides jumped and immediately straightened under his stricken stare.

"Why is there an entire cauldron of gravy?" he asked, his voice faint.

"Well, you see … we kept trying to thicken it, and then it would be too thick so we'd add water and—"

Fin held up his hand and stopped Peter's explanation while rubbing his mouth as though to stop himself from shouting. Sir Harris was the first one to try and speak again.

"Are you angry?"

Fin shook his head slowly.

"Is it because we've chipped just about every piece of plateware?" Hannah asked uncharacteristically timidly.

"No."

"Is it because the ale is gone?" Sir Harris asked hesitantly.

"THE ALE IS GONE?!" the redhead exploded.

All the aides except for the future duke leapt back.

"No, but don't you feel better knowing that it isn't!"

"I want you … to run laps around the castle." Fin's voice came out mildly strangled as he stared dementedly down at the auburn-haired knight.

"It's quite hot out today and—"

"NOW!"

Sir Harris sprang into action immediately and darted out of the kitchen, leaving Fin to face the rest of his aides while gesturing toward the overabundance of pies filling every shelf and ledge available in the kitchen, then to a large wooden barrel that was filled with old loaves of bread.

"How did … all of this happen?"

"Well … we made a dozen loaves of bread not realizing that you needed salt …" Sir Lewis began hesitantly.

"Then we made about ten rhubarb pies but … er … we didn't know the leafy bits were poisonous until Ruby pointed that out," Sir Andrews continued.

"The window got broken when I tried to toss Sir Taylor a pot …" Hannah admitted while fidgeting.

"But we did finish all the meals! They weren't … all terrible. Everyone was fed three times a day thanks to a couple other maids coming to help," Heather, who was visibly sweating, exclaimed desperately.

Fin slowly turned around and walked to the chairs by his cooking table. He then half collapsed into one and gripped his head while leaning his elbows on the table.

"You served … brussels sprouts and salted meat … for every meal … except breakfast?"

"Right! We served fruit and eggs and that seemed to go over quite well," Sir Taylor affirmed while nodding to the other aides.

Fin didn't say anything for a good long while, ignoring the uncomfortable silence that was building.

"Are you sure you're not angry?" Hannah asked while fidgeting even more.

"No. I'm not angry. It wasn't any of your faults that you didn't know what you were doing. I was unaware that you all knew so little, and so the blame is placed squarely with me."

The aides all visibly let out a sigh of relief, until Fin lifted his face once again and stared at them all with a half-crazed glint in his eye.

"I think I need to start teaching you all how to cook. From now on, you are all to be my students, and I will have you know … you have had it easy until now, but that is done." He rose, the manic energy around him making both Sirs Andrews and Lewis grip on to Sir Taylor fearfully.

"W-Why does it feel like we are being punished?" Heather asked as she glued herself to Peter's side.

"This isn't a punishment; this is a chance to improve your skills in the kitchen." Fin's voice was light and casual, but his eyes were wide and unblinking.

Hannah let out a small squeak and took a hasty step back as Fin once again stepped closer to them.

"Do you know what we are going to learn first?" he asked, his eyes frighteningly wide.

"W-What?" Peter stammered while reaching out and clasping Hannah's shoulder.

"How to scrub every inch of your kitchen."

"Wouldn't it be faster with your magic?" Sir Taylor risked while arching a bushy black eyebrow.

Of everyone present, the large burly knight seemed the least disturbed by Fin's reaction, earning him a long-suffering appraisal from the man.

"It would be. However, in instances when I am … absent, you will need to be able to do everything required without it."

Sir Taylor shrugged.

"Alright, lads, to the buckets. Cook, where are the brushes? We couldn't find those."

Fin blinked as everyone, but Sir Taylor moved into action.

"Have you been drinking?" the redhead asked uncertainly.

"Nay, Cook."

"Your … disposition is strange today."

The knight lowered his voice and shot a brief glance over his shoulder to affirm the others were preoccupied.

"How is the queen?" Sir Taylor's eyes had a sudden deep knowingness to them that unnerved Fin greatly.

"Tough to say. The princess seemed fine," the redhead answered, doing his best to keep his tone even.

Nodding and sharing a look of complete understanding, Sir Taylor clapped Fin on the shoulder before joining the other aides in their duties.

Before the cook had a moment to ponder Sir Taylor's strange behavior further, however, Ruby entered the room. The woman's face was pale, and it was obvious in her posture that something was wrong, making Fin immediately ready himself for the worst possible news.

"Mr. Ashowan, His Majesty has summoned you."

The silence in the kitchen was deafening.

"Everyone, by the time I get back I want you all to have finished scrubbing this entire place. I should be back in time to prepare dinner. Lunch should be a simple soup and bread."

The aides all nodded solemnly before the redhead turned and walked out of the kitchen at Ruby's side.

As the pair moved through the corridors together, Fin began to notice that he was getting an increasing number of stares and whispers. Wearily, he figured that word of his being a witch had probably already torn through the castle like wildfire, and so he did his best to avoid looking at anyone directly.

"Silly gossipmongers." Ruby sighed with a shake of her head. Her usually rounded cheeks seemed a little thinner somehow. Perhaps the stress of recent weeks had taken too great a toll on the woman.

"About the queen?" Fin asked, feigning ignorance to figure out where the woman stood.

"No … I think they should be talking about that to be perfectly honest. Instead all they want to talk about is how apparently most of the nobles believe you to be a witch."

Fin kept his expression controlled, but he decided it was time to just live with the truth of it. So far things hadn't been going terribly …

"I *am* a witch, Ruby. Why do you think I never needed more aides? For an entire castle, you think I'd only ask for four people? That's ridiculous." He couldn't help but tease her a little.

Ruby didn't respond but froze in her tracks and gaped up at him. Unable to continue walking with him.

Fin decided not to respond to her shock, instead choosing to let the news sink in a little more naturally.

The poor woman must've been incredibly startled, however, because she didn't even bother to catch up to Fin as he continued on his way to the king's chamber.

As he walked, he tried to control his growing anxiety and wariness about what the king could possibly need him for …

The guards nodded knowingly to Fin, even giving him a bit of a smile before he entered the room, where the musk of unwashed sweaty bodies and the lingering metallic note of blood overwhelmed his senses.

The scene was more or less exactly as he had last seen it. The king sitting at the queen's bedside holding her hand, while Katelyn Ashowan knelt with her hands hovering over the queen's abdomen.

Bowing quickly, Fin announced his arrival.

"You called for me, Your Majesty?"

"Yes. Eric is inconsolable right now, and you are the only person I can think of who can both contain him and try to keep him calm."

Fin straightened in abundant surprise.

"Your Majesty, are you asking me to take care of the prince in place of his governess?"

"Yes. I can't have him shrieking up and down this hallway just now. I'll talk to him this evening if … if Ainsley hasn't woken up," he explained, his hold on the queen's hand tightening.

"I understand, Your Majesty." Even though Fin didn't understand at all. The king needed to see his son and daughter …

Even if just for an hour.

It wasn't Fin's business to say so, though. So instead, he turned and reached out to take the handle of the door to make his exit, when he suddenly stopped and turned around.

"Your Majesty, what … what is the princess to be called?"

Norman raised his face, his cheeks sunken in and his eyes dark.

"What do you mean?"

"Her name. Eric wanted to know." Fin felt a cold sweat trickle down his back.

"Call her whatever you want. We can change it later if Ainsley wakes up."

Fin was about to reply, and not in a calm rational manner, when his mother cast him a warning glance over her shoulder that had him clamping his mouth shut.

So without a third look back, he left the chamber, even though he had more than a few words he wanted to share with the king regarding his attitude toward his daughter.

When Fin first entered Eric's chamber, he found the boy's governess cowering behind a chair while the lad threw any item he could at the doorway where Fin stood.

Quickly catching the book that had been launched with impressive force, Fin stared at the prince with raised eyebrows. Eric's furious tantrum stopped when he saw the redhead, who glanced over to the governess. Fin couldn't help but wish to question her previous experience with children, as every time he saw her, she seemed unable to handle the young boy effectively …

"Eric, what are you doing?" Fin stepped into the room and closed the door behind him with a frown. His disapproval was all too clear.

"No one is telling me anything!" the child shouted, his face red and tearstained.

"So you terrify your poor governess and destroy your room? Is this how a young man should behave?" His hands were on his hips while Eric's were curled into fists.

"What else can I do! I want to see my sister! And my mom! Where's Dad?!" Fresh tears were flooding down his face.

"If you see your sister right now after you have just destroyed your room, she will be very scared. Is that what you want to do?"

Eric looked ready to shout some more, but under Fin's direct stare the fight suddenly went out of him.

"No … No, I don't."

"Good. Now I want you to apologize to your governess this instant, and together we are going to clean up this mess."

The woman stood gratefully from her hidden location; her conservative black dress looked terribly warm for the summer, and wholly impractical for chasing around an energetic eight-year-old boy.

Setting the room back to rights and calming the prince down took far longer than Fin had anticipated, and so he sent a message to his aides that he would be back to the kitchen later than he had hoped to begin the supper.

Fin proceeded to ask Eric to read to him from one of the texts he was supposed to be studying for that week, and once the lad seemed more like himself, the redhead decided a visit to the newborn princess wasn't a bad idea. The governess, who Fin learned was called Farrah, he sent to rest for the afternoon after she had been informed of the king's orders pertaining to the prince. The woman's relief was thinly veiled.

When the duo entered the princess's nursery, Eric could barely contain his eagerness as he bounced up and down on the balls of his feet trying to see in the cradle as Physician Durand continued performing another examination.

"Ah, good day, Your Highness, and— Oh, Mr. Ashowan! Pleasure to see you again."

Fin managed a smile at the man as they shook hands.

"How does the princess fare?" he asked as Eric peered down at his sister's small sleeping face.

"Remarkably well. She seems determined to grow up in as little time as possible."

Eric smiled excitedly. "Good! I want to show her how to ride a horse, and the best hiding places. Well … not all of them. I need some if we ever play together."

The men smiled fondly at the boy's eagerness.

"I spoke with the king regarding the princess's name," Fin started, his smile dimming slightly. "He told me to name her myself. Says that he will change the name if Her Majesty—" He stopped suddenly and glanced down at Eric who was fortunately too distracted with his sister to notice.

"That is a rather large responsibility. Perhaps leave the matter?" the physician suggested, though it was clear he didn't like that the child was being overlooked either.

"I have a better idea. Eric?"

The boy looked up at him still grinning ear to ear.

"What should we name your sister? Your father says he isn't sure yet, so do you mind telling us what to call her until he knows?"

The prince's eyes grew as round as saucers.

"Really?! I can name her?!"

"Until your father thinks of a different name. Then again, maybe he will like what you think of." Physician Durand's eyes twinkled.

Eric stared at his sister now, frowning. The boy was quiet for a long moment before he suddenly broke out into a triumphant grin.

"I know! I'll name her after mom's mom! Mom always said she liked Grandma's name!"

The physician and cook shared looks of surprise. It was a surprisingly mature notion for an eight-year-old.

"Grandma's name was Alina! Papa will like it because it has an 'A' just like Mom's name!"

Fin tousled the prince's golden locks before looking down at the baby girl.

"You know what, Eric? I think that's the perfect name for her. Alina it is."

Physician Durand bowed his head reverently to the princess.

"Very well, Princess Alina Reyes, daughter of our beloved King and Queen Norman and Ainsley Reyes, sister of Prince Eric Reyes, it is our pleasure to meet you."

Fin bowed to the cradle, and Eric puffed his chest out in pride; he knew he had picked the perfect name. His father would surely think the exact same way, he just knew it.

CHAPTER 29
BEGONE OR BEWITCHED

Fin sat in the rocking chair by the cool fireplace as Eric continued to prattle on to his sister about his day, the world, his friends, and the castle.

"I'm glad the prince has taken to the princess." Physician Durand puffed on the pipe in his hand while sitting in the chair opposite Fin.

"Can't say I'm surprised. Eric is a great kid." Fin closed his eyes and leaned his head against the back of the chair, his body heavy.

"You did well in the meeting today. It'd be a good thing if this was the start of witches and humans working more closely together in my opinion. The possible advancements that could be made would be incredible."

"Mm-hmm," Fin replied wearily. He still hadn't recovered his full stamina after his match with Adamma and his body was screaming at him to rest.

"You know, Mr. Ashowan, I don't think it will be long before someone thinks to include you in more serious political matters; perhaps you should—"

A loud commotion cut the elder off and had Fin on his feet immediately while Eric leapt back from the cradle, startled.

The princess didn't like everyone's sudden distress and let out a small cry of her own to tell them so.

"What in the world—"

"Please mind the children," Fin called out as he crossed the room in long strides, opened and closed the door behind himself, and headed toward the loud shouts and bangs.

As he drew closer to the king's chamber, he noticed what looked to be seven armed knights facing the two guards, their hands on their weapons. In the middle of all the shouting stood none other than Lord Gauva, his face a mixture of irritable and smug.

"What's happening?" Fin asked as he drew near.

"YOU! Just who we were waiting for!" Lord Gauva turned immediately, his eyes bright as he brandished a finger at the cook. A glimmer of uncertainty, fear, and righteousness was clear in the man's gaze.

Fin knew that look.

He had seen it many times before.

It was the look of someone looking for his blood ...

He didn't have to guess why.

"Why is a mere *cook* allowed in and out of the king's chamber when no one but your mother and Physician Durand should be allowed!"

Fin's palms began to sweat, and so he put his hands in his pockets.

"My ability makes it easy for me to boil water, stack towels, and better explain my mother's ability while she is incapable," he added dryly.

"Oh, you explained plenty! No one but you three have the ear of our king and queen lately! Does no one else find this strange?" The men all grunted in agreement save for the two guards at the door who were beginning to look worried, which made their grips on the hilts of their sheathed swords tighten.

"Summon the king then." Fin nodded to the guards who both swallowed with great difficulty.

"His Majesty refuses to leave his wife's side," one of them explained briefly.

"Aha! Does that sound like our king? Ignoring his call to duty? Hiding when the kingdom is on war's doorstep just because his wife is—"

"Mind how you speak of the queen," the guard on the right growled fiercely.

Lord Gauva at least had the good sense to look chastened.

"Perhaps ask the king if Lord Gauva might be granted access to witness his well-being," Fin addressed the guards again, though if he were perfectly honest, the king didn't seem in his right mind at all. It might hurt his cause if anything ...

"Mr. Ashowan, I'm not leaving my post to deliver a message with the likes of these men here. They're speakin' about dragging you an' your mother away for questioning," the one guard explained while fixing the lord with a sharp glare.

"He will do no such thing. I will be the one to go ask His Majesty then." Fin's calm voice was a façade. The mention of anyone taking him or his mother anywhere to be "questioned" was forcing him to dig his fingernails into his palms to stay calm. He needed to stay in control no matter what. Losing his temper would not help anyone or anything …

Entering the chamber, Fin saw that his mother was lying down sleeping beside the queen, the soft glow over Her Highness's body weaker, but still there.

Both Kate and Ainsley looked pale, and Fin could tell his mother had been generous in the timeline she had given the king. It wouldn't be long before her magic would no longer suffice …

"Your Majesty, there is a small mob outside the room demanding that my mother and I be removed for questioning given that we are witches," the redhead announced after his bow was wholly ignored.

"Who might that be?" The quiet in the king's voice didn't fool Fin for a moment; the man was not entirely sane. A combination of grief and lack of sleep or proper food was taking a heavy toll.

"Lord Gauva."

"Sounds like something he'd do. Very well. I will go address him. Whatever happens, however, Mr. Ashowan, I do not want *anyone* stopping your mother's work, understand? That is an official command." As Norman stood, his haggard face regarded the cook emotionlessly.

Fin gave another small bow and kept his head bent as the king stepped by him and exited the chamber.

Lord Gauva fell back a step at the sight of the king.

Gone was the composed, well-groomed man who was their leader, and before them stood a ghost. Norman's gaze was deadened, his complexion resembled a sickly paste, and his tunic was rumpled and askew.

"I … I was right. Look at what their magic has done to you, sire! We will see them hanged at—"

"CEASE." Norman's voice boomed far louder than anyone would've thought he was capable of at that point. "My wife, your queen, lies on her deathbed, and these people you rush to condemn are the only ones keeping her amongst the living. Lord Gauva, you have overstepped your rank grossly. You will take your men and leave this instant or be charged with treason." The king turned back to the room, not noticing the uncertain glances everyone present gave save for Lord Gauva whose eyes were narrowed and his fists clenched.

"Your Majesty will forgive me when this spell is broken."

With a wave of his hand, three of the baron's men pushed the door open just as Norman had opened the latch.

Once the group saw the inside of the room with the queen looking every bit a corpse, and Fin's mother lying beside her, the golden threads of magic flowing between them, the redhead knew blood was about to be demanded.

"GRAB THE WITCH!" Lord Gauva roared, thrusting the king and Fin aside and pointing at Katelyn who didn't stir.

One of the knights brought by the baron lunged through the doorway at the healer, only the water pitcher on the table beside the bed suddenly shot up in the air and careened into his head, knocking him back a step.

The men then turned slowly to stare at Fin whose heart was in his ears.

There was nothing else he could do. They were committing treason; they were going to hurt him and his mother and endanger the queen …

Fin stepped forward and the men drew their weapons.

"Someone summon Captain Antonio and Mage Lee," the king ordered one of the guards who was beginning to draw his own sword.

"Your Majesty, once I am outside with them, please shut the door," Fin called out, his eyes never leaving the baron's men who suddenly noticed that the redhead's eyes were beginning to glow …

Norman quickly stepped out of the way, and suddenly a blast of a blue lightning shield wrought with ancient symbols surged through the air and sent the knights sailing back out of the doorway.

"AHA! I knew you were hiding your true colors!" Lord Gauva called out proudly. His triumph disappeared, however, the moment Fin exited the chamber and turned his eyes filled with blue lightning to him.

"Gods … we never should've stopped hunting your kind. Men, attack!" Lord Gauva breathed in disgust.

All seven knights tried to charge forward, only to find they couldn't move past some kind of invisible barrier.

Each man tried to rush through, or stab at it, but each time the blow was repelled. In fact, the shield somehow was increasing its span and was forcing the attackers back down the corridor away from the king's chamber.

"You ... You! How *dare* you accost a man of my breeding! You may have drained the mind of our king, queen, and even that knight Sir Harris but—"

"Why do you think I did *anything* to Sir Harris?" A strange echo reverberated through the halls when the witch spoke.

"That young man is to be a duke! I saw the topic of our next meeting in Mr. Howard's notes, and yet I saw Harris only a few hours ago running laps around the castle just because you told him to!"

"He isn't a duke yet. He is still under my command until he rises to power," Fin replied through gritted teeth. In truth it was quite a bit harder controlling his abilities and not blasting them all out the nearest window.

The shield continued herding the men back down the corridor until they were nearly forced against the west wall.

"I ... will ... see you hanged!" the baron hissed despite his men accidentally dropping weapons as they all tried to push against the shield.

"What is the meaning of this?!" Captain Antonio's voice broke out behind Fin, but the redhead couldn't stop. If he did, they'd attack, and he wasn't taking any chances.

"Go talk to His Majesty!" Fin called without turning around.

Mage Lee had arrived at the same time as the captain and was watching stunned as Fin successfully repressed the men, then strode forward until he stood beside the cook.

"I take it Lord Gauva is not an admirer of yours?" Lee asked while folding his arms casually over his chest, his staff loosely clutched in his hand.

"It's difficult not to send them flying."

"Show off," the mage muttered before casting a sideways glance at the younger man and noticed that he was in fact sweating quite profusely.

"Would you like some help?"

"No."

"You know us mages are perfectly—"

"Why aren't you asking me what happened?" Fin snapped irritably.

"Oh, dear boy, I don't need to ask! Lord Gauva was frothing at the mouth earlier. I'm only surprised he didn't grab a few pitchforks as well," Lee clucked, his tone almost bored.

"Glad ... you see ... the humor in all this," Fin managed, though his hands were starting to shake.

Captain Antonio exited the king's chamber and strolled over to where Fin stood, his blue eye glaring at Lord Gauva.

"Baron, you are being charged with treason and attacking Her Majesty the queen, as are all your knights."

"His Majesty is bewitched by that man right beside you! What is wrong with all of you?! Why aren't you seeing him for the monster he is!"

Captain Antonio glanced at Fin and his eyebrows did rise at the sight of the glowing unnatural lightning consuming his eyes, but then he turned to face Lord Gauva once more.

"I grant you Mr. Ashowan could use a bath, but it is a little extreme to refer to him as a monster." The captain then lowered his voice so that only Fin could hear. "Stop whatever it is you're doing, the knights should be coming up the stairs behind them now."

With a small nod, the redhead released the barrier, and all the men were pitched forward at the loss of force pressing against them.

The only one to stumble to his feet, however, immediately launched himself at Fin. The unit of castle knights appeared in the nick of time from the servants' stairwell and seized the assailant's arms before he could take a single step, holding him back. The knight's face was growing purple as he continued to resist his arrest, his eyes glued on Fin as though he were possessed.

"I … will … cut you down, witch! You and your wench of a mother!"

The knight was suddenly blasted out of the arresting knights' hands with great force against the wall behind him, rendering him unconscious. Both the captain and Mage Lee shot the cook flat glances.

"That was an unnecessary assault on my nephew! Captain! Arrest that man!" Baron Gauva seethed, clearly grasping at straws as two knights seized his arms.

Captain Antonio sighed, then turned to Fin, a deep weariness in his eye.

"For that I will have to put you in a cell for a night."

"What?!" Fin demanded in great alarm.

The captain once again dropped his voice. "I want the other nobles to be enraged on your behalf. It'll alienate Lord Gauva further and help you in the long run. I also want to do this by the book so that no one can say you got preferential treatment. You assaulted a knight above your station while he was already under arrest. His Majesty will obviously pardon you and have you released by dawn once the paperwork clears."

Fin turned, his hands on his hips as he readied himself to argue. Yet as he opened his mouth to defend himself and stared into Antonio's pleading blue eye, he immediately felt the fight go out of him. He really shouldn't have lost control when the knight was baiting him …

"Are there a lot of rats down there?" Fin asked wearily.

"One or two. Sir Doffer trained them to shake hands, though, and they are quite well fed," Antonio explained as he signaled two knights to bring shackles for the redhead.

"What are the cots like?"

"Try not to think about them," Antonio replied evasively.

Mage Lee leaned over with his arms crossed to join in on the conversation, a dreamy smile on his face. "As a cook you have an astute sense of smell, don't you?"

Fin glared as he was fitted with shackles along with Lord Gauva and his knights.

"Tell me how your evening goes, Mr. Ashowan; I'm going to go have a hot bath." Mage Lee gave him a mock salute.

Fin sighed and hung his head. He hated politics.

As Captain Antonio had him led toward the servants' stairwell, Fin looked over his shoulder, a weary yet sly smile climbing up his face before he disappeared around the corner.

"I hope your plan works, Captain, because you're going to have to explain to my mother why I'm locked up tonight."

Mage Lee burst out in a loud cackle as the captain grew rigid, his one blue eye widened, and his expression fell into one of obvious dread. He had clearly forgotten that ever so small, important detail ...

CHAPTER 30
VEXING VISITATIONS

Fin eyed the pile of damp hay in the corner warily before moving his gaze to the stained chamber pot that could have been white ... at some point.

"I thought you mentioned a cot, Captain?" Fin called over his shoulder as the clack of his cell door being locked rang out.

"All I said was to try and not think about them," Antonio countered innocently.

Slowly turning back around to show the military man his less than thrilled expression, the redhead was promptly distracted by the loud entrance of Baron Gauva and his men.

"UNHAND ME, YOU! I WILL NOT BE STORED DOWN HERE WITH THESE CRETINS! I MUST SAVE HIS MAJESTY!"

It took three knights to physically subdue the lord as he tried to pull free with his shackled hands.

"Lord Gauva, unless you want to share a cell with five other Troivackian men, you will reside here until His Majesty decides where your new ... quarters shall be." Captain Antonio's cool voice silenced the man only briefly.

"This is preposterous! I could be held in my estate just outside of Austice, I—"

"His Majesty wants you kept nearby and under close watch given your treasonous actions today." Mr. Howard stepped through the dungeon doorway with his own set of armed guards who carried torches for him.

Fin turned from the dramatics and was pleased to note that there were windows in this dungeon, albeit barred small ones. They still cast a respectable amount of light, meaning he wouldn't have to speculate over the time.

"You're locking me up beside the witch?!"

Fin's back stiffened as he pretended not to hear the incredulous tone in the baron's voice.

"You'll be sharing a cell with a couple of your knights," Mr. Howard explained idly while reading over the scroll in his hand.

"This is absurd!" The baron blustered a few more curse words until Mr. Howard raised his clear blue eyes and fixed him with a flat glare.

"What is absurd is you committing treason over something as ludicrous as witches having the power to control minds. Not to mention you pulled this little stunt with Her Majesty's life hanging in the balance and a war about to break out," Mr. Howard replied curtly.

The baron's purpling face looked ready to explode, when a streak of black fur rushed through everyone's legs, and through the bars of Fin's cell.

"Oh Gods, what is that?!" Lord Gauva demanded while brandishing a finger at the feline that had itself wrapped around the redhead's legs.

"A cat," the witch replied shortly before scooping his familiar up in his arms.

As the tirade continued on behind him, Fin looked at Kraken who seemed quite eager to talk to him for once.

"*Witch! I have not seen you in two days and now find you here! What have you done?*"

Fin glanced over his shoulder and ensured that no one was close enough to hear him over the din of the baron and his men.

"It's fine, this is more for politics than my being in trouble. Everything will be cleared by the morning."

"*While I am not exactly fond of this new setting, I must admit the rats do seem lovely and plump.*"

Fin hesitated then sidled over to the cell door.

"Captain?" he called softly as Mr. Howard continued dealing with the chaos of the rest of the dungeon.

The man leaned back so that his back rested against the bars of the redhead's cell.

"How upset will Sir Doffer be if his rats were to … er … go missing?"

The captain's lone eye swiveled over and noted Kraken in Fin's arms. He gave a smile that could have also been a grimace. "I'll ask, but maybe don't let him out of your sight for a while." He gestured to Kraken with a jerk of his chin then moved away.

Walking back farther into his cell, Fin resumed his conversation with his familiar.

"Don't eat the rats. One of the knights here is rather attached to them."

Kraken gave his witch a long stare before blinking slowly.

"You humans grow stranger every day. Very well then, Witch, I have come to give you some news. Your whiskers might be a little bit ruffled about it all, but I swear everything was done for the overall good."

Fin raised an eyebrow and waited.

"I'm the one who set the fire and smoked out the strange-smelling enemies."

"YOU WHAT?!"

Everyone in the dungeon fell silent and turned to the witch who had his back to them and was staring angrily at the feline in his arms.

"You could have been killed! Why in the world did you—"

"Because of my deeds you and your fellow humans are safer, aren't you?"

"Yes, but that isn't the point! Why didn't you come to me with this?"

"These plans were in motion before we could properly converse, and it was a time-sensitive operation. However, I heard yesterday that you were looking for them on your own … and I am glad for it. There are more in the city, and there are humans of this land that conspire with our enemies."

Fin's mind was floundering over his familiar's report. "Who?"

"Is the witch talking to a cat?! A beast that could eat our souls?!"

At this everyone, including Fin, turned their attention back to the baron.

"And I thought that bard was over the top," Fin muttered loud enough to be heard, making the captain and his knights snort in laughter.

"Mr. Ashowan, are you conversing with your flea-ridden pet?" Mr. Howard turned around looking vastly unamused.

Fin sighed before setting Kraken back down. "We need to talk. Stay here." He whispered low enough that no one else but the cat could hear before moving over to his cell door.

"That conversation would be better when I am not behind bars," Fin addressed the king's assistant ambiguously.

"I won't lie to you, Ashowan; seeing you stuck here like this is the high-light of my day. If I could commission a portrait of this moment, I would." Mr. Howard folded his arms and strolled over, looking incredibly smug.

"Just remember that me being down here means you have to keep eating the food my assistants cook."

A brief haunted look crossed the man's face before he shook his head.

"I still have ale and wine."

"You and I know you really just want some pork chops and fresh herb bread with that ale."

The two continued glaring at each other.

"Mr. Howard, I'm glad that you at least had the good sense not to romantically pursue the cook. Even if you obviously care for him," Baron Gauva grumbled.

Fin burst out laughing while Mr. Howard swung around, violent intent bright in his eyes.

"I am not interested in the cook! I—"

The assistant was interrupted by the arrival of Keith Lee, who was escorting a hooded figure, though they paused in confusion at the overly crowded dungeon.

"I didn't realize the dungeon was such a popular part of the castle," the almost mage announced quite seriously.

"I am here to take Baron Gauva's statement, then Mr. Ashowan's. The captain is here as a witness and interrogator if need be." Mr. Howard shot a half-crazed glance to the baron who was standing at his cell door with his hands wrapped around the bars.

"Ah, I see. Well, why is it Lady Jenoure's maid is here?" Keith gestured over his shoulder as the figure was in the process of lowering her hood to reveal Clara.

Before anyone could think to ask a question, Clara was uncere-moniously shoved aside as Lady Emily Gauva rushed forward; several knights were trailing behind her as she quickly found her husband and descended upon him.

"Rafael! What is the meaning of this! You committed treason?!" she demanded, her eyes burning in fury.

"He's a witch! He must have cursed our king's mind and—"

Keith snorted derisively. "Please, magic is a gift from the Gods. They would never bestow a gift that would take away someone's free will."

For once, Fin didn't loathe every word that came from the young man's mouth.

Emily Gauva turned to stare at the cook who was leaning casually against his cell wall while the chaos unfolded around him, studying him for a brief moment before turning back even more infuriated to her husband.

"What in the Gods' names has happened?"

"Emily, my dear, you need not—"

"Rafael, one more word that isn't an explanation and I will scream. Captain Antonio, what all has transpired?" she demanded with her hands placed on her hips. Her silken gown the color of a setting sun stuck out like a sore thumb amongst the grime of the dungeon, and yet it also somehow made her all the more imposing.

"Just as your husband said. He attempted to charge Her Majesty's bedchamber against the king's orders and placed Her Majesty the queen in grave danger."

A look of pure horror filled the woman's face before she turned to the baron.

"You … You've ruined us," she whispered the words, but everyone could hear the utter despair in her voice.

"I haven't ruined anything! That witch and his mother are powerful and have the ear of the king! Look, even Lady Jenoure's servant comes for him. Lady Jenoure is the sister of Earl Piereva, you know; she could be plotting with him to—"

"Enough!" Emily snapped as tears wet her eyes. "I don't like that Jenoure trollop any more than the next person, but she is no traitor. She's probably just having an affair with the cook … Rafael, how could you do this without talking to me?!"

Fin's face drained of color and his heart skipped a beat as he waited for someone to turn and realize that Lady Gauva had hit the nail perfectly on the head. However, fortunately for him, everyone seemed to be a tad more focused on the more serious crime of the day …

"The mage boy there just said it isn't possible that the king and queen have been bewitched! Why didn't you investigate more thoroughly before charging in?!"

"He was informed at today's meeting by Mage Lee himself, Lady Gauva, as well as by Mr. Ashowan," Mr. Howard recited dutifully.

Emily then proceeded to bombard her husband with questions on his actions, all the while ignoring those around her.

Captain Antonio leaned down to Mr. Howard as the lady carried on and whispered, "I love when the wives do the interrogating for me."

Even Fin chuckled at that one as the men all shared knowing smiles.

Meanwhile, Clara discreetly moved over to Fin's cell and leaned forward, inviting him closer to her.

Sidling over as casually as possible so as not to draw further attention, Fin bowed his head against the bars.

"Is *she* okay?" he asked quietly, not wanting to risk uttering Annika's name.

"Oh, she's just about ready to declare war on the castle, but otherwise fine. She's stressed enough right now, you know." The maid eyed Fin with a glimmer of accusation in her eyes.

"I know. I didn't really have a choice. The king ordered me to stop the baron no matter what, so I did."

Clara sighed and shook her head. "Given that no one seems all that angry with you, I take it things are alright?"

"I landed a blow on Baron Gauva's nephew as they were being arrested. The captain says one night in here will help me politically with the nobles."

"Hm … Possibly." Clara considered the notion with her usual smooth expression not giving away anything. "It's true then? That you're a witch?"

Fin hesitated for only a moment before giving a small nod.

"Well, that explains a few things. Aren't witches educated by their coven?"

Frowning, he nodded again.

"My grandfather used to hunt your kind, sorry. He paid close attention to them even after their prosecution was made illegal."

Eyeing her carefully, Fin wondered if he was going to have issues with Annika's maid.

"Don't look at me like that. My grandfather was an ass. Luckily my father didn't take after him at all. Aside from embezzling taxes and illegal trading …" She gave a dainty single shoulder shrug before changing the topic. "So you'll be released tomorrow. I'll go tell *her*, and please, for both our sakes, spend the night at the estate tomorrow. Every time you're late or don't return she develops a new outlandish reason that isn't ever as strange as the reality."

Fin chuckled. "Is she staying safe?"

"No. She's still going around trying to find … something. Ask her yourself. Don't worry though, she hasn't survived this long for no reason." Clara drew her hood back up.

Fin pursed his lips. He didn't want Annika putting herself in danger, but he recognized how hypocritical it would be of him to say so.

"Pardon me, but why *are* you here?" a frowning Mr. Howard called out, interrupting the exchange between Clara and Fin.

"Oh! I think I know! You said your name is Clara, yes? I remember my father was talking about their wedding nearly a week ago!" Keith piped up, making Fin's eye twitch involuntarily.

"Fin, you two are married?!" Captain Antonio exploded, standing straighter. "You're going to break your mother's heart with this; you should have told her!"

"I thought he was gay?" Baron Gauva called out, equally confused.

"My lord, some people prefer to have both!" one of the knights imprisoned with the noble offered helpfully.

"Well, it was awfully fast after Mr. Howard rejected him; perhaps she is with child?" Lady Emily Gauva offered while turning to study the maid, her recent troubles momentarily forgotten in light of the new gossip.

"We're not married!" Fin held up his hands defensively, while also being torn between laughing and banging his head against the bars of his cell.

"Nor am I with child," Clara added acidly to Lady Gauva who shot her a haughty look in response.

"Then why are you here?" Captain Antonio demanded more authoritatively.

"I was unaware it would be so … active down here," Clara replied after giving a dutiful curtsy to the captain.

"That doesn't answer the question," Mr. Howard pointed out suspiciously.

"I am … here … because …" Clara was obviously not used to being the one lying to nobles as she kept her eyes fixed on the ground.

"Let me guess, the cook is Lady Jenoure's paramour?" Emily Gauva scoffed openly.

"No!" both Fin and Clara burst out in unison.

"Look, Clara and I recently … attempted courting … only she just came down here to end things with me." Fin jumped in desperately, knowing that there was no other way to throw them off the scent. "I suppose being arrested isn't what most women like in a man."

There was a beat of silence where it was unclear whether or not the lie would be believed.

Then, for the second miraculous time that day, Keith jumped in to help.

"Arrested and abandoned all in one day … that is unfortunate, Mr. Ashowan. Perhaps I can offer you some advice?"

CHAPTER 31
THE QUEEN'S GIFT

Norman sat with his forearms braced on his knees, his gaze fixed on Ainsley's still face. He knew there wasn't long. He knew Katelyn Ashowan was nearing her limits, and that when she was no longer keeping his wife with them amongst the living, it was unlikely she would wake up.

"Your Majesty?" Ruby's voice broke the quiet.

Forcing Norman to turn his bleary stare to look at her.

"The prince is outside the chamber as you requested." The Head of Housekeeping watched her king and felt sorrow twist her innards. He looked near death's carriage himself. He had barely eaten, slept, or drunk in two days, and the light in his eyes had been completely extinguished. She wondered if it really was a good idea for the young prince to see his father in such a state.

"Thank you, that will be all." Norman dismissed her as he stood, sensing that the woman was fighting the urge to say something unnecessary.

Ruby curtsied with her lips pursed, and dutifully exited the room, giving the king another moment to pull himself together.

With a deep breath, the monarch crossed over to the door and pulled it open to see his son standing waiting with two armed guards on either side of him. The prince looked uneasy, and were it not for his formal education, he most likely would've been fidgeting rigorously.

"Eric, I'm going to let you see your mother—"

"Really?!" The little boy's face broke out into a relieved grin, and Norman found himself cursing the fact that Fin was locked up for the night.

Kneeling down before his son, he reached out and gently brushed the boy's golden curls. Ainsley had once told him that she had been blond as a child …

As the king searched Eric's small face, he realized how much the prince took after himself instead of the queen, and he was grateful for it in that moment.

"Eric, your mother isn't … well. So when you go in, you have to be very quiet, alright? She is asleep, and we need to let her rest."

The child's smile dimmed. "When will she wake up?"

"I … don't know. But I want you to see her right now, alright?"

The boy's lips trembled. "Do I … Do I have to say goodbye?"

Norman's heart shattered. He didn't think there had been anything left to break, but as he drew his son in and hugged him, he found the pain in his chest intensified.

"Just say what you feel," he replied before quietly waiting as Eric tried to calm down enough to go in to see his mother without being loud. It took a few moments, but eventually the prince had regained control, and Norman set to explaining about Katelyn's presence before taking him inside. Fin's mother had fallen asleep nearly an hour earlier, and so it was the perfect time for a more private family moment …

The only sound in the room was their footfalls as they entered, but when Eric laid eyes on his mother, the king immediately worried that he was going to start crying loudly. However, at the last moment, Eric seemed to remember that he needed to not disturb the healer or the queen and bit down on his lip quietly. His small hands balled into fists at his sides, and he walked stiffly over to his mother's side of the bed with his father's hands guiding him from behind.

Norman gave him an encouraging pat on the shoulder, before taking a seat in the chair he had been in before getting up.

"C-Can Mom hear me?" Eric whispered, his voice warbling.

"I don't know, but it doesn't hurt to try."

Slowly, the boy reached up, and with trembling fingers he grasped his mother's hand. Her skin was cool to the touch and made him give a small sniffle.

"M-Mom, I … I want you to wake up, please. I made a mess earlier, but Fin helped me clean it, but I'm sorry anyway. I scared Farrah, but I already apologized, I swear." Eric wiped his nose using the back of his sleeve before he moved closer to his mother. "I named my sister; I think you'll like it too. I named her—"

"That's enough, Eric." Norman's stern voice made the boy jump.

Bending down and planting a hasty kiss on his mother's forehead, the prince paused by her ear and whispered something that the king wasn't able to hear.

Then, he stepped back, and said, "I love you, Mom. Please come back soon."

When the boy turned back to his father, his eyes filled with tears and his lip quivering, he threw his arms around him. The father and son shared a long embrace, each of them unable to properly say what they were both thinking and feeling in that moment.

When the time came for the king to finally escort his son from the room, Eric turned to him, his face tearstained.

"Alina should get to say goodbye, too."

Norman froze and his insides clenched painfully.

"Is that what you named …"

"My sister?" Eric supplied helpfully. "Yes. That's what mom's mom was called, right?"

Norman nodded slowly; unknowingly, his hand clamped down a little too tightly on his son's shoulder as he steered him to the door. Once the guards had taken charge of the prince again, the king returned to the room. His eyes cast to the floor as a deafening white noise blared in his head.

"Your Majesty?"

Turning wearily, the monarch saw Katelyn Ashowan sitting up slowly; the woman's drawn face was somber. For a moment he feared she was about to tell him that he'd missed Ainsley's last breath.

"What is it?"

"The princess should meet her mother. It might be her only chance." The healer's voice was quiet.

Norman felt anger surge in him. He knew there were matters beyond anyone's control, but Katelyn Ashowan was supposed to save everyone …

"Later," he answered tersely.

Surprisingly, the healer didn't even bat an eye. There was a calm stoniness to her that showed that, beneath her bubbly personality, lay a seasoned physician …

One who had dealt with death and the turmoil it wreaked more times than she could count.

"Your Majesty," Katelyn began speaking again, but Norman exploded before she could finish her thought.

"No! There is no reason to bring her in here! We continue on. Besides, she will not remember the exchange. There is no reason to—"

"When she is older, you will see just how important it is," Katelyn cut in, her voice quiet yet firm.

The king shook his head, his hazel eyes beginning to glare at the witch.

"No. I have said it is not what matters right now. You will perform the duties I have asked of you without your unsolicited opinion," he snapped, stepping closer to the bed where she sat, still looking completely unflappable.

"Say the queen does awaken. What will her first question be?" Kate asked evenly, her eyes filled with knowingness.

Norman's face drained of what little color it had left.

He knew exactly what Ainsley would ask.

She would want to know how their daughter was …

And he wouldn't be able to answer.

Then, she would look at him in such a way that would bring all sense back to him and he would immediately …

"I don't want her here." The monarch's voice was hoarse, and the steeliness in his eyes faltered.

Katelyn stared at him wisely for several more moments before then turning her attention back to the queen's sleeping form. She didn't say a word as she resumed her position with her hands extended over the ruler, and once again bolstered the golden glow around her.

"If I … If I see her …" Norman's voice cracked, and it broke off as he tried to speak.

Reaching out with shaking hands, he touched his wife's feet that were covered by their quilt. Her large feet that had trodden on his toes more times than he could count, and each time he'd tease her … make her laugh until he'd hear her snort …

"If I see our daughter, I'm frightened that I will fall in love with her, and that I …" Norman blinked and turned his gaze to the chamber window, unable to say the words.

"That you won't regret how having her meant losing the queen?"

Norman nodded. Unable to speak past the lump in his throat for several painful moments.

"Ainsley doesn't deserve to die alone. Or for me to think even for a second that her death was …"

Giving his head a violent shake after a long quiet moment, the monarch stalked over once more to the chamber door, flung it open, and barked to the nearest guard that he was to fetch the princess.

When he returned to the foot of the bed, he was visibly shaking, but he was staring with great intensity at Ainsley's face. His own features were a mask of stoicism.

Norman thought his heartbeat could be heard around the room, but Katelyn said nothing as she continued weaving her magic over his wife.

So consumed in his own mind and emotions in the short span of time that felt like years, the king jumped at the sound of the door latch being lifted.

He immediately strode over to the window, his back facing the room as Physician Durand stepped in with a pile of blankets in his arms. Buried deep within their softness was the princess who was once again awake and staring around herself, though her eyes were struggling to focus on anything.

After closing the door behind himself and stepping farther into the room, Physician Durand shared a meaningful nod with Katelyn before turning to the king.

"You summoned the princess, Your Majesty?"

"Yes, show her Ainsley's face, then be gone."

"Sire, perhaps you can rest the princess on the queen. She has been listening to Her Majesty's heartbeat for many months now and it might—" Physician Durand started patiently.

"Do whatever you deem fit," Norman's thin grasp of his emotions was quickly slipping.

"Your Majesty, could you please take the princess and position her? Physician Durand's arthritis is most likely already hurting him," Katelyn suggested softly.

"I don't believe that for a second, but if you both are going to try and convince me of more nonsense, I'll do it," the king snapped while turning around and striding over to the physician who was more than a little taken aback by the harshness of his tone.

Without looking down, the king scooped his daughter up into his arms. The movement was so swift, however, that he managed to startle her into crying.

Her weak cries followed by an immediate cough made Norman freeze. All pain and fury in his face disappeared in an instant as he laid eyes on his daughter for the first time.

The tension visibly left his shoulders, and instead he began gently rocking the child to try and soothe her on instinct.

"She coughed; is she alright?" His voice had softened considerably, and the princess's cries immediately faded away as she suddenly turned toward the sound of his voice.

"The lungs are underdeveloped when a child is born so early, but thus far she seems to be in otherwise good health," Physician Durand explained kindly.

Norman unconsciously moved closer to Ainsley's bedside, his gaze fixed on the baby in his arms as she began to squirm.

"She's much smaller than Eric was when he was born." Norman's voice was gaining a small croak.

Despite her eyes being unable to focus, the princess stilled once again when he spoke.

"She recognizes your voice," Katelyn observed with a small smile.

Norman's cheek began to quake as he continued staring down at his daughter who had pulled her arm free of the blankets and was experimenting with making a fist.

Reaching with a trembling hand, Norman planted his thumb in the infant's palm and watched as the tiny fingers failed to encircle it.

His heart leapt to his throat, and then …

Then, he succumbed to the tears he had kept at bay for far too long.

Staring down into his daughter's face, Norman sobbed, and, slowly, he planted a watery kiss on her forehead, his beard tickling her face.

As he knelt down beside the bed, he carefully moved the princess to his wife's chest. He set her small head so that her tiny ear was pressed close to Ainsley's heart, and he watched through his tears, his hand still resting on her small back, as the baby once again stilled and let out a contented sigh.

"It's our girl, Ainsley," he whispered as he then reached and stroked away the hair from the queen's forehead.

The room was quiet as Norman wept and he gently held his wife and daughter, unable to stop the flood of love and sorrow that rushed through him.

He gazed at them for as long as he could, trying to burn the image into his brain for the rest of his life.

"Eric named her after your mum. I think we'll keep it, yeah? Alina. Maybe Lina for short, hm?" he asked brokenly as he then began rubbing soothing circles on the baby's back. "Don't worry, right now her feet look perfectly small." Norman tried to laugh but failed. Instead, he contented himself with watching Alina's eyes move over him, and her fingers brush against Ainsley's exposed skin.

As much as everyone in the room wished they could hold on to the moment forever, the baby began to fuss.

Her head had begun turning to try and find a source of food.

Norman didn't move at first, his sobs growing worse as he resisted taking back his daughter.

Dissatisfied and hungry, Alina began to cry, and he knew he couldn't wait much longer. Norman lifted Ainsley's hand, kissed it, then gently picked up his daughter.

Leaning his forehead against hers, listening to her cry, Norman finally turned to Katelyn who was staring intently at the queen.

"If you can't go on much longer, Mrs. Ashowan, it's alright," he whispered defeatedly as his daughter continued to flail about in his arms.

Katelyn didn't say anything for a moment, but when she did turn to him, her face was completely serene before saying: "I don't need to continue."

Norman's eyes dropped to Ainsley's face, and he watched with bated breath, as her eyebrows twitched ever so slightly into a frown, and her brown eyes then, ever so slowly, opened.

CHAPTER 32
LATE-NIGHT TALKS

As Captain Antonio approached the king and queen's bedchamber, his face grim, he refused to meet anyone's eyes as they watched him pass. Nobles whispered behind their hands, and servants gave him a wide berth as though fearful that he would somehow place blame on them for Baron Gauva's actions. He was so intent on not looking at anyone directly that when he finally reached his destination, he failed to notice the bright smiles the guards wore.

"Please tell His Majesty I have arrived," Captain Antonio ordered while keeping his one eye fixed on the grain of the door in front of him. He had to be strong. If the queen lay dead, there was no telling how broken Norman would be ...

When the guard disappeared into the shadowy room, the captain could hear the faint sound of sobbing, and immediately he found himself fighting off the surge of warmth in his eye.

"You may enter, Antonio," the king's voice called out quietly.

Stepping over the threshold and closing the door behind himself, Antonio at long last moved his gaze to where the queen lay. Knowing it would be far crueler to delay the inevitable.

Instead of the peacefully arranged corpse of the woman he had come to love as a niece, Antonio instead found himself staring at Norman

239

kneeling by the bedside holding Ainsley's hand, his face tearstained as she gazed at him wearily …

She was smiling.

Alive, and smiling.

Antonio's composure failed and the knot of emotion in his chest vanished so quickly that he couldn't help but burst out saying, "Oh, thank the Gods."

Norman smiled at his friend and gestured Antonio closer.

"I was hoping to lie beside my wife and rest with her; however, we didn't wish to disturb Mrs. Ashowan. Given that her son is currently … busy, I gathered you were the next best person for the job."

Antonio's eye turned to Katelyn's sleeping form, and immediately he felt his joy dim.

She looked near death herself … She had clearly pushed herself for the sake of the queen.

"She can rest for as long as she needs in Lady Jenoure's former chamber. See to it that Ruby takes care of her as though she were royalty. We owe her Ainsley's and Alina's lives."

Captain Antonio's eyebrows shot up. "Alina is the new princess's name?"

"It is. Eric thought of it, and we feel it suits her. Though we will most likely call her Lina for short."

"Yes, knowing Norman, he will be mixing up her name and my own horribly if we don't give him a bit of respite," Ainsley teased, her smile warming the captain's heart.

"Aye. A good name." Ainsley and Norman were unable to keep their eyes off each other as Norman bent his head and planted a gentle kiss on the back of her hand.

Wanting to give the reunited couple their privacy, the captain moved toward the side of the bed where Katelyn lay. As he scooped her carefully into his arms, she didn't stir even once as she was shifted from the soft bed into Antonio's firm arms.

Cradled against his chest, Katelyn felt small and vulnerable to him. Even her skin felt cool to the touch, and the captain could feel his mind begin to leap into action on ordering her a bath and hot meal the moment she awoke.

Bowing his head slightly, he then wordlessly took his leave of the royal couple.

When he exited the chamber, he noticed the guards saluting Katelyn despite her not being conscious. As he moved the short distance to Lady

Jenoure's former room, he passed Physician Durand who also bowed to the fragile woman in his arms.

Antonio continued walking silently, when he felt Katelyn begin to stir, and so he glanced down briefly into her drawn face in time to see her eyes open with obvious difficulty. She blinked in confusion before lifting her face to him, and the captain immediately felt his heart skip a beat.

"What's … happening?" the healer asked faintly

"You're to take a well-deserved rest."

"Oh … but … why are you carrying me?" Katelyn attempted to look around herself but was obviously too weak to do so properly.

"Because you deserve to be treated as royalty for what you have done," Antonio explained quietly as he hesitated before their destination.

Clutching her ever so slightly closer to himself Antonio maneuvered her so that he could open the door with one hand quickly before hastily returning his hold around her back.

"I just … did my … duty…" Katelyn protested softly before once again falling into a deep sleep.

Chuckling to himself, Antonio approached the made bed and laid her down upon its satiny surface.

Working with the utmost care, he tucked Katelyn under the cover and gently brushed the stray strands of hair from her face. He smiled down at the woman who had made him, for the first time in decades, feel things he believed he had no right to feel any longer.

The very first night she had met him, he had been irritable and weary. He had not been in any mood for Sir Taylor's antics, but when Katelyn had welcomed him in and they'd all played simple drinking games … he found himself more and more intrigued by her mind.

Their first day courting she had asked why he had worn a hat that covered his eyepatch, and when Antonio answered that it was because most people feared him, she laughed and said: "I've met men who should be feared, but, Captain, you are quite obviously one to be loved. Take off that silly thing; it's far too hot out to wear that. While you aren't fearsome to me, if you start to smell I am not going to hold my tongue."

Moving back to the corridor, Antonio flagged down the nearest passing maid and gave her his orders for Katelyn's treatment upon awaking.

He then returned to her bedside, the magnetic pull she seemed to share with him as strong as ever.

"I'd like to be honest with you, Katelyn. You are a fine woman. A strong woman. However, I must confess that I am out of practice with all of this.

It is strange how easy and wonderful it is to be with you … my last wife I had to go through brutal training for seven years before I could marry her, you see. But she was worth it. Every second … sorry. I don't mean to talk about her excessively. I suppose I just mean that I don't quite know what I'm doing. Especially with you being a witch and *especially* with Finlay being your son. I've gone drinking with the man; he is … well, more people should be frightened of him, that's for certain." Antonio took a moment and cleared his throat.

"What I am trying to say … well … I would like to have however many days I have left in this life with you. This relationship has moved quickly, but I cannot fathom a better way to spend the rest of my time. I knew the day I met my first wife, and I knew the night I met you."

Letting out a long breath, Antonio turned toward the chamber door. He was keenly aware of his racing heart.

"Once you have recovered, and perhaps once I speak about this with Finlay, I would like to ask you a question. For now, I just want to practice."

Stiffly, he made it to the chamber door, then had the brilliant idea of how to get out of a truly difficult conversation later on. Dropping his voice so that it could barely be heard, Antonio gave her one final message.

"Oh, I locked Finlay up in the dungeon for the night. For political reasons. I'll see you when you—"

"FIN IS WHERE?!" Katelyn suddenly shot up out of her sleep, her bloodshot eyes homed in on the captain who had leapt back against the door in shock.

His mind worked furiously to try and think of a reasonable excuse for having imprisoned her son, while also beginning to rethink which of the Ashowans he should truly fear in that moment.

"I don't give a damn if it's for politics or for a prank, you will release my son this instant!" Katelyn was wielding a long thin finger in Antonio's face.

"He was fine with the plan! Did you ever stop and think about whether or not he might *want* to be more involved in more respectable positions in the future?" Antonio fired back while lifting his hands up to try and ward off any attack she might launch at him.

"That is for him to decide! He can choose how he may want to go about it as well—one that does not involve him being in a *cell*!" Despite Katelyn's haggard appearance, a small tinge of color entered her cheeks.

"I mean no offense when I say this, Kate, but Finlay is terrible in politics! He is too blunt to get anywhere on his own. I know it is tough to see, but I did this because I want to help him! I care about him, and … and you. I wouldn't do this to pull some childish prank. Can you not trust me on this matter?"

"Antonio, as lovely as you are, and as much as I've enjoyed our time together, I will not let you make these decisions for us! You have no right. He is *my* son, and I will see that he is protected and that he is not jerked around by those in a position of power!"

The captain's hands dropped, and he fixed Katelyn with an even, calm stare.

"I am not like Aidan, Kate. I told Fin my plan, and I'll have you know, I was legally within my rights to have him locked up. He attacked a knight who was already in the process of being arrested. This will help him in the long run. Sometimes in life you can't just be about defense. Sometimes you need to take offensive actions to come out ahead."

Katelyn squared her shoulders and crossed her arms over her chest, and the military man could see her working all too quickly to regain composure of her emotions. He didn't want to fight her … he just wanted to take care of her. Gods knew she deserved to be taken care of and perhaps spoiled more than a little.

"Your son is a grown man. He did not openly object to my idea. Ask him yourself in the morning. For now, you need to get in that bed and go to sleep." He loomed over her, his eyebrow raised sternly.

"Oh, is that what you are *ordering* me to do? *Because you are the authority on everyone today*?" she snapped angrily.

"Yes. Because you are sleep deprived, starving, and in desperate need of a bath. Fin can last one more night then take his own well-deserved rest." As Antonio took a step forward with his head tilted, his gaze sharpened. "Now, are you going to get back in that bed on your own two legs, or am I going to have to carry you back?"

Katelyn's hands moved to her hips, and her challenging expression faltered.

"I can move perfectly fine on my own, and I need no strong-arming into doing anything!" While Kate tried to keep her tone imperious, there was a flicker of doubt across her face.

"I am glad to hear it, lass." Antonio folded his arms across his chest and waited expectantly.

"Well, are you just going to stand there, or are you going to go release my son! And I am no lass, I am old enough to be a grandmother!" Kate bit out while taking an unconscious step back.

The captain smiled. She wasn't reacting to him with fear, and that was something he had sincerely worried about when they'd eventually share a disagreement.

"Well, you're not *my* grandmother, and I am a good few years older than you. So, to me you're a lass. Now, I'll give you until I count to three before I put you in that bed myself, and I intend to make sure you stay there."

"This is absolutely preposterous, and you have yet to release Fin. I will not—"

"Three."

Hastily, the captain swept down and scooped Kate up in one fell swoop over his shoulder.

"HOW DARE YOU— ANTONIO! ABSOLUTELY NOT! NO! I AM NOT A BABE TO BE BURPED! IF YOU DO NOT PUT ME DOWN THIS MINUTE, I WILL NEVER MARRY YOU!"

Antonio froze, then with a short heft, he had Katelyn back in his arms cradled against his chest so that he could better see her face.

"I didn't know if you'd heard the whole thing," he admitted sheepishly.

Seeing the captain suddenly turn bashful, Katelyn found her irritation immediately dissolving.

"I did ... and I ... I mean ... You know I'm still married."

"I do. Which is why we will have to petition the king to dissolve the union as abandonment, or as a retroaction to Helmer's treatment of you and Finlay. Though the latter will be a far more grueling process."

Kate's lips pursed, and it was clear that a long list of emotions was bubbling up in her chest.

"We do not need to rush any ceremony, and I know that we never really talked of this ..." Slowly, Antonio set Katelyn down on the bed, then seated himself beside her.

"It has only been ... two weeks!" Kate burst out after taking a moment to properly count the days.

"Aye, but we are coming at this with some experience under our belts, lass." Antonio's blue eye twinkled.

"My son always comes first."

"I know. Though he might be gaining an extra family member to pester him— My own mother still lives."

Kate nodded. "I remember you mentioning her."

Antonio then turned so that he could face the witch fully, his knee coming to rest on the bed. "Have you told Finlay that you know of his father's coming?"

"I haven't. With any luck, the two now look nothing alike and I won't have to tell him. The last time they saw each other … well …" Katelyn shifted uncomfortably.

The captain hadn't told her Fin was already well aware of his father's pending arrival. He didn't need to get caught up in that mess … even if he *had* been the one to confess to her that Aidan Helmer was coming.

"You don't have to tell me if you don't feel up to it," Antonio added softly.

"I'm ashamed of who I was back then. That I let that man abuse my son that way. All because I kept reasoning to myself that, because I was healing Fin and myself, it wasn't as terrible as it could have been. As though physical scars were the worst part, and because Aidan wasn't home often. I didn't believe we would be able to make ends meet if it were just Finlay and myself, even though in truth I was better off relying on my own talents than trying to support his movements …" Kate had begun gently rubbing her thumb over the blankets idly. "It feels so much bigger than yourself when you are in that kind of marriage. It wasn't even me that made him leave in the end."

Antonio frowned. "Who was it?"

"Fin. He had never shown any magical abilities for years, and then one day … he had enough. Blasted his father clear off the island."

The captain knew better than to comment how that feat was both impressive and frightening. Instead, he took Katelyn's hands in his own and gently brushed his thumb against the back of her knuckles.

"I won't try to take away your guilt because that isn't for me to do, but … I can say that you have saved countless lives since that day. Your son grew up well, Kate. He *is* grown up now, though, and it is okay to once again think about what you may want for yourself. So … I won't need you to answer my proposal today, or even tomorrow. Remember, I had presumed you were asleep," Antonio noted with a subtle teasing tone. "But do think about it."

She gave a small nod while furrowing her brow.

Satisfied with that response, Antonio began to wordlessly tuck Katelyn back into the bed, a small smile on his face as he worked.

Once finished, he straightened and headed back to the door. Before making his exit he turned back to the witch and said, "A bath will be brought up for you once you are awake, along with a hot meal. Though sadly it will be the cooking of the kitchen aides."

"Whose fault is that I wonder?" Kate muttered darkly.

Antonio chuckled. "Sleep well, lass."

Staring at the armor plate that spanned his back, the healer's eyes darted to Antonio's hand on the handle of the door, and suddenly she heard herself call out.

"Antonio would you ... would you stay?"

Turning and shooting her a dubious look, the captain didn't dare assume anything for a moment.

"To sleep!" she insisted while blushing like a young maiden.

Chuckling again, Antonio made his way back to the bed and began removing his armor quietly.

Once the task was completed, he slowly clambered into the bed and lay with his hands folded atop his belly. Once he was resting beside her, Kate nestled down into the covers and closed her eyes. Somehow, despite having enough on her mind to fill several books, she fell asleep almost instantly. Though her final thoughts did circle the notion that, perhaps being married again ... if it were to someone like Antonio ... it could be ... well ... wonderful.

With her mind and her heart for once working slowly in the same direction, the one thought that delayed her sleep, albeit for a moment, was: *Gods, we may want to wait a little while before telling Fin ... perhaps a week or two after he gets out of the dungeon.*

CHAPTER 33
CAREFUL CALCULATIONS

"You. Explain," Fin demanded with narrowed eyes.

Kraken rolled around in the grime of the cell a few more times for good measure before finally meeting his gaze.

"*I already explained that there wasn't enough time to include you in my plan with the fire,*" Kraken chirped impatiently.

"No. About there being other traitors in Austice."

"*Well, those enemy men didn't just appear. Boats brought them. People knew where to hide them. You need to find the ring cat. That place with all the strong-smelling women ... some of the men escaped there.*"

"You mean Madam Mathilda's establishment?"

"*I don't bother with human names. Your mate has been searching for all of these things on her own. She is a tiresome one to keep an eye on, let me tell you ...*"

"Is she safe?" Fin demanded, alarmed.

"*As safe as she can be. My new position of authority under Fat Tony has afforded me some perks ... I must compliment your choice of mate if I am purfectly honest. She is as quiet and clever as some talented cats I know. Doesn't lose her whiskers under pressure.*"

Fin rubbed the back of his neck while frowning. Thanks to Kraken he knew what Annika was up to, but it was dangerous … She was trying to find out who was associated with helping the invaders all on her own.

He felt more than a little angry that she couldn't confide the risky work she was undertaking, but also recognized the cost of treason … particularly when the prime example of that little betrayal was bemoaning his fortune mere feet away.

"Wait, who is Fat Tony?"

"The leader of one of the cat gangs of Austice. Don't worry, he is a reasonable cat compared to some."

"Why are you in a gang, though?"

"To ensure your objectives are met."

"What objectives?"

The feline let out a small breath that could've been interpreted as a sigh.

"A safe and happy home, witch. When we bonded, I knew this about you instantly."

Fin blanched.

He never would've thought such an abstract notion could be understood by a cat.

Then again, the familiar wasn't an ordinary cat …

"What is it *you* want, Kraken?"

The familiar blinked up at him, then stood and sauntered over to Fin, his tail swishing with every step.

"I want to sleep beside you in a warm soft bed and be fed delicious food without any worry. I want you to be happy, because you are annoyingly difficult to please. What I have discovered in my short time with you is that to help you, I must be the best I can be."

Fin blinked in awe.

He had always known familiars were especially attuned to their owners, but to *hear* one's love and wish for one's well-being (albeit expressed quite dryly) was stunning.

"Well … thank you."

"Oyy! Ashowan! As a witch, are you able to make any wench you bed more beautiful? I hear some witches can do that!" one of the knights sharing a cell with Lord Gauva called out suddenly.

Fin sighed; he had blocked all sound from leaving his cell while speaking with Kraken, but he immediately regretted not preventing sound from coming in. Lifting the barrier all together, he replied, "No, I can't. Good night."

"So ... the baron said you could fold clothes, and we all saw, or rather felt the shield thing ... but ... why aren't witches, you know ... ruling everything?"

Fin closed his eyes and let out a small breath. He knew it wasn't a bad question, but it had been a long day, and he didn't particularly feel like talking with the men who had tried to hurt his mother.

"We aren't here to rule, we are here to maintain balance between humans and nature. To ensure you do not forget what you are a part of."

"Ah ... but ... how does you being a— Sorry, what was it?" The knight addressed someone else in the cell. It was too dark to tell who given the late hour.

"A house witch," came the bitter reply from Lord Gauva.

"Yeah. How does you being a 'house witch' bring us closer to nature?"

Fin opened his mouth to give a churlish retort, then realized that once again the man was asking a good question.

"Well, what is important in life? Respecting what the earth gives us, and the power it holds, but also ... what that balance brings us. My powers show how to harmonize all things. Food from the earth, fire for the hearth, breath of air, and nourishing life-sustaining water. A good home harnesses all of these."

"Why the shield then?!" Lord Gauva barked.

"A home is also supposed to be safe," Fin growled in response.

The dungeon fell quiet as the men all heeded his words. The redhead leaned against the damp stone wall and closed his eyes, knowing that there wasn't any chance he would be able to sleep peacefully.

"Are you going to help us win against Troivack?" The somber voice of Baron Gauva resonated against the stones.

"No."

Fin cracked his eyes open slowly.

"But I'm going to cook one hell of a dinner for everyone when we do."

The men once again fell silent, and at last, it seemed it was for good. Fin closed his eyes and felt Kraken clamber up into his lap. The silky top of his head pressed into his limp hand expectantly.

With a small yawn, the witch began scratching gently under the familiar's chin and felt the satisfying purr rumble in Kraken's belly. At least one of them didn't mind being stuck in a cell for the night ...

~~~~~~~

Norman stared at the wilted lettuce on his plate dejectedly, then lifted his gaze to his goblet of wine and opted to take another hearty gulp of that instead.

"Kevin, remind me why you were so happy about Finlay Ashowan being locked up again?" Norman asked his assistant while pushing what he guessed was meant to be salad farther away from himself.

Kevin Howard regarded his own plate that had the green … ish … vegetables, and then looked over to the white … brown pile of mush that could have been potatoes? Or turnips …

"I … I still stand by my earlier sentiment. A night where we know where he is and he isn't causing trouble is worth it!" Despite the vehemence in the man's voice, there was an air of unease about him.

"Kevin, I won't be having anyone speak ill of the Ashowans today. I owe him and his mother everything. I think I should look into having him knighted at the very least," Norman warned his assistant sternly before taking another goblet of wine and looking at the pile of paperwork that had grown significantly over the days he had been absent from meetings and daily tasks.

"I know, Your Majesty. I don't mean to … disparage the man … not entirely," Mr. Howard added on belatedly when Norman shot him a wry expression over the rim of his goblet. "It's just whenever he goes to *do* anything it becomes a headache."

Norman sighed and shook his head.

He was exhausted and ready to crawl into bed beside his wife—even though there was a pillow barrier currently built down half of their bed so as to prevent Ainsley from accidentally moving excessively in her sleep and disturbing her stitches.

However, the duty of a king never stopped. Not really …

"So we have received word that Duke Cowan is sending what percentage of his knights?"

"Thirty-five percent, sire. I've already submitted his inventory and stock report to Lord Fuks to collaborate with the other houses that have submitted their contributions to the war. It's been difficult to organize, between arresting the Troivackians we've already found and utilizing some of the wartime supplies and transportation in order to imprison them. The main contributors are Baron Taylor, Baron Haversher, Marquis Sibell, and surprisingly, Duke Rhodes."

Norman's upper lip curled. "Duke Rhodes is going to use this to drag matters out and try and ask for favors later."

"Without a doubt," Mr. Howard agreed.

With a sigh, Norman rubbed his forehead and slumped forward in his seat.

"By your estimation, how long do you think we can fund the war without raising taxes?"

"Tough to say … the Troivackians are attacking because their food reserves and farmlands are dwindling dangerously. If we manage to protect our supplies well, we might be able to outlast them, but who knows if they've been smuggling food back through the soldiers that we've discovered. None of them have been forthcoming with details, or they only know a very small amount of the grander plan. Perhaps a year, if we manage things well."

Norman nodded somberly; he was about to start asking for more exact numbers when a knock rang out in his otherwise quiet study.

"Your Majesty, Lord Ryu of Zinfera is here with news from the Zinferan emperor!" the guard outside the door called in.

Smiling wearily at Mr. Howard, who understood the king's sentiment without a word, the king replied, "Send him in!"

Lord Jiho Ryu stepped into the office looking every bit as dignified as he did at all hours of the day.

Bowing to the Daxarian king, he straightened, his face unreadable.

"Your Majesty, congratulations on the birth of the princess. My emperor also sends his regards, and we both are relieved to hear of the queen's survival."

Norman acknowledged the formality with a single bob of his head and waited for the important piece of news that could determine their likelihood of survival in the pending war …

"The emperor is, or *was*, rather dissatisfied with learning that Lord Nam would not in fact be inheriting a dukedom," Jiho began slowly.

"Was?" the king asked impatiently.

"I informed the emperor that you had learned of the multiple debts and loans Lord Nam had to his name, and how it would be almost completely eradicated by Lady Marigold's dowry. I expressed that while you were apologetic that he should lose the title, you believe that pertaining to Lord Nam in particular the deal is a fair one."

Neither the king nor Mr. Howard bothered trying to goad the man to speak faster; Norman could sense that the most important point was coming.

"I also mentioned that I would be given the title of baron here in Daxaria, and my lands here would be subject to taxes in both kingdoms for the next ten years. The emperor agreed that this was a fair compromise, and that our two kingdoms have formed an acceptable bond."

Norman straightened in his chair, his finger tapping his armrest in silence for several long minutes.

Then, a smile slowly stretched across his face.

"I must confess, Jiho … I see why your emperor values you so. You've offered a wonderful compromise, and I just so happen to have a baron house that has had its family members recently stripped of any right to its lands and assets. How do you like the title Baron Gauva?"

Lord Ryu smiled politely and bowed. "It would be my honor, Your Majesty. I understand you may wish to withhold bestowing the title to me publicly until after the emperor's troops arrive."

"You are wise indeed. I will have the official transfer of title and ownership drawn up and sent to the emperor as evidence of the deal before the end of the week."

Mr. Howard's face paled, but he scribbled down the note dutifully, though he eyed the large stack of papers before him with his eyes ever so slightly glazed.

"Thank you again for your skillful handling of the situation, and a good night to you, Lord Ryu."

The Zinferan bowed and left the king and his assistant, his footfalls silent as he strode out the door.

Norman stared after him with a smile still on his face.

"Your Majesty, I was unaware you had offered him a barony." The stress in Mr. Howard's was clear enough that Norman moved his hazel eyes to lock eyes with the man.

"That's because I didn't. All Lord Ryu and I agreed upon was that I was willing to give the happy couple an annual stipend for the next ten years, and to bring to the emperor's attention that I knew of Lord Nam's … questionable decisions."

"So you're saying … Lord Ryu interjected himself into the deal to benefit?" Mr. Howard asked indignantly while turning to stare at the closed door as though he meant to summon the Zinferan lord back.

"Yes, though this benefits everyone as well as gets Lady Marigold and Lord Nam out of my hair. Furthermore, he has firmed up loyalty with both the emperor and myself without entangling Lady Jenoure. This also saves me having to find someone for Baron Gauva's title and wealth who is loyal and can handle the responsibility. It's a solution that appeases multiple people and we have a baron who will not abuse his power as he is attending to matters in the Zinferan court. He most likely will acquiesce to leaving his knights at my disposal as well. Yes, Lord Ryu is … impressive. Without a doubt."

"Wouldn't it have been just as easy to have him marry Lady Jenoure?" Mr. Howard grumbled as he snatched another document to begin reviewing.

"Well … perhaps. However, the Zinferan emperor benefits from this deal more financially, and … I benefit in the most important way."

Mr. Howard's blue eyes snapped up with a frown, his confusion clear.

"My wife doesn't lose her best friend and confidante." Norman leaned back in his chair, his fingers laced over his belly.

While Mr. Howard was caught between openly rolling his eyes at his king's obvious adoration of his wife and maintaining his respectful air, Norman didn't pay him any heed.

In truth, the second-biggest asset to the new arrangement was that Lady Jenoure could continue being the source of underground information and carrying out secretive missions without risking a foreign husband learning of Norman's moves. Or worse yet, controlling Annika's activities unnecessarily and complicating matters.

No. Lady Jenoure was by far a greater vassal single, and free to be exactly as she was.

Thankfully, she didn't seem all that interested in marrying again anyway …

CHAPTER 34
GROUP THERAPY

The cell door squeaked open as honeyed sunshine spilled through the narrow window opening high on the cell wall a certain redheaded witch was leaning against.

Cracking open his eyes that felt as though they were weighted down with sandbags, Fin glanced up to see instead of the captain, a knight he didn't recognize accompanied by Mr. Howard.

The assistant looked smugly down at Fin's disheveled self and watched as the witch stood with a grunt.

"Have a pleasant evening?" Mr. Howard asked, looking a little too delighted.

"I heard from one of the knights the queen awoke," Fin commented instead with a small smile.

The assistant's pleased expression faded to one of sincere relief. "Yes ... alive and well thankfully."

"Where's the captain?" Fin asked while rotating his shoulder to try and ease some of the stiffness from it.

At this, Mr. Howard froze.

"It would seem ... your mother didn't take kindly to you being incarcerated. He has overslept as a result."

Fin grinned wryly and the assistant waved him forward while rolling his eyes.

"Come on. We are to meet with His Majesty and the others this morning."

Fin raised a quizzical eyebrow but didn't receive any more of an explanation as they made the long journey up to the council room.

"Any chance I could get some food at this meeting?" the redhead asked while attempting to rub the kinks out from the back of his neck.

"There is food, but your assistants made it."

Wincing visibly, Fin didn't say anything in response.

At long last they reached the council room, and upon entering Fin noticed immediately that the king looked like his regular self again, and everyone else in the room looked jubilant. There were mysterious baked goods that were strange in color in the middle of the table, but Fin still grabbed one nonetheless as his stomach rumbled loudly.

Captain Antonio pointedly looked away from Fin, while Lord Fuks raised a chalice to him, and Mage Lee smirked. Trying to busy himself, Fin attempted to bite into the food in his hand and nearly chipped a tooth. He opted to carefully set the item back down on the table with the utmost care.

"Welcome back, Mr. Ashowan. I apologize for your time spent in the cell," Norman began as he also raised his goblet to the witch.

"I understand, Your Majesty. Did my incarceration rack up support like we'd hoped?" Fin's eyes were fixed on Captain Antonio's profile as the man continued to avoid meeting his gaze.

"Well, the women nobility are certainly in an uproar on your behalf. As are the maids … Their husbands are intimidated into agreeing … is how we're interpreting it," Mr. Howard explained in a businesslike tone as he finished dipping his quill in ink to begin his note-taking.

"On that note, I am sorry to hear that your courtship with Lady Jenoure's maid suffered," the king added sincerely.

Fin's cheeks turned crimson, but before he had a chance to say anything Mage Lee was upon him.

"What?! You two were such a lovely couple! A wedding between the two of you would have been such fun … perhaps she reacted to your arrest hastily. If you go now and—"

"No, no. It's alright. I'm not sure we were well suited," Fin interjected desperately while Norman tried to hide his smile.

"Ah, I am sorry to rub salt in the wound, Fin. Mage Lee has a deep love of weddings …" the king explained with a bemused glance toward Lee.

"Don't worry about it, Your Majesty. If we could carry on with the meeting, though, I wouldn't mind seeking out a bath soon." Fin bowed his head to the king, hoping that he didn't sound too demanding.

"Ah, yes. We have much to discuss in light of recent events …" Norman straightened in his chair, the twinkle in his eye dimming slightly as more serious matters entered his mind.

"Mr. Ashowan, your father's vessel experienced some poor weather, and so he is expected to arrive even later than originally planned."

Fin's expression remained blank, and so the monarch plunged on, not wanting to dwell on the unpleasantness.

"We have negotiated with Sorlia merchants to have the Troivackian soldiers that have been discovered boarded in secret onto their boats and set out to sea. We will keep them as far from shore for as long as possible while the war carries on in hopes that this helps our cause. As of now, we have discovered just over two thousand men in total thanks to a handful cracking under our interrogations; however, that is not quite half of our estimated numbers."

Everyone nodded while frowning.

"I received word during my search that there are Troivackian allies amongst the merchants and … brothels of Austice that should be investigated more closely." Fin announced this while tactfully omitting that Kraken was his informant …

Mage Lee straightened in his seat. "So *that's* what you were doing in Madam Mathilda's! Looking for the Troivackians!"

All eyes turned to the mage.

"How is it you knew Fin was inside a brothel, Lee?" Mr. Howard asked, a wild smile on his face.

"I had to offer him assistance when he was drugged and about to have his legs broken!" the mage burst out despite his cheeks reddening.

"Why was it they did these things, Mr. Ashowan? I was aware of an impromptu festival you started but this comes as news to me." Norman steepled his fingers while leaning forward with a small frown.

"I was asking to speak with the head of the brothel. Apparently that was grounds to have me treated as Mage Lee described. Which is all the more suspicious," Fin muttered, not liking the demonically happy assistant who was scribbling things down furiously.

"No shame in a healthy young man dabbling with the ladies!" Lord Fuks interjected loudly. "Though that might also have something to do with your sweetheart deciding she didn't want to marry you ..."

Fin groaned; the morning was proving to be one long headache ...

"Do you think you might be able to find out more about what this brothel madam was doing? I have already begun having merchant and noble ships searched, and their captains interrogated. However, we have yet to find anything here in Austice aside from those in the winter market, and not much luck from what I've heard in our other fair cities," Norman addressed Fin seriously.

"I can return to the city and try." Immediately the redhead wondered how quickly he might be able to return to Annika's estate and whether or not she'd be home ...

"Alright, well that settles those matters regarding Mr. Ashowan. Lord Fuks, you have the expense estimates for the war sorted now with the food ration plans? Wonderful. Now—" Norman began addressing his council but was cut off suddenly.

"Captain Antonio! Did you not wish to have a discussion with Fin?" Mage Lee interjected suddenly, his features a little too lively for the witch's liking.

Antonio looked as though he were going to punch the mage. Lee at least had the decency and good sense to tone down his obvious excitement after seeing the captain's blue eye turn sharp.

Fin faced the captain expectantly. He guessed that his mother had demanded that the military leader apologize for having her son locked up, and so he wanted to get the whole unpleasant ordeal dealt with.

Instead, the captain awkwardly cleared his throat and slowly turned to face the youngest member of the meeting.

"Mr. Ashowan ... Finlay ... Your mother and I had a lengthy discussion last evening. One that has made it a necessity for us to ... broach more sensitive topics." Antonio didn't risk taking his eyes off Fin, whose expression was flatter than the crepes he occasionally made for breakfast.

"I ... wanted a more private word; however, I was concerned about what your reaction could be. I hoped that having more people here for support might prove beneficial to—"

"Captain, please get on with it." Fin's tone was hollow. He really hated drawn-out apologies.

"Well, it seems I ... that is, your mother and ... I ..."

The fearsome warrior looked to Norman for help, only the king appeared to be all too happy to wait for him to figure out what to say.

"Well, your father is coming, and while he is here ... there has been mention of ... proceedings that might—"

"Antonio, are you really that scared of him?!" Mr. Howard burst out impatiently.

"I must agree with His Majesty's assistant. Gods, man, this is more torturous than the kitchen aides' recent attempts at cooking," Lord Fuks added exasperatedly.

The captain cleared his throat awkwardly and an uncharacteristic amount of red began to climb up his neck.

"No need to apologize about last night, Captain, if it's this difficult for you; think nothing of it." Fin sighed. It really wasn't worth drawing the meeting on. "I've had worse nights than last night in the cell, and—"

"Finlay, I proposed marriage to your mother. She, er ... She agreed."

The room fell silent.

All eyes were on Fin who went still as a statue. His eyes transfixed on the captain who didn't dare move, as though he were a fat mouse caught in front of a hungry and disgruntled ginger cat ...

"You've only been courting for a few weeks." The voice that left the witch's mouth was hoarse.

"Aye, but ... when you know you know. Especially at our age we don't like to squander what little time we have," the captain managed with difficulty.

"So ... you mentioned my father ... because you want my mother to file for an official dissolvement of their union," Fin started slowly.

"Yes."

"I plan on consenting when your mother formally submits the plea," Norman offered casually. "Then she is free to marry whenever and whom-ever she chooses."

Fin's eyes met with the king's, and for once the monarch decided to instead closely inspect his marvelous ceiling.

"Isn't it wonderful, Finlay? You were already probably going to be knighted sometime soon, and once you're officially related to the captain that will help with your standing amongst the other knights. His Majesty did offer Captain Antonio the title of baron and some land some years ago for his retirement, but given his background, he respectfully declined so as to not rock the boat with the other nobility," Mage Lee explained brightly.

"His background?" the witch asked faintly.

"Ah, yes … my mother is Daxarian, but my father was Troivackian. A nobleman. It is one of the reasons I go by my first name instead of my last name, which sounds distinctly Troivackian. My full name is Antonio Faucher. You cannot tell now that my hair is mostly white, but it used to be quite dark. I am also larger than most Daxarians you may have noticed … I am not titled currently, which is why I am free to choose myself a wife of any ranking. Though once we marry and perhaps win the war, I may consider His Majesty's offer again … if to offer a more comfortable life to the both of you …"

Fin slowly stood, silencing the captain who looked ready to end the awkward encounter by any means necessary. Bracing his hands on the table in front of him with his head bowed, Fin took a moment to quiet his thoughts.

"I will be going back to Austice for the next few days to see what I can learn from Madam Mathilda. Please inform my mother. Good day, Your Majesty, Lord Fuks, Mage Lee, Mr. Howard … Captain." Fin stood and bowed without meeting anyone's stare.

As he turned and marched to the door, Lord Fuks called out to him.

"Perhaps consider calling the captain 'father' in the near future! It could be a wonderful chance to bond and—"

Mr. Howard lunged for the elderly man and clamped his hand over his mouth hastily.

"No need to have us all killed," the assistant hissed under his breath.

Fin hesitated only for a moment after Lord Fuks's outburst, before continuing to exit the chamber and embarking on his new mission of fleeing the castle grounds as quickly as possible.

Norman turned toward the captain, his expression pleasantly mild. "Well … he didn't burn down the castle or blast you into the Alcide Sea."

"Nor did he curse you out or refuse to accept the marriage!" Mage Lee added optimistically.

"Honestly, I think you two will get along famously once the shock wears off." Lord Fuks waved his hand dismissively while taking a mouthful of water from his goblet.

"In hindsight, perhaps you should've waited until he'd had a bath and an ale following his time in his cell," Mr. Howard thought aloud, making everyone but the captain shoot him incredulous looks.

"Shall we discuss the budget report for the war, Lord Fuks?" the captain addressed the nobility quietly, his face and posture somehow both tense and relaxed at the same time.

After one last exchange of worried glances, the men delved into further details pertaining to the war with no further mention of the betrothal. The group wordlessly agreed to spare the captain from any more helpful advice for the rest of the morning.

Fin crossed the threshold of Annika's estate by midafternoon and was greeted with a flurry of maids insisting on drawing him a bath and setting out fresh clothes.

He didn't deny their hospitality but asked where their mistress could be found before answering the dozens of questions they put to him.

"Oh, she's in the solar with her maid!" Delores informed him hastily while trailing behind his labored steps. "You should rest, Mr. Wit! It has been a long day for you from the look of it, and you smell ... er ... *look* like you could use a washing before seeing her!"

Ignoring the poor woman's pleas, Fin continued on his path toward the solar, but he only made it halfway up the grand stairs. Annika suddenly appeared breathless at the top, her dark hair floating wildly about her, and the cream-colored muslin dress she wore fluttering in the great wind she had made from dashing down the corridor.

Fin looked up at her and felt as though he were seeing the sun for the very first time.

Breaking into a smile, Annika rushed down the steps and into his arms.

The moment Fin had her in his embrace, he felt everything bad that had happened over the past few days disappear, and instead he melted into the warmth of his lover. He breathed in the spicy smell of her hair that he had come to love so dearly and relished in how she melded to him as though she belonged there.

"Do you think you could stop worrying me to an early grave?" her muffled voice asked after a moment.

"I'll do what I can."

The rest of the staff around them were completely forgotten as the couple continued their embrace, though none of them minded. They were all more than a little happy to see their mistress and, hopefully, their future master perfectly healthy and safe together once more.

CHAPTER 35
WARDROBE WONDERS

Annika stared at Fin's sleeping profile, unable to keep the smile off her face. He had always risen just before dawn, regardless of how hard he had worked, or what time he had gone to sleep (unless drugged against his will …). Apparently after one night in a cell he was able to easily sleep well into the morning, and the viscountess couldn't deny the delight it gave her to sip her coffee and watch his defenseless slumber. It was fortunate that Fin had left a stash of the ground beans and had taught Raymond how to prepare them to his mistress's liking for moments such as these.

Annika had already submitted inquiries on purchasing the beans in bulk and acquiring the land that produced them back in Troivack, but such practical matters were far from her thoughts just then. Rather the lady was rather content staring at the man at her side.

Fin's slanted eyes, even when closed, were beautiful. His mouth that let out whatever he happened to be thinking while he was awake hung slack and motionless.

One blessing Annika had discovered during their recent times together, and that she was grateful for, was that Fin didn't snore.

He did sweat, though …

Casting an appraising eye at the damp pillow beneath his head, she then turned her gaze for the tenth time to the open balcony doors where a cool sea breeze drifted in.

Despite no one being conscious to witness it, Annika lifted her single shoulder in a shrug. She heard that men sweat while sleeping, but her previous husband had been quite elderly and he tended to be on the cold side …

After a few more moments of enjoying the smell of the fresh sea breeze and the peaceful warm coffee, Annika acquiesced that she needed to rise and resume her work. Even if she wanted to linger in bed with Fin and wait for him to awaken.

Slipping out of bed and onto her feet, she stepped over to her wardrobe and drew out a pale blue muslin dress with a long slit up her leg. Casting another glance at the wardrobe she had recently … *improved*, she closed the cedar doors and set to dressing herself.

Fin had expressed his preference for Troivack's summer styles for women on more than one occasion, and she couldn't fully explain the burst of glowing emotion she always received when she saw him staring her up and down helplessly. Pinning part of her ebony tresses back with a bejeweled clip, Annika picked up her coffee mug and left the room quietly.

Making her way to the solar she found Clara already seated with a fresh batch of missives carrying various reports from the Troivackian interrogations and short notes from her various sources around the continent.

"You should begin with this." The maid waved a scroll with the king's seal.

Stepping forward hastily, Annika snatched the parchment and unfurled it. Her eyes flew across the page and at the end she gradually collapsed onto her settee with a faint blush in her cheeks.

"What is it?"

"The queen is fine, and the princess is to be named Alina. Ainsley says she is excited for me to meet the new baby. I also need to begin investigating any merchant ships with ties to …" Annika let out a small sigh, unable to hold back her small smile. "Madam Mathilda."

Clara blinked several times. "Why is it you are blushing? Are you ill?"

Annika's cheeks deepened in their rosy hue.

"No, I just … I keep thinking how I already knew all this thanks to Fin."

Clara was unable to stop herself rolling her eyes to the ceiling. "Not that your newly discovered feminine side is without its charms, but perhaps we could put it to the side while working, hm?"

Annika's smile faded, and she gave the maid a flat look. "You're right, but mind your tone."

Clara's face became shuttered before she once again donned the dutiful maid persona.

"I will meet with Tooley down by the docks after the dinner hour to see which ships are most likely to be tied to the madam. By then most of the men will be well into their cups," Annika mused out loud before turning her gaze to the other reports in front of her.

It would be another long and stressful day, but ... perhaps she would get to see Finlay in the evening, and that knowledge alone made her immediate future just a little bit brighter.

That is, if he managed to keep out of trouble for once ...

Fin stared at the filled tub before him and glanced down at his bare chest.

The serving staff had to have brought it in and prepared it while he slept, but that also meant they'd all seen him in a state of undress. While the witch knew it was entirely common for them to do so for nobility, he couldn't help but feel more than mildly embarrassed.

Then again, Fin gave his underarm a courtesy sniff.

Annika most likely had ordered it.

The cell had not done him any favors, and so, pressing his embarrassment back in his mind, the redhead climbed into the warm soapy waters that surprisingly didn't have any of Annika's scent. Instead the staff had added smells such as sandalwood ... perhaps mint? It was quite refreshing actually.

After a good scrub, Fin felt the last of the grime fade from his person, and so he eagerly exited the most luxurious washing he'd ever been privy to.

Scanning the room for his clothes, he noticed that they weren't anywhere to be found. With a sigh he opened Annika's wardrobe, hoping to find something to cover himself enough to summon a footman or maid. He froze.

Inside Annika's wardrobe, beside her light Troivackian dresses and a couple of her more modest Daxarian garbs, were tunics. Men's tunics ... and trousers. All in his size. Fin blinked in astonishment.

When had she had any of this made? Why would she ...

Fin snatched the items he required without much thought and dressed himself quickly before backing toward one of the lavish chairs in front of the fireplace and collapsing into it numbly. Resting his forearms on his knees, his reality suddenly drenched him like a bucket of clear cool spring water.

He and Annika were going to get married.

He was going to be her husband … Which meant the servants in the house were either going to have a new master or were going to have to bid farewell to their mistress if he botched the entire thing.

"Gods … what have I …" Fin rubbed his face.

He knew he had anguished over this very thing long before he and Annika had dived into the whole affair, but then he had jumped in and hadn't really dealt with the actual events. Instead they had been caught up in their own bubble of happiness that was entirely removed from the real world. The serving staff never criticized, never questioned. His aides kept quiet and offered silent support, but one day … it wouldn't be so easy.

Fin glanced around the chamber and tried to imagine it being his. That the estate should be his home …

It didn't fit.

Somehow he still felt like a dalliance who shouldn't deign to even dream about laying claim to any of the riches surrounding him.

Only … all of it came with Annika, and he knew without a doubt she was his.

At the same time, however, he didn't even know what to call her! They were sharing a bed any chance they got, but they weren't technically courting or betrothed.

"Gods, we haven't talked at all." Fin stood suddenly. Urgency coursed through him as he pulled on his pair of boots; fortunately they were the ones he had been wearing all along.

Stalking from the room, he stopped the nearest maid and demanded where he could find Annika. The woman gave him a strange look, but told him she was in the solar, and so he made his way taking impossibly long strides.

As Fin burst unceremoniously into the room, Annika and Clara both jumped and turned in time to see him rounding the sofa. He then swiftly bent down and tossed Annika over his shoulder—not entirely unlike a sack of potatoes—and then proceeded to exit the room before either of the women could get a coherent word out.

Once Clara had recovered from the shock, however, she darted to the door and shouted at his back, "Good Gods, I just got her to stop smiling like an idiot!"

Sighing exasperatedly, the maid turned back to the room and stomped over to the crystal decanter that held Troivackian moonshine. Pouring herself a small cup she muttered, "Godsdamn lovers and their Godsdamn nonsense ..." Then she smiled a little before taking a practiced sip of the dangerous clear liquid.

Once Fin reached Annika's chamber, and placed her back on her feet, his hands went to his hips as he stared down at her with one of the most perplexing expressions she had ever seen on him, and his breath slightly labored.

"Fin, I know some women prefer a bit of rough handling prior to bedding someone, but I was in the middle of—"

"We need to talk. Now. Work and new crises keep cropping up, and—"

"Not to mention a certain fondness for sharing an enjoyment of—"

"—each other's company, yes." Fin blushed, unable to let Annika finish her sentence. "However, we have not talked of what we are doing to ensure our future together, nor have you told me anything about your days recently. We can't keep the world at bay forever. We need to know what we're making together; otherwise, I may be trying to make a roast while you try to make a pie and that just will not work."

Annika raised an eyebrow; her bewilderment didn't need to be expressed.

"What is your plan with us?" Fin threw up his hands.

Annika was still a little disoriented from being literally hauled out of her solar, but she wondered what was causing this sudden desperation ...

"Has something happened I am unaware of?" she asked slowly.

"I've been asking you this question for weeks."

"Yes, but you seem rather flustered—"

"There are tunics and trousers for me in your wardrobe," he cut in as though that answer cleared up any confusion.

"Do you ... not like the trousers and tunics?"

"No, it isn't that!" Fin rubbed his face in frustration. "Annika, what is your plan with us?"

Feeling more than a little put on the spot, and still baffled over the redhead's exasperation, she tried to find the best place to begin.

"Well ... as you may know, I set up Marigold and Lord Nam. Now that the queen is clear of death's carriage, I expect my plan to be in motion once more. Lord Ryu, I know, read my missives and has spoken with the king about forming a new deal with the emperor. He had some great suggestions, but I am waiting to hear how that went. Assuming it went well, though? It is guaranteed no matter what; I no longer have to marry. The next phase of the plan is regarding making our match acceptable."

"You already talked with Jiho?" Fin frowned at that bit of news.

"Yes, I would have told you, but you've been rather busy. Being arrested and all."

Fin gave her a wry look before gesturing for her to continue.

"Back to the second phase of my plan ... One option is I surrender two-thirds of my wealth as a penalty tax and just marry you without going through the proper channels. It would help fund the war and honestly save us both a lot of trouble, but that would mean I'd be so fallen from grace I wouldn't be allowed anywhere near politics or the queen."

"Not an option," Fin agreed firmly. "So what is the next possibility?"

"The other option is to get you knighted and place you in circumstances that let you shine. You could become a baron in a year if you happen to succeed in helping some of the war efforts I've mapped out. Once ennobled, I can help you anonymously here and there with some financial decisions with the land you'd be given with your title. After building a small fortune, we'd be able to marry. I'd fall out of the inner court circles for a while, but I'd be able to see Ainsley a few times a year should she travel nearby. Not ideal, but if we manage to rely on your growing relationship with His Majesty, Earl Fuks, and the captain—"

At the mention of Antonio Fin's eye twitched. Fortunately, Annika was too lost in her explanation to notice.

"—Along with your coven, you could prove a valuable consultant."

"There are more qualified witches to offer insight to the coven."

"True, but none that have a track record of saving the king's family. Or getting into drunken adventures with him for that matter ..."

Fin feigned innocence at the last barb, but then straightened.

"Annika, approximately how long do you predict this taking?"

"Six years if we do everything carefully. Three if we don't mind being the biggest scandal of the next few decades. A lot also depends on the war."

Fin's mouth hardened into a firm line as he stared down at her calm brown eyes, and the beautiful slope of her shoulders.

"Too long."

Annika started backward in surprise at the forcefulness of his words before regaining her composure. "Well, please enlighten me of your superior plan," she replied hotly.

"Captain Antonio proposed marriage to my mother."

Annika's jaw dropped.

"After the war, he is saying he will become a baron and take on the lands His Majesty has tried to give him several times. So we just need to end the war as quickly as possible."

Spluttering, the viscountess tried to find the words for the shock she had just received.

"We shouldn't just rely on the captain and your mother, though; that was an awfully quick betrothment and often these things fall apart rather quickly. We should still—"

"I'm glad us ending a war is more manageable than my mother's second marriage turning out well," Fin remarked dryly. Annika looked appropriately sheepish before she spoke again.

"That isn't what I meant, and you know it."

Letting out a sigh, Fin reached out and drew her close, hugging her to him, and burying his hands in her long black hair. "There is one important part of both our plans that needs to be addressed."

Annika's muffled "What?" was all the prompting Fin needed to release her. He wanted to be sure he heard her perfectly clear the next time she spoke.

"Well, you see, I realized I haven't known what to call you since we started seeing each other. Yet everything we discuss is assuming our future is bound together, so I think we missed an important step of the process." Fin's hands were back on his hips as he regarded her seriously.

The viscountess didn't have time to fully gauge what he meant before he asked what should've been the most obvious question in the world.

"Annika, will you marry me?"

CHAPTER 36
BREWING STORMS

Annika's breath had been taken from her body.

"Wh-Why did you ask me like that!" she finally managed while unable to fight off the small pulse of dizziness that floated across her vision.

It was Fin's turn to look surprised.

"Is there a different way to ask? One fellow back on Quildon tried to propose with sonnets and I don't think either of us wants to see me try that approach. There is requesting your hand through your male family members, but I think your brother is hard to reach in prison ..." Fin reasoned out while growing slightly more amused at the obvious state of fluster he had cast her in.

"But ... just like ... that ... after toting me out of the solar. Just ... I know you tend to be direct, but Gods!"

Fin looked to the ceiling for a moment to try to stop himself from laughing.

"Annika. You've planned six years of our lives out. How is it so strange? Or were you hoping I'd be content to remain as your long-term ... paramour?"

"No! I already said I wanted us to be married after all of that, but it has been only two weeks!"

Fin fixed her with a flat gaze.

"So should I take this as a no? I'll admit that might put a damper on my day ..."

"Of course it's yes, you arse! It's just ... of all the ..."

"Annika?"

"What?" she snapped, still clearly at a loss for words as she began wringing her hands uncharacteristically and her eyes looked oddly wet ...

"Can I kiss you now?"

"I need a moment!" she burst out, her cheeks deepening in color. "Why is it you ... you can reduce me to a twittering idiot without any effort?!"

"I'd like to think it's because you love me, but you may have other reasons."

"Why are you so calm?! And confident?!" Annika demanded, her tears finally spilling over.

"Is my being calm and confident with you a problem?"

"I just don't understand what has changed!"

"Everything has, love." Fin's blue eyes somehow darkened in seriousness as they regarded the woman in front of him.

Annika stilled then. When the two locked gazes, a deep meaning and understanding suddenly passed between them. Time seemed to stop in the quiet as they both felt overwhelmed by their connection, and the greater knowledge that things were going to have to start growing more serious soon.

So intense was the moment that when the sharp rap on the door echoed into the room, they both jumped.

"Mr. Wit, Mage Lee is here demanding to see you."

Fin let out a small breath and turned to the door. His hand had grasped the handle, his back to Annika who took note of her racing heart as she tried to sort through her jumbled thoughts.

Then the redhead made matters far more fevered when he abruptly turned around, cupped her face, and kissed her. His thumb brushed against her smooth, somewhat damp cheek.

"I'll try to be back before midnight," he whispered before turning back to the door and exiting without another word, leaving Annika to lift fingers to her lips and dazedly realize that she was engaged.

Engaged to a cook ... but not just any cook.

To a house witch.

~~~~~~~~

Fin had made the wise decision to take the servants' stairwell on his venture down to greet Mage Lee, who was waiting in the front hall and gazing about himself curiously.

"I'm beginning to wonder if you're stalking me," Fin called out, drawing the mage's gaze to him as he pressed his hands into his pockets.

"Ashowan, I thought your courtship with Clara was over. Imagine my surprise when I overhear from your kitchen aides that you have returned to Viscountess Jenoure's house," the man huffed with a salt-and-pepper eyebrow raised.

"I hadn't told anyone where I was going," Fin pointed out, fixing the man with a keen stare.

"No, but they speculated you would be here," the mage retorted, folding his arms across his chest stubbornly.

"I had left some of my clothes here and so came to pick them up. I didn't feel like returning late to the castle, so I requested to stay another night. After I investigate Madam Mathilda, I will be returning to my post in His Majesty's kitchen." The redhead had rehearsed the lie on his trek to greet the mage and was grateful for his years of practiced discretion.

"I see. Trying to win Clara back?" Lee challenged with a knowing smile. "Came to tell her you might be in line to inherit a title in a few years, hoping to change her mind?"

Fin rolled his eyes.

"Why are you here, Lee?"

At this, the old man grew suddenly uncomfortable. His arms uncrossed and he suddenly leaned on his staff as though weak, but Fin knew it was more a sign that he had ulterior motives.

"I ... beseech you ... on behalf of everyone in the castle ... please, please come back and cook as soon as possible, and don't ... don't leave for a very long time. Even if Clara agrees to take you back, we'll give you a raise so that she doesn't have to work and can live comfortably on your pay ... We can't take it anymore." The man looked to be on the brink of a breakdown as the grip on his staff tightened.

All color drained from the redhead's face.

"I just said I will be returning once the investigation concludes. What in the world did the kitchen aides do?"

The elder's face grew pale. "Mr. Ashowan, have you ever heard the term *food poisoning*?"

"Oh Gods."

"Yes … your mother has her hands full trying to mend some of us, but she is still weak from her time with the queen. She healed His Majesty, and a handful of the rest of us, but … Please. Please never let them touch so much as an egg ever again."

Fin closed his eyes and took in a deep breath.

"Very well. We'll negotiate this raise once I return. I will do as His Majesty instructed, however, and try to find out what I can about Madam Mathilda for now."

"I will come with you."

"Perhaps I should give more weight to the stalking jest …" Fin replied while exiting the front doors of the estate without waiting for the mage. It was an overcast muggy day, and the taste of lightning was in the air.

"Last time you went you were drugged and would be hobbling about on crutches were it not for me," Lee reminded, walking quickly to catch up to the witch and showcasing how fit he truly was.

"True, but I don't intend to drink or eat anything they offer me this time."

"You also could use my authority to make a little more headway."

"Last time I was there Annik— Lady Jenoure's men lent me a great deal of authority, wouldn't you say?"

The mage glanced at Fin oddly then as they stepped onto the gravel of the drive; he had stopped walking and the witch was forced to turn around to stare at him.

"What is it, you daft old man?" Fin demanded, hoping to the Gods it wasn't about his slip of the tongue a moment before.

Moving forward cautiously, the elder eyed Fin's tunic, which was black. A terrible color for a summer day, but then again, he hadn't really thought about it when getting dressed.

"This is expensive material," Mage Lee observed before lifting his narrowed gaze to him.

"I wore it when I took Clara out courting." Fin's reply was too quick. Too desperate.

"Where are the other clothes you came to retrieve?"

"She had … er … She'd burned them."

The old man's eyes began to grow a little wider. "Finlay …"

The witch swallowed with great difficulty, and it was then the gardener happened to stroll by. "Good day, Mr. Wit! Raymond wanted me to tell you the biscuits are coming out just fine now!"

"Afternoon, Alvin." Fin greeted the man with a small wave, his stomach wrenching in twenty different directions.

"Why does the staff here keep calling you Mr. Wit?"

Instead of answering the mage, the redhead did the only thing he could do in that moment and ignored the question entirely. He placed both hands back in his pockets and resumed his journey around the fountain toward the road that would take him back to Austice.

The mage jogged after him with ease. He was even more spritely than Fin had originally surmised. Perhaps he dyed his beard white … surely no elderly man could move so swiftly.

"Finlay! You need to answer me this instant!"

Fin did not.

He continued his stroll without even glancing to the mage at his side.

"I brought a horse here, could you just— Blast. Finlay!" the mage barked irritably.

Still, the redheaded witch continued his steady pace down the first hill to Austice. The mage tried unsuccessfully to pester him several more times, until they reached the sea level stretch of road before the final hill.

Finally fed up with his latest evasive technique, Mage Lee darted in front of the witch and blocked his path. The cook tried to sidestep him several times before finally lowering his blue eyes.

"I thought you were banned from Madam Mathilda's."

"Ashowan." Lee's voice was tight as he stared at him wildly. "I am beginning to suspect you are up to something that is a grave concern to not only myself, but even His Majesty."

Once again, the witch remained silent before he brushed past the mage.

"Just tell me you aren't having an affair with Lady Jenoure. Tell me I'm crazy."

"You're crazy." Fin called over his shoulder without stopping.

Mage Lee struck his staff into the ground, and a wall of wind suddenly sent the cook flying back toward the mage, the crack of it echoed up the cliff. Fin managed to land with one knee on the ground and grunted as he felt the bone bruise.

"I thought magic was not to be used lightly by the mages," the redhead muttered.

"Because it's you, I'm making an exception." Lee glowered at him before continuing. "Ashowan, this is a very serious matter. You will not run from this conversation."

Pushing himself to his feet with a wince, the witch turned a blank expression to the mage. Lee didn't like it. He had seen that look on people's faces when being interrogated before.

So instead, he changed his approach.

"Alright, if you aren't going to speak, then you are going to listen to me very carefully." Lee's voice was incredibly low, a slight gravelly note entering his normally soft speech.

"If this is an affair with Lady Jenoure out of boredom, cease. It will bring nothing but trouble and shame to her. You will be released from your position as the Royal Cook and forced back to your island." Mage Lee watched as Fin's expression failed to betray a single emotion, but he knew better. He could feel the deep anger simmering beneath the witch's surface, and the mage was glad that the cook hadn't an ounce of power in him at that moment.

"If you or her, or both of you, are in love, Gods help you. You have a ways to go before this could be seen as a possible match. Then again …" The mage eyed him suspiciously. "Did you come to her after hearing that Captain Antonio might be leaving a baron title to you?"

Fin continued to say nothing.

"Godsdamnit, Ashowan! There is enough chaos happening! Could you not have satisfied your itch with another lass closer to your—"

Fin grabbed the mage by the front of his robes and hauled him up until he was an inch from his nose. "Never make mention of my itches again, hm?" He then released Lee and continued on his way as though nothing had happened.

"If you intend on coming to see Madam Mathilda with me, I suggest you hurry along."

Straightening his robes and closing his eyes, Lee sent a brief prayer to the Gods, muttered a curse, then jogged to rejoin Finlay at his side.

Elizabeth Nonata was examining her ledgers with a gold-rimmed magnifying glass when the first pattering of rain could be heard against her window.

Her dog Cassian's head raised at the noise and tilted, his nose beginning to twitch.

With a sigh, she dropped her hand down and watched as the animal pattered over to her and licked her fingers affectionately.

"I'm glad you're braver than my previous dog. Old Tanner was double your size, but I've never known a more timid brute in all my days," she remarked idly, recalling how her last dog would dive for her desk during any thunderstorm and stay curled up and trembling with her needing to pet and soothe him.

With a sigh, she stood and stretched; crossing over to the window she watched the local riffraff dart toward the various pubs and storefronts to save themselves from the pending deluge.

"Hopefully this rain cools off some of the heat. The stink of the main floor is starting to waft up here," Elizabeth observed, thinking how she needed to cut back the amount of perfume her girls were allowed to don.

The women seemed to think the more perfume they used, the less they'd have to smell their evening companions, but in reality the smells merely souped together until Elizabeth was left gagging. The first rumble of thunder drew her eyes to the heavens.

"I don't know why, but I have the strangest feeling like this is going to be a hell of a storm."

Cassian's claws clipped against the floorboards as he made his way over to sit beside his mistress. He knew he would have to leave her soon, when the lower level grew busier and she wanted him to guard her private quarters. So he relished whatever time he could have with her.

Then, as she began to turn away from the rain-washed glass, Elizabeth noticed two figures strolling toward her establishment. Even though it was the middle of the day ... and the bar was closed for restocking and cleaning for at least another hour ...

Squinting, the first flash of lightning cracked the sky, giving her enough light to see a glint of coppery hair being pushed back, and the wink of a mage crystal disappearing under her eaves by the front door.

"Oh good Gods ... not again."

CHAPTER 37
ROUSING A REBELLION

As Fin strolled into the brothel from the storm that rumbled outside, he did his best to wipe his feet on the worn rug in front of the door. Not that it was doing much good when the rest of him was dripping wet. He had to admit, however, that Mage Lee was having a worse time of it with his heavy robes being weighed down from gallons of water. Unlike Fin, though, he had the magical means to dry himself upon stepping into the brothel. He did not offer the redhead the same courtesy, and he even shot the witch a *that's what you get* expression.

Fin rolled his eyes at the pettiness and looked around the room.

Almost immediately, he saw Elizabeth Nonata racing down the steps from the second floor loudly declaring "Nononononononono," with her forest green dress hiked up to allow her a faster descent.

Rounding on them from across the room as soon as her foot touched the ground, she immediately snapped her fingers, and three beefy men Fin didn't recognize from his previous visit stepped forward.

"These two are not allowed on the premises. They bring nothing but trouble." Elizabeth Nonata folded her arms over her chest and scowled darkly at the pair.

Mage Lee stepped forward, his expression somber. "Ms. Nonata, I am afraid we are here on His Majesty's orders. He sent us instead of the knights to give you the chance to do the right thing. We both know how the law's presence in this establishment doesn't benefit you or Madam Mathilda."

The assistant didn't say a word as she brandished a finger over their shoulders toward the dark drenched street through the open doorway.

"Then I will deal with the knights. The two of you caused enough setbacks during your last visit."

"Ms. Nonata, I had wanted to take a more subtle approach than my companion here," Fin said, shooting Lee an irritated side glance. "We just need to speak with Sandy. If the involvement of your brothel and her treason is surface level, you will be looked upon more favorably."

Elizabeth rolled her eyes and moved her hands to her hips. "I fired that wench. I can't afford the type of unsavory business she brings, can I?" There was an accusatory glint in her eyes.

"Where did she go?" Mage Lee demanded urgently.

"It is not my business to know. You're welcome to go pester some of the other brothels. Now, leave. Also, you, the one making a pond of my entrance. If your name is Fin, tell your 'friend' to stop harassing my staff for your whereabouts."

"What friend?" Fin asked, alarmed.

"A lowly looking chap … named Red, I think. You are clearly *not* the lowly rank I initially judged you to be given those clothes, so perhaps he is a manservant you dismissed."

Mage Lee's expression was incredibly smug as Fin shifted at the remark pertaining to his attire.

"What did Red want?"

"I don't know, nor do I care. Out," Elizabeth repeated, pointing over their shoulders. Two of the large men moved forward, while the third one went and stood beside the woman commanding them.

Fin took another step into the room and blocked Lee from view, as though protecting him.

"That is the wrong direction." Elizabeth's brown almond-shaped eyes flashed.

"Funny, I'm usually quite good with directions." Fin shrugged his shoulders with feigned casualness.

"Most men think they are until they get married. Which is why this business is so successful. Get. Out."

"Ms. Nonata, I am quite certain you know where Sandy is, and we would like to discuss how severe this matter is, because despite us mentioning treason you don't seem to be concerned."

"Oh, please, the both of you are con artists. You probably commissioned knights to pose as Viscountess Jenoure's men as a backup plan. I would be happy to send her an urgent missive informing her that such a bold imposter is here in my grasp."

Fin let out a long breath before fixing the woman with a weary gaze.

"If you do, I can guarantee she will be annoyed with me, but you … she might be a little more aggravated with. I don't recommend being the focus of that kind of attention from Lady Jenoure."

"Glad to see you know her so well," Lee muttered ruthlessly behind the redhead before addressing the assistant once more.

"Ms. Nonata, you know that I am the Royal Court Mage to His Majesty; I can credit this man's story."

"At this rate, Lee, it is more likely that the staff you like to show off is fixed with a glass crystal rather than a true mage's. It seems the far likelier story considering you have not once presented any official documents or seal indicating your status. I really shouldn't have offered you so many perks without being more thorough."

At this, Fin turned around and stared incredulously at the mage.

"I haven't been so incensed in years! Of course I am a real mage!" Lee shook his staff, making the crystal atop glow.

Elizabeth scoffed. "Parlor tricks."

Fin clenched his fist at his side, but he continued his direct gaze at Elizabeth Nonata while staying tensed in the event that one of the two guards nearing him would pounce. "Perhaps we should go back and return with your official seal, Lee," he remarked flatly.

"Bollocks to that! She knows who I am, I will not stand this insult!"

Sighing, and silently cursing the mage in his mind, Fin turned back to the assistant.

"We need to discuss this matter in private, Ms. Nonata."

By then, a handful of the women had exited their rooms yawning and were staring down at the peculiar scene. Many of them had mussed hair and dark makeup smudged under their eyes, but one, still fresh faced and energetic, suddenly called out.

"YOU! YOU RAT BASTARD!"

Everyone jumped at the sudden shriek, and when all eyes turned, they saw the young woman in a cream shift and weathered green robe pointing at Fin, her eyes mad with fury.

"You're the one who tried to end my career!"

"I offered you a better one!" the redhead exclaimed, turning his palms up in puzzled defense when he realized it was Chloe.

"You think I want to slave away in a hot kitchen for half of what I make here?!" the woman demanded while gripping the banister that wrapped itself around the entire second floor.

"You intend to do this until you die?" Fin asked, his hands moving to his hips.

"No, I'll marry or become a madam!"

When Fin shook his head, he heard a small snort of disbelief from Elizabeth Nonata and Mage Lee. However, the witch glared at the assistant, which effectively silenced her.

"Is that what you peddled to her? Made her believe she had a future in this business?"

Elizabeth Nonata's cheeks deepened in color. "I am not arguing this with you, *Out!*"

The burly two men surged forward and reached for Fin's arms, only for him to turn tightly out of the way at the last second, leaving Mage Lee to be seized instead.

The witch then shoved the trio out the entrance back into the pouring rain and closed the door as they tried to regain their footing. Fin turned back to Elizabeth and continued toward her calmly while the women above them gasped and began chattering amongst themselves.

The third and final guard present moved to grab Fin, but the redhead managed instead to land a strong uppercut to the guard's groin.

"Sorry about that," he whispered as the fellow gagged and recoiled on the floor. The redhead then turned to the assistant who was beginning to look slightly more panicked.

"Ms. Nonata, if any of the women under your protection now, or recently, proves to be in any way connected with thousands of Troivackian soldiers being smuggled into Daxaria, I want you to think about what that would mean for your beloved business." Fin's voice was low when he reached Elizabeth, who now was notably pale and drawing out a small dagger. "Now, if you still have nothing to say to me, I will leave. The knights will be here by this evening."

"Suits me just fine! There is nothing of interest here, so we may as well get some paying titled men coming in!"

Shaking his head, Fin slowly turned—making sure to be wary of the knife in Elizabeth's hand—and walked purposefully back to the door, which was already open with Mage Lee standing in its frame, glaring daggers at the witch. The two men who had seized the elder lay unconscious in the street.

About to admit defeat and inform the king more drastic measures needed to be taken, Fin glanced up at the prostitutes who stared down whispering behind their hands, and an ironclad resolution suddenly gripped him.

Turning back to the room, the third guard was just beginning to get back to his feet, though it was obvious he was still battling the gut-wrenching nausea. Fin placed his hands on his hips and lifted his face up to the women.

"If you think this is a lucrative profession, you are wrong. I don't see a single one of you over the age of twenty-five at the most. Now, if you insist on pursuing this line of work, why not ensure you will be properly cared for?"

"Mr. Ashowan, what in the name of the *Gods* are you doing?" Mage Lee's panicked whisper matched Elizabeth Nonata's expression of dawning horror. Somehow she knew the redhead was about to cause even more trouble ...

"Just make sure no one tackles me," Fin uttered before once again addressing the prostitutes who were growing in their numbers as more and more of them woke up from the commotion.

"What do you mean properly cared for? We're the best-paid prostitutes in the city!" one of the older women called out.

"Does your pay improve the longer you work?" Fin demanded, his volume marginally increasing.

The woman who had spoken glanced at Chloe and openly scowled. "Nah. It decreases usually when the new youngs come in."

Fin shot a deadly glance at Elizabeth Nonata who was beginning to lift her dagger again but froze under the ire of his stare.

"How is that fair? You've worked longer, become more experienced, and what actually happens when none of the patrons think you are to their taste?" he insisted, staring directly at the prostitute who seemed all too eager to be listened to.

"I'll go to work at one of the other brothels, or become a maid somewhere ..."

"For even less pay I'm guessing? Not to mention marriage prospects by then I imagine are difficult," Fin pointed out loudly as Elizabeth tried to shout over him, only for Lee's staff to glow briefly, effectively intimidating her once again into silence.

By this time the girls were all beginning to speak amongst themselves worriedly.

"What you all need is stable pay, and perhaps a fund you all contribute to for when you are no longer able to work. Or are between work."

"No longer able to work?! That means they will be retired and living off those still working until they die! It could be fifty years!" Elizabeth called out derisively.

"Or it could be a fund that helps to offer them options. Education. What if they then had the means to become accountants? Seamstresses? Housekeepers? Or even physicians?"

"A *woman* physician?" one of the younger women called out quietly, her eyes round.

Elizabeth Nonata scoffed.

"My mother is one, and she is currently serving the king," Fin announced loudly. The news effectively made Elizabeth grow still, but it was the opposite for the prostitutes. A flurry of excitement broke out amongst the women as they excitedly conversed about a brighter future after their time served.

"Could these ... benefits be applied to the rest of us as well?" Fin glanced behind him and saw a reedy bartender leaning forward eagerly from the shadows.

"Yes, it could."

"What would stop girls from coming in and quitting and just being paid out immediately?" The query came from Mage Lee, who seemed genuinely intrigued by the speech.

"The girls would have to meet the standards set by the employer and serve their full term unless injured or sick to the point where they are unable to perform their duties."

"This is preposterous! Madam Mathilda will never permit this, so the lot of you better stop listening to this menace and get back to your rooms!" Ms. Nonata hissed.

"It isn't preposterous if you all walk out of here today until your demands are met," Fin pointed out while turning a slow smile to the assistant who was practically frothing at the mouth.

The room went deathly quiet.

"We'll be relieved of our positions," Chloe whispered fearfully.

"You're Godsdamn right you would be; take them out!" Elizabeth was addressing the guard who had by then recovered from the blow Finlay had laid, but the man was listening with too much interest to adhere to her demand.

"Not if you all leave at once. Where is Ms. Nonata going to hire the sheer volume of professionals such as yourselves in a matter of, say, three hours? She will then have wealthy merchants pounding down her door and find that this business is completely empty. Even if she manages to hire some other women, you all have built relationships with these clients. You'll have become well-known to them ... what happens when you are all gone?"

Elizabeth's face was beginning to turn red as she stepped forward with her dagger in hand only for Lee to gently tap his staff against the floor and send the woman back by a couple feet with a block of wind.

For a moment all the women fell silent at having witnessed magic for the first time in their lives, and yet once the shock had faded, they all leaned forward even more eagerly.

"This is entirely within your power, ladies. However, you would all have to leave. Not just some of you. All. You need to unite as one group, because Ms. Nonata and Madam Mathilda are powerful, but not against *all* of you," Fin explained while making sure to make eye contact briefly with every woman present.

Glancing at one another, the first woman who had addressed Fin suddenly pressed her fist to the air.

"Godsdamnit, ladies, I don't care how mad this sounds. For Ms. Nonata to be this scared, there has to be some sense to it! Let's do it! It isn't like we have long here, anyway!"

A miracle happened then, and every single prostitute met the others' gazes ... and nodded. Like soldiers preparing for battle, they all promptly returned to their rooms and exited them again in proper street clothes.

Elizabeth's jaw dropped as the girls filed down around her.

"You ... I will never hire you back! Any of you! How dare— Grab them!" Ms. Nonata addressed her henchman who still stood at her side in a daze. When he turned to face her, however, there was a glint in his green eyes.

"I always ... wanted to become a puppet maker ..." He then proceeded to walk away, joining the steady stream of prostitutes, maids, and bartenders.

Giving her a sly, satisfied smile, Fin waited until the last of the women strolled past him before turning to take his own leave.

"I'll take you to Mathilda, but you bring those women back here, now!" Elizabeth boomed forcefully.

Without turning around, Fin pressed his hands in his pockets and smiled at Lee, who was staring at him with a mixture of awe and bewilderment.

"Oh, no, Ms. Nonata. You wanted the knights to be the ones to interrogate your employer. I have a new goal in mind now. Good day."

CHAPTER 38
FIN'S FANS

The queen was the exact color of an uncooked flank steak, and the king the picture of a guilty person. The royal couple sat before Katelyn Ashowan, who stood regarding them with a cool expression that was not at all how they had come to know her.

"So," the healer began patiently. "The reason the princess was born before my guessed timeline was because, despite my orders, you two engaged in marital relatio—"

"We were careful! It wasn't—" Norman began defensively but was quickly silenced by Ainsley's warning hand on his arm.

"Your Majesty, while I applaud your deep love for your wife, it was beyond reckless."

"In fairness, I had forgotten that the act was completely banned. We didn't do … everything … just a little—" Ainsley managed before the burning in her face turned scalding and forced her to stop.

With a sigh, Katelyn dropped her forehead to her fingertips.

"This is neither here nor there at this point, but Your Majesties, there is another matter I haven't brought to your attention as there were more serious issues."

All at once the embarrassment of the couple drained and was immediately replaced with worry. Norman reached over and clasped Ainsley's hand while fixing Katelyn with a stern gaze.

"During the birth of the princess, and consequent healing of the queen, I'm afraid there was a great cost." Katelyn's eyes flitted over to Ainsley whose stoic expression hardened even further, but she nodded to encourage the witch to continue.

"Your Majesty, you will never be able to conceive again. I had to remove too much …" The healer trailed off, unsure of how much medical talk she really needed to use.

The couple stared at her stunned, and a flicker of the uncertain bubbly woman Katelyn Ashowan was when she wasn't a physician appeared. Despite her training, the healer was beginning to fortify herself in the event the royals decided to not only banish her but hang her for such a massive consequence.

"I … we understand, Mrs. Ashowan. If you wouldn't mind, please give His Majesty and me a moment? Please resume healing the castle occupants' food poisoning as best you can." The queen nodded to the door, and Katelyn obliged after a brief curtsy.

Turning to Norman with tears in her eyes, Ainsley leaned her forehead against his shoulder and swallowed with great difficulty. Wordlessly, he reached up and gently stroked the back of his wife's head, not knowing what he could say.

After a few moments of the occasional tear dripping off the queen's cheek onto her husband's sleeve, she spoke.

"I'm so relieved."

Norman stiffened at her announcement, making the queen lean back and stare at him with open anguish. "Does that make me a terrible person?"

Reaching up to cup her cheek, the king wiped away the remaining tears on her pale face.

"You have been, and always will be, the best person I know. Even before I knew you, and even after I'm gone."

Nodding, but crying a little harder, Ainsley returned her husband's embrace and thanked the Gods that never again would she have to hold a dead babe in her arms.

Striding into the council room an hour after consoling his wife, Norman wasn't prepared for the sight that met him.

The room was packed full, wall to wall … with noblewomen.

His primary council sat at the table, and every single one of them looked as though there were a hundred archers with arrows notched and trained onto their skulls.

Mr. Howard was shaking his head with his eyes closed when Norman eventually ventured a questioning glance at him. The monarch also noticed that Mage Lee was missing. It appeared a good amount of the nobility were healed from their unpleasant bout of food poisoning from earlier, though most of the people who had suffered had been those who had tried eating the undercooked bacon for breakfast the previous morning. Most of the noblewomen had forgone the fare and appeared to be in much better shape than their husbands.

"Good day, everyone," Norman began while wondering what fresh hell had occurred in less than a day. Everyone who was seated rose and bowed, while the women curtsied. "Is there a particular reason why we have so many esteemed guests here today?"

"Your Majesty, it is regarding … the house witch. Mr. Finlay Ashowan," Mr. Howard managed while sounding as though he were being choked.

"Son of a mage," Norman muttered under his breath so that only his assistant could hear before once again addressing the crowd. "What is the issue with Mr. Ashowan?"

The room exploded as everyone began talking heatedly at once.

The king held up his hand and silenced them all, then pointed to Lady Laurent who seemed to have stepped forward from the plethora of noblewomen as some kind of leader …

"Countess Laurent, if you could please explain on behalf of the women here." Norman gestured around the filled room.

The woman swallowed with great difficulty and refused to look at her husband who was watching his wife with open dread.

"Well, you see, Your Majesty … we are all disgusted with how Mr. Ashowan was treated with regard to Baron Gauva's betrayal. He acted in self-defense and was carelessly tossed in a cell after he has been nothing but a model servant to you and the royal family. Especially now that I hear he was in fact an uncredited hero who helped Mage Lee stop Hilda. Us ladies do not understand why he is being treated as a criminal and forced to take a leave of absence."

Norman turned to look at Mr. Howard, whose arms were folded and eyes gazed off into some distant horror.

"My lady, Mr. Ashowan was promptly released once I realized he was wrongly imprisoned. Our cook requested some time off and we gave him a few days in our fair Austice," Norman explained, though he could see on the lady's face that his words were doing little to calm her agitation.

"After our husbands were poisoned in the cook's absence, us women were talking amongst ourselves and … well …" Lady Laurent glanced over her shoulder and received several affirmative nods from the wide array of noble females behind her.

"We think Mr. Ashowan should be given a raise and knighted."

Norman blinked and stepped behind Mr. Howard's chair while placing his hands on its back.

"Might I ask when Mr. Ashowan gave you all such a strong impression?"

"Well, for one thing, he doesn't poison us," Lady Laurent began dryly. "For another, he makes the best food we have ever eaten in our lives. He has saved us all, and he treats the prince with kindness and genuine friendship … He has many wonderful attributes."

Norman turned to stare at Captain Antonio who looked caught between laughing hysterically and being frozen in shock.

"I see. We will take your thoughts into consideration once Mr. Ashowan has returned." The monarch managed to say without a hitch in his voice.

"Your Majesty, we will be back if Mr. Ashowan returns and no changes have been made!" another noblewoman, whose name Norman couldn't remember, burst out.

"My lady, are you threatening our king?" Mr. Howard asked slowly while finally straightening in his seat.

"N-No." The blond lass shrank back into the crowd. She was most likely one of the daughters of the noblemen …

"His Majesty has assured you all that he will take your concerns into consideration. Please show yourselves out as right now our country is on the brink of war, and we have far more pressing issues than the castle cook." Mr. Howard stood and gestured to the door imperiously.

The women stayed rooted to their respective spots until Norman stepped closer to his own chair and glanced around the room at them all.

"My assistant speaks the truth. We have greater threats right now. However, your kind words are heeded." He made sure to add the last part with a slightly warmer tone, but the king indicated the door all the same.

Slowly, the women began to shift out of the room and leave their husbands and fathers to their business.

Still unable to fully understand what had just happened, Norman seated himself and basked in the momentary quiet as the lords around him all shifted in their seats.

"Did none of you think to stop your—" the king began quietly only to be interrupted hastily.

"Are you able to command the queen when she decides to do something?" Lord Laurent snapped, his ears a shade of purple that was rather concerning.

Sensing that everyone present was more than a little embarrassed at the show of rebellion the women in their families had shown, Norman made the wise decision to wait before saying anything further on the matter.

Instead, he tucked his chair in, and opened his mouth to begin the meeting, when in burst a knight under the direct command of Captain Antonio.

"Your Majesty!" he shouted while bowing deeply.

Everyone looked up startled, and yet somehow … before the knight even spoke, Norman had a hunch about what could have caused such panic.

"Royal Cook Mr. Ashowan and Royal Court Mage Lee have sent a messenger to summon us knights to conduct a search of Madam Mathilda's brothel, but he, ah … there is another issue …"

"Of course there is." The words were out of Norman's mouth before he could stop himself.

All the men around the table looked at their king in alarm. He waved off their concerned stares and gestured for the knight to continue. Truly, there was nothing the redheaded menace could've done that would surprise him anymore …

"Mr. Ashowan seems to have convinced all of the … erm … prostitutes to quit work until they receive better working conditions, and funds to better their employment options after aging out of the brothel."

Norman's jaw dropped.

Fin sat beside Mage Lee, protected from the rain by the brothel's eaves, and continued scrawling out the numbers the prostitutes gave him regarding their payments and expenses. The group mingled in the street directly outside Madam Mathilda's brothel and only cleared the road for local traffic. Otherwise the women were quite vigorous in stopping any of the regular patrons from entering the brothel by informing them that there wasn't a bartender or wench in sight once over the threshold of the house.

The witch and mage had procured some parchment from a nearby business and, with the help of stacked crates and two empty ale barrels acting as two chairs and a table, had begun the arduous task of calculating a fair wage for them all. Many of them only appeared comfortable because of Lee's presence, and after an unenthused request from Fin followed by several busty women's pleas, the mage acquiesced to help until the knights came.

"What exactly is your plan here, Mr. Ashowan?" the elder asked after the second hour of their documentation.

"To unite these women and create a better life for them."

Lee let out a long sigh. "I mean about how you are supposed to find Madam Mathilda."

"She won't be forthcoming, so I figured I might as well spend my time doing something else worthwhile."

The mage continued looking dubiously at the redhead, until he shook his head and turned back to the parchment in front of himself.

"Not to mention, I'm pretty sure we can ask any of these women if they've happened to see or hear anything regarding the Troivackian men."

The mage turned back to him with a slow smile spreading. "I see, and will it be you who conducts these questions?"

"I can, but I think it'd be best if you talk to the ones you are … er … familiar with."

Lee had the faintest of blushes, but he nodded while clearing his throat.

"Very well."

After another few moments of watching Fin talk to the last of the women and jot down their information, the mage folded his arms across his chest.

"You love *her*, don't you?"

Fin sighed and set the cheap quill he had been using down then stretched his ink-stained fingers. There was nothing to indicate he had heard Lee's question.

"Does she love you back?"

The redhead then cracked his neck, still without responding.

"Did I ever tell you about the first time I met Candace?"

At long last Fin replied, "You haven't."

"She was the daughter of a wealthy merchant who didn't believe she should waste her time studying to be a mage."

"A wise father."

"Shut up." Lee cuffed Fin on the back of his head then continued. "My father was his assistant, but I hadn't ever been invited to the house … until he heard I'd been accepted to the academy. I was fifteen … and when I saw her …"

The mage sighed. "She has surprised me at every turn."

"I don't doubt it. She surprised me, too, when I learned you two go to brothels together."

Mage Lee coughed violently, and after a moment, he finally managed to compose himself again to continue.

"My point is, even overcoming the bridge between extreme wealth and moderate, no titles or services to the king involved, that was difficult enough to make acceptable. You cannot bridge the social gap like I did in this case," Lee explained, watching the redhead's profile that once again grew blank. "This is not a possibility for the two of you."

The witch surprised the mage then by suddenly laughing.

"Well … you know … I'm not saying your assumptions regarding the viscountess and myself are at all right, but by now you should know one absolute truth about me."

"And what is that?" Lee narrowed his eyes but was disarmed by Fin when the young man rested his elbow against the small table they had created and leaned in closer so that no one could overhear his next words.

"Anything a mage can do, a witch can do better."

CHAPTER 39
MEETING MATHILDA

The streets of Austice were aflutter with gossip over Madam Mathilda's brothel workers. Some believed that the infamous business owner had fired everyone, others that there was an outbreak of a venereal disease. Then there were those who made their way down to the establishment to see for themselves just what had happened.

What none of them were prepared for was the gaggle of knights that had blocked off the street, or for the heated discussion between a particular tall redhead and the king's assistant.

"Mr. Howard, these women deserve better treatment. This place is considered to have the best working conditions, and yet it ruins all other job prospects and—"

"I don't care! Our priority is finding what the madam knows; I am not interested in helping whatever nonsensical chaos you've bred this time!"

Fin's hands were planted firmly on his hips as he stared down at Mr. Howard. The man looked dead set against him, and Mage Lee had faded into the crowd at some point, unwilling to help.

"The knights are questioning Mathilda's assistant as we speak. You have time to go through what I've recorded and tell me what they should be making, reasonable raises, and what they could afford to put toward the post-education fund."

Mr. Howard's flat expression didn't indicate that he felt similarly, so Fin changed tactics.

"You're the best person for this job."

"That, I won't dispute."

"Great! Then you won't mind taking a look and letting us know!"

"Mr. Ashowan, I am not going to—"

A trio of nearby prostitutes sidled over to the arguing pair then. Two of the girls draped themselves gracefully over Mr. Howard's tensed shoulders, while the third one squared off in front of him.

"Is it true you're the king's assistant?" A waiflike blonde on his left brushed her lips near Mr. Howard's ear, making the man twitch.

"You know we want to properly thank you for helping us." A buxom brunette on his right lifted his arm and began gently stroking his fingers.

The third woman present was the one who had rallied the women in the first place, and Fin had since learned she was named Giselle. Though her working name was Gigi. She addressed the redhead then.

"We've been thinking of calling the group Whores United."

"Isn't that just a threesome?" the blond woman asked, blinking in confusion.

Fin winced as he noticed Mr. Howard visibly recoil at the exchange.

"Perhaps we just call it United … Workers," the redhead managed to get out while keeping an unreadable expression.

Giselle gave a single shoulder shrug. "Suit yourselves."

She then turned to Mr. Howard who looked like a deer staring down the shaft of an arrow.

"Now, perhaps Mr. … Howard, was it? Perhaps we can work out an agreement."

The assistant looked to Fin, and the witch could see that while the ladies could work their charms on Lee, Kevin Howard did not enjoy such attentions.

"Perhaps Mr. Howard would like to hear about what kinds of wine Madam Mathilda offers for her … er … *esteemed* guests?"

Giselle shot Fin an incredulous look, but then noticed that the assistant's face suddenly relaxed a little.

"Of course! We have some of the best-quality wines reserved for such customers. Girls, why don't you show our new friend inside, I'm sure the knights working there won't mind a cool ale themselves."

Fin grinned as the trio then proceeded to usher Mr. Howard past him toward the doorway, though as he brushed by the witch, the assistant uttered, "This isn't over, Ashowan."

Chuckling, Fin turned back to the street that, while damp, was at least no longer victim to the wall of rain that had plagued its cobblestones earlier that morning.

"Mr. Ashowan?"

A knight Fin didn't recognize, but who looked quite serious, stood in the doorway of the brothel. "Ms. Nonata and the captain would like to speak with you."

With a short nod, the cook followed him back into Madam Mathilda's business and up the stairs to the assistant's office. If any of the knights thought it strange that Fin was present for their work, or that he seemed to be the one directing the prostitutes, they said nothing. Since the princess's birth and the discovery that he was a witch, there had been a shift in their respects toward him, so no one bothered questioning his involvement.

Once inside the room, the witch spared the captain only a brief glance. That was all he needed to determine that Antonio was not having an easy time of it with the woman, who looked equally irked.

"Ms. Nonata here is insisting that only you be the one to meet and speak with the madam," Antonio growled.

Fin couldn't hide his shock as he turned to the woman who was openly glaring at him.

"Why me?"

"Because I think you of all people should know who you are messing with!" she declared while folding her arms imperiously.

"Would that be a threat?" the captain asked with a hard gleam in his eye.

Elizabeth Nonata paled slightly, but quickly regained her composure. Fin couldn't blame her; he had never seen the captain in such circumstances before and was quickly discovering that he could be an incredibly frightening man.

"No, but Mr.— What was your name again? Ashen?"

"Ashowan," the captain snapped, making Elizabeth jump and shoot Fin a look of wonder. After all, it wasn't every day someone crossed paths with someone close to both the captain of all Daxarian knights and the Royal Mage.

"Right. Mr. *Ashowan* here has completely upended Madam Mathilda's business, and I think the very least he can do is look her in the face and explain why."

"Ms. Nonata, you do realize that in the event evidence is discovered that you were smuggling in Troivackian men on one of the boats your madam has invested in, this establishment will be completely shut down?

Then following that discovery there would be a devastatingly short trial, where both yourself *and* your employer will be imprisoned for obstruction and shortly thereafter hung for treason."

The assistant visibly gulped.

"I did try to warn you that I was the lesser evil ..." Fin murmured innocently while also inching away from the captain who looked ready to arrest the woman right then and there.

Elizabeth shot Fin an acid glare before addressing Captain Antonio.

"I-I'm aware. However, we have nothing to hide! I've already given your men the information regarding which ships funded by the madam are docked here in Austice, and the schedule for the two that are out on their trade routes."

"Regardless, I will be present when Mr. Ashowan questions the madam." Antonio's tone left little room for debate, and so with a small sigh, and an even smaller nod, Elizabeth straightened her shoulders.

"Very well. Follow me." The assistant swiftly strode out of the room and began strolling down the balcony.

Both Fin and the captain wordlessly followed, and when they passed by some of the knights who stood guard, Antonio waved them off.

Once they reached the stairs, Elizabeth veered toward the nearest room on her right and entered.

It was a shabby room compared to the rest of the house, with worn floorboards that were in desperate need of a polish and stained walls that Fin didn't want to think too much about. Elizabeth faced the back wall, where an equally dreary tapestry hung, and lifted it to reveal a door-shaped crack that ran around the wall. It would've been tough to spot even if someone had happened to look behind the tapestry ...

Elizabeth then issued an irregular knocking pattern and proceeded to push the hidden door open.

Fin frowned as he tried to remember the buildings near the brothel and realized that they must be attached ... meaning Madam Mathilda owned the establishment beside her own. An unremarkable cobbler worked below if the redhead recalled correctly ... perhaps his wife was the madam?

Antonio moved through the secret doorway before Fin, following Elizabeth Nonata into an empty apartment that had graying floorboards, and a single grimy round window. The assistant didn't stop moving, however, and instead continued across the span of the room until she reached the next wall.

Then, reaching upward she pulled free a short rope that had been tucked between two stones and pulled open a trap door in the ceiling attached to a ladder that lowered down silently to the ground.

"What is the purpose of this empty room?" Antonio asked with his hand still clasped around the hilt of his sword.

"We send the girls here who might need to hide."

"Don't you have guards for that?" Fin pointed out suspiciously.

"Sometimes the girls have family members that they'd rather hide from than have forcefully ejected, and we respect their wishes," the assistant quipped.

"Why did you knock if this room was empty?" Antonio stepped closer to Elizabeth, which in turn made her fidget.

"I knocked because sometimes the madam is in here listening. I wanted to give her a warning if she happened to be waiting to speak with me about all the ruckus."

The captain's eye narrowed threateningly; he wasn't buying her story, but the assistant waved him up toward the open trap door.

"Go see her for yourself and ask."

Antonio's footfalls were heavy as he moved purposefully to the ladder, his armor gleaming in the pale light coming in through the window.

"Gods, I feel sorry for your wife," Elizabeth muttered at the captain's back when he had moved up the ladder out of earshot.

Fin closed his eyes and did his best to not respond to the glib remark, when he was reminded that his mother would be said wife someday. Instead, he nudged the assistant to follow after Antonio, which she began to do with an indignant sniff. Once she was up the ladder completely, the redhead followed.

When he finally stepped into the room above the empty apartment, Fin realized that the attic space they were in was completely dark, but there was a doorway to their right rimmed with light.

"Good Gods, is this a maze?" Captain Antonio demanded as Elizabeth hurried forward.

"As the madam's assistant it is my job to keep her safe."

There was a strange hitch in her voice as she opened the door, and in the warm glow that cascaded out of the doorway, Fin was then able to see that she was gripping her skirt with her free hand until her knuckles were white.

"Lizzie? Whatever seems to be going on in the street? Is there another festival?"

A strange voice called out, and after a brief look at each other, both the captain and Fin stepped into the brightly lit room that was …

Pink.

Every scrap of cloth in the large apartment was the same shade of pink, and past the large four-poster bed in the middle was a desk with a golden framed mirror perched atop, where a woman with long sandy-colored hair sat facing the glass, a pink feathered fan open and shielding her face in the reflection. If Fin had wondered who was responsible for the decor in the brothel, he now realized the answer was before him.

"Mathilda?" Elizabeth asked quietly, rushing into the room quickly and blocking the view of the woman before Fin could get a better look.

"Oh, Lizzie, what have you done?"

That strange voice again …

"Things are a-a little hectic downstairs, but that redheaded oaf I told you about? He's here, and we have to answer his questions."

Fin frowned at being called an oaf, but soon ignored that as he craned his neck to try and once again get a better view of the madam.

"My dear, whatever for?"

"They think we are shipping in Troivackian soldiers."

"Oh, what nonsense. Should I summon Jonesy?" Madam Mathilda stood then, revealing that she was remarkably tall for a woman, and while her fan still covered her face … there was something different about her.

"No! No, don't fetch Jonesy." Elizabeth sounded terrified at the notion, which made Fin and Antonio share a meaningful glance before turning their attention back to the scene unfolding in front of them.

The assistant then slowly pivoted back to face Antonio and Fin and, with the madam's hand resting on her arm, she guided her forward.

Fin noticed Mathilda's dress was a gaudy mix of patterns all in various shades of pink, red, and orange, and yet she wore boots … men's boots.

By the time the fan had been lowered Fin knew roughly what he was about to see, and apparently so did the captain.

The pair of them stared into the whiskered face of a man, who had painted a dark mark on his cheek and wore a long strand of pearls around his neck.

"What is the meaning of this?" Antonio demanded angrily, making Elizabeth unconsciously jump and step in front of her employer.

"Captain Antonio, Mr. Ashowan, th-this is Madam Mathilda."

Fin blinked.

"Well, you brutes certainly know how to gape like the best of my clients. So tell me, what is all this nonsense about Troivackian soldiers?" the man asked while raising a haughty eyebrow and looking back and forth between them while gently pressing Elizabeth back to his side.

"Madam Mathilda." Fin was the first to recover as he cleared his throat. "One of the girls you used to employ named Sultry Sandy is believed to have distracted me from monitoring a pair of Troivackian men that were believed to be from the military here to attack Austice citizens."

"I see, and are you aware of what 'Sultry Sandy's' profession was at the time, young man?"

"I'm aware, but it was plain as day I wouldn't be able to afford her … services. So there was no need for—"

"The quality of your clothes is quite fine. I think she appraised you well enough."

"I was not wearing fine clothes at the time."

Fin could feel Captain Antonio's eye rake over him, and he did his best not to suddenly appear shifty under his scrutiny.

"I see, well. Why is it you believed those two men were soldiers? What nefarious deed had they done that made you so bothered by them, hm?"

"I believe we're the ones here to ask the questions." Antonio stepped forward then, making the assistant leap between him and the madam yet again.

It was then that Fin really looked at the assistant. Then studied the madam a little closer as well, and after a few moments, had a theory …

"Are you two related?"

Elizabeth visibly paled, and the madam turned on him with a bemused smile. "That's the first sign of intelligence you've given me. Yes, this is a younger sister. Now, once again, tell me, why is it my establishment is under such discourteous investigation?"

Fin winced, he could tell that the conversation was going nowhere quickly, and judging from Antonio's expression, he didn't have long before things escalated.

CHAPTER 40
NOW YOU SEE ME

"Why did you sack Sandy if she had done nothing wrong?" Fin asked, trying to ignore the odd flirty look Mathilda was giving him.

"I found out she was giving out favors to some men for free, which doesn't set a very good reputation for my business." She winked.

"Why do you hide your identity so thoroughly?" Fin wondered aloud hastily, hoping to distract her with the seriousness of his questions.

"Oh, please, you silly man." Mathilda laughed and crossed her legs. "I don't even need to bother answering that."

The four of them had taken to the seating area of the madam's apartment, a cozy nook beside the only window in the room, which was boarded up and covered with lacy curtains.

"Do you own all these buildings that your mad maze runs through?" Antonio growled, earning a reproachful glare from Elizabeth at the blatant disregard of her earlier request that only Fin question the madam.

"I do."

"Are all these establishments listed under your name?" The captain continued ignoring the assistant's displeasure.

"No."

"I see." Captain Antonio continued studying Madam Mathilda with a wary frown. "I will be conducting a search through all the buildings you own on this street and will need the names they are listed under."

Mathilda let out a small laugh and waved her hand as though none of it mattered in the slightest. Despite her being compliant in their requests and questioning, there was something a mite off about the whole thing ...

What particularly bothered Fin was how Elizabeth Nonata kept nervously looking at her sibling.

"Madam Mathilda, if someone should like to smuggle in or hide Troivackian soldiers, what is the most effective method?" the witch asked slowly.

"Well, how would I know? I ship in fine wines and silks; I dabble in some perfumes."

"And drugs," Fin pointed out, tilting his head to the side, and watching closely as Madam Mathilda's expression twitched.

Elizabeth stilled and appeared to be holding her breath.

"Drugs, well ... of ... of course this establishment offers all ... all kinds of ..." Mathilda's superior expression suddenly grew vacant.

"I think we have answered enough of your questions! This is bordering on harassment; why isn't a magistrate here?" Elizabeth jumped out of her chair, a panicked glint entering her eyes.

Fin was about to open his mouth to ask what was happening, when Mathilda's hand suddenly shot out and grabbed the assistant's arm firmly.

"What the hell's going on?" Mathilda's voice was completely changed, instead of the light effeminate tones from before it was rough ... gravelly ... masculine.

Captain Antonio's hand was on the hilt of his sword in an instant.

"No! Nothing!" Elizabeth turned to face Mathilda and dropped to her knees. Gently clasping her sibling's hand, she lowered her voice, though given the close quarters Fin and Antonio heard each word clearly. "Jonesy, nothing is wrong, I swear. They just had to ask a few questions. They're leaving now."

"Ms. Nonata, your charade is up. Now you need to take us to the real Madam Mathilda or I will have you both executed before the sun sets. Am I clear?" Antonio's voice boomed in the small space, and even Fin winced from the edge in his tone.

"I don't think so." Mathilda or Jonesy—Fin wasn't even sure anymore—rose from his seat. He threw down the feathered fan roughly, his movements completely different from before. "Bess, did these louts hurt you?"

"Good Gods, man, you were here the whole time!" Antonio rose, his body tense and ready to do some serious damage.

Fin dropped his gaze to Elizabeth who looked close to tears. There was a strange nagging sense of ill ease brewing in his mind ...

"Ms. Nonata, I think you need to explain what is wrong with your brother," the redhead urged quietly, his focus solely on Elizabeth.

Antonio shot a brief perplexed glance in Fin's direction, then redirected his gaze to the assistant and waited for her to answer.

"There is nothin' wrong with me. Now the two of you get out before I break open that window an' toss you out." Jonesy snarled, shifting in his seat.

Elizabeth's shoulders slumped forward before she turned, visibly shaking, to face Fin.

"My ... My brother has ... there are different versions of him. They c-come out at different times, and ... it started when I was still young, and there just seems to be more than there was at first ..."

Captain Antonio was frowning, but he no longer looked ready to stab Jonesy when he registered the sincerity in Elizabeth's tone. Slowly, he sat back down.

"Look. We haven't done anythin' wrong. Get out." Jonesy glared openly.

"They're here from the king. Don't ... don't do anything. W-What about letting Sid do the talking? Please?" Elizabeth remained on her knees, her hands gently gripping her brother's forearms.

Jonesy shook his head and opened his mouth, ready to argue with her, but his sister then squeezed his arms a little more desperately, her fear palpable. Giving his head another small jerk, it looked as though the man was trying to clear his vision, until Jonesy's expression once again fell blank. A dazed far-off look appeared in his eyes as his posture slumped forward.

A moment later he blinked and lifted his eyes. A sharpness in his look told Fin that this had to be yet another person, and so the redhead glanced at the captain who was watching the whole scene with an unreadable expression.

"What's happening, Ellie? Jonesy was cursing about some problem ..." No longer Mathilda or Jonesy, but yet another personality asked.

"Sid, you need to explain to these men about your ... your condition. Please." He looked skeptical over Elizabeth's brief explanation, but once he registered her panicked expression and position on her knees, he visibly caved to her insistence.

"Fine. Just let me change into something that is not so horrendous," he muttered before turning and heading to a chest on the ground a few feet away.

Rummaging around, he drew out a stained cream tunic, trousers, and a leather thong he used to hastily tie his hair back.

In a matter of moments Sid was back in his seat and was studying the two men keenly as though taking in as much about them as he could.

"Well, as you may have heard, my name is Sid. I am here when matters become ... tangled. When things are fine and business pertaining to the brothel needs to be handled, Mathilda likes to speak out. She's a conniving bitch, but she takes care of the girls and knows how to best lure in new customers. If you start to piss off any of the others, you'll meet Jonesy. An idiot who loves to gamble far too much, but he will get rid of any problems that arise."

There was a long stretch of silence where no one said a word, until Fin finally found his voice.

"Do you mean to say you have many people living in your head?" He glanced to the captain and was surprised to see he still wasn't showing any reaction to the news.

"In a way. Jonesy appeared when Warren was sixteen, and since then, more of us have ... come forward to help out when we can. That was a decade or two ago now I believe."

"And who is Warren?" Captain Antonio asked, his voice controlled.

"Warren is this young woman's brother. We exist to protect him." Sid gestured smoothly to Elizabeth whose eyes were fixed on the ground and hands were clasped in her lap.

"What does Warren need to be protected from?" Fin wondered aloud slowly.

Sid considered the question carefully before answering, his fingers laced together casually. "Everything, I suppose. The world isn't a safe place."

"Well, whoever is sitting there, I need to know their involvement in hiding and shipping Troivackian soldiers." Captain Antonio's voice was cool, but he didn't start insulting or discounting what he was hearing, which surprised Fin greatly.

"I'm afraid I know nothing about that. Then again, I haven't needed to come out in ... how long has it been, Ellie?"

"Two months."

"My, my, you all have been doing quite well it seems. Well, no matter, though I think you should investigate Jonesy's bar before claiming complete innocence."

Elizabeth's remaining composure crumbled in that instance. "He wouldn't."

"If Jonesy thought it meant protecting all that we've built, he would."

"What bar does Jonesy run?" Antonio asked, but Fin's mind was already working furiously, and he knew exactly the pub that had an owner as elusive as Madam Mathilda.

"The Wet Whistle," he jumped in, drawing Elizabeth's attention to him.

"That's the one," Sid confirmed with a nod before turning his attention over to the captain. "You're being rather quiet, sir. Usually the armed types aren't the most receptive to strange happenings."

"I've seen men driven mad from grief and pain, and I've seen all kinds of people with tics and oddities that come from a long history of their souls being misused by others. Your affliction is strange, but I've seen stranger in my travels," the captain answered evenly, his blue eye not leaving Sid's face for a moment.

"You don't seem to share memories from your other people ... otherwise, you would know our names and all about Jonesy's bar," Fin observed carefully.

"Clever lad you are." Sid smiled at Fin, revealing a missing eyetooth. "We don't always know what the other has done, it's true. Ellie tries to document our days and interactions best she can, but sometimes we like privacy."

Fin immediately recalled the red book Elizabeth had pulled out to record his statement when he claimed Mathilda had interfered with his business the night he first came to the brothel.

"Why don't your own people record what's happened?"

"Not all of us can read and write. Some of us are ... quite young. At least two of them seem to be children old enough to cling to their mother's skirts. Sometimes if there is something they would find interesting, they overtake this body."

Fin nodded while frowning. He was relatively confident he understood.

It was as though a group of different people all were aboard a ship, but some remained belowdecks while only one could steer ...

"It must be frustrating," the redhead voiced before he could think to stop himself.

"It was a little … off-putting at first, but Ellie here has always been good about helping." Sid reached over and patted the assistant's limp hands as though she were a favorite niece.

Captain Antonio stood then, and with a grim expression he nodded to Fin.

"Well, I understand why you are hidden away now. However … I need you both to be guarded while our search is conducted."

Sid cocked an eyebrow; it was the first time he looked ill at ease.

"Well, sir, I recommend you post some men who are a little more worldly, because otherwise you are going to be getting some very distressed reports."

Antonio gave a curt nod and then gestured at the open door.

"Shall we?"

Fin sat at the bar of Mathilda's with Captain Antonio, Mr. Howard, and Mage Lee discussing what they had discovered about the madam while a unit of knights went to the Wet Whistle.

"Do you believe what he's saying?" Mr. Howard asked while swirling the ruby-colored beverage in his goblet.

"He's either an incredible actor or telling the truth. No, I don't doubt he has more than one person living in his mind, but … I do doubt that there aren't more of them associated with this. Even Elizabeth Nonata, I think, knows more than she's saying. That empty room is too convenient and was oddly clean for not being used regularly as she says," Antonio explained with a shake of his head.

"One thing that is for certain is that it couldn't have just been them smuggling soldiers onto our shores. I've done a thorough search of Madam Mathilda's assets, and the ships she owns are nowhere near large enough for carting an entire army over here. Even with multiple trips." Mr. Howard sipped his beverage and barely suppressed his pleased smile over the wine's quality.

"So we need to figure out who is an enemy here in Daxaria with the resources to contribute to this treason," Captain Antonio reasoned, his blue eye trained on the bar, lost in thought.

"I didn't want to believe it, but is it possible Viscountess Jenoure is actually involved? She certainly has the funds and connections to make such a thing happen. Not only that, but she could have arranged it in exchange for becoming the head of the Piereva family *and* get rid of her ass of a brother if she bargained with King Matthias," Mr. Howard pointed out, and then slowly lowered his goblet as he continued down the train of thought. "In fact … it actually explains … everything."

"She has another brother," Fin blurted out before he could stop himself.

When the men all turned to look at him in surprise—except for Mage Lee who looked deeply unimpressed—Fin quickly added on.

"When I was courting Clara, she mentioned it."

The men all accepted this explanation, except once again for Mage Lee, who rolled his eyes to the ceiling in exasperation. Fortunately, no one other than Fin noticed the response.

"I was definitely forgetting about her brother Charles … though to be perfectly honest it wouldn't be difficult for her to have him killed." Mr. Howard picked up his goblet and drank again.

"Lady Jenoure has been close friends with the queen for years and has inherited great wealth and freedom that she never had before in Troivack. She has not once expressed an interest in returning to her home country …" Captain Antonio explained while shaking his head. "I don't believe she would betray our king."

Fin felt a small breath of relief escape his mouth at Antonio's defense, and so he decided to excuse himself from the conversation to best avoid any other dangerous outbursts.

"Well, I think I'll be heading off. I tried to get the information without involving the knights and failed. Sorry about that." Clapping Antonio on the shoulder, Fin stood and started toward the door, only to have the captain's hand curl around the front of his tunic and hold him still.

"Oh, I don't think so, Ashowan. You need to go talk to your mother. When I had to relay to her that you fled the castle after hearing about our engagement, she was up half the night worrying about you."

Fin's head turned slowly to face the captain, and the other men present stilled.

"How is it you know my mother was awake half the night?"

Antonio blushed.

Maintaining eye contact with the captain, Fin proceeded to peel the captain's hand off of his tunic, his expression bleak.

"This isn't about me, Fin. It's about Kate. Go see her," the captain tried again, but the demand in his voice was replaced with pleading.

"You know, I might have handled the news better if I hadn't been told in a room with multiple eyewitnesses, one of whom was the king." Fin managed to sound casual, but he was standing a little too motionless.

"In fairness to myself, your mother mentioned you blasting a child-hood friend deep into the woods over some silly argument."

"Jiho told her about that?!" Fin spluttered, rounding on the captain and ignoring the highly entertained mage and assistant who watched the whole exchange with gleeful smiles.

"He did. Do you now see how I might have wanted to take precautions once learning that?"

Fin let out a long-suffering sigh before pinching the bridge of his nose and closing his eyes.

"Ashowan, I must say it is nice for once not being the one having to deal with your antics." Mr. Howard sighed dreamily, until the redhead's sharp gaze moved to him, making the man choke on his wine.

"Perhaps this evening you should go home, Fin, hm? Stay out of trouble for once?" Mage Lee suggested while stroking his beard innocently.

"This is none of your business." Fin shot a pointed look at the mage, who responded with an innocent eyebrow lift.

"He's right, Lee, it's a family matter now." Mr. Howard's smile could have guided a lost vessel to shore, it was so bright.

Fin's expression fell flat as his attention shifted to the gleeful assistant and he recalled a wonderful spot in the woods that would be perfect for an unmarked grave. The redhead then noticed Mage Lee's matching smirk and immediately decided death would be too quick for them.

Storming out of the brothel, Fin reluctantly headed to the castle, knowing his mother didn't deserve to suffer just because members of the inner council were delighting in his awkward reactions to her future husband. Besides, the walk would give him the time to craft the perfect revenge for a nosy mage and catty assistant …

CHAPTER 41
WOMEN'S WOES

Annika smiled down into Princess Alina's sleeping face and gingerly reached out with her index finger to lightly tap the baby's small hand. "I've never seen someone so soon after they've been born."

Ainsley smiled and shifted the babe in her arms to rest more comfortably against her chest.

"I'm so happy to see you again," Annika whispered then, her dark eyes moving up to the queen's, the pain and sincerity of her words sobering the mood considerably.

"I'm glad to see you, too. I truly didn't know how it was going to turn out … things just felt … wrong. Did …" Ainsley glanced over at her shut chamber door and lowered her voice. "Did Mr. Ashowan tell you what happened that night?"

Annika blushed and dropped her gaze. Ainsley's eyebrows shot up at the sudden shift in her friend's reaction. She had never known Annika to be so open with her expressions.

"He didn't tell me much other than the state of your health and that you had a baby girl."

Nodding seriously, the queen decided to relay some of the details of the event to her friend now that she was no longer about to board death's carriage.

"Well, I'm told that right after Mrs. Ashowan pulled Alina free, her son was the one to tend to her for hours. He was even the one to introduce her to Eric." Ainsley's hand unconsciously moved to her daughter's back.

Annika was blushing all the harder and was looking intently at the baby in an effort to avoid the queen's bemused expression.

"He was a great help during the birth and with the children from what I hear ..." Ainsley continued, a slow smile spreading on her face as she watched Annika begin to fidget.

"I must say, Viscountess Jenoure, it is quite interesting to see you so ... bashful."

Annika turned around and strolled over to the secret entrance she had come through. "Glad to see you're healthy," she called over her shoulder, her voice sounding strangled.

"Oh, for— Annika! I'm teasing you! Get back here! I need to hear more about this relationship."

Halting her steps, the viscountess didn't immediately come back around.

"I want to know when this whole thing started," Ainsley continued, her tone turning a little more serious. "Norman tells me Finlay is going to be knighted most likely before the war becomes violent, and that if the marriage proceeds between Antonio and his mother, Fin may be in line to inherit a baron title."

Annika finally turned and sidled back to Ainsley's side, her face no longer aflame.

"Yes, though, to be perfectly honest, I didn't plan for Captain Antonio to marry Mrs. Ashowan. I had thought it would take several years before Fin could become a baron ..." Annika sighed wearily and slowly seated herself on the chair beside the queen's bed that Norman had taken to sitting in when coming to visit his wife.

"So how did you two—"

The chamber door suddenly swung open, and Annika was on her feet in an instant with her hood drawn over her face. Ainsley jumped at the clamor and clutched the princess to her chest a little more tightly until she realized it was none other than Katelyn Ashowan.

The woman was carrying a washbasin and halted in alarm when she saw the hooded figure beside the queen. Immediately she opened her mouth to call for the guards when Ainsley hastily whispered, "Shut the door! This is a friend!"

The scream died in Katelyn's throat, and instead she frowned. Following Ainsley's order, the healer closed the door ... only she remained in the room with them.

"Your Majesty, it is time for me to wash and check your stitching," she began while moving carefully closer to the bed.

"Very well." Ainsley's panicked voice instantly began to settle, when suddenly a devilish grin started climbing up her face as she slowly turned her gaze over to Annika who was frozen to the spot.

"Lady Jenoure, would you mind holding Lina while *Mrs. Ashowan* tends to me?"

At the announcement of Annika's identity, Kate's eyes bulged, and her mouth dropped open.

Haltingly, the viscountess lowered her hood, her cheeks once again burning with color.

Kate quickly dipped into a dutiful curtsy to the two women, making Annika grimace.

"Lady Jenoure, it is ... good to see you again." Kate moved over to the bedside where Annika was standing, making her leap back out of the way. The healer set the basin on the bedside table and then eyed the viscountess curiously.

"Er ... ah ... yes. Yes, it is ... good to ... to see you," Annika quickly sidestepped around Kate and stood at the foot of the bed.

"I trust you will not spread any gossip regarding Lady Jenoure's presence in my chambers, Mrs. Ashowan. You see, the inner court finds her a suspicious person due to her brother's recent arrest. However, we have been close friends for years now, and I desperately wanted her to meet the baby," Ainsley explained with a warm smile.

Kate visibly relaxed a little more, but she only nodded in response as she lifted the princess from the queen's arms.

Annika's face suddenly paled when she realized that the healer was picking up the babe with the intention of handing her over.

"Oh, I ... I've never really held a babe before, perhaps I am not the best for—" Katelyn held out the swaddled infant and waited patiently.

"Support the head using the crook of your elbow and wrap your arm under her like so." The healer gently guided Annika's gloved hands to show her what to do while ignoring her protests.

When the princess was properly settled in Annika's arms, everyone waited. The viscountess literally held her breath as they all wondered if the baby would break out crying.

Instead, she nestled in closer to the lady's cloak and let out a small sigh.

Kate had already turned to attend to the queen, and Annika remained rooted to the spot out of fear of disturbing the princess.

"So, Mrs. Ashowan, how did Fin respond to your betrothal?" Ainsley asked, her voice almost musical in its delight.

"He … he stormed out of the castle. I haven't heard from him since." The genuine worry and sorrow in the woman's voice surprised both women.

"I … I'm sure he's fine with it and … and was really just more surprised!" Annika blurted before catching herself and clamping her mouth shut.

Kate turned around eagerly, a hopeful glint in her eyes that paired beautifully with her relieved smile.

"Is that all? Oh, thank the Gods … I had wanted to be the one to tell him, but Antonio said that given Fin's arrest, he wanted to clear the air first. Then of course I foolishly mentioned him blasting Jiho into the woods a few weeks ago …"

"I beg your pardon, Fin did what?" Annika's tone dropped dangerously.

While Kate's face drained of color, Ainsley looked as though she were holding back her laughter.

"He's fine! Jiho wasn't hurt, mostly just annoyed. I am sorry, I really shouldn't have mentioned anything. I—" Kate suddenly turned and looked to the queen who couldn't contain her mirth.

It dawned on Kate then that she and Annika were speaking rather casually … yet the queen didn't seem at all surprised …

"I am sorry, Your Majesty, for bringing my personal matters up. I can assure you that Jiho and Fin have always scuffled since they were boys. I hope you don't think me rude by calling Lord Ryu by his first name, it's just I've known him since—"

"Mrs. Ashowan, I take absolutely no offense to you two discussing matters regarding Mr. Finlay Ashowan. In fact, I would love to hear more about our beloved cook."

Annika glared at Ainsley, while Kate's concerned face gradually shifted to a slight frown.

"Your Majesty …" The healer glanced at Annika who wasn't quick enough in schooling her expression, back to the queen. "Did Lady Jenoure perhaps tell you …"

Ainsley smiled beautifully. "Tell me what, Mrs. Ashowan?"

Kate stared quietly for a few minutes before waving her hand. "Oh, nothing of import. Might I ask where it is you have been staying while being exiled from the castle, Lady Jenoure?"

Annika swallowed nervously before turning her attention to Kate's back as the woman began adjusting Ainsley's knees.

"I have an estate in Austice by the sea."

"Oh, how lovely! I'm sure despite everything going on that it still must be nice to spend some time by ... the ... water..." Kate's work halted, and she turned to look at Annika again with a more calculating gaze. "Do you get many visitors?"

Despite her tone being light, Annika could see the slight stress of aggression in Kate's shoulders.

Ainsley was forced to cover her mouth in an effort to stop herself from laughing before she decided to stir the pot ... just a little.

"I understand you've been in exile, Lady Jenoure, but perhaps you got to go out disguised to see some of the sights. In fact ... why yes! Mrs. Ashowan, didn't you mention that *Fin* was taking a few days off in Austice as well? How fun! Annika did you perhaps *see* Mr. Ashowan during your time away from the castle?"

Annika didn't dare to move and was silently thanking the Gods that she had a newborn in her arms to deter Kate should she become violent.

"I ... I ... erm..."

"What's wrong, Annika? You're usually so well-spoken!" Ainsley was positively glowing.

It was Kate who turned to shoot the queen a dark look before speaking; however, the monarch didn't seem insulted or disquieted in the least.

"I doubt my son would peruse the same streets Lady Jenoure would." The healer's tone was clipped.

Annika stared back and forth between her best friend and her future mother-in-law, completely at a loss, until at long last she gave up.

"Mrs. Ashowan, yes, Fin has been staying with me, and, Ainsley, you're a conniving wench that deserves to choke on tea if you hadn't just come back from the brink of death."

The queen burst out howling in hysterics, unable to suppress her laughter any longer as Kate closed her eyes and let out a long sigh.

"Lady Jenoure, I do not think it is wise for you two to be behaving so brazenly. It speaks ill of both of you should anyone discover the two of you having formed a ... an ... alliance," Kate finished awkwardly while Annika winced and wished that the floor would open and swallow her.

"I know ... we just ... Fin and I needed ... oh, pipe down, you!" the viscountess snapped at the queen who was wiping her eyes and still snorting to herself.

"I would … if I … could … this hurts my stitches … but it is just too … damn … funny!" Ainsley was then set off yet again, and both Kate and Annika were left waiting for her to settle down.

"Fin and I just wanted time to get to know each other without the pretense of hiding …" Annika explained quietly, while blushing deeply for what felt like the hundredth time that day.

"Well, how are you going to stop the staff of your estate from gossiping, hm? All it takes is one maid to talk with another maid," Kate pointed out sternly.

"Oh, none of Annika's staff members can ever step out of line," Ainsley explained while still actively trying not to laugh.

Katelyn's expression turned serious as she stared at the viscountess with obvious assumptions being built up in her mind.

"Why is your staff so beholden to you?"

Annika looked to Ainsley and seriously debated the woman's desire to live another day.

"It … is *supposed* to be a secret," she began slowly. "All my staff members are fugitives or Daxarian-mixed Troivackian bastards. My footmen, my cook, my maids … I'm the only one keeping them from being either impoverished, imprisoned, or beheaded."

"With the king and my permission, of course," Ainsley reminded with a slightly more serious nod.

"I see." Kate frowned thoughtfully.

"Mrs. Ashowan, I … I know this shouldn't come from me, but I do have to leave soon and I need to tell Ainsley that …" Annika didn't know what inspired her to do it, and in the years to come she would call her actions that day "a lapse of sanity."

"This morning, Fin proposed to me."

Ainsley's hand flew to her mouth, while Katelyn stood frozen.

"I … I said yes."

"Oh, good Gods! It's too soon!" Ainsley burst out then, unable to keep out of the discussion, but Annika's gaze was fixed solely on Fin's mother.

"You and the captain have been together almost exactly the same amount of time."

"Yes, but …" Kate's mouth had gone dry, and she immediately began to empathize with her son hearing about her betrothal from the captain. "I've been married before and—"

"So have I."

Kate blinked in astonishment.

"He ... died more than a year ago. He was in his seventies; it ... wasn't sudden ..." Annika tried to explain to lighten the news. "We didn't have any children."

Kate swallowed with obvious difficulty and opened her mouth to reply, when the chamber door opened once again, and in stepped His Majesty, the king.

"Mrs. Ashowan, is everything alright? I thought this was to be a quick—"

Norman stared at the peculiar scene in front of him of Viscountess Jenoure in her trousers and cloak holding his daughter, then to Mrs. Ashowan who was staring at the lady with such a wide range of emotions that he wondered if she had discovered new ones, and Ainsley who looked ...

Like she was having the time of her life.

"Ah, Lady Jenoure ... I thought you were coming this evening." Norman closed the door swiftly behind him.

"I-I had work to attend to this evening so I thought I'd stop in earlier." Annika hastily handed the princess to her father. "I best be on my way then. Mrs. Ashowan has promised not to repeat to anyone that she's seen me. I will take my leave now, good day."

Lady Jenoure then swept over to the false panel, ignoring Kate's startled expression at the hidden door, and disappeared into its opening.

Norman frowned in confusion at her departure, before turning to look back at his wife.

"Is the viscountess feeling alright? She's not usually so flustered."

Ainsley grinned at her husband lovingly, while Kate closed her eyes and appeared to be taking calming breaths.

"Oh, Lady Jenoure is doing perfectly well; I think she was just a little startled by being discovered by Mrs. Ashowan."

Norman nodded slowly, unconvinced that there wasn't more to the strange atmosphere.

"Very well, I'll go retrieve the nursemaid for Lina— Oh, Mrs. Ashowan, I believe I spotted your son heading to his cottage on my way here. Once you're finished tending to Her Majesty, please feel free to go speak with him. I know you've been distressed about his reaction to your betrothal."

Kate's eyes fluttered open, and Norman grew concerned over the intense fury in the woman's face.

"Yes ... *my* betrothal ... We will have much to discuss indeed."

CHAPTER 42
TENUOUS TIMING

After Fin discovered his cottage was empty, he had gone to the barracks to see if his mother was checking up on the men there. Then one of the knights informed him that she was tending to the queen, so he decided to check on his kitchen aides. It was on his way to see them that the redhead noticed his mother had returned to the cottage and was standing outside the door with her hands on her hips.

"Oh no."

Fin had seen that look on his mother enough to know it was a bad sign. He debated fleeing to Annika's estate and returning when Katelyn had cooled down, but didn't like his odds over whether or not she would chase after him.

Slowly, with heavy steps, he began to move toward his cottage, his hands pressed into his pockets, and his head hung a little lower.

As soon as Fin stood in front of his mother, she turned and pointed to the empty cottage behind her.

The redhead let out a long sigh, then crossed the threshold into his house.

Fin strode forward and nodded to the windows and doorway to magically seal off the sound. He could tell this would be a loud discussion ...

Kate stepped into the cottage behind him and closed the door with enough force that the door banged.

"Have you lost your mind?" she demanded, her voice ragged.

Fin turned around with a small frown.

He didn't think it was about him avoiding talking to her about the betrothal anymore ... Was it because Jiho had ratted him out about blasting him into the woods?

"You've been staying with Lady Jenoure for almost a week!" Kate exploded when she could see that her son was obviously confused.

Fin's face drained of color, and he stood up straighter. "How did you ..."

"The viscountess told me herself!" Kate threw her hands in the air and began shaking her head. "If you want to marry that woman, you need to be cautious! What in the world are you two in such a hurry for?! This could completely destroy her reputation, and Gods— What if there is a child conceived? Do you know the shame that—"

"When were you talking with Annika?" Fin interrupted, trying to keep track of his mother's ramblings.

"Not even an hour ago in the queen's chambers. Lady Jenoure came for a secret visit—which I think is another poor idea given that her brother is imprisoned for war crimes. Someone could spot her and try to harm her!"

"Wait ... the queen knows about Annika and me?"

Katelyn made a half groan, half shout, and began pacing furiously.

"Do the two of you never talk?! Her Majesty seemed perfectly aware of what has been happening between the two of you, and she seemed to be having quite a bit of fun about it—"

"She wasn't angry?" Fin asked seriously; the new information brought to light was far more important to him.

"No! Now, I need you to listen to me. You have to be less of a naïve fool and think! I know more about your betrothed's day than you!"

"I haven't even seen Annika since— Wait. She told you we're betrothed?!"

Kate laughed for a moment with a crazed energy moving her features.

"She did! Tell me, is this revenge? Because of Antonio telling you about the betrothal before I did?!"

Fin rubbed his face with both his hands.

It took a lot to make his mother fly off the handle, and to date in his life, Fin had only ever seen her so worked up a total of five times. Usually the best thing to do was escape and let her calm down ... perhaps for a week ...

But Fin was a little too flustered over learning Annika had told his mother and the queen that they were engaged without discussing it with him.

"This is not revenge. I had no idea she was going to tell either of you about the engagement. I was summoned away this morning by Mage Lee to handle some matters in Austice before we could discuss anything more. Now, I came here because *your* betrothed told me you were worried about my reaction to the news of *your* wedding. Which is also … happening … quickly." Fin folded his arms and waited.

Kate's hands flew to her hips, and color tinged her cheeks. "No. You do not get to switch this over to me."

"Then ask me questions instead of accusing me," Fin demanded, raising his voice ever so slightly.

Kate huffed loudly for several moments, just staring at her son.

"Mum, you knew I was pursuing Lady Jenoure. You knew it had gone well; why are you surprised over the betrothal?" the redhead tried again, more gently.

"Because it was so quick!"

Fin shot her a sardonic look.

"It's different, we're old," Kate snapped irritably.

"And I might die in the war."

All color drained from his mother's face, as her hands fell from her hips to her sides, looking as though she had just had her breath stolen.

Fin stared grimly at her. He hadn't confessed his fears to Annika … hadn't wanted anything to touch their happiness … but he needed his mother to understand. Needed her to be happy for him …

"The war hasn't even started yet." Katelyn's voice was quiet, and didn't sound at all confident, making Fin take a step closer to his mother. He knew he had to tell her then … even though he really didn't want to.

"Aidan Helmer is the chief of military for Troivack."

She swallowed with great difficulty. "I know."

Fin frowned, and then annoyed realization crossed his face. "The captain told you, didn't he?"

"Yes. I was going to ask the king to dissolve the marriage when your father arrived so that I could marry Antonio," Kate confessed, her voice still soft as she regarded her son with such obvious love and fear.

Fin let out a sigh before lifting his resigned gaze to his mother. "You know what Aidan's like. He will come after me for revenge after blasting him off the island. I'm just lucky that his ship was delayed by a few days.

It might not be during his visit this time, but if I remember him correctly, he will find some way to punish me."

Kate shook her head, tears welling up in her eyes. "No. No, we will not let him do that. The war could be another year or two away—"

"Mum … it's already started. I can't tell you exactly what is going on, but … I don't think it will be long before the actual fighting begins."

The healer stood, clutching her skirts tightly, her spine rigid. For a long moment she didn't speak or move her watery gaze from her son, and when she did, she sounded as though she hadn't had a sip of water in days.

"I still don't think you should be sleeping with Lady Jenoure before getting married."

Fin managed a small, embarrassed smile. "I'm sorry you had to find out that way."

"I'm sorry that Antonio told you before we talked."

Nodding, Fin opened his arms and raised his eyebrows in question.

With a small sob Kate dove for her son's embrace and clutched him tightly to her.

"Don't you dare let that man take you from me." She wept quietly in his arms, as Fin gently soothed her, rubbing her back gently and kissing the top of her head.

"I don't plan to."

A knock rang out into the cottage, startling both mother and son out of their embrace.

Dabbing the tears off her face with the back of her wrist, Kate opened the door and was surprised to see Captain Antonio standing there with a line of knights standing farther back.

"Sorry to interrupt, lass." He gazed warmly down at his betrothed who blushed and sniffled. "I take it matters are sorted?"

Antonio turned his gaze to Fin, who gave a somber nod of affirmation. "What is the matter, Captain?"

"We spoke to some of the prostitutes and believe that we have found another possible hideout. I wondered if you would like to join in the search. After all, there is talk of having you knighted soon." There was a twinkle in the captain's eye that gave Fin mixed feelings.

"Do I have to wear armor?"

"You're not a knight yet, Ashowan!" Antonio laughed. "No, we'll have you fitted with a leather vest, and if you want an old sword or spear, you're welcome to it. Come now. You started this madness."

Fin gave a slightly grim smile as he stepped out and the captain clapped his shoulder amicably.

As he took a few more steps closer to the line of knights who were all eyeing him warily, Fin could hear his mother worriedly whispering something to Antonio behind him.

The redhead waited for the captain to join him at his side before asking, "What was that about?"

Antonio's good mood had disappeared, and it was obvious that something was wrong.

"Your mother said she heard that your father's ship was delayed … she also said that he used to send a messenger to her back before he left you both, saying he would be late returning home, then come right on time to make sure she wasn't healing the islanders."

Fin's blood ran cold.

He knew his mother had taken some of the abuse quietly, but he hadn't known that particular cruel trick.

"So that means …"

"Your father is probably coming right when he first said he would," Antonio growled.

"Oh Gods." Fin stopped in his tracks and turned to face the captain, who wore an equally severe expression. "That means he will be here tomorrow."

Norman stared at the two men and felt his blood simmer at the news.

"Mr. Ashowan, I am sorry to say this because of your blood relation to the man, but your father is—"

"An ass," Fin finished for the king darkly. "I'll go to the kitchen immediately and have them start preparing for tomorrow. I can try and find Ruby as well so that they have the rooms prepared."

"Captain, I want you to go to the property you found by the harbor and empty it of any and all Troivackian soldiers. Fin, you can go with him, but once you are finished, I want you to come see me. I want to discuss the possibility of you protecting Her Majesty and my children."

"Would it be possible, Your Majesty, for that discussion to happen in the kitchen? There will be a great deal of work to do and as much as I wish my father to try whatever new recipe my aides have invented, I'm sure not all his entourage is deserving of such cruelty."

Norman managed to give a small laugh. "Yes. Send a steward up to me and I will come down. I need to firm up Zinfera's army before Mr. Helmer returns to Troivack, so I will be in council meetings regarding Lord Jiho Ryu becoming a dual citizen and a baron, as well as Sir Harris and Lady Marigold Iones for the rest of the day." Norman addressed Antonio then. "Have a squire bring me your records on Sir Harris's performance while here at the castle, and inform him to be prepared to be summoned."

Fin was taken aback at just having learned his childhood friend was becoming ennobled in Daxaria … though he suspected it had something to do with Annika getting out of marrying him …

"Sire, perhaps we should have some of your knights keep an eye on Lady Marigold and her mother. Word travels quickly in this castle and I would not be at all surprised if one of them tried to have Sir Harris attacked, or worse, killed."

Antonio looked to Fin both surprised and impressed over the political insight. "I agree wholeheartedly, Mr. Ashowan; I was thinking of doing something similar as well."

"The paperwork ennobling Lord Ryu and the tax agreement should have reached the emperor by now, meaning the Zinferan army will begin sending forty-five percent of their army sometime over the next three days," the king explained to Captain Antonio, the stress in his voice abundantly clear.

"This is all good news, isn't it? We have discovered their hidden knights, and now we have guaranteed help from the Zinferans. They should be here in a matter of weeks." Fin began slowly, hoping that he wasn't missing another integral piece to the war somehow.

Norman straightened his shoulders and glanced over his shoulder at his closed chamber door where Ainsley slept soundly, unaware of the chaos brewing mere steps away.

"I don't know why, but I have a bad feeling about this … even if we manage to stay on top of everything and catch Aidan Helmer in his trick … I just feel uneasy." He shook his head.

Fin and Antonio glanced at each other, a wordless understanding passing between the two of them.

They felt the exact same way, and it wasn't just because the rain and thunder had resumed outside.

Something dark was on the horizon, and try as they might to fight against it, it seemed like it would descend upon them quickly.

Both Fin and Antonio bowed to the king, then turned to complete their assigned tasks. With each step, the sober weight of reality began to press down on the redheaded witch.

It would seem his happy carefree days were coming to an abrupt end, and it was time to brace for the storm.

CHAPTER 43
CAUGHT RED-HANDED

Fin stared at the kitchen aides in the faint firelight of the candles and hearth, his eyes somber and his hands in his pockets.

The group all shifted awkwardly, not saying a word as the vibrato of crickets wafted in through the open window.

"So … your father is coming … tomorrow?" Hannah asked slowly, while glancing nervously at Peter.

"He is. I'll be heading out shortly for some work with the captain, but when I get back, we are working on preparing enough food. It'll be like Beltane all over again."

Sirs Andrews and Lewis groaned aloud.

Sir Harris turned with an arched eyebrow to stare at them. "Was it really that bad?"

"Yes," everyone in the room answered in unison.

"Also, Harris, you better go to the barracks. Captain Antonio has a few messages for you," Fin informed him sternly.

The knight looked uncertain by the sudden announcement, but he did as instructed and excused himself from the room after giving an affirmative nod.

Fin began giving out his instructions to the staff who, for once, didn't dispute his orders.

"I'll be back around midnight; try to have everything ready by then so that we can start preparing for breakfast. Remember, with breakfast you cook the meat and dice the fruit *last* and focus on baking the bread first to avoid poisoning people."

The knights all looked off innocently in various directions, Hannah suddenly became interested in her toes, and Heather and Peter had the good grace to blush and wince.

Fin cleared his throat, making sure to cast one final flat look at the aides to let them know he was far from letting the food poisoning incident go.

As he slowly rounded the table and strode toward the garden door, the staff gradually shifted to their duties, all but Sir Taylor who was in the process of nudging Hannah toward Fin.

The blonde looked uncertain, but she gave the burly knight a hesitant nod of understanding.

Stepping lightly after their superior, Hannah caught up to him just outside the kitchen door. "Er ... Fin? Might I ... talk with you?"

The cook turned his head and stared with a mildly concerned expression then shifted to be facing the petite blonde directly.

"It's just that ... well ... are you going to be alright with ... with your father being under the same roof as you?"

Fin felt the pain in his chest that had started building the moment he and Antonio had realized that Aidan Helmer would be descending upon them. There was a reason his hands were shoved into his pockets ... he knew they had a tremor.

"It's fine, Hannah, it was many years ago." Fin tried to turn back around and walk away from the conversation, but she once again stopped him.

"It's still your father. I know even when I don't want something like that to matter it ... somehow still does."

Fin's face tensed as he remembered what Lee had told him a few nights previous about Hannah's own father. He felt a new wave of guilt fill him as he realized he knew far more about her situation than she may want.

"I'm sorry, Hannah," Fin started, immediately making her expression turn tense and hesitant. "A few days ago someone told me about your family history ... it isn't my business to know, and I hadn't asked about it; they just ... told me."

Embarrassment, followed by a deeply pained emotion, marred the maid's face as she took a small step back to the warm glow of the kitchen behind her. Fin's hands clenched in his pockets, and he immediately wondered if he shouldn't have told her that he knew, when she spoke.

"I guess that means you know I speak from experience." Her voice was quiet. "My father was a cruel man, and he sold me to a brothel when I was fifteen. Even though he died before I had to go, and I managed to give them back the money they paid, no one would ever want to marry me in my village knowing that …" She trailed off; a small croak in her throat had started that wrenched Fin's heart sickeningly.

After a moment of regaining her composure, Hannah resumed speaking. "It doesn't matter that he died four years ago. It could be twenty and if he were alive and showed up, I would somehow feel … feel like I did back when I was with him."

"What happened to your brother?" Fin asked softly, hoping to lessen the pain in her eyes.

"My best friend back in my village … she and her husband took him in. I send them money to help, but I didn't want being around me to hurt him. If I had brought him here with me, there was no chance that I would've been able to protect him … that is, until you came."

Fin stilled.

"I might … after the war … be able to bring him here, because you … you made me stronger. You've made all of us stronger. You've made us feel like we belong here. Like this is … an actual home to us. The knights that used to terrify me and make me cry myself to sleep at night are now like my older brothers. When I started standing up for myself, Peter realized I needed help, and now he's my best friend. He was so quiet before, and is so much older than myself, that I never would've bothered. It isn't just that you've helped us all, either; it's that … well … you're … all my family, Fin. You gave me a family I can count on and love. So if you need help, please tell us."

The only sound between them was the clattering that came from within the kitchen, and the singing crickets. Fin stepped forward heavily and drew Hannah into an embrace.

Patting her back, the redhead did his best to swallow down the swell of emotions that threatened to overflow.

"Thank you," he managed hoarsely.

When the pair separated again, Fin moved his hands to her slender shoulders and stared earnestly at the young woman, a small smile on his face.

"I will definitely say if I need help. Even though you've all done more than enough already pertaining to a certain noblewoman ..."

Hannah grinned devilishly, which made her look far more like herself. "How is your courtship going?"

Fin chuckled and dropped his hands to his sides. "We're betrothed actually."

The blond maid's jaw dropped. "What?! So soon? When ... how ... where ... When?!"

"You asked when already, but these are questions that will have to be answered another time. I need to go convene with the captain." Ruffling the top of Hannah's head and making her squawk in displeasure, Fin turned and once again moved away from the castle.

As he walked, he couldn't help but notice that he was able to stand a little straighter, and even his hands felt steady enough to stitch wings back onto a fly.

He could face his father ... He just had to keep remembering that he wasn't alone anymore. Now there were people who accepted and cared about him exactly as he was. The old voice that had always told him such a thing was unattainable was defeated, and that win was something Aidan Helmer wasn't going to take from him ever again.

As they crept along the docks, the creaking of the ships in the dark waters echoed around Captain Antonio and the squadron he had brought.

"Do you see the abandoned inn over there?" the captain whispered to Fin, who was trying to watch his feet so that he wouldn't misstep and fall into the Alcide Sea.

"I can't see anything," the redhead murmured back. It was true that they had opted to go without torches so that if there were any Troivackian soldiers hiding they would not be alerted.

"Do you see where the tavern's torch is lit?"

"Yes."

"Do you see the inn that has collapsed into the water beside it?"

"I thought that was a rock!" Fin couldn't help but exclaim when he realized the half-sunken lumpy crest at the end of the Austice road was their destination.

"It's one of the reasons we never suspected anything strange. The entire building looks as though it is about to crumble into the sea with one good storm, but if that pub were connected to it somehow ... well ..."

Fin nodded in understanding as he moved toward the destination with more certainty, eyeing its precarious balance on the rocks with renewed interest.

With them were perhaps ten knights, and another ten were waiting up the street that could easily arrive should they be called upon.

Once in front of the sunken building, the captain pointed to the ground to draw everyone's attention to the foot-wide crack between the land and the building that dropped straight down into the sea. Nodding in understanding, the men carefully stepped over the gap and filed into the building as quietly as possible.

Fin and the captain, being the last ones in, then had to creep around the severely slanted floors while maintaining their footing in the dark.

Piles of broken chairs and tables were pushed against the walls, and more than the occasional loose or rotted floorboard shifted beneath their feet.

Fin's heart was in his ears as the slight shuffling of men moving through the building uninterrupted blended with the swish of waves beneath them. There was a tension in the air the redhead wasn't familiar with, and not having any light to navigate by was frustrating, but he knew it wouldn't be for long.

Now that they were in the building, and the door behind them closed, Antonio finally called out: "Torches."

Five bursts of light suddenly appeared around the room, showing how absolutely frightening the inn truly was.

Cracks ran across the ceiling and in the corners, and several spots looked wet and waiting for an errant step. As the group surveyed their surroundings, it became plain to see that no one had lived there in quite some time, and not only that, but the stairs to the second story were no longer attached to the upper landing at all.

"I don't like this," the captain growled beside Fin, making him give a small start.

"Sir, there's a pair of trousers and other odd clothing pieces along this back wall," one of the knights called out.

Antonio frowned.

"Captain, what if … this building is only for hiding the men when knights come to the next-door tavern?" Fin asked suddenly as he eyed the wall of the inn that was still relatively intact. "Only half of this building has collapsed fully away from where it was … what if it's like Mathilda's maze in the attics?"

Fin nodded to the wall that could have been shared with the tavern back before the erosion of land beneath them. In all honesty, the precariousness of the creaking floor beneath him made him a little eager to be back on solid land.

"This place wouldn't be able to safely hide more than twenty men at most," the captain voiced pensively.

"Yes, but if the pub had an apartment above and a basement built into the rock where they keep their ale barrels … they wouldn't need this place to house all of them."

The captain's lone blue eye swiveled over to the wall that Fin had gestured at where many of his men had already started searching after hearing the redhead's idea.

After a few moments, another knight called out.

"Here, sir! It doesn't open straight into the pub, but … well … come take a look."

Both Fin and the captain moved over to the broken set of shelves that the knight had pressed open to reveal a second door that undoubtedly led to the pub but was obviously locked shut.

Grinning ruthlessly, Antonio turned to Fin. "Feel like grabbing a drink?"

The plan was simple; all Fin had to do was go in, and see if any Troivackians were in the pub. Then he was to take note of who did anything that could be a warning to any hidden soldiers when the captain made his entrance. Given that the establishment was owned and run by Madam Mathilda's alter personality, Jonesy, the bartender may not have been the one who knew anything …

Fin sidled up to the bar and slowly seated himself. Ordering himself a tankard, he watched how the occupants of the pub appeared to be a handful of weary sailors and the occasional seedy characters. Pretty standard patronage … and not a Troivackian in sight.

He eyed a door to the side of the bar and glanced at the bartender as he poured the frothy beverage with a complacent expression that matched his sallow coloring.

Fin looked around the pub and considered the surroundings more carefully.

Despite the room being well lit, and the bar obviously well stocked, it occurred to the redhead then that the establishment, despite its prime location beside the docks, wasn't all that busy …

"Here you are," the bartender said, setting Fin's drink in front of him, then immediately snatching up the coin Fin had dropped on the bar surface.

"Thanks; surprised you don't have more people in here." The witch tried to relax his speech cautiously.

The man with his balding head and deep scowl lines glared in response. "We close early."

Giving a single shoulder shrug, the redhead picked up the ale and pretended to take a drink. He didn't need a repeat of the night at Madam Mathilda's.

He was about to start trying to find a gap in time to sneak into the closed-off room, when an unsuspected cry boomed out: "OYY! FIN! LAD! I'VE BEEN SEARCHIN' FOR YOU!"

The redhead spilled his ale; he was so taken aback by the shout, and several heads swiveled around to see the newcomer.

Once he had landed his drink safely on the bar, Fin looked over hastily to see who was disrupting the plan.

Red, the man who had tried to mug Fin when he had first begun looking for the Troivackians, stood grinning at him as he strode into the tavern.

"I was searchin' at Mathilda's for ye ever since the festival. What a spectacular night that was, eh? Did you hear that the brothel closed down?"

Fin blinked and was still reeling from being startled.

What in the world was Red doing so far south in the city … ? Alarm bells were clanging very loudly in Fin's head.

"Yeah, I, uh, ran into one of the girls. She said you kept going back asking for me. What was that about?"

"Well, you see, I had wanted to talk to you 'bout how you were lookin' for those Troivackian men." Red held up a single finger to the bartender who was watching the entire situation like a cat monitoring pending danger; in other words, gearing up to scurry away.

Once Red had a pint in his hand, he seated himself on the stool beside Fin and leaned both elbows on the bar.

"I know those Troivackians, they lifted your change that day, an' well … I felt bad. Wondered if you wanted a bit 'o work. You made the best food I'd ever tried …"

Fin waited as all the pieces of the puzzle began to shift closer together as Red referenced the mugging story he had made up when they had first met …

324

Someone had sent Sandy to distract him, and when Annika had shown up and gotten rid of her, Red had shown up and redirected him.

Red had been talking with his son and friend about the Troivackians when they'd first met … And now, he was conveniently located at the same tavern the final group of soldiers were allegedly hiding in.

"After all, you seem to know quite a few people around the city, like those knights out front." Red took a sip from his ale and turned to face Fin, a strange gleam in his eyes.

Fin heard the door beside the bar open and heard the weapons being drawn.

"Pity it had to be like this," Red announced as the bartender suddenly ducked beneath the bar while clutching two bottles of what the redhead guessed to be expensive liquor.

Fin noticed in the reflection of his steel tankard someone approaching him from behind.

"It is indeed, Red. Too bad, I was looking forward to meeting your missus."

Fin ducked suddenly, and narrowly avoided the sword that sang past his ear; turning with his tankard in hand, he threw the item into the face of his attacker.

When he faced the group that had emerged from the storage room of the tavern, he counted ten, but he knew there were most likely more hiding.

Fortunately … the front door sprang open, and this time Captain Antonio emerged with the knights behind him.

Red shrugged. "Sorry to say, lad, we have a few more in the reserves."

The pounding of an extra dozen feet could be heard as they clambered down from the apartment above, and up from the basement.

"Oh, we know." Fin then heard the undeniable splintering of wood from below as the group of Antonio's knights that had remained in the dilapidated inn blocked off the secret exit. Red frowned at the sound, clearly understanding that things had just run frightfully awry.

Fin smiled, though he gave an apologetic shrug.

"Don't worry, we wanted it to be a fair fight."

CHAPTER 44
RED SKY IN THE MORNING

As the fighting raged on, Fin mostly managed to deflect blows and stay out of the Troivackian soldiers' way using stools and tankards as weapons until the captain handed him back the spear Fin had chosen before leaving the castle.

The Troivackians that continued pouring up and down from the cellar and apartment above made the tavern grow more and more disarrayed and splattered with errant drops of blood; though it seemed no one had died yet, there were a number of stab wounds and broken noses.

The knights were absorbing most of the Troivackians' attacks, but occasionally an innocent patron of the tavern got caught in the crosshairs. Fin ducked under a heavy fist that had swung closer to his face and delivered a cheap shot to the man's groin before lunging toward the remaining three sailors who were trying unsuccessfully to leave the violent scene.

"Follow me. Stick to the walls," Fin managed to explain over the din.

Sure enough, slowly but surely, they made their way through the crowd with Fin parrying and shoving the occasional soldier who stumbled across his path. For the most part, the Troivackians who had joined the fight more recently mistook the redhead for a civilian despite the spear in his hand, and so they didn't bother trying to fight him when faced with the other soldiers who wore chest plates and helmets.

Once Fin and the sailors managed to clear the pub doorway, they nearly crashed into another two knights who were standing guard to prevent anyone else from entering or exiting.

"Mr. Ashowan, are these men with the Troivackians?" one of the knights Fin had never met in his life called out.

"No, they just got caught in the crossfire," the redhead explained briefly before the sailors thanked him and proceeded to flee.

"I'll go check to see how the men are doing in the inn," Fin explained before darting back to the half-sunken building where shouts and cries rang out.

"We think another group of Troivackians are nearby; we just saw a cloaked figure dart into the building," the knight called out as Fin moved to step over the gap between the doorway and land.

"It was only one of them, but we were told we had to stay here. See if you can get him out."

The redhead froze.

A lone cloaked figure running into danger …

She wouldn't … no. Why would she be here … ?

Fin dove into the building, and sure enough, he saw a small, hooded figure throwing knives and ducking blows from four Troivackian soldiers. It appeared that the Daxarian men had crossed fully over into the tavern and the four were the only ones who had managed to squeeze back through the fray to the inn with the hope of escaping.

Gritting his teeth, Fin stepped in and, using his spear, swiped out the leg of one of the soldiers, who banged his head and immediately fell unconscious, while Annika felled another. The two remaining Troivackians widened their distance to make them harder targets for the mysterious cloaked being and the tall redhead wielding a spear.

"You … shouldn't, ugh, be here," Fin ground out while dodging the blows with great difficulty. The only advantage he had was he had a weapon and the Troivackian hadn't made it to the higher ground of the inn. Otherwise, he could tell that the men would've outclassed him in combative technique.

"Neither …" Annika ripped the dagger she had lodged in one of the fallen men's shoulders and swiftly ducked another blow before plunging it into her new attacker's thigh. "Should you!"

"Yes … I, oof." The Troivackian soldier had landed a rather painful blow to Fin's abdomen, and were it not for the gravity of the building working with him, he was quite certain his shove wouldn't have been enough

327

to make the Troivackian stumble away from him to give him breathing room. "Should be."

Annika launched herself up from her crouched position and tried to ram her head into the soldier's jaw, only he wrapped his arms around her and began to squeeze her, crushing her.

Fin shifted the spear in his hand, and even though he saw his own assailant charging up toward him, he jabbed the weapon into the neck of the man who was attempting to snap Annika in two.

Promptly after his successful attack, the redhead was tackled brutally to the floor, though he managed to hear Annika's assailant crumple to the ground.

As the soldier on top of Fin began to straighten on his knees to pummel him, Annika rose from behind him. The last Troivackian's eyes suddenly widened and grew vacant before he slowly collapsed over the redhead.

With a grunt, Fin managed to shove off the body, noting the knife plunged through his back to his heart.

"What do you mean you're supposed to be here?" Annika panted while hunched over slightly.

"Are you alright?" Fin asked while standing with his own wince of pain.

"Fine, fine. Just a cracked rib or two."

"Go see my mother and have her heal you," Fin ordered immediately while gesturing to the empty doorway and yet also gently raising her hood back over her head.

"I said it's fine. These will heal in their own time."

"Why won't you go see her? Given the fact that you told her we were engaged already, I would think you were feeling quite close with her," Fin panted, lifting an eyebrow while slowly steering Annika to the door by clasping her shoulders.

"Oh Gods … I'm so sorry … I panicked," she explained with a small gasp as Fin ushered her over the threshold. The knights standing outside the tavern eyed the pair curiously, so the redhead turned and blocked her from view.

"Just a local pickpocket who thought they could lift some coin during the fight," he called out. "We need more men guarding this door, though." He added the last hastily before they could say anything.

"No need, Mr. Ashowan. We've rounded up the entire group. They're already being escorted out of Austice." Antonio appeared in the doorway of the tavern and turned to face the redhead with his calm blue eye squinting slightly into the darkness.

"That's good. There is one unconscious Troivackian in there, though the others the Daxarian soldiers took care of," Fin said quickly, thinking of the three corpses he and his fiancée had left behind.

Antonio waved behind himself to have two men go through the doorway and find the lone survivor of Annika's attack, making Fin take a hasty step back and hope that she was still successfully hidden behind him.

"Not bad for your first raid; you did the right thing by taking care of the civilians, though your form and attacks could use some work. We will have to wait to further interrogate that man who you seem to know … Red, was it? Anyway, we have far more pressing matters to attend to this week." Antonio stepped forward and gave Fin a brief nod of appraisal, then noticed his slightly pained expression. "Are you hurt?"

"Got tackled. Bruised my back."

"Ah, well. Considering most of the injuries are of a similar minor caliber, it's a good thing we know a certain healer who doesn't mind giving us a hand."

"Physician Durand is quite talented."

Captain Antonio shook his head and chuckled before clapping his hand on Fin's shoulder, and making his knees buckle as a sharp stab of pain ran through his back.

"Sorry." When he noticed Fin's pained expression, Antonio quickly removed his hand and stepped back. "Now, who was the hooded woman you guided out of the inn and let run off?"

Fin felt his face pale.

"Was it that pesky agent of His Majesty?" Antonio dropped his voice so that no one else could overhear them.

"You … know about her?" Fin asked slowly.

"Oh, I know His Majesty has a woman who scouts out some of our raids and reports numbers for us to prepare for. If I see a small, hooded figure, I am never to attack unless they aren't able to identify themselves as 'the Dragon.'" Antonio stared off into the distance where Fin guessed Annika had fled, for the captain was right and she was no longer hiding behind him.

"I'm surprised you know about her, though." The military man eyed Fin with interest. "I only learned of her existence when the king told me that, due to the war, she would be more active in the field."

"It was an accident. I, uh, found her wounded one day and gave her a hand." Despite the pain in Fin's back from the fight, he could feel a cold sweat building along his spine.

"Ah," the Captain nodded understandingly, but he was still eyeing the redhead curiously. "Well, let us return, shall we? Your father will be upon us by dawn, and we wouldn't want to appear as though we're eager to see him."

Fin glanced over his shoulder at the vessels that bobbed in the water behind him and felt sickening dread well up inside his gut. "No. I suppose we wouldn't."

The gangplank lowered, and Troivackian crewmembers began filing off the ship carrying various trunks and baskets, before then lining up on the dock to wait. The captain of the vessel was next off the ship as he then stood across from the gangplank and bowed.

Captain Antonio squinted against the bright morning sun as the tall shadowy figure strode leisurely down the gangplank with two rows of soldiers behind him. When he drew nearer, Antonio lowered his hand and stared at a man who, without a doubt, was Finlay Ashowan's father.

The resemblance was uncanny.

The narrow face with high cheekbones, the shape of his mouth, the hair that had obviously once been red, but was instead a light blond and white, his slanted eyes …

The eyes stopped Antonio and made him want to let out a sigh of relief. As the Troivackian chief of military drew closer, his gaze fixed on the captain, it became clear that instead of the piercing blue of Fin's, his father's were black as coal.

As Aidan Helmer continued to stride up the dock to land, Antonio could see other little differences that somehow made him feel better and better.

While the cook didn't tend to smile a great deal, he didn't have frown lines etched in his forehead, either. Another difference was their distinct style … while Fin dressed in plain practical trousers and tunics, his father … well, his father wore a rich burgundy vest and fine black tunic with matching pants.

When the Troivackian chief of military finally stood before the captain, the two bowed to each other as equals.

"Good to meet you, Captain, I have heard wonderful things about your prowess here in Daxaria's military." Aidan Helmer greeted Antonio with a practiced smile.

"I am glad to hear it. Shall we head to the castle now?" Antonio gestured to the road where on either side, several rows of his own knights stood. Beyond them sat a fine carriage.

The captain had insulted Aidan by not being equally complimentary or making small talk regarding the journey. His reward for it was a flash of ire in the Troivackian chief of military's eyes.

About what I expected from what they've told me, Antonio mused to himself.

"Oh, no hurry, Captain, I know I sent that letter a few days ago saying I would be delayed, so I'm sure His Majesty would like some more time to prepare. I can tour the city while arrangements are—"

"Not at all. We expected that you would arrive on time." Antonio showed his own smile then. Cold, and cutting.

Another small twitch of Aidan's eyebrows showed the captain that he had succeeded in annoying him.

"How ever did you come to that … *fortunate* guess?" Aidan asked as they stepped toward the waiting carriage.

"We received the same rainstorm you must have encountered, and it didn't seem to be any more than a drizzle," Antonio made up on the spot thinking of the day of the thunderstorm where he and Finlay had gone to question Madam Mathilda.

"I see." There was skepticism in Aidan's tone, but the captain's stoic expression didn't betray anything, so Aidan pressed on. "It is unfortunate I must return to my home shores under such circumstances, but perhaps my visit will prove more endearing than one might anticipate."

Antonio didn't like the far-off look Aidan had in his eyes, nor did he like the slight smile that pulled at a corner of his mouth.

"How long has it been since you've been on Daxarian land?"

"Oh … about twenty years."

"That's a long time to be gone and not return."

"It is. I may even try to track down that darling wife of mine while I'm here." Aidan sighed and tutted to himself as though thinking of an errant child.

Antonio's blood began to boil, but the captain had years of experience keeping his composure as he moved closer to the carriage. "Does she know you are here?"

"Oh, I doubt it. Though I think she is somewhere nearby … after all, I wouldn't be here if it weren't for her message."

Antonio almost stopped walking he was so shocked, but there was no hiding his frown.

"What message?"

"Oh, the message detailing Earl Piereva's abhorrent behavior while here. All the accounts were written down and organized so efficiently that your king simply added his seal and forwarded the report to us." Aidan smiled then, sensing that he had rattled the captain somehow.

Antonio's stomach churned; there was no way Kate could have done such a thing and not told him …

"I know that woman's handwriting intimately, but it was how I got the message that left me without a single doubt as to it being her."

The men had finally reached the carriage and a footman was hastily opening the door for their guest, his eyes downcast.

"What method was that?" the captain asked, forcing himself to sound only casually interested.

"His Majesty didn't mention it? He had the message expediently delivered to me from a certain air witch my wife was friends with many, many years ago. In fact, perhaps she is staying with her now that I think about it. After all, our son is in his late twenties and most likely doesn't want his mother living with him. Captain, would you mind perhaps looking for a woman named Sky? It would be so very kind of you if you might reunite me with my wife."

Antonio didn't respond, only inclined his head ever so slightly as Aidan Helmer climbed into his carriage.

As the vehicle lurched into motion and began its long journey up the center road of Austice, the captain watched with his back ramrod straight, and his face immobile. After a few moments, he allowed himself to think and breathe again when he was certain he was back in control of his impulses. Though, despite not bellowing out ferociously like he wished to, he did still make a less than peaceful decision.

That man will not live past the war. I swear it.

CHAPTER 45
TAKING THE OFFENSIVE

Ainsley watched as her husband finished buttoning his tunic up to his throat before donning the fine blue velvet coat that had been laid out for him. She could see the nervousness in his slight frown and distracted gaze as she continued cradling their sleeping daughter in her arms.

"I have a question I have been wanting to ask you for a while now, and … I need to ask it now before I lose you completely to the stress of having Troivack's chief of military under our roof."

Norman turned to face his wife, and it was clear that pulling himself from his many thoughts was difficult enough.

"Why is it that you chose to send Finlay Ashowan to investigate the whereabouts of the Troivackian soldiers instead of one of your knights or a mercenary? He isn't a trained soldier, and off the castle grounds he has no magic."

Surprisingly, a glimmer of good humor spread to the king's eyes, and his shoulders relaxed.

"I did have other knights searching, but Austice is a military city; all the soldiers are known, and it would take me too long to find a trustworthy mercenary after Lady Jenoure had to send hers away. Fin had asked me for a bit of a rest, and so … I thought … might as well see what he finds. After all, things seem to turn out … well … if he is involved."

The incredulous eyebrow raise his wife gave him urged Norman to expound on his answer.

"There is a lot of chaos before the beneficial results, but somehow even those events wind up as good stories in the end. For example, never in my life did I think I would have an official Royal Secret pertaining to ten fountains located all over the grounds."

Even Ainsley couldn't suppress a small snort at the memory.

"Well … there is another reason I had as well."

The queen tilted her head with interest.

"Finlay can protect the castle grounds because they are his home, but what if … what if I gave him an even bigger radius to think of as 'home'? I wondered if he spent more time out in Austice, if perhaps he could feel that way about the whole city."

A glint of conniving interest sparked in the queen's eyes. She, too, had been wondering about such a thing.

"Have you asked Mr. Ashowan about this?"

"I've avoided it as there was always so much to think about, and he has until recently been incredibly private about his magic … but … it is starting to feel more urgent that I ask him. Once his father leaves, I will broach the subject."

Ainsley nodded somberly, but as she studied her husband's face, a sly smile tugged at the corner of her lips. "I'm beginning to realize the amount you've kept to yourself during my final months of pregnancy with Lina."

Norman closed his eyes with a small wince and strained smile. "Sorry, love."

"I understand why; I'm not upset. To be perfectly honest, though, sometimes I need a distraction from other troubles, so in the future … don't carry your burdens alone. Remember, I'm the one who got you into this whole mess of being king," she reminded him playfully. "If it were up to you, we'd be fat and lazy on your homelands blissfully ignorant of the kingdom's plights."

Norman laughed. The stress his position brought him had molded deep worry lines in his face, he at times lost sleep, and other times he loathed the moments he lost with his son …

But Ainsley always reminded him it was worth it.

They had created a kingdom together that, while not without its issues, was built on trust, loyalty, and fairness. It was still a mess—implementing great changes tended to take many years of hard work—but Norman could honestly say it was better than it had been when he'd first been crowned.

"As much as I love to admire you in your new coat, go welcome that soiled loincloth known as Aidan Helmer, and tell me all about him." Ainsley smiled ruthlessly, and Norman grinned back.

The truth was over the years, many people forgot that when Ainsley wasn't wracked with grief or occupied by taking care of herself while pregnant ... she was an incredibly sharp, and capable woman.

The birth of their daughter and the subsequent consequence of the queen no longer being able to have children meant that the many nobles and members of the kingdom were in for a surprise in the coming weeks ... one that Norman was more than a little excited for.

Aidan strode into the castle's entrance already displeased.

The king hadn't been waiting nervously on the steps like he should've been, *and* they had been prepared for his arrival.

Either my wife or son warned the king of my methods ... how ... annoying.

Footmen carried his trunks, and maids scurried by and recoiled from his charcoal gaze.

Strange. Most women find me alluring ... Even as an enemy representative this seems odd ...

A woman stepped forward then. Plump, plain, but her gaze was direct and her spine straight.

"We are pleased to receive you, Mr. Helmer. I am Head of Housekeeping, Ruby. His Majesty is awaiting you in the throne room," Ruby announced while studying him with a keen interest. It was remarkable how much he looked like Finlay ...

Aidan's slitted gaze surveyed the woman with deeper displeasure. She was all too entitled for her role. It was supposed to be the king himself that was to greet a foreign diplomat! This welcome suggested that the ruler of Daxaria believed himself to be in a far superior position for the coming war than he was.

Without acknowledging the woman called "Ruby," Aidan continued in the direction she had gestured, assuming that footmen would appear to guide him in the proper direction.

Unlike the Troivackian castle, this one had clearly not been built for its royalty to reside in throughout the year. Austice was a military city, and so when the King of Daxaria had declared that it would be his main residence five years prior, it sent many interesting messages out to his citizens, as well as his foes.

The building itself had smaller rooms, narrow passageways, and a strange layout that Aidan didn't like one bit.

He kept these thoughts to himself, however, as he strode down a northern corridor that appeared to be lined with guards and serving staff.

As he walked, he noticed several interesting things.

For one, the stones beneath his feet were barely worn.

Did they not have people in the throne room that often?

Where would he deliver his decrees upon his people?

For another thing, not a single member of nobility had come to exchange pleasantries with him. The lackadaisical handling of hospitality further irritated the fire witch.

Once in front of the throne room doors, Aidan raised an eyebrow at the guards standing at the ready.

The men stared through him as though he weren't there, but they opened the doors regardless.

"Presenting Mr. Aidan Helmer, Chief of Military of Troivack."

Instead of a booming imperial voice, Aidan's gaze cut to a man with sandy brown hair and clear blue eyes who already looked irritated. When they locked eyes, the Daxarian notably stiffened, then muttered something to himself that Aidan couldn't hear and slowly walked up toward the throne to stand behind the king.

The throne room was … small.

Perhaps only thirty nobles were present and standing comfortably. While the king's golden ornate chair was regal and imposing, it somehow felt as though Aidan's audience with the monarch was purposefully made as insulting as possible.

Aidan bowed, but not to the proper depth, and when he straightened, he fixed the king with his dark eyes and waited. He was supposed to speak and thank the royal for welcoming him to his kingdom. Instead he stood silently.

No one said anything or dared to even breathe.

You began the nature of this insult, Aidan hissed in his mind.

"I see you have arrived safely, Mr. Helmer." Norman's hazel eyes seemed to gleam dangerously, as though he knew exactly what the witch in front of him was thinking.

"Indeed, Your Majesty. It is unfortunate that we must formally meet under these circumstances."

"Quite so. Lord Piereva is being kept in a secure location in Austice. Once we agree on who shall dole out the punishment, I'm sure you will be eager to return to your home."

"While Troivack is my current home, I must say it is quite wonderful to have returned back to the shores that raised me."

A ripple of tension moved through the room.

"Head of Housekeeping, Ruby, will show you to your quarters. We will see you at the dining hour."

Aidan bowed again and turned toward the doors; the nobility all shared meaningful looks once he passed them, as they all formed opinions that they felt would explode from their mouths at any given moment.

"Oh, pardon me, Your Majesty, but is my wife, Katelyn Ashowan, still under your employ at this time?" Aidan turned around and smiled at the king.

The nobles were unable to contain themselves as they all burst out in surprised whispers.

Norman didn't bat an eye, however.

"It is not your place to question which physician serves the Daxarian monarchy. I hope you do not forget yourself while visiting us, Mr. Helmer. Lord Piereva created enough of a mess already, I'd hate to discover you have come with similar intentions."

Infuriatingly, Aidan didn't respond to the chastisement as Norman had wished him to.

Instead, the fire witch smiled. "My apologies, Your Majesty. I just am eager to see my wife and son. I'm sure you can understand my impatience."

Then with another bow, Aidan turned and left the room.

Norman's stomach churned as everyone around him began chattering amongst themselves, their worry over the Troivack chief of military heightening the tension in the air. Letting out a long sigh, he summoned Mr. Howard's presence to his left.

"Keep Mrs. Ashowan's whereabouts hidden at all costs until the time is right. Inform the staff that no one is allowed to breathe a word about her or Fin with Helmer here."

Aidan entered the banquet hall and felt his earlier judgment of the castle shift. It was an appropriately large room, and a significant number of nobles had descended in their finery for the meal.

The king sat waiting at his table with his chalice clutched in hand as he watched the fire witch draw nearer.

"Good evening, Your Majesty." Aidan bowed.

"Good evening, Mr. Helmer. My assistant, Mr. Howard, will show you to your place."

Aidan followed the same man who had first introduced him to the king and guided him to a seat only two nobles down from Norman himself.

The room had fallen quiet as this happened, but many still were murmuring to their friends and spouses about the visitors. The men Aidan had brought with him were all lowly soldiers … he had left his assistant on the ship. A most strange decision …

As the servants began to file into the hall carrying dishes that smelled heavenly, everyone turned their attention to the meal.

Exclamations echoed throughout the room.

"He's back! The cook is back!"

"Oh, thank the Gods …"

"Rolph, are you weeping?!"

Aidan raised an eyebrow curiously. Had his son gone somewhere? Why were they all so emotional about his return?

Just then a lone bowl was set in front of him, making him wrinkle his nose and scowl.

"What is this?" Aidan demanded while gesturing to the other bowls of soup that had been laid out that glowed with the enticing warmth of potatoes and butter, whereas his resembled a strange gray seafood stew …

"Our cook prepared this especially for you," the serving wench who had laid the plate down squeaked nervously.

What is that son of mine trying to pull …

Waving the lass away, Aidan snatched up his spoon and lifted the food to his mouth, when the scent reached his nose. He froze, his face draining of color as he then slowly lowered the spoon, still full, back down to the bowl.

"Is something amiss?" Norman asked, his tone sharp.

After a brief moment of wading through his memories, Aidan smiled charmingly. "Not at all, sire. I think I may forgo this course for tonight is all."

Norman's eyes narrowed before he dropped his gaze to the bowl and realized Fin had served his father something different than everyone else …

Still holding grudges, are we? Aidan thought to himself, his smile growing brighter as he closed his eyes and thought back to the last day he'd seen Finlay.

He had come home … a particular fish stew had been prepared … and shortly thereafter, the boy who had been a sniveling lump clinging to his mother's skirts had exploded with power.

Aidan was quiet through the rest of the meal; however, as the final dessert vestiges were removed from the tables, he turned to the king, a dark glimmer in his eyes.

"Your Majesty, this food far exceeds my wildest expectations. I would be deeply appreciative if you might summon the cook so that I may give him my praise."

For some strange reason, multiple men at the table stiffened at the request. One was an elderly man with a ridiculous name who was infamous for being a touch mad. Earl Fuhcs? Fooks? Something like that.

Then there was the king's assistant who had a far-off look in his eye as though a great doom awaited him. The captain of Daxaria's knights had hesitated for a moment, and even the disgusting mage had shown some kind of reaction.

Aidan waited. He knew such a kind request would be too difficult to publicly refute without being the epitome of rude.

"Very well, we will summon Mr. Ashowan." With a nod, the king sent Ruby scurrying from the room, and a strange wave of excitement fluttered through the noblewomen.

Sitting back in his chair as they all waited for several long moments, Aidan swirled the contents in his goblet around.

"Our cook is a busy man, so we will not keep him long," the king warned with an obvious edge in his voice.

Aidan shot the monarch a sly smile.

Looks like my boy has been rubbing elbows with the nobility …

He then bowed his head, a gleeful glint in his black eyes. "Of course, Your Majesty."

The room suddenly quieted, and without looking, the fire witch could hear the long steady strides drawing closer to the table.

"You called for me, Your Majesty?"

The room fell silent, as the tall redheaded cook stood with his shoulders straight, and his bright blue eyes raised to the king's table.

Lifting his chin, Aidan laid eyes on his fully grown son for the first time in twenty years, and before the king could utter a word, he burst out laughing.

He was perfect.

CHAPTER 46
FILIAL FRICTION

When Fin had entered the banquet hall, he had noticed the swirl of whispers around him, though they were so quiet they most likely didn't reach the king's ears. A few words and exclamations he was able to hear as he walked by, but it was surprising he noticed anything over the hard pounding of his heart.

"… He looks just like …"

"… Related?"

"Different … name?"

Fin kept his eyes trained on Norman who was regarding him gravely, as though apologizing for forcing him into such an uncomfortable situation.

The laughter that rang out suddenly made his insides clench and twist. He had forgotten how that laugh sounded after so many years …

"Mr. Ashowan, it would seem that the Troivackian Royal Cook has insulted more than Lord Piereva's taste buds. Mr. Helmer here can't help but be amazed at your superior skill and wished to commend you," Norman announced, while attempting to sound jovial.

His expression remaining a mask of indifference, Fin turned to stare at Aidan. His palms were sweating, but they were safely stowed in his pockets as he looked at his father for the first time since blasting him off the island.

Fin's own face aged twenty years older stared back at him except ... except for the black eyes that made him feel as though he were about to be sick.

Aidan stood from the table, a half-smile on his face as he rounded it, and effectively silenced the remaining whispers in the hall as everyone watched, shocked. There was no doubt that he and the cook were father and son once the pair stood toe-to-toe.

Fin held his ground even though his insides quaked, and bile rose into the back of his throat. His father on the other hand looked completely at ease, his handsome face still wearing a half smile.

"You've grown to match my height, I see," Aidan observed quietly with a nod.

Fin stared back blankly, not saying a word. He couldn't bring himself to talk when he knew his voice would come out as nothing but a croak. There was the growing smell of lightning in the room, and a few nobles noticed their arm hairs were beginning to rise on their own. Norman glanced over to Mage Lee, who met his questioning gaze with a worried one. The situation was undoubtedly dangerous.

"Your stew was a nice homecoming message."

Is that why you didn't eat any of it? Fin's mind snapped, and he wanted to say it out loud, as carelessly as his father spoke, but couldn't. So instead, he opted for stoic silence, not letting his eyes leave his father's face for a moment.

"You've got some talent cooking for your king." His mocking tone could only be heard by Fin, who immediately interpreted his words with ease.

How could you serve a mere human man?

"Now, now, my boy, it is rude not to reply when an esteemed guest addresses you." Aidan clapped a hand on Fin's shoulder, and blue lightning immediately began to fill his gaze.

"Sire," Captain Antonio exclaimed suddenly, forcing Norman to tear his gaze away from the calamity unfolding before him. "The silverware ... the plates ... they're burning hot to the touch."

Norman looked back to Aidan and noticed waves of heat beginning to pour from his body as he gripped Fin's shoulder.

"Mr. Helmer, if you are quite done having words with our cook, I believe he has other duties to attend to," Norman called out between them, his voice ringing in the silence of the hall.

Fin blinked, the lightning disappearing from his gaze before he wrenched himself free of his father's grasp and turned to exit the banquet hall.

Aidan stared after him with a bemused smirk on his face before he turned and made his way back to his place at the table.

"I apologize for the awkwardness, Your Majesty, I'm sure you could see that *my son* and I are in need of a more private discussion."

"You will not interfere with my cook's work under any circumstances. If he wishes to speak with you, he is free to approach you," Norman ordered, making Aidan's infuriating smile, at long last, drip off his face.

"Your Majesty seeks to bar me from my own family?"

"I seek to protect my citizens from a man who, were I a vindictive individual, could be tried as a traitor," Norman replied back coolly. "Or were you forgetting?"

"Your Majesty, I am here to punish the treasonous *Troivackian* man known as Earl Phillip Piereva, surely you do not wish to insult me gravely with the suggestion that I had anything to do with—"

"What is your job, Mr. Helmer?" Norman cut him off, staring at him levelly.

"Your deplorable manners are noted, Majesty," Aidan replied, though his lip twitched as though wishing to sneer.

"You are the chief of military, are you not? For Troivack?"

Aidan's jaw clenched shut.

"That position is assigned when there are talks of war, and you, Mr. Helmer, have been Troivack's chief of military for a few years now. Would that not mean you sought out King Matthias for the position to bring war to Daxaria? Is this not a prime example of treason?"

Aidan said nothing for a few moments before he picked up his wine and took a drink.

"When I arrived on Troivack's shores, it was many years ago. I have long since become a citizen of the kingdom. A promotion is to be commended for a foreigner; it means I rose up from the bottom ranks."

"I see. Then you are admitting that you are a foreigner here in Daxaria now?"

Aidan paused and slid a suspicious glance to Norman whose face remained unreadable.

"I have said as much."

"How long did it take you to be promoted through the ranks?"

"I have been in Troivack for nearly twenty years—"

"Excellent." Turning to the guards at the door, Norman waved his hand.

Aidan was about to demand just what was the meaning of the unseemly behavior, when in walked Katelyn Ashowan.

He stilled.

She strode forward confidently, her brown wavy hair brushed to a gleam, and her warm gaze fixed on the king. She wore a plain but respectable cream dress, and despite having aged twenty years, she looked … well, rather the same she had the last time Aidan had seen her, save for the strands of white in her hair.

She cut her hair shorter … it suits her, Aidan thought dazedly for a moment, before he realized the oddity of Katelyn appearing so suddenly.

The nobles were beside themselves with the drama, and immediately whispers broke out again.

"Mrs. Ashowan, your request to dissolve your marriage to Mr. Aidan Helmer has been approved on grounds of abandonment. Mr. Howard will issue you the official record."

Aidan's head whipped around to stare at the king, outraged.

"This is preposterous! This is not a formal trial to make such a decision—"

"Mr. Helmer, I believe we got off on the wrong foot; however, you are attempting to interfere with my governing a grave matter with my citizen."

"You're trying to force a divorce between me and my wife!" Aidan was on his feet in an instant. "I simply went away, I always intended to—"

"You joined another kingdom and sent no correspondence to your wife and child for more than twenty years? If it were five years, perhaps I could consider this plea; however, I cannot see a single king or magistrate that will deny the grounds of this dissolvement." Norman waved him off, and the temperature in the room rose notably.

Mage Lee stood, his staff's crystal faintly glowing as he frowned at Aidan in warning.

"For the love of the Gods, sit your ass down." The outburst came from none other than Katelyn Ashowan.

Aidan turned on her, the ire in his eyes deadly.

"You despised us, let it end, and leave us be. We have nothing for you. Stay in your new kingdom and enjoy your life." Kate's chest rose and fell quickly, but her gaze had turned steely as she stared up at her former husband.

Aidan leaned his hands on the table and stared so fiercely that he didn't blink. "This is far from over, Kate."

"Like hell it is. Thank you, Your Majesty, for your kind ruling. I will retire for this evening." Curtsying, the healer turned and strode swiftly out of the room, leaving Aidan to turn his anger back to the king.

343

"You will face consequences for your reckless behavior, Your Majesty."

Norman turned with a small smile and keen shine in his hazel eyes. "Just as you have begun to face yours. Now. Do sit, a nice sherry is to be served before dinner is resolved."

Fin stood in his kitchen with his hands braced against his beloved worktable, his heart still racing in his chest. Even though he had known his father would summon him, it hadn't made the experience any easier. His aides behind him all exchanged worried glances, when a small fluffy shadow brushed against Fin's leg.

Looking down into the wide pupils of Kraken, Fin sighed and bent down to scoop up the cat.

"Witch, you are sweaty, and your heartbeat could outrace a mouse's. Whatever is wrong?"

"My father is here."

The feline didn't say anything for a moment, as the aides behind Fin slowly began to leave the room. They still weren't completely used to their employer's discussions with his cat.

"Are you not pleased to see the male who sired you?"

"No. In fact I want to blast him all the way back to Troivack." With a sigh, and still cradling the feline, Fin sank into the nearest seat by his table.

"Why don't you do that, then?" Kraken asked, clearly confused.

"Because it would be breaking the law for me to assault a foreign diplomat."

"What if nobody finds out?"

"My powers when it comes to expelling people aren't always subtle." Fin chuckled bitterly to himself.

"I learned about poison while we stayed at your mate's home, would you like me to—"

"Why in the world were you learning about poison?!" Fin stared down at his cat with great alarm.

"There was a great amount of experiments conducted the night you returned smelling strongly of perfume and females."

Fin paused, then remembered he had been drugged the night he visited Mathilda's.

"Oh … Annika was trying to make sure I wasn't going to die?"

"I believe it was something to that effect, yes."

"What did you lear—"

Fin's question was cut short by the castle door opening then.

Drawing his eyes upward, he felt his stomach drop at the sight of Aidan Helmer in his kitchen.

The man had his white tunic sleeves rolled up, and his maroon silk vest hung open when he held up his hands. "I come in peace. I only want to talk with you."

Fin felt Kraken roll out of his arms as the house witch stared at his father without saying a word.

"I know it was startling seeing me like that for the first time since you were a child, but I had to be completely certain the rumors were true, that you were in fact the cook for the king."

Fin still didn't say anything, just continued staring as the man stepped farther into the kitchen, approaching him casually.

"I'll admit I got a little carried away; your king can be … careless, and my temper was tried by him." Aidan tilted his head to the side, a charming smile slowly climbing up his face as he studied his son.

"What do you want?" Fin's voice sounded as though it came from another person, but he didn't dare blink or look away.

"I want to talk to my son. It's been twenty years, and while I have heard all kinds of things about you … I haven't gotten to know who you've become for myself."

Fin continued staring at him blankly for a moment, as Aidan then folded his hands and leaned a casual elbow on the table. Standing up, Finlay turned and strode to the garden door.

A curling tendril of flames appeared and danced in front of his eyes then, beautifully blocking his path.

Fin turned around, a slightly manic glint in his blue eyes, while Aidan smiled and shrugged innocently.

Before Fin could do anything, however, the fire witch suddenly jumped up with a small yelp.

"Something just *bit* me! Do you have rodents down here?"

"No." Fin turned back around, after noting the bushy swishing tail hidden under a nearby potato sack, and placed his hand on the door handle, only to snap it back with a hiss. It was scalding hot.

"Finlay, I just want to talk. It hurts to know my son, a witch, is here toiling away as a peasant for a mere human king. I can offer you a great life back in Troivack. Money, work of your choice, women … That reminds me, I haven't heard, but do you have a wife yet? Do I have any grandchildren?"

There was something derisive in his eyes, and so without further ado, the broom that had been propped up in the corner by the door suddenly flew over and up the back of Aidan's tunic, effectively dragging him from the room while spluttering.

Fin made sure the door slammed and locked shut after the removal of his father, then he turned and left by commanding the garden door to open for him.

"Come on, Kraken," he called over his shoulder before closing the door behind himself. "I want to go check up on Mum and make sure she's alright. Apparently she and him at least aren't married anymore."

As Fin walked through the darkness toward his cottage, he did his best to calm down and stop the trembling in his hands. He didn't want his father to still affect him … didn't want to feel weak against the monster.

Upon arriving at his humble abode, Fin found Captain Antonio standing waiting for him outside the front door. "We've moved your mother to somewhere safer for now. We know you can protect her in the cottage, but she doesn't want to be a prisoner here on the grounds while your father is in the castle. She's found some lodging in Austice; I can tell you where later."

Fin nodded quietly and noticed the curious glint in the captain's eye in the torchlight.

"She's doing well. Riled up, but glad to be rid of him."

Fin nodded again, relieved. "Good. She deserves to be free."

"How are you?" The captain's voice was firm, but … tense. It was clear he was worried about his future stepson.

Fin gave an ambiguous shrug and a strained smile. "I'll survive. Good night, Captain. It's been a long day."

Grimacing slightly, but understanding the young man needed time alone after the ordeal he had just faced, Antonio clapped Fin on the shoulder, nodded his own farewell, and departed.

As soon as the witch entered his darkened cottage, he sensed Annika waiting in the shadows.

Magically sealing off the shutters and doors from intrusion and sounds, a fire roared to life in the hearth, revealing the viscountess to be by the table. The minute her wide, worried brown eyes met his weary blue ones, she rushed into his arms, embracing him tightly without a word.

Fin knew while he had made it through his first day with his father being back under the same roof, it was most likely not going to be the hardest. So he embraced Annika tightly and did his best to forget all the unpleasantness for at least the night.

War was on the kingdom's doorstep, but his mother was finally free …

As Fin kissed the top of Annika's head and breathed in her spicy scent, he couldn't help but be grateful knowing that while there were still mysteries and dangers waiting outside, he had friends, family, and a wonderful fiancée to help him through the hardships.

He could face Aidan again, and this time, it would be different. He was sure of it.

He just wanted a decent book to read ...

Not too much to ask, is it? It was in 1935 when Allen Lane, Managing Director of Bodley Head Publishers, stood on a platform at Exeter railway station looking for something good to read on his journey back to London. His choice was limited to popular magazines and poor-quality paperbacks – the same choice faced every day by the vast majority of readers, few of whom could afford hardbacks. Lane's disappointment and subsequent anger at the range of books generally available led him to found a company – and change the world.

'We believed in the existence in this country of a vast reading public for intelligent books at a low price, and staked everything on it'
Sir Allen Lane, 1902–1970, founder of Penguin Books

The quality paperback had arrived – and not just in bookshops. Lane was adamant that his Penguins should appear in chain stores and tobacconists, and should cost no more than a packet of cigarettes.

Reading habits (and cigarette prices) have changed since 1935, but Penguin still believes in publishing the best books for everybody to enjoy. We still believe that good design costs no more than bad design, and we still believe that quality books published passionately and responsibly make the world a better place.

So wherever you see the little bird – whether it's on a piece of prize-winning literary fiction or a celebrity autobiography, political tour de force or historical masterpiece, a serial-killer thriller, reference book, world classic or a piece of pure escapism – you can bet that it represents the very best that the genre has to offer.

Whatever you like to read – trust Penguin.

read more
www.penguin.co.uk